Essarts
(ruins)

Fonquevillers
(ruins)

Bucquoy
(ruins)

Gommecourt
(ruins)

Hébuterne
(ruins)

Puisieux-au-Mont
(ruins)

Serre-lès-Puisieux
(ruins)

Miraumont
(ruins)

Beaumont-
sur-l'Ancre
(ruins)

chonvillers
(ruins)

Beaumont-Hamel
(ruins)

Grandcourt
(ruins)

River Ancre

Hamel
(ruins)

Thiepval
(ruins)

Mesnil
(ruins)

N

1 mile

PHILIP GRAY

Two Storm Wood

Harvill *Secker*

LONDON

1 3 5 7 9 10 8 6 4 2

Harvill Secker is part of the Penguin Random House group of companies
whose addresses can be found at global.penguinrandomhouse.com

Penguin
Random House
UK

First published by Harvill Secker in 2021

A CIP catalogue record for this book is available from the British Library

penguin.co.uk/vintage

ISBN 9781787302617 (hardback)
ISBN 9781787302624 (trade paperback)

Typeset in 11.5/15.76 pt Van Dijck MT Pro
by Integra Software Services Pvt. Ltd, Pondicherry

Printed and bound in Great Britain by Clays Ltd, Elcograf S.p.A.

Penguin Random House is committed to a sustainable future for our business, our readers
and our planet. This book is made from Forest Stewardship Council® certified paper.

For my family.

Why does she come so promptly, when she must know

That she's only the nearer to the inevitable farewell;

The hill is steep, on the snow my steps are slow —

Why does she come, when she knows what I have to tell?

D. H. Lawrence, *A Winter's Tale*

— One —

The beds were screened off in this corner of the ward, and the shutters half-closed so that the daylight fell in watery bands on the ceilings and walls. Where family portraits had once hung there were now ghostly rectangles, punctured by electric light fittings screwed into the plaster. Outside, the calls of nesting rooks carried across the grounds.

Major Richardson stopped at the first bed, where a man lay, eyes closed. 'Is he asleep?'

Captain Price opened his file. 'He had morphine an hour ago, a quarter-gram. He'll be out for a while yet.'

Richardson leaned closer to the man's face, squinting through his spectacles at the aftermath of four operations. The bandages had been off for a fortnight but the disfigurement was as bad as ever: the sunken cheek, the taut, shiny brow, the mouth folded into a permanent sneer. He had seen worse – men with no faces at all – but he wished he could have done more. He liked to be sure the lives he saved were worth living.

'Any visitors?'

'His fiancée, a girl called Eleanor. She came down most days when things were dicey.'

Price remembered her well: pretty, neatly dressed, an expensive-looking bonnet pulled down low over her eyes, as if she were afraid of being recognised. He had escorted her through the ward on her first visit, struck by her obvious unease. He had reassured her that her intended was not in immediate danger, thinking that must account for it, but she hardly seemed to hear him, intent on whatever battle she was fighting with herself.

'And now?' Richardson asked.

'She doesn't come at all.' Price lowered his voice. 'She sent him a letter. In hindsight, we should have intercepted it.'

1

Richardson frowned. 'She broke it off?'

'Something about him not *playing the game*.'

'What game?'

'Pre-marital abstinence, in a word. She'd heard something about the brothels at the front. Seems his reassurances weren't enough.'

Richardson shook his head. 'They wouldn't be.'

'A pretext, you think?'

'Of course. Look at him.'

Price took in the brutal caricature of what might once have been a handsome face. He had always hoped that men like this, who had sacrificed so much in the line of duty – the disfigured and maimed – might enjoy some special exemption from further hurt, some special consideration from those who had stayed behind, but human nature had often disappointed him.

'How did he take it?'

'He hasn't said a word, according to the nurses.'

'That bad. Any other visitors?'

Price shook his head. 'He has no immediate family. Parents died when he was a child. I took the liberty of checking with the War Office.'

'Unfortunate.'

'They were killed. Tragic story. Sort of thing that leaves a mark.'

Price would have liked to discuss it further. He had developed an interest in nervous disorders and other conditions that were usually the province of psychiatry. Unfortunately Richardson, the hospital director, rarely had time for theorising.

'You think he'll try to end it?' he said.

Price dug his hands into his pockets. 'From where he was to where he is now, it's a long way down. He had quite a war: MC, mentioned in dispatches.'

Richardson's grunt was non-committal. 'Suicide requires a plan, and resolution.'

'He's strong.'

'Physically. Wouldn't have come through otherwise. Mentally, only time will tell. With all the morphine, anything could be going through his head. I wonder if he even knows the war's over.'

At the mention of morphine the patient's eyelids drifted open. The pupils were starkly pale against his weather-tanned skin.

Richardson straightened up. 'Colonel, good to see you catching up on your sleep. Don't let us disturb you.'

The man blinked lazily, then turned his head towards the patient in the other bed. A major in the military police, he lay propped up on pillows, mouth half-open, sleeping noiselessly, a saline infusion plumbed into his arm, a sheen of sweat on his brow. He had no legs below the knee. His wheelchair stood beside the bed, his uniform deliberately folded on the seat, ready for use. A nurse was standing over him, taking his pulse.

On the other side of the screens a door opened. A smell of boiled food drifted into the room.

'You're making excellent progress, Colonel,' Richardson said, but his patient's eyes were already closed.

The major started coughing, a wheeze rising from his chest. The amputations had been carried out in France, after his truck had been hit by a shrapnel round. The field surgeon had been too conservative, leaving a pair of tiny fragments in the left leg. After several months, in which the patient had appeared to recover well, infection had set in. Richardson feared the corrective operation had come too late.

The nurse looked up at him and slowly shook her head.

Price came over. 'That cough. We should move him, just in case.'

'He won't last much longer,' Richardson said. 'A few days at most.'

'All the same ...' Price sounded apologetic, but the threat from influenza was real. Most of the other patients would stand no chance in their weakened state. An isolation ward had already been set aside.

'All right, see to it. First thing in the morning.' Richardson turned. 'Damned shame, though. I heard these two fellows got on well. It's friendship that makes these things bearable, often as not.'

That night the major came round. His fever had abated a little. He felt cool and light-headed. Was he really awake or just dreaming again? In his dreams he had his legs and felt no pain. He dreamed about returning to his wife in Hammersmith, to his office at Scotland Yard. People greeted him with smiles

3

and rounds of drinks. They wanted to hear his stories from the war. The only difficulty was knowing where to begin.

He looked down at the foot of the bed: the blankets lay flat under the dim electric light, nothing where his legs should be. A familiar wave of despair broke over him. He glanced at the wheelchair: it was still there, its heavy iron frame a rebuke to his hopes, his inability to accept and adapt. The only thing missing was his uniform: his cap, tunic and greatcoat, distinguished by the red flashes of the provost marshal's branch. The uniform reminded him that he was still part of the army, still a person of rank with rights and duties. But they had taken it away. Why had they done that? What did it mean?

He managed to sit up. Beside the next bed someone was dressing. It took a while for him to realise that it was the colonel, the poor devil who had lost half his face to a German grenade. He had only been able to speak for the last few days, but he had been a good listener, never tiring of the major's old case-histories from before the war.

The colonel was putting on a uniform – but it wasn't his own uniform. It was the major's.

'I say, Colonel? What the devil are you doing? Those are—'

The colonel turned, raising a finger to his lips. He was up to something, some sort of prank. But he had no right to take what wasn't his.

The major coughed. His lungs were inflamed, raw. Pain racked his chest. 'Put those back. Damn it, those are . . .'

The colonel was standing over him, his ravaged face silhouetted against the electric bulb. He was holding a pillow in his hands.

'This'll help you sleep,' he said, coming close.

He held the pillow over the major's face, pressing it down with the weight of his body until the dying man's arms went slack and he stopped struggling. It only took a couple of minutes. When it was over, he laid the major's arms neatly by his sides, carefully closed his eyes, straightened the bedcovers and slipped silently out of the ward.

———

Nobody

—— Two ——

England, March 1916

She did not see him at first. He was hidden beyond shafts of sunlight streaming down from the stained-glass windows. She had slipped up the spiral staircase into the organ gallery, expecting it to be empty. When he stepped out of the shadows, she jumped.

'Excuse me. I didn't mean to startle you.'

The young stranger was tall and broad at the shoulders, but his clothes were loose on him, as if handed down, and there was a smudge of dust on his collar. In the sunlight his hair was a pale shade of gold.

Amy Vanneck was still slightly out of breath from the climb. 'I just wanted . . . I heard the music.'

She had been drawn into the chapel by the sound of a choir. She and her mother, Lady Constance, were on an informal tour of Cambridge colleges, conducted by Aunt Clem, whose husband lectured in biology, but the sisters had gone off in search of somewhere they could 'spend a penny', as her aunt quaintly referred to it. The choristers, half of them schoolboys, had filed past on their way out, leaving Amy, as she thought, alone.

The stranger was carrying an untidy bundle of sheet music and pencils. She supposed he was the choirmaster, or the organist, although he could not have been more than twenty years old, scarcely older than her.

'It was beautiful, by the way,' she added before turning to go.

'Wait.' The stranger stepped closer. One of his pencils clattered to the floor. 'Do you . . . ?' He scrambled to keep the music from going the same way. 'The organ, do you play at all?'

'Not really. I always wanted . . . Well, it doesn't matter.'

The stranger was looking at Amy intently. Young men had never looked at her very often, except in passing. She was small, raven-haired and nothing like as pretty as her older sisters – a state of affairs that had its compensations: she had never waved a loved one off to war, for one thing; did not have to wait for news of them, dreading the arrival of a notification slip from the War Office: *It is my painful duty to inform you that a report has been received* ... She could hear about battles and offensives and 'pushes' without a cold hand of dread closing around her heart. If the stranger was staring at her, it must have been because women were not often seen in this place, this hallowed male preserve. After all, the only concession to the feminine in the whole building was a solitary image of the Virgin in coloured glass.

The stranger shook himself. 'No, please. Feel free.' He stepped back, inviting her to sit down at the keyboards. 'It can be a little temperamental, but it makes a good sound, most of the time.'

Amy peered down into the body of the chapel. She did not relish the prospect of explaining herself – being alone with a strange man, out of sight of everyone – but her mother and aunt would be gone a little while yet.

'No one'll hear,' the young man said. 'Or they'll just think it's me. I'm Edward, by the way – Edward Haslam. I teach music at the boys' school. St Thomas's? We're joining forces with the college choir this year. Easter services and all that.'

'Amy Vanneck.'

Fleetingly they touched hands. He was clean-shaven and had hazel brown eyes. When he smiled, she thought she glimpsed the boy in him, shyness beneath an adult veneer.

She eased herself onto the bench and took off her gloves. The organ had three manuals and a bewildering range of stops. She had wanted to take up the instrument when she was at school, but her ambition had been given short shrift. The 'king of instruments' was apparently unsuitable for a young lady, being loud, domineering and forever associated with the sacraments. She had been forced to make do with piano lessons. It was much the same when she expressed an interest in studying medicine, only this time her mother had been the obstacle. 'A young lady of your station doesn't spend her time cutting up bodies, living or dead,' was her final verdict. 'Your father will never agree, in any case.'

The music teacher was waiting expectantly. Amy took a deep breath and played a dark minor chord. Nothing happened. Not even a puff of air came from the pipes.

'Um, might I suggest ... ?' The teacher pulled out a couple of stops. 'Try these.'

Amy blushed. She tried another chord, this time in a major key. A fanfare of bright notes echoed through the cavernous space. She let her fingers run up and down the keys, at first slowly, then faster. When she pushed down on the pedals, she felt the deep sound reverberate through her whole body.

'I've no music,' she said. 'Have you a hymn book?'

'A hymn book?' There was disappointment in the teacher's voice. 'I suppose there must be one somewhere. On the other hand ...' He pulled out a score from the stack he was carrying and placed it in front of her. 'Why not give this a go?' The name of the piece was *The Topliner Rag*. 'It's from America. The latest thing.'

It had to be a joke. How could anyone play ragtime in a place of worship? Edward Haslam was teasing her: expecting her to blush and demur, like the sheltered, strait-laced girl she must have seemed to be.

'Or if you'd prefer something more—'

Without another word, she launched into the music. The solemn chapel was instantly transformed into a fairground. Oblivious to her wrong notes, the young man set about trying different combinations of stops, calling out the names as the sound became wilder and stranger. Soon they were both laughing.

'Amy?' Her mother's voice cut through the music. 'Where is that girl?'

Amy froze. 'I must go.'

At the top of the spiral staircase she looked back. Edward Haslam was still watching her. He silently mouthed the word *Goodbye*.

Amy's mother was showing signs of fatigue. She had been determined to see all the architectural high points in one go, as if it were a penance. Amy suspected it was something she intended to do only once, like having a bad tooth removed. Duty done, there would never be a need to go through it a second time.

'Who were you talking to, Amy?' she asked, as they set off across the court.

It was a struggle to keep up with her.

'Nobody. I just wanted to try the organ.'

'Was that you? That awful noise?'

'It was only a piece I found.'

'Extraordinary.' Her mother shook her head. 'And *where* are your gloves?'

9

Amy had left them behind. 'I'm sorry. Go on ahead. I'll catch you up.'

She hurried back into the chapel. Edward Haslam was already on his way out, gloves in hand. He was smiling, as if her forgetfulness were a prize.

'Thank you.' Amy took the gloves.

'Miss Vanneck?'

She stopped.

'There's a musical soirée tonight. A friend's house. Some wonderful players. You'd—'

'I'd love to, but ...' Amy's mother and aunt were almost at the gatehouse. Her mother turned. 'I can't.'

If he was pretending to be disappointed, it was a good act.

'If you change your mind, I'll be outside the Round Church at six. I'll wait for you, just in case.'

There was no need for Amy to refuse a second time, because the whole idea was ridiculous.

The others were waiting in the shelter of the porters' lodge.

'So you *were* talking to someone,' her mother said. 'Who was that man?'

Amy frowned as she pulled on her gloves. 'I told you, Mother. He's nobody.'

Her mother watched the teacher go back inside the chapel. 'Yes, I expect he is.'

———

By late afternoon Amy's mother had recovered enough to attend to her correspondence. Originally the plan had been to spend at most a fortnight in Cambridge, but Lady Constance seemed in no hurry to return to her husband and the family estate in Suffolk. With so many gone to the war and social life curtailed, it was perhaps a little uneventful, even for her.

Amy sat at the window in Aunt Clem's upstairs sitting room, leafing through one of her uncle's textbooks, a study of the human nervous system. She found it hard to concentrate. It was still light outside, but a mist was gathering, hiding the far end of the street. She glanced at the clock on the mantel: it was a quarter to six.

'Where is the Round Church exactly?'

Aunt Clem looked up from her sewing. 'Just around the corner from St John's. We passed it earlier.'

'And St John's is . . . ?'

'Next to Trinity. Why do you ask?'

Amy returned to her book. 'I think I read about it somewhere.'

Another lie, her third of the day, designed, like the others, to hide her encounter with Edward Haslam – an encounter that meant nothing and would lead to nothing. She turned a page. A new chapter was entitled *Neurons, Size and General Morphology*.

Ten minutes to six. Amy pictured Edward Haslam getting ready for their rendezvous, knowing that it would never happen but unable to extinguish the romantic hope that, against all the odds, it might. He would put on a smarter set of clothes, if he owned one. He would brush his hair and polish his shoes, and then – she smiled at the thought – have to dig out the black polish from under his fingernails. Then he would bicycle off to the Round Church, arriving at least five minutes early, just in case.

The clock read five minutes to six.

She could not meet him, even if she had wanted to. What possible excuse could she give for stepping out alone? Even the shops were closed by now. And to be absent for a whole evening? That would require a mountain of lies, more than she could hope to muster. As for telling the truth, that would do her no good, either. She would be forbidden to go. Who was Edward Haslam? What did she know about him? Who had introduced them? *We are not that kind of people, Amy. You should know better.* Amy did not want to imagine the scene.

How long would he stay there before giving up? Ten minutes? Fifteen? At twenty past six he would cycle off alone to his musical soirée, disappointed perhaps, but not surprised. And there he would meet another girl – a girl who was free and unafraid – and he would forget all about the one who had wandered into the chapel.

Aunt Clem's husband came into the room as the mantel clock chimed six. He was a man in his fifties, with a white beard and kindly eyes. 'I meant to say: this came for you while you were out.'

In his hand was a letter in a small blue envelope.

'For you, Amy.' He frowned. 'Is something the matter?'

'No, nothing. Thank you, Uncle.'

The letter was from Kitty Page, an old school friend who lived in Cambridge. They had arranged to meet the following morning, but Kitty wrote to say that she had gone down with a fever and that her anxious parents had insisted she stay in bed.

Amy stood up. 'Kitty's not well. She has the flu.'

'Oh, I am sorry,' her mother said, without looking up from her writing. 'Do send her our best wishes.'

'I think I should go to her,' Amy said. 'She's been laid up all day, very bored.'

'If you must.' Her mother's pen continued to scratch its way across the page. 'Be sure to keep your distance. You don't want to catch anything.'

———

She borrowed Aunt Clem's bicycle and pedalled hard, the heavy iron machine juddering as it rolled over the cobblestones. The air was cold against her cheeks. Single chimes rang out across the town: a quarter past six.

The dank streets were almost empty. On King's Parade the shop awnings were up. Outside Trinity a group of officer cadets were marching towards the Great Gate, the sergeant major's commands echoing up and down the narrow lane. Amy swerved onto the pavement. Nobody passed her until she reached the end of the road.

The Round Church was easy to spot: squat, circular, impractically small. Even among the half-timbered houses it looked like a relic from a bygone age. Out of breath, Amy wheeled her bicycle towards the entrance. A single lantern burned above the door.

Edward Haslam was not there.

She stood in the deepening twilight, the truth coming home to her as her breathing slowed. She'd been wrong: twenty minutes was too long to wait. He had already gone. Or perhaps he had never turned up in the first place.

You stupid girl, Amy. You stupid, stupid girl.

She climbed back onto her bicycle, realising only then that she was not alone.

''Scuse me. Miss Amy, is it?'

It was a boy, fifteen or so. He wore a cap, and his shirt had no collar. He had been sitting on the low wall at the corner of the churchyard.

'Yes?'

'Gentleman said to give you this.' He pulled a piece of paper from his top pocket. 'Said to wait half an hour. Paid me sixpence.'

Amy unfolded the paper. At the top was printed 6 PORTUGAL PLACE. The message beneath had been written in pencil. She went and stood beneath the lantern.

Dear Miss Vanneck,

If you receive this note, it means you came to meet me. I would have given the world to be there, as I promised. But a colleague of mine just received word that his son was killed at Arras. His wife is away and he is utterly distraught. I am afraid to leave him – of what he might do. William was their only child.

I do not expect you to forgive me, but know at least that I did not break my promise lightly. War poisons everything that it does not destroy. That's why I will never take part in it, as long as I live.

With deepest regret,

Edward Haslam

The boy was still loitering at the corner, no doubt hopeful of another commission. Amy put the letter in her coat and went to pick up her bicycle. In her pocket was a sixpence.

———

— Three —

Northern France, February 1919

It was a flare gun, distance about a thousand yards. No one had forgotten the sound: the percussive punch, the crackle like static. Captain Mackenzie got to his feet and lifted the tent flap. A white Very light was climbing into the sky, haloed in rain. Over the broken ground dark shadows gaped.

Sergeant Cotterell was beside him. 'What's that about? Something up with the coolies.'

On the far side of the ridge a Chinese labour company was gathering salvage: rails, piping, copper, brass – anything with scrap value. They took away stores of munitions, but unexploded ordnance was left where it lay. Like the bunkers and the barbed wire, it was regarded as *fait de guerre* and the responsibility of the French.

Mackenzie raised his binoculars. The search party was strung out in a line below the ridge, a distance of six yards between each man. From this distance they might have been giant tortoises, the way they lumbered towards the skyline, heads down, backs bowed beneath rain-darkened oilskins. In their wake, five yellow flags, knee-high, flapped in the wind, each one marking the site of a find.

The flare sank below the horizon. A trail of smoke drifted on the wind.

'Better get up there. Have a stretcher party at the ready.'

The rain was coming down harder, hiding the horizon behind drifting grey veils. A wagon driver, Sergeant Farrer, was struggling with his horse, slipping and sliding as he fought to keep it from bolting.

Corporal Reid, the company clerk, was keeping his distance. 'Something's spooked it, sir. Must be a storm comin' in.'

Mackenzie glanced at the sky. It was getting dark. The horse was in a frenzy, but Farrer – a lanky bug-eyed youth from a Lancashire regiment – kept talking to it, caressing its neck when it came within reach. He had a way with animals, which was just as well, as he hardly said a word to the other men.

Mackenzie climbed up the embankment that marked the road to La Signy Farm, mud sucking at his boots. After the frosts of winter the ground was softening, the water pooling in the chalky soil, gathering in the shell holes and the earthworks. Rain would restart the process of decay. Identification would be more difficult and harder on the stomach.

He pulled his coat closer about him. Keeping the squads at full strength was difficult enough as it was, even on double pay. The work took a heavy toll. The volunteers became sullen and withdrawn, unable to sleep, violent quarrels breaking out over nothing. They had all seen their share of battle, but it was as if the reality had only now hit home. Mackenzie went easy on them. He turned a blind eye to minor infractions, even the occasional absence. He reminded them often that the work was important, that it might mean everything to the families back home. It was all he could think of. It was what he told himself.

In the distance Aldridge's squad were still working their way towards the crown of the ridge, which was topped with scraps of blasted vegetation where once there had been woods. By now his men knew what to look for, beyond the obvious markers. Items of equipment on the surface or protruding from the ground were a good indicator. Grass took on a vivid blue tint. Standing water turned greenish-black or grey. Rat holes were always examined closely: scraps of bone around the entrances often meant a shallow grave was close by, though in such cases there was frequently nothing left to identify. The Directorate of Graves Registration provided a list of field burial sites, the occupants of which had to be exhumed and relocated if they could still be found. But there were also the missing: bodies still lying in shell holes and dugouts or hidden among the brambles, dead men who had received no burial – five thousand for every mile of the front, Mackenzie had calculated. That wasn't counting the Germans; but then, nobody counted them.

A pistol shot echoed in the distance. Every man in the squad straightened up. The sound had come from the same direction as the flare. Mackenzie heard shouting.

Moments later Sergeant Cotterell came splashing down the communications trench. 'The Chinks found something. Their adjutant come over. He's waiting at Mark Copse.'

'What did they find?'

'Wouldn't say, sir. Said to fetch you right away.'

They went back into the communications trench, zigzagging through a junction of firing and support lines known as Elephant & Castle. They passed Aldridge's squad coming down off the ridge and made their way towards the ruins of the village. They found the adjutant shivering beside a broken gun carriage. He was short and narrow-chested, officers in the Chinese Labour Corps being recruited for their knowledge of language and custom, not their physique.

'Rawlins, sir,' he said, tucking a Webley into its case. Mackenzie realised he had left his own revolver in the tent. 'The CO sent me over, asks if you could assist.'

'With what?'

'Best see for yourself, sir.'

'Can't it wait till morning?'

Rawlins shook his head and set off, leading them across what had once been no-man's-land. The others followed in single file, eyes fixed on the ground, as they had to be. Unexploded shells were prone to shift in wet soil. They could work their way towards the surface, rotating as the earth softened beneath them. Timed fuses were the greatest threat. The scratch of a spade or a solitary footstep might restore the pathway to the blasting cap, triggering detonation. A change in temperature could have the same effect. Two weeks earlier, near Langemark, volunteers had lit a camp fire, intent on brewing tea, unaware that a high-explosive shell lay buried beneath their feet. Ten men had been blown to pieces.

After two hundred yards they picked their way through a swathe of collapsed wire, dark and rusting, behind which lay the old German lines. Shelling had reduced the fire trench to a ditch, full of loose earth, rags and splintered wood.

They turned down a short communications trench, scrambled over broken timbers, pressed on along the support line. In places the ramparts were intact, but the mud was thicker and darker, like the bottom of a pond. Finally they reached a junction with another trench, wider and deeper than the others. Beyond it stood a dozen tree trunks, weathered to grey. This section of the German line had once been a strongpoint. On the army maps it was called Two Storm Wood.

'Something shifted up here,' Rawlins shouted, pointing down the northern wall of the trench. 'After we went over it. Ground opened up.'

'A tunnel?'

'Could be.'

This area of the front had been heavily undermined, the tunnels packed with explosives, not all of them used. Mackenzie had asked Corps HQ for the plans, but such information had always been closely guarded, and his request had gone unanswered.

'Some men came back for firewood,' Rawlins said. 'Missed the entrance the first time. Must have been hidden before all the rain.'

They went around the next traverse. The beam of a torch swung through the gloom and fixed on them. Rawlins said something in Mandarin and the beam swung down. Two Chinese men were standing before them, stocky dark-skinned labourers with chevrons on their coats and canes in their hands. Discipline among the Chinese was rarely a formal affair, except where serious crimes were concerned. Instead, violence was meted out spontaneously by *paitou*: gangers of the same race. Some of the rank-and-file were no more than boys anyway, armed with forged papers, such was their eagerness for several years of well-paid work – though Mackenzie often wondered if they had known what they were letting themselves in for.

The gangers were jumpy. More words, incomprehensible to Mackenzie, passed between them and Lieutenant Rawlins. One of them handed Rawlins the torch.

To their right, partly hidden by a heap of corrugated iron and timbers, lay the entrance to a dugout. The frame had taken shell damage. Rawlins shone his torch into the hole.

'Down there, sir.'

He made no move to lead them. The gangers stood motionless, the rain running down their faces.

'Where's your CO?'

'Called away, sir. Some of our boys took off. Word got out.'

'Word?'

The adjutant simply stared into the dugout. 'Down there, sir,' he said again.

Mackenzie hated these underground places. Before the Armistice they had kept him in one piece, but the fear of being buried alive never left him.

The heaviest-calibre shells could collapse a dugout thirty feet down. He could not sleep underground unless utterly exhausted, and even then he would dream of that lightless death, lungs filling with dirt, the choked-off screams of men.

Sergeant Cotterell had his own torch. He was already stooped over, one foot planted over the threshold. Holding onto the lintel, he lowered himself through the hole. Mackenzie snatched the other torch from Rawlins and followed. A succession of muddy steps led down into blackness.

They went slowly, checking all around for wire trips and hidden explosives. The Chinese could easily have missed them. Through the fug of damp earth, Mackenzie caught a sickly hint of decay.

They reached the first turn.

'Clear so far.' Cotterell's voice hummed in the narrow space.

'Keep going.'

The sound of the rain above them slowly faded away. Silence closed in, relieved only by their own breathing and the creak of timbers. The smell was stronger now: acrid, fatty. Mackenzie reached for a handkerchief. Like his men, he had learned always to carry one soaked in carron oil. He sucked in the harsh, medicinal vapour, his hand pressed hard against his mouth.

During the war he would have feared a bullet or a grenade, resistance from a cornered enemy. It was different this time: older fears played on his mind. When he was a boy, holidaying on the south-Kent coast, he and one of his brothers had discovered a brick tower on an empty stretch of shore, the structure derelict and listing, like a hulk run aground. They had forced open the door, disturbing something that lay in the darkness. They could not see what it was – an animal was his first thought – but then he had glimpsed bony knuckles clutched around a blanket, heard a whimpering breath: pitiful, but human. He had run away, his brother close behind; run and not looked back until the tower was out of sight, fear giving way at last to shame. He had not wanted to see, that was the truth of it, to comprehend the wretchedness cowering alone in that cold, dark place; to expose his conscience to the horror. Finally the two of them had resolved to go back with clothes and food, but then they had heard talk of a madman escaped from some fortress asylum and they had abandoned their plan. The incident was never spoken of again. His brother was dead now, in any case.

Sergeant Cotterell had already reached the main chamber. His footsteps echoed around the walls. Unlike the British, the Germans reinforced their dugouts with concrete and steel. They had ventilation shafts and water tanks. The General Staff had not wanted British soldiers getting too comfortable underground.

Mackenzie's torch flickered and grew dim. His pulse was loud in his ears.

'Sergeant?'

Still covering his nose and mouth, Mackenzie eased himself down the last few steps. Grit crunched beneath his boots. From somewhere up ahead came a voice: muttering, cursing. It had to be Cotterell.

'Sergeant, where are you?'

The beam of the torch caught an overturned chair, a rope hanging over the edge of a table, the wide-eyed stare of an abandoned gas mask. The table was caked in a clinging filth. Dark streaks on the wall beyond resembled the daubings of a lunatic child.

Cotterell was quiet now. It was as if he had vanished. How big was this place? Were there passageways, tunnels? If so, where did they lead? How many men had once taken shelter down here?

'Sergeant?'

Mackenzie turned. A gap in the wall marked the entrance to the next chamber. Pale light flickered across the floor. He moved slowly towards it, breath held, trying to make no sound – just as in a trench raid, except that he had no weapon.

Cotterell stood in front of him, the torch making a pool of light at his feet.

'What is it, man? What did you see in there?'

Cotterell did not answer. He walked back to the steps and disappeared without a word, leaving Mackenzie alone. Beyond him, in the second chamber, the captain sensed movement, an almost imperceptible disturbance in the air, like the beat of wings.

———

—— Four ——

Most of the other officers had left the dining room when Major Parry took out the pamphlet and slid it across the table. 'Third in a month, sir. I thought you should see it.'

Brigadier Henley had been watching the street. Brigade HQ had been established in a hotel on the rue Despret, which the Germans had used as a hospital for gas casualties, but in four years, it seemed, nobody had thought to clean the windows. Reluctantly he put down the nutcracker and squinted at the lines of uneven type. 'Bolshie stuff, is it?'

'The political objectives aren't clear. What it's calling for, if I read it right, sir, is some sort of purge.'

'A purge?'

'Of the ruling classes – the powers that be. The language is rather biblical.'

A staff captain sat at the far end of the table, smoking a cigarette as he nursed his fourth glass of claret. 'Work of a lunatic. Shrapnel in the brain.'

The captain's drinking had become noticeable in recent weeks. Before the Armistice it would have earned him a reprimand, but with the enemy gone and the brigade demobilising, the matter had been left to stew.

'Perhaps so,' Major Parry said, 'but it might strike a chord with some of our boys.'

'Our boys?'

'Third paragraph, sir.'

The brigadier took out a pair of spectacles and leaned over the pamphlet. He read out loud: '*Some have power by right of birth, which is no right, but deference and cowardice make it so. Others buy their way to power.*' Henley grunted, dabbing at the ends of his moustache. '*Few are those whose spirit has been forged by war: chieftains, who gather men to their banners as naturally as the swarm to the hive. In time of war they are feared more than the enemy by those who rule us.*' The brigadier shook his head. 'I still don't see what—'

'Read on, sir.'

Henley frowned. '*What became of that hero, of La Bassée and Longeast Wood, who rode the black horse over Bazentin Ridge and . . .*'

The staff captain looked up, impressed by the brigadier's sudden silence. 'That was Colonel Rhodes, wasn't it?'

'I fear so,' Parry said.

'*He was rewarded with treachery. Our masters knew what we know: that their ruin is written in the blood of the fallen.*' Henley put the pamphlet down. 'What utter nonsense. A Hun grenade did for Rhodes.'

'He was alive when they shipped him back to England,' Parry said.

Henley shook his head. 'Severe head injuries. Worse than dead.'

The staff captain picked up his glass. 'Rhodes was a fine battalion commander – the best. The Seventh were nothing before him, and nothing much afterwards.'

'Your opinion is noted,' Parry said.

'Opinion be damned; he was a legend, a Hector. Should have been on the General Staff.' The staff captain emptied his glass. 'Touch of the tar brush, of course – Indian Army and all that. Expect that's what put the kibosh on it.'

Henley was lost in thought. Lieutenant Colonel Rhodes had in fact been offered a post on the staff, at Third Army, but had turned it down. It was the first hint that his ambitions might be grander than becoming any mere commander of infantry; that what mattered most to him was his reputation with the common soldier, not the army top brass.

Henley pushed the pamphlet away. 'Where did this come from?'

'Unclear. There were copies circulating in Charleroi. An NCO saw something like it in Boulogne before the mutiny.'

Henley shook his head. Since the Armistice the newspapers had been full of stories about demonstrations and strikes over pensions and pay – at the pits, on the docks and the railways, even at the Metropolitan Police. Five thousand troops, impatient for demobilisation, had mutinied in Calais. In Wales, rioting by Canadian soldiers had left five men dead. The Guards Division had been withdrawn from Germany and was on its way back to London – the only formation the government thought it could still count on.

'Tell the battalion commanders to watch out for anyone distributing,' he said. 'But no general searches. We don't want to start something.'

Someone knocked at the door. Dawson, the mess sergeant, walked in and saluted. 'Sorry to trouble you, sir. I wasn't sure if you'd—'

'What is it?'

All the men present were serving in the East Lancashire Division, but the sergeant was the only one whose speech suggested as much.

'You've a visitor, sir. A woman.'

'A woman?'

'A lady, sir.' Dawson stepped forward, holding out a scrap of paper. 'I asked her to write her name down.'

Henley took the paper and read it.

'No women in the mess, Dawson,' the staff captain said. 'What are you playing at?'

———

Amy Vanneck stood alone at the end of the hallway, shivering in her black overcoat, clutching the cane handles of a travelling bag. On either side of her, beyond closed doors, loud male voices echoed, punctuated by the clack of billiard balls. The air had a leathery taint, besides the pervading smell of tobacco, the unmistakable smell of a masculine world, of spit and polish, tradition and discipline. She tried to imagine Edward there, tried to picture him at ease, fitting in, so that she might feel less out-of-place herself.

It was four days since she had made the crossing to Boulogne, four days on railways and dirt roads, four nights dozing in carriages and waiting rooms. She had reached the fortress town of Maubeuge, seven miles away, that morning. A shabby boarding house accepted her money for a room. But rest, she had found, was impossible. After one brief attempt, she had washed and changed her clothes and taken the first train to the Jeumont, where Edward's brigade was now headquartered.

France was not how she had imagined it: it was vaster, emptier, shabbier. The towns and villages she glimpsed through carriage windows were shuttered and unwelcoming. There were few trees or hedges to soften the stark brick settlements that seemed to weigh on the land like an alien presence. Even Amiens, shrouded in a gritty winter mist, was not the busy provincial capital of her imagination, but grey and half-deserted, shell damage visible on every street. After a few minutes in the heart of the city she had returned gratefully to the Gare du Nord. Among the other weary travellers she felt a little less alone.

A shrill cry of command echoed down the street outside. Boots thumped unevenly on cobblestones. An NCO was putting some recruits through their paces, his voice thick with disdain. For a schoolmaster, Edward had never been that keen on order and discipline. It was music he loved – any kind of music. Once, in his cottage, she had been woken by a strange, insistent sound. She had hurried downstairs to find the kitchen table covered in old bottles and glasses, filled to different levels with water and arranged according to pitch. Edward, half-naked, was tapping out the Dance of the Swans from *Swan Lake* with a pair of bone-handled spoons.

'What do you think?' he had called out, without stopping. 'Think I might earn a few coppers in the marketplace?'

'I'm not sure Tchaikovsky would approve.'

'Pyotr Ilyich? He'd love it. It'd be a liberation. Escape from the bloody Bolshoi, and not before time!'

With that, he had switched into the Infernal Galop from *Orpheus in the Underworld*. That's what music was for him: liberation, release – she had seen it clearly then for the first time. It spoke to the heart and from the heart, untrammelled by rules, conventions, etiquette. Edward had tried to instil the same idea in his pupils, he told her. 'Music says what it wants to say, even if you can't.'

Amy had taken him at his word when he told her that the army was his idea of hell. And yet to hell he had gone.

A door banged shut. The mess sergeant reappeared. 'Follow me, if you would, Miss.'

———

On the floor above was a large dining room. Logs were smoking in a marble fireplace, over which hung a landscape painting, dark with soot. Awkwardly two men stood to greet Amy. The younger was little more than Edward's age, smartly turned out, bespectacled. The other had to be Brigadier Henley. The men introduced themselves and offered her a seat.

'Thank you for seeing me, Brigadier.'

Henley glanced at the pearl tiepin in Amy's lapel. His eyes were clear and dark, but not without warmth. 'Sergeant, bring Miss Vanneck some ... Would you care for some tea or ... ?'

Amy cleared her throat. 'No, thank you.'

The men sat down again.

'Miss Vanneck, am I to understand you came here unaccompanied?' Henley said.

'I'm meeting a friend in a few days' time.'

'May I ask where?'

'In Amiens.'

Amy hoped she sounded certain, not merely hopeful. The fact was, she had written to Kitty only after arriving in France. Nor was she sure how her letter would be received. Before events at home had forced Amy's hand, before her hurried departure for the Continent, they had planned to make the journey together. It was not merely a matter of solidarity. Kitty had reasons of her own for making the trip: her brother John, a lieutenant in the Hampshires, had been killed on the Somme the previous September. He had been given a field burial close to the front line, but the army could no longer locate his grave. No explanation had been given to the family, or any assurances that a further search would be made. It was something they were simply supposed to accept. Kitty had been distraught, outraged. Her beloved brother deserved better: a proper grave, a headstone with a name, a site that could be visited. She would see to it herself, if she had to.

But all that had been months ago. The pain of grief might have eased in that time. Perhaps Kitty had come to accept the idea of her brother lying in an unmarked grave, or beneath a stone that read *Unknown but to God*. He was only one of thousands, after all. The fact that Amy was already in France would make it easier to back out. Kitty had only to ignore her friend's letter, or pretend it had never arrived. Perhaps it was too much to expect anything else.

'Amiens, you say?' The brigadier looked perplexed. 'And in the meantime, you're quite alone?'

Amy nodded.

'Does your father know you're here?'

'Of course.'

'And he approves?'

Amy nodded. 'He understands: if there's any chance of finding my fiancé – of making an identification – it must be taken.' Henley and Major Parry looked at each other. 'Edward was missing in action on the seventeenth of August last year.'

For several seconds there was silence in the room. It was as if Amy had said something disturbing or bizarre. The field of battle, even now, was another preserve: of soldiers, of men. She had seen few Englishwomen on the ferry from Folkstone, and after Amiens none at all. Perhaps this was why. Perhaps they felt what she could not: that the men they loved belonged out here, in martial company, whether living or dead.

The brigadier's chin dipped towards his chest. 'I see. So you've come to find his ... to find *him*?'

The trace of a smile appeared on Major Parry's lips.

Amy nodded. 'Captain Edward Haslam, of the Seventh Manchesters.'

Parry's smile vanished. He glanced at Henley, but the brigadier remained quite still.

'And, assuming you succeed in finding him, then what?'

'Then I shall see that he has a marked grave.' Amy swallowed. 'Isn't that his due?'

Henley nodded. 'It is, of course. But how to do you propose to go about this task?'

'I want to find out where Edward was last seen. That's the first step.'

'And the second?'

'Records – anything by way of records. Perhaps something has been missed or misreported. Perhaps he was found, by someone. Mistakes can happen, can't they?'

Henley nodded. 'On occasion, I suppose. And what if there's been no mistake?'

'Then I will go to the place where he was and search.'

Henley frowned. 'You surely don't intend to visit the battlefields? I'm afraid that would be quite impossible at this stage.'

Amy's mouth was dry. A decanter of water sat in front of her, but she was afraid to ask for a drink, afraid of looking any weaker than she already did. 'Doesn't the army have men working there now?'

'Soldiers, Miss Vanneck, and coolies. They're accustomed to the conditions. They have the requisite constitution. With respect, you do not.' By way of a concession, he added, 'I don't mean you personally, of course. I refer to the fairer sex in general.'

Amy did not argue. For all she knew, the battlefields were still under martial law. 'I was hoping it might—'

'In any case, shouldn't this be a matter for his family?' Henley said. 'His mother? His father?'

'Edward's parents are both dead.'

Henley sighed. 'I see.'

'I received some information from the colonel of his regiment.'

'Major General Barnard?'

Amy reached into her bag and handed the letter to Brigadier Henley, watching as he skimmed through the preliminary expressions of regret, before focusing on the lines that mattered:

On 7th June the 42nd Division was posted to the line two miles north of the River Ancre. Over the next six weeks, raids by elements of the division succeeded in pushing the enemy back a thousand yards. Having lost key points below the Serre Ridge on 16th August, the enemy counter-attacked the same night. The division was heavily engaged, and it was only the next morning, when the enemy had been repulsed, that Capt. Haslam's absence was noted.

The line at this time was in a state of flux, and losses were high. The 42nd Division spent seventy-five consecutive days in the line, a period that would have placed operations, and the men themselves, under exceptional strain. It is not the army's normal practice to keep divisions in the line for so long.

I regret that your fiancé's fate remains unknown. However, the army has undertaken to search the front in a manner which was not possible during the hostilities. Should more information come to light, it will be passed to you.

In the meantime, it should be some comfort to reflect that Capt. Haslam fought valiantly and unstintingly in the service of his country, and for those he loved.

Henley folded up the letter and handed it back. 'Very thorough. I'm not sure what more I can add.'

Amy had made several enquiries of the regiment, none of which had received a response. It was only when her Uncle Evelyn had interceded on her behalf that Barnard had seen fit to write.

'I was hoping Edward's comrades might know more,' Amy said. 'They might have seen something.'

Henley took a cigarette from a silver case. He was lighting up when Major Parry murmured something in his ear. The brigadier frowned, then opened the case again. 'Miss Vanneck, I don't suppose you ... ?'

Amy shook her head. Her mother had always told her that smoking was the badge of a fallen woman.

Henley put the case away and pushed himself back in his chair. 'Miss Vanneck, I must commend your resourcefulness in getting this far, and you do have my sympathy, but I'm afraid this is a matter you simply must leave to the army.'

'But isn't the army going home?'

'Be that as it may, a considerable effort is under way to clear ... to *recover* the dead and the missing, and to identify them where possible. The presence of civilians in operational areas can only impede that effort.' Henley's tone softened. 'And I'm sure you wouldn't want that.'

'But how many men are unaccounted for? And how many are searching for them?'

'I don't have the numbers to hand, but identifying the dead is the top priority, I assure you.'

'I heard there are cemeteries in Flanders full of graves without names.'

Henley glanced at Major Parry, as if willing him to explain, but Parry remained silent. 'It's in the nature of war, I'm afraid. Especially one fought on such a scale, over much the same ground.' He cleared his throat. 'We may have to face the fact that many of the missing will remain missing, however we might wish it were otherwise.'

Amy's hands were clasped together in her lap. 'Is there any chance Edward was taken prisoner?'

The brigadier plucked a sliver of tobacco from his tongue. 'I'm not acquainted with the circumstances, I'm afraid, but if that were the case, he'd have been released by now. Besides, last August . . .'

Again he looked to Major Parry. 'Last August the brigade was going forward for the most part,' Parry said. 'Very few of our men were captured, and certainly no officers.'

Amy caught the disdain in his voice, as if capture implied surrender, and surrender implied cowardice. 'My uncle said it was important I talk to members of the battalion.'

Henley stared at her through the twisting bands of smoke. She took care not to look away. 'Your uncle being . . . ?'

'Sir Evelyn Vanneck.'

She had used the name deliberately, hoping it would work on Brigadier Henley as it had worked on Major General Barnard. Her uncle had trained as a barrister but worked at the Foreign Office. He travelled more than anyone Amy had ever met, as part of various delegations to conferences and diplomatic conventions, the substance of which he was never at liberty to discuss. When Amy was a child he would return with exotic gifts that used to fascinate her: a bearded soldier doll from the Russian court, the figure of a prancing horse made of Venetian glass, a patterned chess board from Samarkand – blue, he said, like the mosques of the Silk Road. But then the war had come, and his visits had all but stopped. Amy had managed to introduce him to Edward, when Sir Evelyn was in Cambridge and she was staying there with her aunt. She had hoped Edward would meet with her uncle's enthusiastic approval, but in the event Edward had been reticent and her uncle preoccupied. Nothing about the encounter was reassuring.

Brigadier Henley's forefinger tapped gently against the edge of the table. 'Well, since you're here, Miss Vanneck, I suppose it wouldn't hurt to talk to the CO. He might have something to satisfy your curiosity, though I wouldn't count on it.'

'May I ask why?'

'I'll let you find that out for yourself.' Henley stood up. 'You must forgive me, but I'm afraid I have duties to attend to. Major Parry, be so good as to escort Miss Vanneck to Seventh Battalion HQ. Tell the CO to give her what information he can.'

'Yes, sir.'

'And then see she gets back on her train.'

———

The 7th Manchesters were camped in a field on the northern edge of the town, within sight of a stone church, their yellow tents huddled in rows around a flagpole. Headquarters had been set up in an old mill, outside which stood a small crowd of civilians, kept at bay by two sentries who saluted as Major Parry edged his way through.

'Your CO in, is he?'

'Yes, sir.'

'Good. This way, Miss Vanneck. *Prenez du recul, s'il vous plaît!*'

Reluctantly the crowd stood back. Inside it was darker and quieter, the chill air thick with a smell of damp earth, a typewriter hacking away unseen. Wooden steps led to an upper floor. They were halfway up when a burly civilian with a scarf round his neck appeared above them, followed by a hard-faced woman in a black hat.

A sergeant was behind them. 'Move along now, toot sweet!' Seeing Major Parry below, he saluted. 'Begging your pardon, sir. Didn't see you.'

The civilians pushed past.

At the top of the steps was an office. Amy saw a roll-top desk, filing cabinets and a factory clock on the wall with rusted black hands.

Parry rapped on the door frame. 'Trouble with the locals, Colonel?'

An officer sat sprawling in front of the desk, trying to light a pipe. 'The usual: selling liquor after hours. Don't take kindly to the red-knobs shutting 'em down.'

He looked up and saw Amy standing in the doorway. He had pitted skin and elfin ears, but for Amy it was getting hard to see past another khaki uniform to the individual beneath.

'Miss Vanneck, this is Lieutenant Colonel Webster,' Parry said.

Amy offered her hand. Edward had never mentioned an officer called Webster. She assumed he was new to the battalion. The sergeant major followed her in.

'Miss Vanneck was engaged to Captain Haslam, sir,' Parry said. 'It was Haslam, wasn't it?'

'Yes, Edward Haslam.'

Amy searched Webster's face for some trace of sympathy or regret, but found none.

'The captain was posted as missing in action last year,' Parry said, 'in August.'

'The seventeenth of August,' Amy said.

'Miss Vanneck wants information on the circumstances, Colonel. The brigadier asks if you could assist.'

Webster glanced at Amy, as if doubtful this could be true. She had an idea what he was thinking: here must be one of that new breed of woman – assertive, unfeminine – who, after their participation in the war effort, felt entitled to go wherever they wanted and do whatever they pleased.

'All right, let's see.' Webster put the pipe between his lips and took out a key. 'Do take a seat.' He gestured towards an upright chair. 'The battalion diary might shed some light on the matter.'

Amy sat down. 'Did you know him, Colonel?'

'Afraid not. I transferred from another division last October. Never had the privilege of commanding Captain Haslam – though I understand he was an outstanding officer.'

An outstanding officer. The phrase was a standard ingredient of military condolence. Dead officers were all outstanding. Mediocrity was the preserve of survivors.

'The regimental here's the only veteran,' Webster said. 'How long have you been with us, Sergeant Major?'

'Since October of 'seventeen, sir. I were in D company back then. Didn't see much of Captain Haslam. Knew him by sight's about all.'

'Do you remember when he went missing – what happened?' Amy said.

'Can't say as I do. That were a rough time. We were in the line a long spell.'

'Seventy-five days.'

For the first time, the sergeant major looked her in the eye. 'That'd be about it, Miss. Rotten sort of places, them old battlefields. Give you the creeps, what with the graves churned up an' all.'

'Yes, thank you, Sergeant Major,' Parry said.

Webster had unlocked the desk. He pulled out a large loose-bound book and thumbed through the pages. With its wide margins and ruled lines, it resembled a ledger, the spaces between filled with neat handwriting.

'Says they were in line east of Auchonvillers, two miles from the Ancre.' Webster turned over another page and read out an entry. '*August the ninth: withdraw from Rob Roy to reserve trenches Legend and Dunmow, three thousand yards west of Serre. Relieved by Seventh Northumberland Fusiliers.*'

Edward had once explained the dangers of rotating battalions on the front line. If the enemy got wind of it, they would put up flairs and shell the area, hoping to catch men in the narrow communications trenches. Units usually changed places at dead of night, in silence.

'I'm afraid you'd need a trench map to make sense of these places,' Webster said.

'Could you lend me one?'

'I'm afraid that's impossible,' Major Parry said. 'Trench maps constitute vital military intelligence. The enemy would do anything to get hold of them.'

'The enemy? But aren't they … ?'

'Regulations are regulations,' Parry said. 'I'm sure you understand.'

Amy repeated the names in her head: *Rob Roy, Legend, Dunmow*. How far from that stretch of line did Edward lie: a hundred yards? A mile?

'What about after that?'

Webster turned back to the diary. Even from where she sat, Amy could see that the entries had become shorter.

'The brigade moves forward again night of the twelfth to thirteenth. *Heavy enemy counter-attacks to regain lost outposts, all repulsed.*' Webster ran a finger over the cramped, angular handwriting, then turned a page. '*August the fifteenth: in reserve.* It says there was some shelling. Four shrapnel injuries. And the sixteenth …' He turned another page, frowning. 'Nothing. Just a casualty list. This must have been when the CO was wounded.'

'The CO?'

'Lieutenant Colonel Rhodes.' Webster squinted at the writing. 'It says, yes … *Dawn on the seventeenth, enemy attempted to regain the old trenches west of Serre, having commenced with gas and shelling. Lt Col Rhodes found severely wounded by a grenade. With two battalions of New Zealanders, countered and regained the lost positions around ten o'clock*.' Webster turned the book so that Amy could see it. 'Your fiancé is listed here.'

She read his name: *Capt. E. J. Haslam*. Beside it was the single word *Missing*. For a moment she had his face before her: his brown eyes, his smile, the smell of his skin. All of them gone now, for ever.

There were four names above Edward's. Opposite the first two was written *Wounded*, opposite the next two *Killed*. They were all officers. Casualties among the other ranks – the privates and NCOs – were not listed by name. Their fates were summarised in a single line: *O.R. 23 killed; 19 wounded*.

Amy felt unsteady. 'Is this all you have?'

'If there was more information,' Parry said, 'it would have been shared with his family.'

'Colonel Rhodes isn't . . .'

'His wounds were severe.'

'Could I speak to the man who replaced him?'

'I'm afraid not. Major Blomfield is dead. Killed on Beaucamp Ridge about six weeks after he assumed command.'

'Then some of Edward's comrades, in C Company . . . Edward mentioned some of them. I wrote down all the names.'

Amy took out a piece of paper from her pocket and offered it to Colonel Webster. With a glance at Parry, he took it. 'The difficulty is, Miss Vanneck, the battalion suffered rather badly at the end of September, attacking the Hindenburg Line.'

'How badly?'

'The enemy were in well-prepared positions. Machine-gun nests, concrete – and wire, of course. Our brigade pushed through, but the others got hung up assaulting the high ground. Our boys ended up being strafed from two sides. The Seventh got the worst of it, I'm afraid.'

'On the first day we lost three hundred men out of four hundred and fifty,' Parry said. 'And twelve out of sixteen officers.'

Colonel Webster looked at Amy's list. 'I'm sorry, but I don't think any of these men are still with us. The battalion was back in the thick of it in October, and we had casualties then too.'

Amy felt the blood drain from her face. Edward's battalion no longer existed. His comrades had been expended and replaced. This was what the brigadier had been reluctant to tell her: that she was too late.

Major Parry stood with his hands behind his back, watching her closely. He was assessing her, trying to read her. 'I'm afraid the brigadier was right, Miss Vanneck. Your presence here can really serve no useful purpose. I'm surprised your father thought it might.' He had seen through the lie, and wanted Amy to know it. 'I'm only sorry you weren't better advised.'

———

Amy made her own way back to the station, her head swimming, her footsteps heavy. She had placed a lot of hope in the 7th Manchesters, but her hopes had been misplaced. To the surviving officers, Captain Haslam was just a name in a ledger, one that meant next to nothing. If she was going to find him, she would have to do it without their help.

A solitary electric bulb burned in the ticket office. Outside, on the narrow platform, everything was dark. A nearby estaminet was doing good business, piano music and rowdy voices drifting out into the night.

A gust of wind blew a crumpled pamphlet against Amy's boot. She stooped to remove it, found herself looking at dense lines of type, large but uneven. Where the type was clear, she read:

Our masters knew what we know: that their ruin is written in the blood
of the fallen.
Our natural leaders were betrayed, but they shall return. The seeds have been
planted, and soon will be a reckoning in blood.
Comrades! The time is at hand. A sword has been forged in the furnace of battle,
and it will cut the canker from our land. Be ready!
WE ARE THAT SWORD!

She slumped down on a bench beneath the station clock. Up ahead, where the rue de la Station crossed the line, she spotted a solitary woman wandering past the officers' mess. She got as far as the corner, then headed back the way she had come. She was almost out of sight when another, taller figure stopped in front of her. Words were exchanged.

It was then Amy realised she was not alone.

'You here, Miss?'

Further up the platform a light swept through the darkness.

'Yes, over here.'

The voice drew closer. 'Sergeant Dawson. The brigadier said to see you onto your train. You all right, Miss?'

Amy recognised the mess sergeant at Brigade headquarters. 'Yes, of course.'

'Wouldn't you rather wait inside, Miss? Cold out here.'

'I'm all right, thank you.'

'Whatever you say, Miss.' Dawson glanced back over his shoulder. 'So I heard it was a trench map you were after. This is the last one they did around Serre.'

He placed a folded map in her hand. The paper was bulky, pale white and fibrous. On the front was printed the red-and-white diamond of the 42nd Division.

'Aren't these maps secret?'

Dawson laughed. 'There's a few lying around the mess. Good for souvenirs is all.'

Amy reached into her bag. 'I should pay you.'

'No need for that, Miss,' Dawson said, but when Amy held out a twenty-franc note, he stuffed it quickly into his trouser pocket. 'Have any luck, did you, with the battalion? They tell you anything?'

Amy shook her head. 'There's no one left. No one even remembers him.'

A whistle announced the arrival of the train. Dawson led Amy down the platform. The carriages were mostly empty. Only three people got off, two of them soldiers.

Dawson held open a door. Even in the gloom, Amy could tell he was holding something back. He closed the door again, but before she could move to a compartment, he rapped on the window.

'There's a corporal from C Company, name of Staveley.' He spoke softly. 'Crashed a motorcycle. They took him to a CCS in Maubeuge. He might know a thing or two, if he's still—'

The whistle sounded again. The train was already moving.

'Staveley. Thank you.'

'Only don't tell him I—' Dawson's words were obscured behind the noise of steel on steel. 'Best not use my name at all.'

Amy wasn't sure she had heard him right. She stayed at the window of the carriage until nothing remained of the station and the town but a few dim points of light in the darkness.

———

—— Five ——

Clearing Station Number 55 occupied an old insane asylum on the eastern approaches of Maubeuge, a blank symmetrical building of brick and stone, its windows barred with iron. Two rows of tents, separated by duckboards, stood in the grounds, gusts of wind tugging at dirty canvas, offering glimpses of the spaces within: empty camp beds, chairs tipped over on their sides; no patients or staff. Beyond the high garden wall, visible through a wrought-iron gate, lay a cemetery, the turned earth bare beneath black wooden crosses.

The main building echoed to the sound of coughing and the clack of heels. One of the windows in the entrance hall was open. It swung back and forth, banging against the frame.

'Miss Henderson?' Amy jumped. 'If you could get changed right away. We were expecting you at eight.'

She turned to find a woman dressed in the white uniform of a nurse. 'I'm sorry. My name isn't Henderson.'

'Who are you then?'

Amy gave her name and offered her hand, noticing only when it was too late that there was mud on her gloves. The woman merely frowned. She was middle-aged, gaunt.

'You're not from the Nursing Service?'

'No.'

'What do you want here?'

It seemed visitors were not welcome.

'I'd like to see Corporal Staveley.'

'Staveley?'

'Of the Seventh Manchesters.'

'Why?' The nurse looked down at Amy's dress. Her hem was black. The cart that had carried her from the middle of town had been loaded with coal. 'You're not family?'

Amy shook her head. 'My fiancé served with the corporal in C Company. His commanding officer, Lieutenant Colonel Webster, suggested I visit.'

She hoped this would be enough: a name dropped, the veiled suggestion that her visit was prompted by compassion.

'Staveley? Are you quite sure?'

'He may remember my fiancé. There's almost no one else left.'

The nurse sighed. 'I see. My name is Adams. I'm the senior sister.' From somewhere above them came a piercing cry of terror, followed by hurried footsteps. 'Your fiancé, is he . . . ?'

'Missing in action.'

Sister Adams nodded. 'Well, I suppose a little conversation can't hurt. But don't expect to get much sense out of him. The corporal's mind . . . Well, you'll see for yourself.'

She led Amy to the back of the building and up a narrow staircase. Two doors gave off the landing above, both equipped with locks and bolts. A corridor on the other side was lined with tiles up to shoulder height, like a butcher's shop. A small window looked out over the cemetery.

'Is he very unwell?'

'Something's not right with him – apart from the burns, I mean. Shell shock perhaps.' Sister Adams reached into her pocket for a key. 'He went to Amiens on an errand. Claims he had a vision. An hour later he rode his motorcycle into a brick wall, in broad daylight. He'd have burned to death if there'd been more fuel in the tank.' They had stopped at another door. It was painted dark red. 'He needs the kind of help we can't give. Sometimes I think he'd be better off with a priest.' Sister Adams unlocked the door. 'Wait here until I call you. And be on your guard. He can be . . . unpredictable.'

The room on the other side was gloomy. Bars of pale light slanted across the floorboards. Some kind of fluid had been hurled against the opposite wall, leaving a grainy brown stain. Amy felt a draught, a sharp smell of urine. She heard the sister's voice, gentle words of entreaty. She wondered how badly burned the corporal was.

Sister Adams reappeared, opening the door wide. 'Here she is, Jack, a visitor for you.'

The patient was lying propped up on pillows, the partially bandaged head turned towards the window. His visible flesh – the left cheek, an inch

37

of forehead, the mouth and nose – was puffy and stained brown with iodine. His left eyebrow was completely gone, in its place a patch of shiny purple scar tissue. His arms rested outside the covers. The left was bandaged, three fingers missing. In the right hand was a small metal object, which he worked at with a ragged thumbnail.

Amy accepted a seat beside the bed. Staveley's gaze was fixed on the road outside, the road that led to Amiens.

'Miss Vanneck's fiancé was in your battalion,' Sister Adams said, brightly. 'I'm sure you've a great deal to say that would interest her: many memories of the Manchesters.'

Staveley did not stir.

'I've told her you've been decorated, with the Military Medal. Why don't you tell her how you got it?'

A breath pushed though Staveley's nostrils.

'Tell her about the medal,' Sister Adams insisted. 'She's come all the way from England.'

Staveley's head turned a little. Half of his top lip seemed to have folded in on itself, leaving a row of misshapen incisors permanently exposed. Amy found it hard to look at him.

'He rescued an injured officer from no-man's-land,' Sister Adams said, 'right under the enemy's guns. Conspicuous bravery, they said.'

The corporal's chest heaved, his breath making a wheezing sound. He looked back towards the road.

'My fiancé was Edward Haslam,' Amy said, 'Captain Haslam. They told me you were in his company.'

At last Staveley's eyes found hers.

'That's true, isn't it, Jack?' Sister Adams said.

'I just wanted to know if you were anywhere near him when . . . If you have any idea what became of him?'

From Staveley's mouth came a dry, clicking sound. 'Rose.'

More a grunt than a word.

'He's thirsty,' Amy said.

Sister Adams picked up the earthenware jug that stood by the bed. 'Are you thirsty, Jack? I'll get you some more water.'

She carried the jug away.

'Who's Rose?' Amy said gently. 'Is she your—'

'*Rose.*'

Staveley's arm made an awkward circle over the covers. He wanted Amy to come closer. Did he think she was Rose? His sweetheart, his wife? She leaned towards him. Perhaps his eyes were damaged too. Maybe it was hard for him to see.

His hand made another impatient loop in the air. Amy edged closer still, close enough to detect a trace of decay behind the antiseptic. Staveley's tongue worked behind the yellow teeth, searching for moisture.

'*Curl. Rose.*'

He held out his hand. In it lay a little naked figure in gilded metal: a baby with a pot belly and a wooden head. Its green, staring eyes were two glass beads. It was a lucky charm, a 'fumsup'. Amy had seen them for sale in England.

It came to her: the first word Staveley was trying to say was *Colonel.*

'Don't try to talk until you've had some water. Sister Adams is—'

The charm fell from Staveley's hand. Amy was reaching down to pick it up when he lurched towards her. '*He'll find you!*'

Amy stumbled backwards, colliding with the bedside table. When Sister Adams hurried back into the room, Staveley was slumped back against the pillow, his chest heaving.

'What's all this? What have you been up to, Jack?'

Amy straightened the table. 'It's my fault. I should go.'

Sister Adams poured out a glass of water and held it to her patient's mouth, supporting his head as he gulped it down.

'He shouldn't be here,' she said. Staveley was unable to seal his lips around the rim. He made a sucking, gurgling sound. 'He should be moved to England, but the papers never come through.'

The corporal sighed, his body relaxing in the sister's arms.

'I'm sorry to have troubled you,' Amy said. 'I can see myself out.'

She reached the door.

'Remember him.' The voice was hoarse and faltering, but Staveley was alert, with her in the here and now. 'The c-choirmaster.'

'That's right.' Amy returned to the bedside. 'Did he tell you about that?'

Staveley shook his head. 'It were ...' He took a couple of shallow breaths. '... what we ... c-called him for ... a joke.'

'But he was a choirmaster, at a boys' school. That was his job before he signed up.'

Briefly Staveley's mouth formed itself into the parody of a smile. 'Fancy that.'

'Music was what he loved most,' Amy said, 'until . . . until he came here.'

Staveley's head tilted. Amy heard the bones in his neck click. 'Sang a different tune then, eh?'

'What do you mean?'

'Just a few minutes more, I think,' Sister Adams said.

'Mr Staveley?'

Staveley's eyes narrowed, a flash of malevolence behind the rheumy slits. 'Sure you still want . . . ?'

'Want? Want what?'

'Him.' His breathing was laboured. 'No matter what?'

'Of course.' Amy was not sure what he meant. 'Of course.'

Sister Adams went to a trolley where dressings and syringes lay waiting. 'I'd like him to sleep, if he can.'

Staveley sighed. His gaze returned to the road.

Amy tried once more to regain his attention. 'Do you know what happened on the sixteenth of August? Corporal Staveley? Do you remember that day? By the River Ancre. A German counter-attack on the Serre Ridge. Captain Haslam was reported missing in the morning.'

Staveley nodded to himself. 'Still there, I'd say.'

'Where exactly?'

'There's places.'

'Places?'

Staveley cast a furtive glance at Sister Adams. His voice dropped to a whisper. '*Underground.*' He coughed. 'Dugouts. Huns built 'em. And tunnels. Miles and miles, under no-man's-land. Men went down there – deserters. Come out at night. Scavenge, like animals. Kill what they find.'

Sister Adams touched Amy on the shoulder. 'Take no notice. It's one of those stories that went round. Not a shred of truth in it.'

'But could there be tunnels?'

'Very likely,' Sister Adams said before Staveley could answer. 'There were tunnels in lots of places. It doesn't mean a thing.'

Footsteps in the corridor. Another nurse hurried into the room. 'Major Harrington wants you in theatre, Sister.'

Sister Adams nodded. 'Perhaps now, Miss Vanneck, would be the time to . . .'

'Of course.'

'I told you: his mind isn't . . . I'm sorry.'

Amy got up. Staveley was still watching her, eyes narrowed, as if assessing her. She reached for his hand. 'Where did you last see Captain Haslam? Please try to remember.'

Staveley took a deep breath. 'Go home.' He spoke softly. 'Too late soon.'

'Too late?'

'He'll find you.' His tone was matter-of-fact, as if it did not concern him one way or another.

'Who? Who'll find me?'

'Like a worm on a hook.'

Sister Adams sighed. 'Now, Jack, don't start.'

'You'll die here.'

'Jack, that's enough.' Sister Adams began arranging the blankets, pulling them up tight across Staveley's chest. 'Miss Vanneck didn't come to hear your nonsense.'

Staveley took a long, shuddering breath and slumped back against his pillows. 'Why'd you come?'

Amy realised that she was shaking. 'I want to find him.'

The corporal nodded to himself. 'Take him, you mean. Take him back.'

Amy swallowed. Sister Adams was watching her. 'No, I'm . . . I couldn't do—'

'Liar!'

Staveley's throat made a rasping sound that might have been a laugh. Then he was coughing again, racked with pain.

'The corporal needs to rest now,' Sister Adams said firmly.

Staveley turned his head towards the Amiens road. Amy said goodbye, but he did not seem to hear her. She was at the door when he spoke again.

'Look for him under Two Storm Wood.' His voice was calm, an edge of cruelty to it. 'Look for your damned sweetheart there.'

———

Sister Adams escorted Amy out. The questioning had disturbed her patient – or disturbed her – and the briskness of her demeanour suggested she was not pleased. 'I warned you not to expect any sense from him,' she said, as they reached the top of the stairs. 'You should forget what he told you.'

'Is there such place as Two Storm Wood?'

'In his head perhaps.'

'He seemed so sure about it.'

Sister Adams turned. 'Do you know what happened in Amiens, before he tried to kill himself? Do you know *who* he saw?' Amy shook her head. 'The Devil. That's what he said: the Devil at the Gare du Nord. Does that sound like a man you can believe?'

———

The Horseman

—— Six ——

When they met in the early days it was never for long. She had taken a job at the telephone exchange, filling in for men gone off to the war. He usually worked late at the school. All the while her mother, who had still not returned to Suffolk, was watchful and demanding, and not easily evaded. An hour, a half-hour – sometimes a week going by between them – that was all they had. Amy's experience of Edward was made up of fragments, time stolen from under the nose of propriety. And now that he was gone, her memories of him were fragments too, moments that had stuck in her mind – sometimes unaccountably – but which seemed to erode a little every day, like islands giving way to the sea.

One Saturday Amy's mother hurried away to London on a matter of family business, taking Aunt Clem with her. They would not be back until late. Amy got word to Edward as soon as she could: *Meet me at the Crusoe Bridge at twelve o'clock.*

She put on her smartest clothes and a new straw hat, dressing up for the occasion because she assumed they would be going into town: to a café or the pictures, or to a tea dance in one of the big hotels, things normal couples did. Edward would want to make up for lost time. But when she reached the bridge – a narrow, iron structure with trees and meadows close on either side – there was no sign of him. She would never forget the panic that took hold of her at the thought that he had simply decided not to come. Until that moment she had never acknowledged the hopes she had placed in him. Had she been taken in? Had her imagination run away with her? She had no experience of men, of romantic love. Her friends, like Kitty Page, knew no more than she did; and Amy's two older sisters, both now married, had always preferred to share their secrets with each other. Standing alone on the bridge, facing the possibility that Edward had already moved on, was the moment she understood: it was love that made her afraid.

'Amy, is that you?'

All the fear: gone in an instant. She hurried to the rail. Edward was in a rowing boat, standing precariously, looking up at her. He was in shirtsleeves, no collar or tie.

'Edward?' It was hard not to laugh. 'What are you doing down there?'

Bright sunlight reflected off the water. She had to shade her eyes.

'There was something I wanted you to see, on the river.' He took in her appearance, and his. 'But you're not really dressed for it.'

He was disappointed, embarrassed, aware perhaps of seeming boyish when what the occasion demanded was worldliness and sophistication.

'Never mind. Stay there.' To Amy the thought of a tea dance – the smoke, the jostling bodies, the rituals and the steps – had lost its appeal. 'I'm coming down.'

The banks were slippery, and she got muddy climbing into the boat. They rowed upstream for half an hour or more, the river narrow, winding and thickly shaded. Three years on, she didn't remember what they said to each other, only the sight of him pulling on the oars, practised efficiency in the way he leaned back with each stroke, instead of paddling like the blazered day-trippers she had often seen in the town. Watching him labour at close quarters, feeling his strength translate into the liquid motion of the boat, she saw a side to him, a physicality that was new. Soon they had left the rooftops and spires far behind. No one passed them as they went.

Further on, they left the boat and set off across a meadow where cattle were grazing. The wind was warm but gusting, so that Amy had to hold on to her hat. Edward took her hand as she climbed over a sty.

On the other side he brought a finger to his lips. 'Down there.'

They were beside the river again. In front of them lay a sheltered loop of water separated from the main course by a fallen tree that had trapped enough silt to form a narrow mud bank. Halfway along, well hidden from almost every side, was a platform of grass and sticks upon which stood an adult swan.

Edward crouched down behind a willow, beckoning Amy to follow. 'They hatched just yesterday, seven of them.'

'Seven?'

She had not noticed the cygnets at first. Their down was grey like the mud. They sat huddled in a circle at their mother's feet.

Another adult swam by, making short, high-pitched calls.

'That's the cob. The anxious father.'

'If he's the cob, what's she?'

'She's the pen.'

The female stood tall and flapped her wings. She was beautiful: pure white, large and powerful. She launched herself onto the water. One by one the cygnets followed, three of them clambering onto her back. They swam out onto the river, the cob bringing up the rear.

'Is it true swans mate for life?'

'Usually.'

'It sounds romantic.'

'We like to think so, don't we? But I'm not sure there's much room for sentiment in the natural world. Cobs'll drown a cygnet if it's weak or sick. I think it's their version of quarantine.'

'That's awful,' Amy said.

Edward shrugged. 'We can admire them all the same, can't we? I mean, *look* at them.'

When the swans were out of sight, they left the river and took a path westwards besides fields of ripening barley. Long afterwards Amy remembered the hedgerows, thick and tall, and teeming with finches; the bitter taste of bottled ale, the drift of high cloud between his gentle, unhurried kisses – above all, a sense that her old life was coming to an end, that a different, unfamiliar one was about to begin. Two years earlier the outbreak of war had felt momentous, even in rural Suffolk, though nothing changed much in her daily routine. But this was different. It was change that came from within – a kind that could not be reversed.

She had told her family nothing of Edward Haslam's existence. They would want to know how the affair had come about. It was too much to hope that her mother would approve, especially when deceit had so clearly been involved. Most likely she would remove Amy to Suffolk at once. As for her father, he would defer to his wife as he did in everything, his one preserve being the management of the estate, which he would not trust to anyone else for fear of being swindled, even though he himself was neither knowledgeable nor competent. And even if Amy could persuade them to relent, she would be watched from that moment on, her every encounter with Edward effectively public. Edward would surely hate that, just as she would. But she could not go on hiding the affair for ever. Sooner or later she would have to tell the truth.

'If we stayed here,' she asked, as she lay with her head on Edward's chest, 'if we stayed out here in the country and didn't go back, how long do you think it would take for them to find us?'

'I suppose that depends on how many people came to look.' His hand was on the back of her neck, his fingers making ringlets with her hair. 'In your case, I expect that would be quite a few, I'm afraid.'

'And in yours?'

He took a while to answer. His hand came to rest against her skin. 'I suppose a lot less. Come to think of it, I'm not sure anyone would come at all.'

———

The sun was veiled in cloud as they rowed back to town, the evening chill bringing up the gooseflesh on Amy's arms. They left the boat and took the footpath across Coe Fen, skylarks still twittering high above them as if reluctant to surrender the day. They walked in silence, Amy weighed down at the prospect of saying goodbye, at the resumption of their separate lives. The power of her feelings seemed to run ahead of her, beyond what was sensible or safe, feelings she could not expect Edward to share.

As they approached the road he took her hand. 'Are you all right, Amy? You seem sad.'

She tried to make light of it. 'Just a little melancholy. Isn't evening the time for it?'

'Yes, but not *this* evening. I've never been happier.'

'That's very flattering, when I'm about to leave you.'

'That wasn't what I meant.'

'What did you mean?'

He stopped. His face shaded the chestnut trees that lined the path. Then he leaned forward and kissed her. It was not their first kiss, or the longest, but years later she could still remember it. She remembered being happy.

On Trumpington Road they stopped again. Amy had expected to see the house in darkness, but there were lights burning in the parlour and the upstairs sitting room. Her mother and aunt had returned early. Amy did not dare get any closer with Edward at her side. Even if it were only Aunt Clem who saw her, there would be interrogations, warnings. Her past deceptions would be discovered.

Edward looked up at the lights and let go of Amy's hand. 'Have you said anything yet, to your mother and father? About us?'

'Not yet.'

Edward kicked at the ground. 'I thought not.'

'I tell them as little as I can. Always. It gives them less to disapprove of.'

'But why should they disapprove? What's wrong with me?'

Amy looked at him. 'Well, for one thing, there's your egregious lack of a title.'

Edward laughed. 'Of course. Careless of me. I should have gone to the trouble of getting one. Do *you* mind?'

'Of course not. Young men with titles are all bores. I've met enough of them to know.'

'I meant about your parents – them not approving of me. Do you mind about that?'

He was serious. The realisation hit her as a soft blow to the heart.

'I said, not to *begin* with. Once they got to know you, of course they'd like you. I know they would.'

Edward nodded, his gaze still on the ground. At the far end of the road the lamplighters were starting their work.

'What if they didn't?'

—— Seven ——

France, March 1919

Amiens squatted under a drizzling sky. Returning refugees were camped along the shattered boulevards, skinny livestock tied up behind wagons piled high with furniture. The smoke from their braziers drifted by the rooftops, gusts of wind blowing ash and cinders into the faces of passers-by. Rubble from bombed-out buildings – every street had a few – had been gathered into piles that spilled over the pavements. The air had a rancid smell.

Amy went early to the Gare du Nord. She had spent much of the night studying the trench map Sergeant Dawson had given her, deciphering its unfamiliar language of markings, lines and symbols. It was dated from April the previous year, four months before Edward went missing. The trench networks were marked in colour – blue for British, red for German – though by all accounts the area had changed hands several times during the final year of the war. Firing lines, support lines, communication trenches, they had been extended, destroyed and re-dug so that the resulting pattern looked like an unravelled sweater. The trenches had names – Flag Avenue, Cheapside, Lonely Lane – beneath which lay the original topography: the hamlets, farms, woods and streams that were now marked only in faint outline, like memories, their existence qualified by the single word *destroyed* in brackets. She could see no mention of Two Storm Wood.

She found Kitty Page huddled under a clock in the ticket hall, clutching a large suitcase, fending off a gang of ragged boys intent on helping her carry it. There was a red blush on her pale, freckled cheeks.

'You're here, Kitty – you're really here!'

Amy put her arms around her friend and held her close.

'Didn't you get my telegram?'

'Yes, but I wasn't sure you'd—'

'I caught an earlier train – stupid of me – and then that was delayed. You wouldn't believe the journey I've had. I swear it's a miracle I haven't lost my bag.'

Kitty chattered as if they were two friends on a trip to the seaside. Perhaps it helped her feel safe in an alien city. She had been withdrawn at school and short of friends – not one of the popular girls. For a long time Amy had hardly noticed her, the way she sat in corners, avoiding everyone's eye, holding an open book in front of her like a shield. But now here she was, journeying from England for the very first time, alone. She had done a lot of growing up since her brother died.

'I've been so worried about you,' Kitty said, 'not knowing anything. But you're looking well, Amy, *very* well.'

In Amy's experience, when someone said you looked *very* well, that meant you looked ill.

'You too, Kitty. You're a sight for sore eyes.'

'I'm a wreck. I almost missed the train. Do we have a place to stay here?'

'I've found a place. It isn't grand, but . . .'

'My old Baedeker recommends the Hôtel du Rhin.'

'You brought a Baedeker?'

'And a map of Picardy, from Stanfords.' Kitty picked up her suitcase. 'I thought we might need one.'

The rooming-house keeper, Madame Pinégal, served supper by candlelight in the tiny dining room, but did not eat with her guests. '*Vous avez plein de choses à vous dire, Mesdames,*' she said, placing a dusty bottle of Barsac on the table. She closed and bolted the shutters before saying goodnight. A small fire burned in the grate, but the room remained cold.

'I didn't expect Amiens to be so damaged,' Kitty said when they had finished eating. 'Was there fighting here?'

'The town was shelled last year, during the German offensive. Madame told me about it. The cathedral was hit nine times, but it's still standing. You can't get inside for all the sandbags.'

Amy had found a row of market stalls in the street behind it. She had bought provisions and an American army torch.

51

'Do your family know you're here?' Kitty said.

'I expect they'll have guessed.'

'Won't they look for you?'

'I doubt it. They know it wouldn't do any good.' Amy reached for the Barsac and poured out two glasses. It was sweet and honeyed, a pre-war vintage. But after the sweetness came an aftertaste: bitter, like rotten almonds.

The last time she had seen her mother, she had been holding the letter from Major General Barnard, feigning sympathy and interest, as the occasion demanded. Amy had been taken in, at first. It had always been her mother's opinion that Edward Haslam was a chancer who clung to the Vanneck name like an *arriviste* limpet, spoiling Amy's prospects of a suitable match. The idea of introducing such a person – a person with no respect for social distinctions and no fortune to compensate – had all too clearly filled her with panic. But all that was before Edward had received his commission, before he had given his life for King and Country.

'You left so suddenly.' Kitty was looking into her glass. 'I thought you'd forgotten about me, about our plan.'

'I had to, I'm sorry. I couldn't stay in England a day longer.'

'Why not?'

Amy had known the question would be asked. She had her answers all prepared.

'I was afraid they'd stop me, Kitty. There was an argument, you see.'

'With your mother?'

This much was true. Barnard's letter revealed not only where Edward had been lost, but where his brigade's headquarters were now established. After the months of waiting, of silence, the wealth of information felt like a sign from above. Amy had hurried to pack a suitcase. She was coming down the stairs again when she had heard urgent voices in the sitting room: her mother angry, aggrieved, her father concerned that they should not be overheard. Amy had stopped and listened. A few minutes later she had left the house without saying goodbye.

Kitty was watching her as she drank. 'She wasn't happy with your going, I suppose.'

'She thought it was absurd. Because Edward wasn't worth it. She never changed her view of him, not even when he was gone.'

Kitty fell silent. Amy picked up the bottle and refilled their glasses. 'Now, tell me how you got away.'

Kitty shrugged. 'It was simple enough: I lied. The family think I'm in Paris, with Gaëlle Blanchet. You remember Gaëlle from school?' Amy recalled a short, red-haired French girl who wore perfume, though it was against the rules. 'There'll be hell to pay if they find out.'

'Unless you succeed. In which case, how could they be angry? They'll at least have a grave to visit, thanks to you. They'll know where John is.'

Kitty nodded. 'I couldn't bear to think of him lying somewhere, without a name or a headstone or anything. It's as if he's alone, and forgotten – forgotten already. It isn't fair.'

Kitty had always been close to her brother. For a while she had harboured the secret wish that he and Amy might get married, or so she said. Amy knew she was not John's type, but the news of his death had shocked her all the same. He had always seemed too affable and good-natured to be killed.

'Did you talk to Edward's comrades?' Kitty said.

'I tried. There aren't many left. The men in charge now – none of them remember him.'

'They couldn't help at all?'

'They were polite enough, but I knew what they were thinking: that I was a silly girl with no understanding of war. They thought I was here out of curiosity.'

Kitty put down her glass. 'Curiosity?'

'John and Edward belong to the army, that's what they think. We've no business here. We should be sitting at home, mourning quietly and not asking questions. Then, if we're lucky, we can expect to see the names of the men we loved on a military monument: name, rank and regiment. Soldiers for eternity. *Here* for eternity.' Amy felt the tears prick at her eyes. 'Edward wasn't a soldier. He was a musician. He taught *music*.'

Amy's glass went over, she wasn't sure how. Wine spilled over the table and onto the floor. The drops were loud against the oak boards.

'I'm sorry, Kitty.' Amy put her head in her hands.

'It's all right.' Kitty reached across the table. 'I feel the same way. Why else would I be here?'

She slowly righted the glass and filled it from the bottle, followed by another for herself. When they were almost empty again, she said, 'If I think how you used to be, before Edward, it's like you were hiding. It's only been a couple of years, but you're different now.'

'Am I?'

'I never thought you'd actually come out here. That's the truth. I know you loved Edward, but I thought you'd drop the idea.'

'I thought the same about you.'

Kitty smiled. 'And yet here we are.'

'Edward used to say that fear was the enemy of freedom. We had to let go of it, not be afraid of what people think.'

'And you did.'

Amy stared at the candle burning between them. The words had come easily: the promises, the reassurances. How much had they been worth? 'You never really trusted him, Kitty, did you?'

'What do you mean? I always—'

'I'm not blaming you. You were always on our side. But you had doubts.'

Kitty's fingers worked at the base of her glass. 'I saw you taking risks for him, more and more risks. I was afraid he might let you down. People like him, with a childhood like his, they find it hard to ... I don't know how to say it: *give of themselves*. I'm glad I was wrong.'

For a long time Edward had said next to nothing about his upbringing. His mother had died when he was very young. His father had died fourteen years later. This much he had told Amy, before shrugging and changing the subject, as if he found it tedious, the events distant, like an old address. But then one summer afternoon, two days after his birthday, Amy had spotted him riding his bicycle through Madingley, where he lived in a small rented cottage, a bouquet of flowers resting on the handlebars. It was a stormy day, the limes and chestnuts hissing in the wind. Rather than call out to him, she had followed, curious – anxious, in fact – to know who the flowers were for. Edward had left his bicycle outside the church of St Mary and walked round the far side to where an iron fence separated the hallowed ground of the churchyard from a field of wheat. When Amy caught up with him, he had already placed the flowers on one of the graves and was standing beside it, lost in thought. The name on the headstone was Emily Haslam. At her death, Edward's mother had been twenty-six years old.

Amy had felt ashamed of herself for intruding, but Edward had smiled when he saw her and taken her hand, as if it were the most natural thing in the world. Beyond the barest facts, it turned out he knew very little about his mother: her likes and dislikes, the kinds of things that made her laugh, whether she had been quiet or chatty, sentimental or down-to-earth, relaxed or anxious. 'I was barely three years old when she died,' he had said, as they wheeled their bicycles through the village. 'It's strange to be so close to someone biologically and still have no real sense of who they were. She brought me into the world. But I've no way to pay her back. So I bring flowers on her birthday. It's the least I can do, don't you think?'

For once Edward seemed happy to talk about his past: how his father – once a quartermaster in the Manchester Regiment, then a partner in a small printing firm – had been unable to raise him alone; how he had been placed with grandparents, then for a year and a half at a small orphanage in Huntingdon, before finally being settling with a widowed aunt on the Isle of Ely. To Amy it sounded hard and lonely, but Edward had insisted she was wrong: 'Every time I fell, there was somebody to catch me – decent people, never cruel. Not all children are so lucky.'

'But your father, you never saw him again?'

'He showed up from time to time. He was often unwell – old before his time, people said. For a long time I hated his visits. I didn't know what to feel, I suppose. In the end I felt sorry for him.'

'You weren't angry? I think I'd have been angry.'

Edward had shaken his head. 'He loved her very much – my mother, I mean. That's what they told me. She was everything to him. He was devastated when she died, utterly broken.'

'But you were his son – *her* son. Wouldn't that be a reason to keep you close?'

Edward had shrugged. 'I can't explain it. That's just how it was. Perhaps I reminded him of her, of her death, and he couldn't bear it.'

By this time they had reached the door of Edward's cottage.

'So, you see, I know about death. I know what it does to the ones it leaves behind. That's why I'll never visit it on anyone else, no matter what.'

'Amy?'

Amy looked up now. Kitty was frowning at her.

'I mean it, really: I was wrong about him.'

Amy let go of the memory. 'Enough about that. What about you, Kitty: what have you found out? Have you heard from John's regiment?'

Kitty put down her glass. 'We had a letter about his whereabouts. Nothing new. There was a lot of fighting in the area, it said. His grave may have been damaged by shelling.'

She took out her map and spread it out on the table, pushing aside dishes and cutlery. Several thousand square miles of Picardy, seemingly sparse and pristine, were laid out before them. Rosières, twenty miles to the east, had already been circled in red ink. Serre-lès-Puisieux lay to the north-east.

'The army has volunteers searching the whole area,' Amy said, 'but we shouldn't wait for them. We should go up there.'

'Keep them up to the mark, you mean? Make our presence felt?'

'Or search for ourselves.'

Kitty insisted they go to Serre first. Amy agreed.

'There's a village called Bertrancourt,' she said, 'just behind the old front line. It used to be a base for field ambulances. Madame Pinégal knows a place we can stay. I found an ironmonger who'll take us in his wagon, provided it doesn't rain too heavily. He said the roads are in a terrible state.'

'And after that?'

'Everyone's desperate for money. As long as we can pay, we'll manage.'

Kitty emptied her glass. A horse went by outside, hooves loud on the muddy cobbles. 'Do you think it'll be very hard, finding Johnny's grave?'

'All graves were marked. Maybe all we have to do is look properly. Maybe the location wasn't recorded right, or there was a mix-up. A lot of graves are being moved.'

'But what if the marker's not there?'

'That'll make things harder, but not impossible.' Amy's heart beat a little faster. Some possibilities had never been discussed, as if to mention them might bring bad luck. 'All soldiers have tags round their necks — two tags. They're buried with one. The other is removed and sent to Graves Registration at Army Headquarters, with a record of the burial. That's how it's supposed to work.'

'Yes, but how does that ... ?'

'If we find an unmarked grave at the spot, we can check it.'

'Check it?' Kitty was shocked, though she tried her best to hide it. 'In other words ...'

'Exhume the body, one way or another. If we want to know who's there, that might be the only way.'

It was hard to talk about the men they had loved rotting in the ground, hard to think of it. But if they could not face the realities, Amy told herself, their journey would be no more than a tour. And they had not come for the scenery.

Kitty hardly spoke for the rest of evening. It was as if she was only now facing up to what lay ahead. Amy wanted only to be where Edward was, to see for herself the land that had claimed him, to feel its soil beneath her feet. It was in silence next morning, each one alone with their thoughts, that the two women left the safety of Amiens and journeyed north-east towards the battlefields of the Ancre.

———

—— Eight ——

The road to Bertrancourt was rutted and stony, with hardly a bend for six miles. Amy and Kitty huddled in the back of the wagon, while the ironmonger sat forward at the reins. Nothing moved over the unploughed fields, where wild grasses grew in weathered clumps from horizon to horizon. They passed a column of military ambulances, heading west, and another cart loaded high with furniture laid up beside a ditch. After that they were alone on the road – as if it led not to the many towns and villages marked on the map, but into a desert.

After three hours the road became narrower and rougher, snaking around a line of low chalk hills, before heading north through the little town of Acheux. It began to drizzle. They sheltered under Kitty's umbrella, gazing at the sparse country, observing in silence the sporadic evidence of war: shell holes, ammunition boxes lying in a ditch, clusters of crosses on the skyline.

Half a mile on, the horses became restive, their pace fitful. The ironmonger had to rein them in hard, cursing as he fought for control.

'What's got into them?' Kitty took Amy's arm. 'Something's frightened them.'

Going round a bend, the horses broke into a gallop. The wagon lurched dangerously as the back wheels crashed over a pothole. It was not until the ironmonger had regained control that Amy saw they were not alone: a hundred yards away a horseman was cantering over the abandoned fields. The horse was massive, at least sixteen hands. She could not see the rider's face, or the colour of his clothes. In the mist he seemed without colour, as if made from clay. How long he had been there, keeping pace with them? The way he kept perfectly parallel with the wagon reminded Amy of a hunter stalking prey. Kitty looked round sharply, as if sensing the same threat. The horseman pulled up and remained motionless, watching them.

They reached Bertrancourt in the early afternoon. It was a large village of thatched barns and brick-built houses, many standing at a distance from one another, as if intent on privacy. At a crossroads they came across a small procession making its way towards the church, where a bell clanged. A man dressed like a postman carried a cross, followed by an old priest in a grubby surplice. Behind them came a coffin on the back of a cart and a dozen villagers, most of them women and children.

The ironmonger pulled off his cap. '*Ça c'est le fermier Chauvin. Labourant son champ, il percuta un obus.*'

Kitty leaned closer. 'What did he say?'

'He says the poor man was ploughing. His plough hit a . . . he means a shell.'

'*Il avait trois enfants.*'

Three youngsters. Amy left the detail untranslated. The procession trailed past them, the children, hollow-eyed, clinging to their mother, who carried herself as if sleepwalking. Nobody looked at the strangers in the wagon.

The Desmoulin farm lay on the edge of the village. The ground all around was churned up, sunken wheel tracks visible in the mud. The letters YMCA had been daubed on the side of a barn in white paint. On the far side of a paddock lay a cemetery full of wooden crosses. They were five miles due west of the Serre Ridge. Edward would have passed through it many times the previous summer. Amy tried to see it through his eyes – sun-baked and dusty, teeming with men in khaki – but it was hard to picture it so full of life.

Madame Desmoulin, a pale, dark-haired woman shy of forty, asked for payment in advance before showing them to a room in the stable block. The room contained a washstand, two enamelled bedpans, a pile of army blankets and a pair of bunk beds into which many names and initials had been carved. Dark floral wallpaper, blistered and peeling, covered one of the walls.

She asked if they would like supper and, when Amy nodded, again asked to be paid in advance.

'What's the matter with that woman?' Kitty said when she had gone. 'Doesn't she trust us?'

'Maybe not.' A dirty glazed window looked out over the yard. Amy took in the condition of the farm: the bleached timbers and bowed roofs, the plaster coming off in chunks from the farmhouse, like a leper's sores. 'Unless they need the money to eat.'

The door to a shed stood open. Monsieur Desmoulin was moving around inside, a knife in his hand. He turned away, revealing a row of rabbits hung up on hooks. Some were already skinned, their lidless eyes huge and staring.

Kitty sighed. 'We should inspect for bedbugs. Madame needs to give us a good bright lamp, if she has such a thing.'

'I'll ask her.'

Amy picked her way towards the farmhouse. The rain was light now, but the wind had a raw edge. Monsieur Desmoulin stepped out of the shed: a tall man, slightly stooped, with a lined face. The knife in his hand was stained with blood. He watched Amy for a moment, as if considering a greeting, then turned and shut the door.

Madame Desmoulin gave Amy a lantern from the parlour. The mattress inspection yielded nothing. Supper, which was served in the kitchen at night-fall, consisted of barley bread with dripping and a watery stew of white beans and grisly meat. Monsieur Desmoulin did not appear for the meal. His wife sat at a distance from her paying guests, eating hungrily but avoiding their gaze. There was nowhere any evidence of children.

Afterwards they used the foul-smelling latrine at the far end of the yard, before taking it in turns to wash. Without her clothes, Kitty seemed frailer: her breasts small and hard, her hips hardly wider than a boy's. Amy watched her from the bottom bunk. The plumpness of her teen years had gone. Now ribs and vertebrae pushed against her pale skin as she bent over the washstand.

'What are you looking at, Amy?' Kitty covered her breasts.

'You.'

'Why?'

'No reason.'

'What were you thinking?'

'I'm sorry.'

'Tell me.'

'You'll be shocked.'

'Why should I be?' Kitty began to dry herself. 'I'm not a child.'

Amy had taken out the tiepin from her coat and was turning it over in her hand. 'I was thinking of you with a man. I was thinking of him touching you.'

Kitty turned away. 'Why?'

'It's easier than remembering. Me and Edward, I mean.' Kitty threw on her nightdress and pulled it down. 'I warned you.'

'I'm not shocked.' Kitty's chin was on her chest as she slowly did up the buttons. At the final one she stopped, her finger absently tracing the edge. 'I think about it too.'

Rain was tapping on the roof, drips falling onto the earthen floor. Now and again Amy mistook the sound for a footstep. Since before supper she had seen no sign of Monsieur Desmoulin. She supposed he was out somewhere, setting snares.

'I've never had a sweetheart,' Kitty said. 'You know that, of course.'

Amy did not know what to say.

Kitty let down her hair. 'I saw all those young men going off to the war, and I thought: no, I'll wait until they come back. I never thought so few of them would.'

When they were younger, Amy and Kitty had forsworn the opposite sex. There had been no open declaration, but it had been understood. Amy was too bookish for the marriage market, and Kitty too tall and awkward. It was better to embrace eternal spinsterhood than wait on the attentions of undeserving men – as long as they did not have to embrace it alone. When Amy broke their unspoken pact by falling in love with Edward, Kitty had not been angry. Instead she had thrown herself into the role of enabler, stepping out with Amy for long afternoons or evenings that were really spent with Edward. She had relished the confidence the lovers placed in her, the secret knowledge that only the three of them possessed. It was, Amy supposed, the next best thing to being in love herself. Was it possible Kitty's being in France was an extension of that same impulse, that same vicarious need?

Kitty pulled a blanket around her shoulders. 'You and Edward, when you were alone together, did you . . . ? Were you really . . . ?'

'Did we go to bed? Is that—'

'It's none of my business.'

'Yes, we did. Did you think we'd wait?'

Kitty sat down at the end of the bunk. With her hair down she looked younger, almost like the child Amy had first known. 'Weren't you afraid people would find out?'

'I was terrified. At first, anyway. But then the fear became part of it.'

Kitty frowned. 'Do you mean, the excitement? Is that ... ?'

'No, not that.' Amy cradled the tiepin between two fingers. The pearl stared up at her, a blind white eye. 'Being with Edward – it's hard to explain, Kitty – it was something for *me*, something *I* wanted. The time I spent with him, that was when I felt the most free. Every time I saw him, it was like coming up for air.'

Kitty ran her fingers through her hair. In the candlelight it was copper and brown. 'But when Edward asked you to marry him, the first time, you said no, didn't you? I never understood that.'

The raindrops from the roof kept up a steady tap-tap-tap, like a pendulum clock.

'It doesn't matter now.'

'You didn't want anything to change, was that it?'

Amy did not answer. She was in the little kitchen in Madingley, finding the sapphire ring in Edward's waistcoat pocket. It had belonged to his grand-mother, he said. She would do anything to relive that moment, to end it differently.

'Were you afraid being married might spoil things?' Kitty said.

Amy turned over, hiding her face in the shadows.

Kitty brought her knees up under her chin. 'I'm sorry. I just want to know what it's like, that's all: to be in love, like you were. I'd like to know how it feels.'

In the stables a horse whinnied. Another, further off, responded in kind. The raindrops went on tapping against the floor, as if measuring the passage of time.

'Try to sleep now,' Amy said, hoping Kitty could not hear her cry.

———

—— Nine ——

No one would take them. They went from house to house, from yard to yard: everywhere the answer was the same – or the only answer was a shuffle of footsteps and the thud of a closing door. Nobody asked them why they wanted to cross the battlefields, what had brought them to the Ancre. It was as if they already knew. The village stood on the edge of a wilderness, a dark ocean that no one dared cross. Maybe the death of the farmer – the one whose coffin had passed them on their way to the village – made them wary, or maybe strangers were just not welcome.

At last, close to the church, they found a farrier shoeing a mare. He stopped working when Amy showed him a hundred-franc note. For that, he said, they could borrow a mule. It was the best he could do.

The beast was a *déserteur* from the Canadian Army and used to being ridden. They packed some provisions and headed out of Bertrancourt along what Kitty's map called *La Grande Rue*, Kitty taking first turn in the saddle. In a field beyond the last house a handful of women were bent double, planting and hoeing, ankle-deep in mud. They stopped working to stare at the foreigners as they passed. Their silence was infectious, like the stillness of the air. Only the sound of hoof-beats disturbed it.

After half an hour the clouds lifted and the horizons widened so that they could see for several miles to north and south. Amy had expected the country to be more open than in England, but this was different. There should have been patches of woodland, a copse here and there. Hadn't Napoleon lined his roads with poplars so that his armies could march in the shade? The trees here were stripped of their branches, standing in sparse rows, lifeless trunks bleached white as bone. The slag of earthworks criss-crossed the great expanse of yellowing grass, like lesions.

A mile on, at the hamlet of Beaussart, behind the ruins of a barn, a bonfire burned unattended, acrid smoke funnelling down the road.

'Are you all right?'

Kitty climbed off the mule. She looked very pale. 'I think I'm ...' Amy took her arm. 'I don't think it did me much good, riding on that animal.'

Amy put a hand on her friend's forehead. It felt damp. 'You're getting a fever.'

'Just seasick, I expect.' Kitty rubbed her hands together. 'I'd like to get warm for a bit.'

She made her way towards the fire, stumbling over bricks and debris. Amy followed, leaving the mule by the road. Beyond the fire stood a farmhouse grander than the rest, with half its roof missing. She looked up at the shuttered windows. The rooms on the other side might still be habitable. She pictured a four-poster bed, mirrors and curtains, dust turning in the air.

In the shadows of the first floor something moved. It made her jump. 'Maybe we shouldn't ... I think we're trespassing, Kitty.'

Kitty strode on. 'No one could live here. It's a ruin.'

Amy stopped. Among the flames, the charred skeleton of a dog lay on its back, limbs pointing stiffly towards the sky. She clamped a hand over her mouth. A memory came to her, something she had read years before, about packs of feral dogs roaming a battlefield, feeding on the dead and wounded. But she was sure it had only been a story.

Kitty was looking back up the road, squinting at something in the distance. The wind had got up, pulling at locks of hair that had slipped out from under her hat. 'Who is that, Amy? Is that a soldier?'

Amy stepped back. It was hard to see anything through the smoke and the rippling air.

'I think he's one of ours. Thank God.' Kitty raised a hand. 'I say!'

Amy's eyes were stinging. She had to wipe them. Through tears she saw a man standing out in the open, several hundred yards from the village, holding a tall black horse by its reins. He wore a khaki cap and a greatcoat.

'If he's English, he's duty bound to help us.' Kitty waved again. 'Over here!'

The man did not wave back. Amy remembered the rider outside Acheux. She felt a squeeze of fear. 'I don't think he's seen us, Kitty.'

'He must have. Why's he just ... ?'

A gust of wind blew ash and cinders into the air. By the time they could see again, the man and the horse had gone.

Kitty scrambled back to the road, but the land to the north was as empty as before. 'Why didn't he come and help us?'

'Why should he help us?' Amy said. 'He has no idea who we are.'

Beyond Beaussart the road came to an end among a cluster of flooded craters. A route around the side had been reinforced with railway sleepers, uneven and slippery. Their boots and the hems of their skirts were soon caked in mud. Then the sleepers ran out too.

A fork leading off *La Grande Rue* was supposed to take them east towards the old front lines, but nothing of the kind was visible. The only landmark was a line of tree stumps strung out along low ground to the south.

'The river should be down there,' Amy said. 'If we keep it on our right, it should lead us close to Serre.'

Kitty's face was flushed and sweaty. 'I don't see it. I don't see a river.'

'Do you need to rest, Kitty?'

She shook her head. 'I don't want to get lost out here.' She was looking towards the east, breathing hard. They were alone, not a living thing moving, even in the sky. 'This is the place, isn't it?'

'The place?'

'The battlefield,' Kitty said. 'I can feel it. I can feel it on my skin.'

Amy held out the map. 'No. It's a mile or two from the first German trenches. We're still behind the British lines, just.'

'So it's over there.' Kitty nodded towards the horizon. The land was undulating but empty. Nothing moved but the grass stalks nearby. 'That's where it happened, all that death and . . .' She frowned. 'It feels wrong: there should be . . . *more*. There should be something.'

Amy stood at her side. She had imagined this place a thousand times, but in her mind it had always been in turmoil: humming with the impact of shells, with machine-guns and the screams of men. She could hear them in her head even now. But the land before her remained mute, as if turning its back. The emptiness was suddenly unbearable.

As she turned, Amy's foot struck something hard. From a patch of nettles a smooth grey sphere stared up at her. She nudged the nettles aside with her foot.

'What is it?' Kitty said.

Amy crouched down. 'A rifle bolt.'

The rifle lay on its side, the stock raised, the barrel mostly hidden beneath the dirt. The trigger and the sights were stained with rust. Writing had been stamped into a metal band around the narrow end of the stock, but Amy could not make it out.

'Is it German?' Kitty asked.

Amy wiped the band with her finger. She saw a crown above the letters G R. 'George Rex. This is one of ours.'

She gripped the stock and pulled. The rifle slid out easily, as if willing itself into her hands. It was dense, heavy, but balanced. Holding it, Amy felt strong, almost powerful. She looked along the barrel, lining up the sights on the horizon.

'Amy, what are you doing?'

'This must be a Lee Enfield.'

A bayonet was fixed below the end of the barrel. It was long, seventeen inches, and narrow, tapered to a sharp point. Amy imagined the wounds, the pared flesh and gouged bone.

Kitty was watching. 'They used rifles to mark the graves sometimes, didn't they?'

She was right. The clump of nettles could have concealed a grave – a soldier buried by comrades close to where he fell.

'We should look, in case there's something with a name.'

A rifle used as a grave marker would not be loaded. Amy gently tugged at the bolt. It would open the breech – she knew that much. But the bolt would not budge. She raised the rifle towards the sky and pulled the trigger, expecting the same result.

The weapon leapt in her hands. She was not prepared for the noise, a compressed fury that ripped through the silence, a shock that she felt like a blow to the heart. Kitty let out a cry and stumbled backwards.

'I'm sorry,' Amy said. 'I thought . . .'

The echo rolled around the sky. Then, inexplicably, it deepened and grew louder. Amy looked up. A fat drop of rain landed on her face. 'Thunder.' She set down the rifle. 'We'd better find shelter.'

She had already spotted a cluster of sandbags on the lee of a small rise. It marked the entrance to a shallow trench, earth piled up on either side. She went in first. After a few yards the trench became deeper, with duckboards underfoot.

'Amy?'

'Down here.'

Kitty tugged at the mule. It was reluctant to follow. 'It's just a ditch.'

'A communications trench. They lead up to the front lines. That's why there's no wire.'

The rain was coming down harder. Dragging the mule, they headed along the cutting, which zigzagged as it passed through the remnants of a copse. In places the walls had collapsed, forcing them to scramble over heaps of loose earth; in others the saturated duckboards had disappeared into the water. After a few minutes they reached a broader, deeper trench with its flanks shored up with wood.

'This is a support line,' Amy said. 'There might be a dugout here somewhere.'

'How do you know?'

'Edward explained it to me.'

Fifty yards on she found a flight of steps cut into the earth. At the end was the entrance to a dugout. A sheet of corrugated iron, listing to one side, shielded it from above.

Kitty caught up with her. She stared into the hole.

'It's a shelter,' Amy said.

A gas curtain hung from the lintel, turning in the wind.

'But what if there's—'

'Come on, Kitty, we'll catch our deaths.'

Amy went down a few steps, eyes adjusting slowly to the darkness. She found a flat space ten feet below, littered with broken timbers. Below that, another flight of steps descended deeper into the earth. The air was heavy with the smell of decay.

Kitty was shivering. Amy sensed it was important to keep her steady, to reassure her that there was no danger. 'We should have something to eat,' she said. 'Are you hungry?'

They crouched on the steps. Amy had a loaf of barley bread and some dry sausage. She set about slicing it up with a penknife. She could make out the interior of the tunnel: stained timbers, sandbags, bits of rubbish, rags. A short, pointed spade – an entrenching tool – lay discarded two steps below.

She listened to the rain: the sound compressing as it funnelled underground. Timbers creaked, as if they were slowly coming alive. She bit into a piece of bread, thinking about the way the rifle had felt in her hands, thinking she might have kept it. A memory of Corporal Staveley coalesced in her mind, the unclosing mouth, the peeling, blistered skin. He said men still lived underground in no-man's-land. But Staveley had lost his mind. He had visions of the Devil and talked to himself.

Out of the corner of her eye she saw something move, but it was only her own shadow on the walls.

'Did you see that?' Kitty pointed towards the bottom of the steps.

'It's just ...'

Dirt and grit fell down the back of Amy's neck. She reached for her torch and shone it above her head. The timbers seemed secure. Then she noticed the points of yellow light behind them.

Kitty screamed. 'There!' She jumped to her feet, knocking the torch from Amy's hand. It tumbled into the darkness, end over end. Amy scrambled after it. Something caught on her boot. She fell forward, landing hard on her front.

The torch was lying in the dirt a few inches from her face. In the beam she saw them, swarming up the steps: rats, long and black, streaming up from the depths of the dugout. She felt their slick bodies nudge past her, their scaly claws, their tails on the back of her outstretched hand. A shudder convulsed her. She rolled over. She wanted to scream, but what good would that do?

Her right hand found the entrenching tool. Her fingers closed around the handle. She gritted her teeth and swung the spade around, clearing a space around her. She got to her knees. More rats, fat like guinea pigs, were coming out of the walls.

Kitty was paralysed, too scared to run. She lost her footing and fell. Rats darted over her back and neck. She shrieked and writhed, hands flailing.

Amy swung the entrenching tool again and again, clearing one step at a time as she advanced towards her friend, harder and faster, feeling the blade connect with flesh and bone, crushing and slicing, hearing the rats' rasping screeches as the steel cut into them.

She hauled Kitty to her feet and dragged her up the last few steps into the daylight. A big rat reared up on its hind legs. She took its head off with a single, pinning thrust. And then they were outside again, running along the trench, dodging round the traverses, scrambling up a ladder to higher ground.

Amy was up first. She stumbled forward, breathing hard, her body shaking. In front of her lay a swathe of rusty barbed wire. A stocky Chinese man in a khaki overcoat was standing on the other side, staring at her, his mouth open.

Amy looked down at herself. Her coat was dark with filth, the belt undone. Her hat was gone, and her hair had come loose. She reached behind to tidy it, only then noticing the blood on her gloves. Letting the entrenching tool drop, she wiped them hastily on her coat.

The man went on staring. Gingerly Amy touched her face: it too was wet with blood.

———

— Ten —

'Most of them are still tagged, sir.' Corporal Reid consulted his notebook. 'Twenty-seven so far. Eleven without. Good uniform detail. No officers.'

The pits behind him held the remains of New Zealanders killed the previous summer. The Huns had buried them two deep, as they often did when rushed, although sometimes enemy officers were separated from the other ranks out of respect for military hierarchy. All of them would have to be searched for effects, labelled and bagged, before removal to a concentration cemetery on the Serre road. Already forty bags lay on the ground. The smell of disinfectant was heavy in the air.

'Make sure we don't miss anything.' Captain Mackenzie shivered. The rain was easing, but if anything, it was darker. Night came quickly on the Ancre, as if reclaiming the land by right. 'I want something from every ...'

'Yes, sir?'

Mackenzie's attention had been drawn to a small group of figures in the distance, approaching from the west. 'Pass me those field glasses, will you, Corporal?'

Reid had liberated a good pair from the corpse of a German lieutenant. The sole of the dead man's boot had just been visible, bobbing up and down at the bottom of a flooded shell hole. Mackenzie had let him keep his prize. Bodies recovered from water were the hardest to deal with. Often the flesh had the consistency of butter, and sloughed off the bones as it was moved. Reid had volunteered to search for the tags, though this courtesy was far from automatic where the enemy was concerned. Lieutenant Arnholt's name was duly recorded, and his skeletal remains bagged up for removal.

Reid handed over the glasses. Mackenzie turned them on the strangers advancing towards them.

'Those aren't women, are they, sir?' Reid asked.

'No, by God, they're ladies. And a Chinaman with a mule.'

One of the women had no hat. Mackenzie wondered if she was a servant. She was *petite*, with dark hair, and young, like her mistress.

'What do they want, sir?' Reid said.

'They must be lost. Very lost.'

Mackenzie looked at the scene that surrounded him: the lines of canvas bags, many still open to the sky; two men in the trench below, levering out a body with their shovels, a mop of black hair on the grinning skull slowly surfacing through the mud. 'Cover that up. And tell the men to stand down.'

They were running short of canvas. Reid had hardly accomplished his task when the party arrived. The Chinese NCO saluted. He was a quartermaster with one of the labour companies working to the south of them: a small, thin-faced man with deep lines in his cheeks. He explained that the ladies were English and had come to look for their dead husbands.

For a moment Mackenzie thought he must be making a joke. 'From England?'

The hatless woman's face was flushed and dirty and she was out of breath, as if she had that very minute stepped out of a fight.

'My name . . .' She cleared her throat. 'My name is Vanneck – Amy Vanneck. This is my friend, Catherine Page. She's looking for her brother.'

The formality of her words struck Mackenzie as absurd, as if they were all of them standing in a drawing room somewhere in the Home Counties. It crossed his mind that the women might be insane.

'Her brother?'

'His grave. Its location has been lost. Somewhere near Rosières.'

Had they noticed the lines of bags lying behind them? Did they know what they contained? The mule began nudging at a clump of grass a few feet away.

The dark-haired woman held out her hand. Instinctively he took it. 'Captain James Mackenzie, Twenty-first Middlesex.'

Her gloves were dirty and torn. A bloody nail showed through a hole. As his grip tightened, Mackenzie detected a distinct tremor. The other woman said nothing.

'Forgive me, but has something happened?' Mackenzie said.

The quartermaster explained the women had wandered into some reserve positions west of Beaumont-Hamel and had disturbed a colony of rats. 'The lady kill some,' he said, nodding towards Miss Vanneck. His mouth widened into a grin. 'That blood on her face – rat blood.'

'It was …' Miss Vanneck dabbed self-consciously at her cheek. 'It was stupid of us. We should have—'

'There are hordes of rats by the river, I don't know why,' Mackenzie said, aware that he too was falling into a conversation, in spite of the circumstances. 'Other wildlife too: feral dogs, foxes, even some wild boar. Nature rushes in where men fear to tread.' He took the hip flask from his coat. 'Can I offer you some brandy? It's rough, but it steadies the nerves.'

Miss Vanneck shook her head.

Mackenzie unscrewed the top. 'I insist.'

She hesitated before taking a long swig. Kitty sipped cautiously, before grimacing and handing back the flask. Corporal Reid and Sergeant Farrer were staring, along with every other man in the squad. Mackenzie searched their faces for some sign of pleasure at the unexpected presence of English ladies, but found none.

'Now, if you wouldn't mind, Miss Vanneck,' he said, 'please explain to me what in God's name you're doing out here.'

———

Mackenzie dismissed the quartermaster and led the women into a tent that had been pitched a short distance away. Corporal Reid went with them. The nervous energy was still coursing through Amy's system. She told herself to calm down. What were a few rats? A nuisance, at worst. She raised a hand to her heart. The tiepin was still in its place, a hard lump beneath the heavy fabric of her coat.

'The front lines were here, give or take a mile, for most of the war,' Mackenzie was saying. His bearing was wary and nervous, and there was a sickly pallor beneath his weather-beaten cheeks. Still, it seemed he was not ready to dismiss them just yet. 'You've seen the devastation. We've recovered about a thousand men so far, most of them listed as missing, or graves destroyed. Graves Registration in Péronne has a record of every field burial – names, dates and locations. We know where to concentrate our efforts, but every square yard has to be checked. It takes time.'

'My fiancé was in the Manchesters,' Amy said.

'We've found a few men from that regiment. Which is to be expected. It's one of the largest in the country.'

'He was a captain in the Seventh Battalion: Edward Haslam. He went missing in August.' Amy fumbled in her pocket for Barnard's letter. 'This is from the colonel of the regiment.'

Mackenzie looked surprised. No doubt he was wondering how she had managed to elicit a personal response from a major general. He looked over the contents of the envelope. 'I'm sorry, but to my knowledge we've not found any remains that match these criteria. Am I correct, Corporal Reid?'

'I think so, sir. Not of the rank of captain.'

'Corporal Reid is our company clerk. He has an excellent memory for these things.'

'You're really sure?'

'As sure as I can be. Many of the remains we find ...' Mackenzie searched Amy's face, looking, she sensed, for signs of discomfort. 'They're not identifiable. We can often tell the rank and regiment, depending on the condition of the uniform: buttons, flashes. If we're lucky we can tell an officer from his boots, or from the Bedford cord on his breeches. It depends. In damp ground, things become difficult for us quite quickly.'

Amy swallowed. They were talking about Edward – the man she had loved, and loved still – in terms of buttons and bones, and scraps of cloth, all of them decaying to nothing, as if he had never existed at all, except in her mind.

'You could have missed him,' Amy said. 'This place is a wilderness. It all looks the same.'

'To the untrained eye, perhaps.' Mackenzie handed back the letter. 'We've developed certain procedures to deal with it.'

'Procedures?'

Mackenzie and his company clerk exchanged a look. Clearly they weren't used to being questioned by civilians.

'We divide each location into plots, five hundred yards square, mark the corners with flags. The company's divided into squads – thirty-two men per squad ideally. Each squad takes a single plot and goes end to end.' Mackenzie hesitated, as if checking to see if the women had heard enough. 'If they find anything, they mark it with another flag: blue for forty bodies or more, yellow for smaller numbers. That's how it works.'

'Have you enough men?' Amy said.

Mackenzie dismissed Corporal Reid. 'I won't deceive you: we could always do with more volunteers. Keeping the squads at full strength can be ... a challenge.'

'How short are you? How short of men?'

'The army offers double pay for this kind of work. Even so, it takes its toll. Hardened veterans can't manage more than a month. They can't sleep, you see. Quarrels break out over nothing. They're sullen, withdrawn. Sometimes they just walk away. But we manage. We stick to the procedure and we carry on. We won't quit until we're done.'

'Or until the War Office recalls you,' Amy said.

For a moment there was silence, broken only by the sound of men working outside: voices of command, the rasp and clank of shovels: small sounds, not the sound of a mighty effort, a nation toiling for its glorious dead.

At last Kitty spoke up. 'Do the men – the dead – do they have things on them, bearing their names? Something that can be checked?'

'Every unidentified body is searched for personal effects. Here, you can see for yourself.'

Mackenzie picked up a stout wooden box and planted it on a table in front of them. It was reinforced with iron bands and latches. He threw open the lid to reveal rows of thick brown envelopes, each one secured with a string fastener. He picked one out and emptied the contents onto the table. Amy stepped closer. In front of her lay a wristwatch, one strap missing, the glass clouded; a small brass chocolate tin, embossed with the image of Princess Mary; a pencil and the fragment of a photograph. Through the stained surface a young woman was just visible, with a child seated on her lap.

'We send these to the Imperial War Graves Commission,' Mackenzie said, 'in case further information comes to light.'

Amy picked up the photograph and looked on the back. Something had been written, but the fragment was illegible. 'This must be his wife. Someone must know her name.'

'I expect someone does,' Mackenzie said. 'But how would we go about finding such a person? Scores of battalions fought here over the years. Where would we begin?'

'If this were in England, wouldn't the police try and find her?' Kitty said. 'Just to know who had died?'

Mackenzie took a cigarette case from his pocket. 'Sadly, this isn't a crime, Miss Page. It's war.'

The woman in the photograph sat stiffly, an uncertain smile on her face. She would be in England now, raising her child alone, still clinging perhaps to some sliver of hope. They would have no grave to visit, or even the certainty that a grave existed. They would have to make do with a form from the War Office, filled in by a clerk.

Mackenzie seemed to read Amy's mind. 'We can only do our best. We've identified almost half the bodies we've found, which is more than most companies do. The fact is, many of the missing will never be found. Their remains are scattered too wide or buried too deep. Or they've been left too long.'

Amy did not want to hear any more. It was all guesswork anyway, a matter of numbers and probabilities. Edward's story might be different. What did Mackenzie know?

'Are there many German dugouts on the Serre Ridge?' she asked.

The captain frowned. 'There were hundreds once. Serre was an enemy strongpoint.'

'And tunnels?'

'Yes, but most of them have been destroyed.' Mackenzie placed a cigarette between his lips. His movements were tense, awkward, as if it took an effort of will to maintain the veneer of propriety. 'Why do you ask?'

'I heard . . .' Amy looked at the broken wristwatch. Her finger moved over the glass. 'I heard men hid down there sometimes – lived down there, in no-man's-land.'

'You mean, deserters?'

'Is it true?'

'No.'

'Just a rumour then?'

'That's right.'

'Why would anyone make it up, if there wasn't some truth to it?'

Mackenzie lit the cigarette. 'You could call it wishful thinking.' He gestured stiffly at the effects laid out on the table. 'So many men were lost at the front, I expect it was easier to believe they were hiding than face the fact that they were dead. In battle, losing your comrades is the hardest thing, almost as bad as losing your family.'

In one of his first letters, Edward had talked about the death of his batman, a corporal called Earnshaw. It was the last time he wrote about losing a comrade. After that, the casualties he mentioned never had names. Amy could not tell if he was hiding his grief or if he had lost the capacity to feel it.

'What about Two Storm Wood?' she said.

For a moment Mackenzie was still, then he began gathering up the effects and replacing them in their envelopes. 'What about it?'

'There is such a place?'

'Piccadilly is a place, Two Storm Wood is just a name. If there ever was a wood, it's long gone.'

'But could men hide there?' Amy said. 'Are there dugouts, tunnels?'

'Probably.' Mackenzie looked at her. 'Who told you about Two Storm Wood? Where did you hear of it?'

Amy hesitated. It felt like she was betraying a confidence. 'I talked to a corporal in the Seventh Manchesters. His name was Jack Staveley.'

'Staveley? What did he say?'

'He said Captain Haslam was still on the battlefield, and that I should look for him under Two Storm Wood.'

'That's all?'

'He didn't explain. He was badly injured. The sister thought he had shell shock.'

'I see.' Mackenzie turned back to his task. 'Well, like I said, these stories are nonsense. You won't find anything at Two Storm Wood.'

Amy took out the trench map and placed it before him. 'Where is it? Can you show me?'

'There's no point.'

'Is it near here?'

'Miss Vanneck—'

'Please.'

Mackenzie pulled on his cigarette. 'Two Storm Wood was a strongpoint in the old German line, just south of Serre. Machine-gun nests, wire.' He slid the map closer. 'The line pivoted around the place, before running down to the river.' He ran a finger along a series of pale-red lines. 'This is it – what's left of it. A lot of it had been destroyed by the time this was compiled.' He folded up the map and handed it back. 'In any case, the whole area's been searched already. You'd be wasting your time.'

'I think we should be on our way, Amy,' Kitty said, 'before it gets dark. Thank you, Captain.'

'What happens if you find an officer you can't identify?' Amy asked.

'As I explained, we have procedures.'

'Edward had a photograph like this one, of me.' Amy was still holding the photograph of the woman and child. 'And letters, and a gold signet ring. None of them would give you a name, but I'd know them. Your men might have found them already.'

Mackenzie turned. 'I'll make a note to check the records when I get back to camp, so as to set your mind at rest.' He held out his hand for the photograph. 'If you leave an address where you can be contacted, I'll ensure that you're informed of any developments. You too, Miss Page. Graves Registration in Péronne might have something. I'd be happy to enquire on your behalf. The man in charge, Major Hargreaves, he's diligent to a fault.'

'We're staying with a Madame Desmoulin in Bertrancourt,' said Kitty, 'but the poste restante at Amiens might be better.'

'Amiens it is, then.' Mackenzie put the envelope back in the box and shut the lid. 'Now if you're ready, I'll have one of my men escort you to your lodgings.'

'There's no need,' Amy said. 'We found our way here, we can find our way back.'

'All the same, I really think—'

'We'll be quite all right, Captain, thank you. You've given us enough of your time.'

Kitty looked puzzled, but did not speak up.

'As you wish.' Mackenzie raised the tent flap. One of his men was on the other side. 'Sergeant Farrer?'

The sergeant stepped aside smartly, eyes cast down.

'There's a road from here running straight back to Colincamps,' Mackenzie said. 'It's the easiest way. Bertrancourt is just two miles further on. It's signposted.'

Kitty stopped in her tracks. A few yards away Mackenzie's men were loading a long, pale bundle onto one of the wagons. Another dozen lay by the side of the road.

Amy took her by the arm. 'Come on, Kitty.'

'Be sure to stay on the road,' Mackenzie said. 'The engineers keep them clear of munitions. So you'll be safe. But don't go across country. Without landmarks it's easy to get lost, even with a map. Between the craters and the wire you can lose all sense of direction, end up walking in circles. Not advised.'

Amy took up the mule's bridle. 'We'll do as you say, Captain. Goodbye.'

Mackenzie was not satisfied. 'Keep your eye on the wheel tracks and don't turn off for any reason. This place can ...' Amy stopped. 'It can play tricks on you. Because of what happened here. If you're not used to it.'

'Then we'll take your advice, Captain.'

Mackenzie nodded. 'So long as you stay on the road, you should be fine.'

———

After a single turn the road straightened out, vanishing into the distance like a strap pulled tight across the land. Scars of wire and chalky earth criss-crossed the terrain on either side. If there was anything living, man or beast, it lay hidden below the line of sight.

They walked for a way in silence, their boots heavy with mud. Mackenzie's men were still working around the burial pit. The khaki figures shrank into the distance and vanished in the mist. Soon the women were alone.

'They were bodies in those bags,' Kitty said, finally. 'Did you see them?'

'Yes.'

'It took me a while to realise. Then I saw the shape of one and it hit me: what was under the canvas.'

'It's what they do, Mackenzie and his men. It can't be easy.'

'I'd go mad. Why not leave those dead men in the ground?'

'Because they have to be identified, if possible. And moved.'

'Why?'

'The French want their land back.'

Kitty shuddered. 'They're welcome to it.'

The mist was thickening and it was starting to get dark. Soon they could not see more than a hundred yards. Amy felt the skin tighten at the back of her neck. In her mind she could hear the noise of battle: the rattle of machine-guns, the whistle and blast of shells, the pleas of dying men. They seemed to rise like vapour from the land.

'Why didn't you want the captain to help us?' Kitty said.

'This road takes us all the way to Colincamps. We don't need a guide to follow it.'

'We'd be safer.'

'There's nobody out here, Kitty.'

'Didn't you trust him? I thought he seemed decent enough.'

'I'm sure he is.'

'Then why . . . ?'

'They were busy. Besides, if we accepted his help, we'd be honour bound to do as he wanted.'

'Go back to Amiens, you mean?'

'Yes, wait and hope – for a miracle.'

Amy quickened her pace. She did not want to talk. It was an effort for Kitty to keep up.

'But what else can we do? We have to accept—'

'We don't have to accept anything. Edward doesn't belong to the army, not any more.' Amy hugged herself, trying to drive out the chill she felt inside. 'I can search for him myself. I can search the graveyards. I can search the lists and the records. Isn't it obvious they're overwhelmed? Mackenzie as good as said so.'

Kitty stopped abruptly. Something had caught her attention nearby.

Amy stopped beside her. 'What is it?'

Kitty was listening intently. 'Did you hear . . . ?'

A voice, far away: bellowing, desperate, pitiful. 'It must be an animal, a dog or a—'

'I didn't see any dogs.'

It came again, a keening sound, closer now: two hundred yards at most.

'It's a wild pig or a fox. You heard what the captain said.'

The creature was moaning, pleading. But it wasn't human, Amy was almost sure of it.

Kitty took a step. 'Whatever it is, it sounds like it's in pain.'

A hollow, grating sound, maybe a bark, maybe a cough.

The mule bucked, yanking the rope from Amy's hand, and bolted.

'No!'

The mule cleared a shallow ditch and vanished into the fog. Before Amy could stop her, Kitty had taken off after it.

'Kitty, wait! Stay here! Kitty!'

The mule brayed. Already it sounded a hundred yards away.

'I can see it! I can see it!' It was Kitty's voice.

'Kitty, come back!' Amy scrambled up a bank of earth. Thirty yards away a line of twisted iron pickets were black against the fog. 'Where are you?' She fumbled in her pocket for the trench torch, then remembered that she had lost it.

She listened and waited, heard nothing over the noise of her own breathing.

'Kitty, for God's sake!'

She ran on. Wire hung from the pickets, most of it pressed flat into the earth. Coils sprang up where she trod, catching on the hem of her skirt. She stumbled down an incline. Rusting metal – green, grey, brown – lay scattered among a carpet of nettles. Her boot splashed into water. It stretched before her: a wide circle, still as glass. Ripples fanned out noiselessly across the surface, lapping against the mud and stones.

'Amy?'

Kitty's voice sounded far away, muffled, scared. It came from her right, from the east.

Amy scrambled out of the crater. She could not see the pickets any more, or any sign of the road.

'Amy!'

Kitty's voice: behind her – or in front?

'I'm here. I'm coming . . . !' But Amy was out of breath, her voice barely a whisper.

The noises of battle were in her head. Even now they refused to be silenced. She started to run again, the ground crumbling beneath her feet. There were craters everywhere. Moving round them, it was hard not to slip.

Kitty had stopped calling to her. Could she have gone on alone? Which way was the road? Amy was not sure any more.

The light was failing. Somewhere, a world away, the sun was going down.

'Back now.' She talked to herself. But in her mind it was Edward who spoke to her. 'Go back, Amy. Go back now.'

She tried to retrace her steps. In places the pointed toes of her boots had left a distinctive print. But after a few yards the trail ran out. All around was only mud and water, churned earth and splinters of chalk.

She was still searching for her footprints when she caught sight of a light in the distance: a small yellow flame, moving unsteadily over the ground. She was about to call out when she realised it couldn't be Kitty: she didn't have a lantern.

The light grew brighter. Amy thought she heard hoof-beats. She opened her mouth to call out again, but the sound died in her throat: she was remembering Staveley's words and the horseman outside Beaussart.

She backed away. The heel of her boot hit something soft and heavy. A line of ruptured sandbags lay scattered behind her. Quietly she stepped over them. Without warning the ground on the other side shifted beneath her weight. Before she could regain her balance, it collapsed. She fell, a landslide of liquid mud sweeping her down. She clawed at the crumbling wall of earth. Dirt flew into her mouth and eyes.

A hard jolt told her she was at the bottom. She was lying in a trench. She tried to get up, but a lancing pain in her right ankle was too much.

Faint shafts of light swept over the fog, drawing closer.

Amy felt her ankle: not broken, maybe just twisted. She could still walk. She could still get away.

Above her a wooden support protruded from the collapsed wall of the trench. She reached for it, hauling herself up. It was only when she was on her feet again that she saw: her hand was closed around a length of bone.

The rest of the body lay on its side, packed into the clay, the shoulders shifting stiffly under the force of Amy's grip. The grinning skull, like the ribcage, was pure white. It was turned towards her, jaw gaping open, as if to speak.

The Provost Marshal

—— Eleven ——

Belgium, September 1917

Whistles sounded up and down the line. From a communications trench eighty yards back, Haslam watched the second wave of Lancashire Fusiliers rise out of the sodden earth and lumber into no-man's-land, vanishing in the twilight among the wire and the smoke. Ahead of them: three enemy strongpoints on the Frezenberg Ridge. The third attempt to take them in a week. 'We are nothing if not persistent,' Colonel Rhodes had muttered at the briefing.

Shells were coming down in front and behind. Shrapnel bursts lit the sky above the supply routes. Ahead, screams pierced the roar of ordnance and the ceaseless splutter of machine-guns: the sound of men being cut down. Haslam wanted to cover his ears.

'Keep it moving!' Sergeant Perry's voice reached him through the noise and the fear. 'Don't drag them boxes!'

The ammunition was heavy. The carrying parties sank up to their calves in the boggy ground. In the shelter of the fire trench, Haslam wiped the dirt from the face of his watch: they were due to move forward to Beck House in four minutes. The pillbox was supposed to have been taken by then.

A bestial shriek brought his head round. A horse, reins and limber dragging at its side, was pounding towards them, eyes wild, its flank slick with blood. Men sprawled to get clear as it toppled into the trench, hooves flailing. Haslam met the animal's fearful stare as it found its feet and took off again towards the rear.

He steadied himself, found a periscope and raised it above the parapet. The mirrors were cracked. Through splintered fragments he searched for the battle. A corpse, days old, lay ten feet from the trench, a glengarry cap tucked into one shoulder strap, belly hollow where the rats had dragged out the guts. Ragged bundles of khaki were scattered across the rims of craters, as far as he could see. It took him a moment to understand that each bundle was a body.

Fifty yards away an arm waved helplessly. A boy, head bloody, helmet gone, was crawling into cover. Then a mortar threw a shower of clotted earth into the sky, and the boy was gone.

Haslam swung the periscope left towards Iberian Farm, right towards Borry: everywhere dead and dying men – scores, hundreds. No sign of progress, no evidence of objectives gained. The Huns were still in their lines. Two minutes and his party was to move. The bile rose in his throat.

Rhodes had foreseen it all, Haslam was sure of it. At the briefing he had been grim-faced. He had spent half the night on the field telephone, going over coordinates for the field artillery. The rest of the time he had been interrogating patrols, getting reports on every inch of enemy wire. Haslam had been in the battalion almost a fortnight, but so far Rhodes had been too busy to speak to him, beyond a perfunctory greeting. Perhaps he thought there wasn't much point forming an acquaintance, given how long it was likely to last.

Something tugged at Haslam's foot. He looked down: the straps of an abandoned pack had wrapped themselves round his ankle. The man who had carried it was nowhere to be seen. The contents of the pack had spilled out across the ground: letters, a chocolate tin, socks and a small golden object: a cherub with a black face and staring emerald eyes – a lucky charm. Haslam picked it up and thrust it in his pocket.

He turned back to the periscope. The smoke had cleared. He was looking at Beck House, a listing hulk of concrete, pitted and scored, sunk deep in the mud, muzzle-flashes flickering from the safety of its belly. Then men were rising against the skyline. He saw Mills bombs flying, some fusiliers were on the far side of the bunker. Smoke, like a cough, puffed through one of the loopholes. The machine-gun fell silent. Then more men were climbing out of the craters on either side, carrying their rifles, arms swinging hard, covering the final yards to the enemy line. One man went down, shot through the neck. A mortar round took two more. The fusiliers went in with the bayonets, vanishing among the earthworks. An officer with a Lewis gun on his shoulder heaved into view, still struggling forward.

Haslam flipped open the chamber of his revolver. Eighteen rounds fired so far, all into a straw target. His hands were shaking. He would need both of them to aim, to pull the trigger, even at close quarters. The day he arrived at the battalion, the adjutant, Major Blomfield, had given him some advice: *You have to hate their guts. You'll be no use here until you do.* It was as if he knew what was on Haslam's mind.

The first kill was the hardest — that's what they said. It would get easier after that, easier and easier until it meant nothing and cost him nothing.

He snapped his revolver shut. 'Move out!'

Sergeant Perry repeated the order. The platoon clambered over the parapets. They carried their loads in leather harnesses, with the straps across their foreheads. In sections, they scrambled towards Beck House, stumbling from crater to crater, cowering among the dead as the shells whistled overhead. Small-arms fire peppered the ground to the right of them, but it was coming from a distance, on the edge of range. Haslam started to believe his luck might hold, that this time they had the enemy beaten. Like the rest of the East Lancashire Division, the 7th Manchesters had learned its fighting in Egypt and the Dardanelles, in vicious campaigns against the Turks. It was something to know that, whatever happened, they would not run.

They were still at least a hundred yards from Beck House when a flooded shell hole opened at Haslam's feet. It was ten yards across, with duckboards laid across one side. The water was dark and still, with a spiral of greasy film turning on the surface. A limbless man lay in the mud on the far side, white face staring at heaven. Haslam froze. It was too much, too horrible to simply walk past.

'Lieutenant Haslam!' It was Sergeant Perry. His voice seemed to bear down on Edward from a great distance. 'Keep moving, sir!'

Haslam ran, boots slipping on the duckboards. In the Ypres Salient men drowned in shell holes, and men drowned trying to save them. The boards bowed beneath his weight, black water welling up between them, the stench rising. Staveley and Farrer were close behind, backs bent, eyes fixed on him — imploringly, it seemed, as if he, an officer, held the key to keeping them alive. Farrer was as new to the 7th Manchesters as he was, a stable boy, not yet eighteen, utterly lost in a theatre of war, the designs of his masters as opaque to him as a secret code.

'Down!'

Out of the corner of his eye, Haslam saw Sergeant Perry diving to the ground. A howitzer shell erupted twenty yards behind him. Haslam hurled himself into the slime, hands clamped down on his helmet. Earth, mud and stones came down like rain.

When he looked back, Staveley and Farrer were both in the water. Staveley had a hand on the duckboards and was trying to haul himself out. Farrer was nearer the middle. He was struggling, calling for help.

Haslam spotted a rifle lying in the mud. He lifted it by the barrel, crawled to the edge of the pool, held it out as far as he could. Farrer thrashed about trying to reach it, but the ammunition boxes were still on his back, dragging him down. The retaining harness had slipped down around his neck.

Haslam waded into the water. At once his legs sank in mud up to his thighs. He could not move another inch. Farrer was screaming and pleading. He went under, then came up again, spewing black water. Haslam reached out with the rifle, holding it by the bayonet with both hands.

'Grab it, man! Grab it, for God's sake!'

Farrer's scrabbling fingers found the stock, but the wood was slippery. He could not get hold of it. Each time he reached, his head dipped below the water. Each time it took him longer to come up again. It was all Haslam could do to look at Farrer, coughing, choking, eyes wide with terror. He knew that the boy was going to drown in front of him, that nothing could be done.

It was then that he saw Rhodes.

The CO was on horseback. He was riding towards them over no-man's-land at a brisk trot, as if there was nothing dangerous about it, as if it were something he did every day. He had no saddle, but guided the horse with long, loose reins that must have started the day hitched to a gun carriage. Haslam realised he was looking at the same animal he had seen running wild: massive, black, with a white star on its forehead.

He's lost his mind, Haslam thought. Staveley's gaping stare reinforced the notion.

Rhodes came over the top of the crater and eased the big horse down the slope, as calm and purposeful as if on the parade ground, the animal responding as if this were the only rider it had ever known. Haslam cowered, waiting for the bullets to rip through them. It was only a matter of time.

Rhodes had transferred from the Deccan Horse, an Indian cavalry regiment, when the Indian Army had shipped out of France. Before that he had performed great feats on the Somme, it was said, putting Huns to the sword in a massed charge. When the CO had asked him why he was joining the infantry, Rhodes had replied simply: 'This is not a cavalry war.'

He had a rope coiled up in one hand. He threw it over the water to where Farrer had surfaced one last time. Farrer made a grab for it just as the water closed over him again.

Rhodes rode back up the slope of the crater, taking up the slack. The rope tightened behind him and then Farrer surfaced, clinging on with both hands, the ammunition boxes still dangling from his neck. When Haslam and Staveley got to him, lying in the mud, they had to prise the rope from his hands.

Rhodes reappeared. He had dismounted and was leading the horse by its broken reins. To north and south the battle still raged, but it was as if the ground in front of Beck House was protected by some invisible shield.

'Do you need help getting back to your battalion?' Rhodes asked the boy, as they pulled the pack off him.

Farrer, coughing, drenched to the skin, straightened up at once. 'No, sir. Thank you, sir. I want to go forward as ordered, sir.'

Rhodes looked out towards Beck House. 'Best be quick about it then. And report to Battalion HQ when you're done. I want you to look after this horse for me. Will you do that?'

Later that day the enemy retook Beck House with three companies of stormtroopers. None of the men holding it came back alive. The emplacements at Iberian and Borry Farms were never reached. Rhodes's battalion covered the surviving fusiliers as they trailed back to the rear under cover of dark, carrying dead and wounded with them. Then, at midnight, the 7th Manchesters were ordered to withdraw to reserve positions a quarter of a mile behind the front line. According to Major Blomfield, the attack had cost eight hundred men.

'The CO had it right,' he muttered, as they were preparing to send out a wiring party. 'Minor operations are futile in this sector. Defences set too deep. He told Third Army in no uncertain terms, but that lot always have to learn the hard way.'

Haslam had never been party to Rhodes's thinking. The commander spent hours closeted with a handful of senior officers and NCOs, dispatch riders coming and going at all hours, but Haslam had no idea what it was all about. He spent his days overseeing kit inspections, practice drills and bathing rosters. As if that were not enough, he sensed scepticism in the way the men dealt with him, a touch of impatience, as if the pips on his shoulders had no business being there. He had not been tested in action, he supposed, had not proved his fitness to lead. It probably did not help that he had arrived four months late at the battalion, thanks to breaking a leg during officer training. And now there was the incident with Private Farrer: Haslam had been in charge of the carrying party and he had almost lost a man without the enemy firing a shot.

He climbed onto a fire step and peered at the dark forms of a wiring party as they crawled out of the comms trench and disappeared among the craters. It was a starless night, the flicker and rumble of distant guns barely enough to disturb the stillness. He knew he should rest, eat something, but he was too wound up, the shock and fear of the battle humming inside him, a single thought growing and hardening like a stone in his gut: *I can't do this.*

He jumped when Private Ingham appeared at his side. 'Sir? The CO wants to see you right away.'

———

Making his way to Battalion Headquarters, Haslam imagined all the things he might have done wrong that day. Had he chosen the wrong route to Beck House? Should Private Farrer's ammunition box have been carried by two men, rather than one? Had he allowed the carrying party to become too spread out? The fact was, from the moment he climbed out of his trench he had not been thinking about anything except staying alive. It had taken every ounce of his willpower to get that far.

Headquarters had been set up under a sturdy brick building – a factory or a church – which had been cut by shellfire to no more than shoulder height, the east-facing wall shored up by a rampart of sandbags ten feet thick. Two sentries had been posted outside. Steps led down into a vaulted interior, lit by paraffin lamps. Stacked crates, a well-swept floor, notices pinned to the walls – the space had an orderly feel after the muddy ruination above. Haslam pictured Rhodes behind a desk, an icy stare as he passed sentence. The commander was easy on his men, they said, and hard on his officers. What could a negligent subaltern expect? What kind of punishment or humiliation? Whatever it was, Haslam hoped Amy and her family would not get to hear of it.

The centre of operations was in the far corner of the cellars, but Rhodes was not there. The regimental sergeant major looked up from the telephone and nodded towards a passageway on his left. 'Down there, sir,' he said, without getting up.

Haslam tried to straighten out his filthy uniform and banged on the frame of an iron gate, over which a canvas had been draped for privacy. The gate swung open. Rhodes's batman, Private Burgess, stood on the other side, holding a freshly polished boot in one hand. He stepped back to let Haslam pass.

Rhodes was standing in front of a basin, shaving with a cut-throat razor. His tunic and shirt were off, braces hanging loose by his sides. It was the first time Haslam had seen him out of full uniform. Obscured only by his undershirt, his shoulders and arms looked massive, like a circus strong-man's. A few inches behind his left ear, Haslam noticed a curved white scar the size of a penny, where the short-cropped hair did not grow – some old boyhood wound.

'I understand you speak German,' Rhodes said, without turning round.

'German? Not exactly, sir. I've—'

'Can you or can't you?'

Haslam removed his cap. 'I've some practice at reading it. Prayers, sacred verse, hymns.'

Out of the corner of his eye, he saw Private Burgess shake his head, as if at the sheer hopelessness of his answer.

'So you could understand it, if you heard it?'

'Well, if it was sung, sir, yes. I expect I could.'

Rhodes looked at Haslam for the first time, the trace of a smile on his lips. 'Well, we'll have to see if we can organise a choir.' He wiped the razor on a washcloth. 'You can go now, Burgess, thank you.'

Private Burgess put down the boots and left, leaving Haslam and Rhodes alone. Haslam hoped it was not a bad sign. He could already picture himself at some listening post in no-man's-land, a few yards from the German wire. Men crawled across on their bellies at dead of night, hoping for some overheard scrap of intelligence. Often they did not come back.

'The division's moving in three days. South to the Somme and the Ancre.' Rhodes began shaving his throat with slow upward strokes. 'It'll make a change from this sideshow.'

Haslam was surprised to hear the Ypres Salient called a sideshow. For months it had been the main focus of British operations.

Rhodes did not wait for him to object. 'The Salient is important for political reasons: the last piece of Belgium we hold. But the Somme's where the war will be decided. That's where the Huns will make their play.' He wetted the razor and tapped it against the side of the basin. 'If we have to fight, we may as well fight where it counts, don't you think?'

Haslam had heard discussions of this sort in England, in the staff common room, at dinner tables: military strategy debated by men whose knowledge of war was limited to what they had read in the newspapers. He had found it repulsive and absurd, but with Rhodes it was different. He was not a man who spoke for the sake of speaking.

'Why the Somme, sir?'

'Because the Hun's objective is Paris. Reach Paris and the war is over, in their book. It's how they won in 1870, and nothing's changed. From their present positions the shortest distance to Paris is from the Somme. So the final breakthrough must come there.'

'You seem very sure, sir.'

'Because I am. When a German talks of victory, he talks about parading down the Champs-Elysées. He can hardly conceive of one without the other. You only have to listen to them talk among themselves.'

'Prisoners, you mean?'

'What did you think?' Rhodes turned his attention to his top lip. Unusually for an officer, he did not have a moustache, though regulations had demanded it for most of the war. Out of uniform, he could have been just another soldier. 'We used to have a German speaker, Captain Miller. But he was wounded at Femy Wood. You'll take his place, help with interrogations, et cetera.'

'I'll do my best, sir.'

Haslam instinctively ducked as the thud of a distant detonation shook the room, narrow threads of dirt falling onto the floor. The razor froze in Rhodes's hand, then resumed its work.

'You look like you could manage a drink. In there.'

Against the wall, incongruous in the setting, stood an armoire, painted eggshell-blue. Crosses of tape had been stuck to each pane of glass for protection. Inside, Haslam found a bottle and some tin mugs. The bottle was clear and had no label.

As he poured, the neck rattled against the lip of the mug.

'I'll join you,' Rhodes said. He was watching in the mirror.

Haslam's cheeks burned. It was hours since the attack, but he was still shaking. He poured again, this time holding the mug hard against the neck of the flask, although that only made the rattling softer. He could not look Rhodes in the face as he handed him his drink.

Rhodes took a mouthful and went back to shaving. Haslam gulped down the spirit. It had a harsh, resinous taste, but there was some comfort in the heat of it.

'You know, it's all right to be frightened,' Rhodes said.

'Frightened, sir? I was just—'

'You'd be mad if you weren't. Or suicidal. Take a seat, go on. We're not on parade.'

There was a chair in the corner with an upholstered seat. Haslam sat down. Instead of discipline, Rhodes was showing him kindness. Under the circumstances, it felt as miraculous as his appearance in no-man's-land.

'Can you sleep?'

'Usually, yes, sir.'

'That's a good sign.'

'It's the rest of the time that's a struggle. As soon as I open my eyes, I start ...'

'Go on.'

Haslam wished he had kept his mouth shut, but it was too late now. 'I start thinking I'm going to die. I'm waiting for it to happen: the sniper round, the shell, the order to attack. Every hour it doesn't happen only brings me closer to when it will.' Haslam hung his head. 'I'm scared pretty much all the time. Not much of an example to the men.'

Rhodes reached for a towel and began wiping the soap from his face. 'And you think it's different for me, because I've a crown on my shoulder?'

'You, sir?'

'I wake up every morning, just like you, thinking I may not see another. I'm frightened by that possibility because it's a real one. I recognise that fear and acknowledge it. Then I put on my uniform and get on with my day.'

Haslam shook his head. 'But today, on that horse. You must have known you were taking a—'

'The Huns had stopped firing – small arms, at any rate.' Rhodes slung the towel over his shoulder and picked up his drink. 'Learning the sound of enemy weaponry can be useful. I recommend it. Each type is quite distinctive – like a ...' He thought for a moment. 'Like an organ stop, if not as melodious. On this occasion they'd been silent for several minutes, long enough to tell me their forward positions were taken. Either way, the operation wasn't as risky as it might have seemed.' He sat down opposite Haslam. 'Of course that's strictly between you and me.' There was a gleam in his eye. 'No one else has to know, got it?'

'Of course, sir.'

Rhodes reached over with the bottle and refilled Haslam's cup. '*Eau de vie*, local produce. Decent whisky's too expensive, and army rum's poison.'

'Agreed, sir.'

Haslam took another mouthful. The alcohol was already dulling his senses. Still he could not stop thinking about Private Farrer, the look of uncomprehending terror, the sense that he had felt of utter helplessness. He wondered if Rhodes was telling the truth.

'I think you'd have done the same thing in my place,' Rhodes said. 'You'd have done what was needed to save that boy.'

Haslam shook his head. 'I'm not so sure. I'm not sure I care that much.'

'You will, though. You'll understand in time.'

'Understand, sir?'

For a moment Rhodes was lost in thought, then he got up and pulled his shirt off the back of his chair. 'An officer must put the welfare of his men above his own, without hesitation. He must ask nothing of them that isn't necessary, and that he isn't prepared to do himself. He must never expose them needlessly to danger. And his men must know this, see it and be in no doubt – because for such a leader they'll do anything.' He began buttoning his cuff, energy in his every movement, though he could not have slept for the best part of two days. 'In other words, he must be like a father to his men.' He looked at Haslam. 'The way a father should be, at any rate.'

Another distant thud shook the building. This time Haslam did not stir. It was suddenly clear that Rhodes knew all about him: his work, his upbringing, even his character. Haslam had begun to feel that he was invisible, irrelevant, but it seemed he could not have been more wrong.

'The metaphor isn't perfect.' Rhodes looked in the mirror as he knotted his tie. 'My father put us all in danger, trusting that God or Providence would protect us. It cost him his life, and our mother's too.'

Haslam had heard things about Rhodes's family: fragments of rumour that passed among the men, unattributed and unconfirmed. Rhodes had grown up in India. His parents had been Christian missionaries. They had been attacked by bandits and cut to pieces. Rhodes, a boy of seven or ten – Haslam had heard several versions – had witnessed their deaths from a hiding place. It was only one of the stories they told about him, and not the most fantastical. Something about the way Rhodes conducted himself seemed to feed men's imaginations.

'Tell me, why the Manchesters?' he asked as he buttoned up the front of his shirt. 'Not your neck of the woods, is it?'

'My father served in the regiment,' Haslam said. 'About thirty years ago now. I thought it couldn't hurt, following in his footsteps.'

Rhodes nodded. 'In my case it was an uncle, about the same time. I suppose it's quite possible they knew each other.'

'Yes, I suppose it is, sir.'

'He never mentioned it? My uncle's name was William.'

Haslam shook his head.

'You could ask him perhaps.'

'My father?' Haslam looked into his glass. 'I can't. He's dead now.'

Rhodes hesitated. 'I'm sorry. Recently, was it?'

Haslam shook his head. 'A while now. He didn't raise me anyway. I don't even remember him that well.'

'I see. That's how it was, eh?' For a moment Rhodes was lost in thought, as if Haslam's upbringing had been a matter of much speculation until then. 'So, orphans the pair of us then.'

'Yes, sir.'

'You weren't actually in an orphanage?'

'Yes, I was, sir. For a couple of years.'

'That so? And yet ...' Rhodes picked up the bottle and looked at it. Most of the *eau de vie* had gone. 'When you put in for a commission, your application was supported by none other than Sir Evelyn Vanneck.' He shared out the rest of the bottle. 'How does an orphan end up with connections like that?'

Rhodes sat down again, his cup in both hands, leaning forward on his elbows. Haslam told him the truth. Told him how he and Sir Evelyn's niece had become sweethearts, how they had become engaged a few days before he left for France, how he had met Sir Evelyn once on a sunny day in Cambridge.

'And did her family accept you, just like that?'

'No.' Haslam found himself laughing. In the past, the recollection had always made him angry. 'They weren't keen – Amy's mother in particular. Of course they were too polite to say so to my face, and I was too naïve to see it, at first. But I might as well have had the mark of Cain. That's the kind of people they are.'

'So I've heard.'

'It was different once I'd got my commission of course. They couldn't object then, not openly. One is expected to support the troops, no matter what their background.'

'I see.' Rhodes sat back. 'So by joining up you rendered yourself bullet-proof, socially speaking.'

'You could say that.'

'And that's why you did it?'

'Yes, sir. That and ...'

'You were more afraid of the Vannecks – of what they might think of you – than you were of the Germans?'

Rhodes laughed. Haslam felt his face grow hot. What if his commanding officer could read him as well as he read the enemy? 'Yes, I suppose I was, sir. In a way.'

'And you were a schoolmaster, reserved occupation and all that. So you had a choice, didn't you?'

'Yes, sir.'

Haslam considered telling Rhodes the truth about the whole affair, a truth he had not shared willingly with anyone, not even Amy. He had the irrational feeling that Rhodes would appreciate the confidence, perhaps even value it.

Haslam had signed up in the autumn, leaving the school a month into the new term. A few days before that, the headmaster had ushered him into his study 'for a chat'. Safely behind his desk, he had begun by apologising for having placed Haslam in an impossible position: one where he had to choose between the interests of his pupils and a natural desire to serve his country in the war – a dilemma that was to be resolved by terminating his position forthwith. Haslam had been too shocked and bewildered to protest. He had walked out of the school then and there, not stopping to collect his hat or coat, leaving even his music behind. Nothing had prepared him for this catastrophe: the sudden loss of his position, his livelihood, the only place that had ever felt like home. He had kept his views on the war to himself, knowing they would not play well with the other staff, still less the governors. The headmaster was no jingoist in any case. Only recently he had gone out of his way to underline Haslam's value to the school, as if to forestall any patriotic urge to enlist. Now Haslam was suddenly dispensable. What had he done wrong? What had he said?

He had walked on and on, with no sense of where he was going, his thoughts in a tumult of rage and fear. What would he do now? How would he support himself? He could not apply to another school without references from his old one, and would references be forthcoming? Everyone would assume that he was simply trying to evade military service, that he was a coward – not the type of man to command respect, even from schoolboys. Why should they respect a man who did not respect himself?

Edward had found himself at the end of the terrace where Amy's aunt had her house. It was the middle of the afternoon; too early for Amy to have returned from her work at the telephone exchange. He decided to wait, intercept her on the street and tell her what had happened.

Standing there on the corner, his panic had slowly ebbed away, to be replaced by a clear vision of the way ahead. He would be called up for the army and would refuse to go. He would declare himself a conscientious objector and face whatever treatment came his way. As an able-bodied man, he would likely be sent to prison for the duration of the war – perhaps longer, depending on the mood of his captors and the nation. He would suffer for what he believed, but a test was overdue. Principles were easy when they cost nothing.

The bells were striking six. He would suffer the stigma, bear the contempt, serve his time in prison, if it came to that. And when at last he came out again, Amy Vanneck – who would have suffered the same stigma in his absence, who would have been shunned by family and friends, left alone in the world to fend for herself – would be there waiting for him at the gates.

Rhodes was watching him, his head on one side. He was waiting for an explanation.

'I just wanted to do my bit, sir,' Edward said.

———

... *That day I saw Rhodes on horseback, braving death, that was when I began to see it: he is not like other commanders, other men. It's the strangest thing, Amy, but where he is, it feels like the centre of the world. When his attention is on you, it's impossible to look away or think of anything else. It has nothing to do with rank. The force of his personality is a vortex: beyond a certain point there's no resisting it, no going back. Truly I think that most of the men are more worried about letting him down than they are about the enemy. His word is law. Certainly King's Regulations don't count for much: the empty mumblings of soft-handed bureaucrats. It has taken me a long time to appreciate this, because I have always been very proud underneath it all, reluctant to follow anyone and slightly contemptuous of those who did. But under Rhodes we are all freed from fear. He fears for us — our bodies and our souls. That is the key. In Rhodes we trust. To cap it all, he seems to think especially well of me. I cannot see why, how I have deserved it, but when he talks to me in private, it is almost as if we are old friends, kindred spirits who share something deeper than the circumstances of war.*

I wish I could explain to you what follows, what it means. The last thing I want is there to be silences between us when this war is over, things we can't speak of or share. That's what I see now, in the letters the men write home. They talk about everything and anything except what we are actually doing out here. Most have given up all hope of being understood, even by those who love them. It troubles me.

Rhodes says this war is a stepping stone. The common soldier is not fighting for what he had — which was damned little — but for a new beginning, where power is not handed down from father to son like a family heirloom. We must make that new beginning or there will be no victory, no sense to it all. I don't know what this new world will look like, how we shall reach it or how it will work, but I believe Rhodes when he says it is coming.

Whatever happens, we cannot go back to where we were. There will be no unseeing of what we have seen, no undoing of what has been done, not for us. We can never again be children, powerless and tractable and without sin.

———

—— Twelve ——

France, March 1919

In the pale circle of light Amy saw a face. Like the lantern, it advanced towards her along the parapet of the trench. Her ankle was swelling painfully inside her boot. She kept still. The slightest movement would give her away.

The figure darkened as it approached through the fog. She saw a khaki balaclava, a thin face, eyes wide and sloping, like some nocturnal animal. The soldier was tall and broad, but the coat looked too big for him. He wore a belt with a flare gun tucked into it. She had seen him before, somewhere.

He stopped a few yards away and crouched down. Amy watched him through a tangle of brambles and wire. He must have seen her footprints, but he wasn't looking at the ground. He was listening.

'Amy?'

It was Kitty's voice. She hadn't left after all. Amy did not dare shout back. The stranger stood up. In a moment he was standing above her, the lantern held high.

'Looking for something, Miss?' he said.

It took a moment for Amy to catch her breath.

'You should've stayed on the road.' The soldier was a northerner. He reached down, offering a hand. He wore mittens with the fingers cut out. 'You don't want to be wandering about here.'

Kitty was still calling her name.

'I'm over here! I'm all right!'

Amy let the soldier take her by the arm. Slowly, painfully, she climbed up the collapsed wall of the trench, avoiding the loose earth and the bones. The trench must have cut through a burial site. The regimental of the Seventh had described exactly that: how the battlefields were worse the second time round.

'Can you walk then?'

'I think so.'

The soldier let go of her arm and turned away.

'Our mule bolted. There was a noise, an animal. I was trying—'

'A stray dog. That'd be it.'

'I thought it sounded ...' But Amy wasn't sure what she had heard any more. Captain Mackenzie had warned them that the battlefield could play tricks on you.

'Found your mule anyhow,' the soldier said.

It was then Amy recognised him. 'You're one of Captain Mackenzie's men, aren't you? Sergeant ... ?'

'He sent me to see you're all right – it being dark an' all.'

She should have guessed. Amy felt she should shake the sergeant's hand, but their difference in station made the whole idea too awkward. 'I'm Amy Vanneck.'

'I know who you are.' The sergeant walked on, holding the lantern low over the ground. 'Best be getting on.'

Amy stopped. 'There's a man back there, in the trench. I mean, his remains. I saw them.'

Farrer kept walking. 'Still plenty round here. I'll let the captain know.'

In a minute they were back on the road, where a wagon stood waiting, hitched to a pair of horses, the steam rising off their flanks. Their mule was already tied to the back.

'The sergeant's going to escort us back to Bertrancourt,' Kitty said. It was clear she was desperate to be gone. 'So thoughtful of Captain Mackenzie. You're limping. Are you—'

'Just a twist. It's not serious.'

The horses whinnied. The darkness still was not absolute, the mist faintly luminous as it covered the land. The soldier grabbed the reins. Without further discussion, Kitty climbed into the back of the wagon, oblivious to the smell of disinfectant and content to occupy a space normally reserved for the dead.

———

They reached their lodgings well after dark. Madame Desmoulin had some soup on the stove, which she served with slices of black bread. Kitty sat down to eat without complaining, but Amy had no appetite. She sat at the table, staring into her bowl. In spite of her weariness, the feeling was still there: of being close to where Edward was, of being within reach. She did not know what Two Storm Wood meant to Captain Mackenzie, why the mention of it was so unwelcome, but it meant something. And in spite of his discouragement, that gave her a pale flicker of hope.

She downed a tumbler of wine, catching sight of herself in a small mirror that hung in a corner of the kitchen. Her hair was caked with mud, her skin spattered with dirt. Two fingernails were split on her right hand. The others were stained with blood. She wondered what Captain Mackenzie had made of her – hatless, bedraggled – and realised she did not care.

Madame Desmoulin was looking out of the window into the yard. '*Pourquoi est-ce qu'il est toujours là?*'

Light played across her face. Amy craned her neck to see where it was coming from. Outside, Mackenzie's man was still there with his wagon, crouching beside one of the horses, his lantern on the ground.

'I'd like to take him some food,' Amy said. 'The poor man must be starving.'

Madame Desmoulin frowned. '*Les soldats ont assez à manger, Mademoiselle.*'

'All the same.'

Amy put some bread and cheese in a napkin and limped into the yard. The sergeant was examining one of the horse's hooves.

'I thought she wasn't moving right,' Amy said. 'Is she going lame?'

Steam was still rising from the animal's flanks.

'Thought it could be a stone. But I ain't found none. No cracking, neither.'

Carefully the sergeant let the hoof descend, as if setting down something precious and delicate. Most of the army's horses, thousands of them, were being slaughtered for meat. Amy had heard about it from Madame Pinégal in Amiens. Only a handful were being taken home.

'I brought you something to eat, by way of thanks. It isn't much.'

Amy held out the napkin. The sergeant looked at it. She saw him swallow. 'I've my own, thank you, Miss.'

'I'll look like a fool taking it back. I expect Madame Desmoulin will be offended.'

Hesitantly the sergeant took the bundle and stuffed it in his pocket.

'Is something wrong with her?'

'Tendon, most likely.' The sergeant's hand came to rest a few inches above the back of the hoof. The horse did not stir. 'She'll be all right.'

'I'm sorry,' Amy said. 'I never caught your name.'

'Farrer. Jonas Farrer.'

Amy recognised the name from one of Edward's letters. 'There was a man called Farrer in the Seventh Manchesters. He almost drowned, at Ypres.'

The sergeant ran his hands up the animal's right leg, flexing it gently at the joint. 'How'd you hear about that, Miss?'

'Edward ... my fiancé. He said a young private was saved by an officer, a Colonel Rhodes, on a horse. He couldn't believe his eyes.' Amy crouched down. 'Was that you?'

'It was.'

The lantern was behind Farrer's back. She could not see his eyes.

'Then you must have known my ... You must have known Captain Haslam.'

'Other ranks don't get to know officers. We get their orders, is all.'

'But do you know what happened to him?'

'Missing, weren't it?'

'Where? Do you know where he was last seen?'

Farrer shook his head. 'Can't help you, Miss. Weren't there.'

'But you said ... Where were you?'

'Field hospital. Broken arm.'

'Did you go back?'

Farrer went on examining the horse's leg, his fingers and thumbs working through the short, matted hair. 'I did.'

It felt like a small miracle to have found a survivor from Edward's battalion. The questions crowded into Amy's head. 'I went to Jeumont, to the Brigade Headquarters. They told me there was no one left. So many died on the Hindenburg Line, and afterwards.'

Farrer nodded. 'We'd lost the commander by that time.'

'Colonel Rhodes?'

'He always found a way. Left nothing to chance – nothing. That's why they kept us in the line so long.'

'Seventy-five days, they said.'

The sergeant got to his feet and started unfastening the harness. 'Pushed them back, one cut at a time – pushed them off that bloody ridge. No one done that before. Huns knew they was second best.' One of the straps came away with a crack. 'Learned the hard way. Captain H had a lot of fight in him, I'll say that.'

It was a compliment, a soldier's condolence, nothing to dwell on – not even true, most likely.

'You mean he was brave?'

'I suppose.'

'What else?'

Farrer's glance cut through her. 'Don't trouble yourself, Miss.'

'Tell me.'

'With respect to you, Miss, a woman don't concern herself with things like that.'

'I do.'

Farrer shook his head. 'The gentlemen are all in the rear – that's what the commander used to say. Stands to reason the ladies are there too, like yourself.'

'Please tell me, Sergeant. What did you mean?'

Farrer slung one of the harnesses over his shoulder, regarding Amy sceptically. 'He were a useful sort to have on a trench raid. That's what I meant. Move in at night. No barrage. Snatch an officer for interrogation maybe, if he comes quiet. Not everyone were good with a knuckle-knife like Captain H. It's not the same as shooting a man at a hundred yards – that's a uniform in your sights.'

He nodded, as if the recollection pleased him.

'That's why the commander gave him a company. No hesitation, see. Quick and quiet.' Farrer made a stabbing gesture towards his throat. Amy's skin tightened. 'Put the wind up the Huns like the Devil: men with their throats cut and not a glimpse of us, like we were ghosts.' He nodded again. 'Put a lot of trust in Captain H, did the commander. Apple of his eye, you might say.'

Amy heard a noise. Kitty was standing a few yards behind her, close enough to hear what had been said. She stared for a moment, then walked away.

Amy got to her feet. She did not want to hear any more. 'I must ... I'll say goodnight now. Thank you, Sergeant Farrer.'

'Goodnight, Miss.' Farrer turned back to the horse. 'You sleep well now.'

Amy hurried back to the stable block. It was late and she needed to sleep – wash first, wash off the blood and the filth, and then, in the morning, decide what to do. She wouldn't think about it tonight. She wouldn't think about what Farrer had said, or the voices in the fog. She wouldn't think about anything.

Kitty was undressing with her back to the door. Amy went to the washstand, filled the basin with water and stripped to the waist, the goosepimples taut on her flesh. She scrubbed her face with her hands. The water came away brown. She looked in the cracked mirror that hung above the stand. Her face was blotchy and swollen, her bottom lip cut. She must have hit her face when she fell.

She heard Farrer's wagon roll out of the yard. She began to shiver, a strange nausea taking hold of her, keeping her from thinking or feeling. She braced herself against the wall.

Kitty had not noticed. 'Do you know something, Amy? I think Captain Mackenzie liked you.'

'Mackenzie?' Amy took a deep breath, then another. The nausea loosened its grip. 'What are you talking about?'

'The way he looked at you. And he was so polite.'

'He wanted to get rid of us.'

Amy sat down on the bunk and pulled off her boots. Her right ankle, it was swollen and tender. In her mind she saw a knife, long and narrow with a curved blade.

'Amy, you must get that seen to.'

'What?'

'Your ankle.'

'It's fine.'

Would the blade be curved, or was a knuckle-knife straight? How long would it be? Farrer had been playing with her. Assassins carried knives; officers carried revolvers.

'Well ... goodnight then, Amy.'

The bunk above her creaked. Slowly Amy pulled on her nightdress.

Edward had never said much about trench raids. His letters had mentioned them in passing, as if they were routine. Before he left for France he had promised to share his experiences of the front line, but somewhere between the Ypres Salient and the Ancre, that promise had been forgotten.

'I saw you talking to that sergeant,' Kitty said.

'Farrer.'

'What did he want?'

'One of the horses was lame.'

'He was watching us before, when we were with Captain Mackenzie.'

'Weren't they all watching us? Beings from another world.'

In the sooty flame of the lantern Amy saw Corporal Staveley, Farrer's comrade in the Seventh, rubbing the fumsup lucky charm between his fingers. She turned the flame down.

'Leave the light, Amy, please. A little longer.'

'All right.'

Staveley had survived the war. He had only tried to kill himself when the fighting was over.

'Amy?' Kitty's voice was tentative, barely audible. 'That man, Sergeant Farrer, was he . . . ? Was he talking about Edward?'

'Yes.'

'Edward wouldn't be able to . . . not the way he said. Not your Edward. I'm sure he'd never—'

'Maybe the sergeant was having his fun. Go to sleep now, Kitty. We'll talk in the morning.'

'All right.'

The creaking of the bunk ceased. Amy began to unroll her stockings. Her heart was still beating fast. She couldn't slow it. It could only be fear – for herself and for Edward – fear of the place she had come to, fear of what it could do.

Kitty seemed to share her thoughts. 'Amy? I'm sorry, but I don't think we should stay here, not so close to the battlefields.'

Amy thought: *we should have come sooner*.

'I never knew it would be like this. John never . . . he never explained what it was like.'

Perhaps Kitty really had not known. Not that it made any difference. Those who had known, like Amy herself, had stayed out of it just the same.

'I thought people would want to help us,' Kitty said. 'I thought they'd be on our side. But they don't want us here, not even the soldiers. I could see it in their eyes.'

106

'So could I.'

'I don't think I'll ever understand what happened here. Perhaps it's better not to. Perhaps that's why John never told me about it.'

'Perhaps.'

'And I'm never going to find him, am I? This place is so vast. And the missing, there are so many of them: thousands and thousands. What can I do? If John were alive, he'd tell me to stay away.'

Kitty's voice cracked. She was crying.

'It's all right,' Amy said. 'We'll go back to Amiens. We'll leave tomorrow.'

'Are you sure?'

Amy lay down and covered herself with a blanket. 'Of course.'

'I'm so sorry, Amy. I think I could go mad here.'

'We'll send a telegram to your family to let them know you're on your way. Maybe they'll meet you at Folkestone.'

'Not yet. We should stay in Amiens a while, make some more enquiries. Maybe Captain Mackenzie will find something.'

'I'm going to stay here, Kitty.'

'Here?' Kitty sat up. 'Alone?'

The lantern was burning low, the flame small and dim. Amy felt the battle-fields draw closer, felt the pull of them, a dark mass, a vortex.

'I have to be here in case they find him, so that he can be identified. And I have to search while there's still time.'

'But Amy—'

'Don't worry about me. There's nothing out here but dead men. What harm can they do?'

'But Captain Mackenzie said—'

'I can't leave Edward here. I can't fail him again. This is my only chance.' The lantern burned brightly, then went out. 'You wanted to know what it means to be in love, Kitty. This is what it means.'

———

—— Thirteen ——

Under the battlefield the tunnels were narrow and low. Mackenzie ran stooped over, following the light, his shoulder snagging on the sharp rocks, fingers caked in blood and chalk. Above him, almost beyond hearing, a ceaseless rumbling of guns resonated through the earth.

'Stop! For God's sake, stop!'

The dust was thickening in the air, catching in his throat. The sound of his raking coughs hummed around his ears like flies.

The young woman was up ahead, holding a storm lantern out in front of her, silhouetted against the ribbed walls. He had to warn her, but she did not look back or give any sign that she could even hear him.

The tunnel got lower and narrower. He was crawling on his hands and knees, coughing still, a ferrous taste in his mouth. He had to stop her before it was too late. He could not let her see what lay ahead, could not let her find the dead.

Then the light ahead was gone. He was alone, entombed in the darkness. The air was thicker and drier. It was hard to breathe. He had to get out, back to the surface. Why had he followed her? Why hadn't she waited for him? He pressed himself against the roof of the tunnel, trying to suck the air into his lungs, to keep the panic at bay. As his breathing slowed, he became aware of whispering.

He couldn't tell if it was behind him or in front. It seemed to come out of the walls. She was right: they were still down here, men – but no longer men. How many? How close? He had to have light. He could not die in that suffo-cating blackness.

Matches – he seized on the thought: he had matches. He dropped to his knees, fumbled in his coat. Which pocket? The left was empty. Had he used them all? They had been damp. Had he thrown them away? The whispering was louder, closer. He tried the other pocket. His fingers found the box.

He rolled onto his back. Hands shaking, he pulled out a match and got ready to strike it. That was when he heard the young woman scream.

———

He awoke to the sound of Corporal Reid hammering on the door of his billet. Dispatches had come in from the Directorate in Péronne, demanding a response by return.

Mackenzie sat up, the dread subsiding. It had been a variation of the same dream, the one that had come every night since the discovery at Two Storm Wood. He was glad to have something practical to take his mind off it. He threw on his clothes and spent an hour making out his report. Then he took a wagon across the Serre Ridge towards the ruins of Miraumont, where most of the company were at work. The clouds were starting to break up, and there was a hard wind blowing from the east.

The Ancre upriver was only a few yards wide, but shelling had obliterated the banks. Water had flooded the surrounding land, turning it into a swamp. The recent rains had made things worse: shell holes had become lakes; trenches had become moats, stagnant and foul. In places Mackenzie's men had cut drainage channels, but many recorded burial sites remained under water, and searching in the boggy terrain was almost impossible.

Lieutenant Aldridge had left his transport in the lee of a chalky rise, beside the rusting wreck of a Mark IV tank. Mackenzie jumped down. He was making his way along the front of a German fire trench, looking for a gap in the wire, when he heard voices.

'Tha's all we need. A cherry knob come to fuck us about.'

Below him two men were smoking outside the entrance to a dugout. One, a corporal, wore the tam-o'-shanter of a Scottish regiment. The other, a private, squatted on his haunches, reading a letter. Approaching from the other direction was an officer Mackenzie had not seen before. He had a kit bag slung over his shoulder and wore the red cap of the military police. Mackenzie hung back. Some breach of regulations must have occurred, but he was in no mood to deal with it.

'Has this dugout been cleared?' the officer asked. He was tall, but his eyes were on the ground, hiding his face. The man reading the letter looked up, but said nothing. 'Do you know?'

'If you're after runaways, you're in the wrong place, sir,' the corporal said. 'The lads round here have been shot already.'

His companion laughed. The Scotsman nodded up the trench. Thirty yards away, accessed by a duckboard walkway, a single yellow flag twisted in the wind. Two bodies lay beneath it. They had been there for months. The maggots had stripped the flesh from their skulls, leaving only the hair and scalp, but the uniforms themselves, though muddy, appeared completely intact. Corporal Hughes was already stooped over them, searching for identification. Lieutenant Aldridge looked on, his hands in his pockets.

The military policeman showed no sign of being disconcerted. 'I'm looking for Captain Mackenzie.'

'Do you hear that, Mister Platt?' the Scotsman said. 'The major here's looking for Captain Mackenzie.' The private stood up, as if prepared for trouble. 'And would he, by any chance, be looking for you, sir?'

'I doubt it.'

'Well, we'll be sure to tell him, if we see him – *sir*.'

Among the General Staff the provost forces were detested more than any other. They were the ones who made the arrests, manned the prisons, presided over the executions. Mackenzie did not want trouble. He climbed down into the trench and hurried over.

'I'm Captain Mackenzie.'

Approaching the dugout, something caught his eye. Floating in a puddle was a wooden sign that read: UNSEEN TRENCH.

The officer looked up. 'Westbrook. Provost marshal, Second Division.'

It was hard not to stare. The left-hand side of the man's face was brutally disfigured, one eyebrow gone, the left cheek sunken and livid. In Mackenzie's experience, men did not return to active duty after injuries like that, but maybe things were different in the military police.

'Second Division?' he said, trying to cover his indiscretion with levity. 'Come a long way, haven't you? Thought your lot were on the Rhine.'

'I'm not here on divisional business.' Westbrook's voice was hoarse. 'Weren't you told to expect me?'

'No.'

'Just as well, probably.'

Mackenzie frowned. 'If some men have done a bunk, they'd be stupid to turn up here. There's nowhere to hide.'

'I'm not after deserters. Whitehall sent me.'

'Whitehall?'

'The War Office. I need information. Graves Registration gave me your name.'

'Mind yer backs, sir!'

They stepped out of the way as three men carrying shovels and a stretcher barged past.

'Information about what?' Mackenzie asked, although it could only be one thing. The thought of it brought up a prickly heat on his skin.

Before Westbrook could answer there came a jolt. One of the stretcher men had put his foot through a duckboard. He cursed, pulling a dripping leg from the sodden earth beneath, then carried on towards the bodies. The broken duckboard hung down, the ends still supported by a length of grey wire. Without explanation, Westbrook threw down his kit bag, crouched down and felt beneath the boards.

'Electric cable,' he said, looking back towards the dugout and then forward along the gangway. His gaze came to rest on the cluster of men gathered around the two dead Tommies. 'Stop!' He barged past Mackenzie. 'Don't touch them!'

Thirty yards away, Lieutenant Aldridge turned. 'Who the hell's that giving orders?'

Corporal Hughes did not look up. He was in the middle of a delicate operation. The nearest of the dead men was missing both his tags; so there was nothing for it but to search inside his clothes for a pay book or a letter – something with a name on it. The mass of the body had already rotted away, the tunic sinking into the void of the abdominal cavity, but the belt would have to be removed before it could be opened. Hughes grasped the belt with both hands and unclipped it with a tug.

The pull fuse was hidden beneath the tunic, secured with a band of wire. It clicked gently and detonated.

The first explosive charge lay under the body, right above the pelvis. It threw Lieutenant Aldridge against the wall of the trench, cracking ribs and knocking him unconscious.

On hearing the detonator click, Corporal Hughes just had time to turn his head to one side. The blast tore off his jaw and hurled the rest of him upwards and backwards. He came down beside the stretcher men. They had been knocked down and lacerated with splinters by the second charge, which had been placed five yards behind them, beneath the duckboards.

Mackenzie had glimpsed the first explosion – a spray of arterial blood; Hughes falling backwards through the air – before the ground in front of him erupted. A piece of wood the size of a bayonet zipped past his ear; then he too was falling, driven by an invisible blow that stripped him of his hearing, leaving only a muted roar.

He felt a heavy jolt and opened his eyes. The roar shrank to a high-pitched whine. The sky above him was spinning unsteadily, heavily, threatening to tip over. The air was full of dust. Someone was coughing. Why the dust, he thought, when there was water everywhere? He tried to move his legs. Nothing happened. He forced himself up on one arm, found that he was lying on his side over the rim of the parapet. His legs had been kicking against empty space. The parapet was dipping and rolling like the deck of a ship.

He rolled onto his back and eased himself down into the trench. The ground felt steadier there, but he was too dizzy to stand. Westbrook and the two stretcher men were slowly picking themselves up. Hughes was still alive, but convulsing, blood gurgling up from his windpipe, spattering against the exposed teeth of his upper jaw. A few yards further away Lieutenant Aldridge was coming round, a hand waving drowsily in front of his face, as if he was being bothered by flies. He was bleeding profusely from a wound above his cheek.

Eyes still smarting, Mackenzie checked the other way: the men he had seen talking to Westbrook were both gone. The dugout was gone too – only earth and fallen timbers where the entrance had been. There must have been a third charge, linked to the other two. He remembered Westbrook finding the cable, the way it had run all the way along the bottom of the trench. He managed to get up onto his knees, thinking as he struggled to find his balance that the booby-trap had been a clever one – ambitious too – even if it was six months late claiming its victims.

One of the stretcher bearers was holding his head in his hands. Another was bent over Hughes, fumbling for something to staunch the bleeding. It looked like the carotid artery had been severed: the man was drowning in his own blood.

'Put him . . .' The provost marshal was on his feet. 'Put him on his side.'

Mackenzie understood: it was better to bleed out than drown, to die without panic. The stretcher bearer blinked at him stupidly, then did as he was told. Hughes's legs kicked out violently, then went slack.

Mackenzie heard a muffled scream behind him. Westbrook was already at the site of the dugout, digging into the fallen earth, feet planted wide, burrowing into the loose earth like an animal. He was bleeding from a cut in his forehead.

'Help me! That shovel, bring it here!'

The stretcher bearer was the first to respond. With a last look at Hughes, he scrambled over, pulling free a shovel that had embedded itself, blade first, in the wall of the trench.

The entrance to the dugout had been capped by a concrete lintel five inches thick. In the explosion it had come down, blocking the way. Westbrook tried to drag it clear, but the weight was too much for him. He snatched the shovel and swung at the earth beneath. As soon as the hole was big enough, he crawled in behind the lintel and braced his legs against it, pushing with all his strength. Already the screaming had stopped. The stretcher bearer jumped clear as the lintel came free and rolled down into the bottom of the trench. The two of them pulled at the earth and debris until a space opened up at the top of the entrance.

They found the missing men on the other side, half-buried under rubble and fallen timbers. The Scotsman was breathing hard and coughing as they slowly pulled him clear. The other man lay motionless, still clutching the letter in his right hand.

Westbrook felt for a pulse. 'What's his name?'

Mackenzie tried to focus on the question. He felt drunk. He hoped he was not about to pass out. Then the answer came to him: 'Platt. His name's Platt.'

'Platt?' The soldier did not respond. 'Help me get him up.'

Westbrook put an arm round the man's shoulder. Mackenzie took the other side and together they hauled him to his feet. Platt's head lolled forward until his chin was resting on his chest.

'I think he's—'

Westbrook drew a hand back. 'Three hard slaps, all right? Behind the shoulder blades.'

Mackenzie nodded, timing the blows to coincide with Westbrook's. With the third impact, the man's whole body convulsed, vomiting up dirt and sputum. He let out a moan and slumped forward again.

Westbrook reached into his kit bag for a water bottle. He poured a little into the palm of his hand and brought it to the soldier's lips. Platt drank between violent coughing, then opened his eyes, the lids livid red against his dirt-caked skin.

'I thought . . .' His voice came out in a whisper. 'I thought—'

'You thought your number was up,' the provost marshal said. 'You were wrong.'

———

—— Fourteen ——

Before she said goodbye to Kitty, Amy went back to the little street market behind Amiens cathedral. The rain had stopped, but a hard northerly wind had taken its place. On the streets and boulevards the people were hunched over, faces covered as if in fear of contagion. At the corner of the rue de Noyon, Amy saw a group of beleaguered English people being escorted by a woman waving a green umbrella. The men all wore black ties. None of them gave Amy a second look as she passed, her muddy coat and boots marking her out as a local. A poster opposite the station advertised 'Cemetery Tours with Guide'.

The market stalls were lined up along a narrow street, protected from the elements by patched canvas roofs that flapped in the wind. A thickset woman dressed in black presided over a stall selling potted meats and a variety of second-hand items: cups and saucers, a wooden mantel clock, candlesticks, blankets and knives. Amy wondered how much of her stock had been looted from wrecked houses or the battlefields to the east.

The woman wasted no time. She picked up the mantel clock and made a point of winding it so that Amy could see the small second-hand turning on its own face.

'*Cent francs. C'est un bon prix, Mademoiselle.*'

Her voice was harsh, insistent, as if it would be entirely unreasonable to do anything but accept her offer.

Amy shook her head. The previous evening, on the boulevard Carnot, she had managed to buy most of the things she wanted: an American Army haversack, a groundsheet, a storm lantern and a water bottle. But one item remained.

Her gaze came to rest on a folding knife with a carved bone handle. She picked it up and pulled out the blade. It was four inches long, with traces of rust on the steel.

'*Allemand,*' the woman said.

She watched as Amy weighed it in her hand, testing the point with the tip of her thumb. Was it enough? Would it protect her? The German who had owned it was dead. In her mind she saw his crumpled body, fly-blown or half-decayed, busy fingers searching through his pockets, tugging off his boots. Were there still pickings to be had from the unclaimed dead?

She put down the knife.

The woman was still watching her. '*Où allez-vous, Mademoiselle?* What you want?'

Amy looked into the coarse, lined face, old before its time: a life devoted now only to survival, with little room for sentiment.

'The Ancre. The Serre Ridge.'

'Serre-lès-Puisieux?'

'*Je cherche mon fiancé.*' Amy felt the need to tell someone, now that Kitty was no longer at her side. Secrecy was just another burden.

The woman looked neither surprised nor sympathetic. She picked up a crate from the ground and put it down beside the mantel clock. It held a collection of heavier items: an entrenching tool, a small iron shovel, a set of scorched fire-irons. None of them seemed of any use. Then Amy saw the knife.

The blade was more than six inches long with a bevelled edge and a narrow elongated point. The handle was metal, with holes for the fingers – brass knuckles and knife combined – the purpose unambiguous. The woman held it in front of her, demonstrating the grip, turning it so that Amy could appreciate the form of the knuckles, the way each loop was crowned with a spike on the outside edge.

It was a knuckle-knife, had to be: the kind Edward was good with, she had been told; the weapon he used on trench raids. *Quick and quiet.*

The woman held it out, handle first. She wanted Amy to try it for size, as if it were a bracelet or an engagement ring.

Amy shook her head. She could not see it in Edward's hands, could not see him using it. It was an instrument for a murderer, not a man of music who went reluctantly to war.

'*Non, merci.*'

'*Dix francs.*' The woman was still holding out the knuckle-knife. '*Essayez le.*'

Amy took hold of the handle. The grip felt secure, the brass loops fitting snugly over her gloved fingers. She ran her eyes along the long steel blade. The strength of her arm, the weight of her body, she could feel them willing themselves towards the point: concentrated, lethal. With such a weapon, small as she was, there was nobody she could not kill, if she was quick, if she was first.

She thought of Edward, imagined him looking at her with that murderous object in her hand. When he had first laid eyes on her, she had been carrying an umbrella and a guidebook. What would he think, seeing her now? What would he say?

A shudder went through her. '*Non, merci.*'

It was as if the knife did not want to be dropped. She had to tug at the handle to get her fingers free.

The woman shrugged, a sceptical look on her face. '*Comme vous voulez.*'

Amy settled for the German folding knife. As she turned to go, her gaze fell on the face of the mantel clock. The second-hand had already stopped.

———————

Fifteen

They buried Hughes at V Corps Cemetery Number 24. A plot of seventy graves, it had been started two years earlier and shelled since then, but many of the surviving markers bore the name of the Yorkshire Light Infantry, which had been Hughes's regiment. He would not have known the men whose remains now lay beside him – he had joined too late for that – but it was the best they could do.

After the brief ceremony Captain Mackenzie returned with the burial party to Colincamps. For most of the war the village had been a couple of miles behind the British lines, and most of the buildings were still standing, surrounded by earthworks, spent munitions and the scars of military occupation. Mackenzie dismissed the men and hurried to his quarters in a nearby stable, only to find Major Westbrook pacing the yard outside.

'You look surprised to see me, Captain,' he said.

Mackenzie was surprised. Of all the men caught by the booby-trap, only Private Salter and Mackenzie himself were still fit for duty. Lieutenant Aldridge would be lucky not to lose an eye.

'I thought you might have earned some leave, after what happened.'

'I'm afraid not.'

They shook hands. Mackenzie detected a stiffness in the other man's movement, likely the result of injury.

'The men think you've come to arrest someone.'

'You don't, I take it,' Westbrook said.

'Who'd send an officer for that, unescorted? It wouldn't be sensible, things being the way they are.'

'I'll bear that in mind.'

'Why *are* you here?'

'Your discovery, below the Serre Ridge.'

'Two Storm Wood?'

'Major Hargeaves showed me your report. I have some questions.'

'That's why you were sent?'

Westbrook nodded.

Mackenzie's report to the Third Army had received a perfunctory acknowledgement from the deputy adjutant general, a Major General Crompton, followed by silence. There had been no hint of an investigation.

'Somebody told the newspapers,' Westbrook added. 'There've been stories – inaccurate, no doubt.'

'I see. Well, you'd better come inside,' Mackenzie said. 'I'll get my batman to make us some tea.'

The stables were dark. The air smelled of wood smoke and rotting hay. Ventilation was provided by two small windows high up on one wall and by five rectangular holes knocked through the brickwork: firing points for riflemen and Lewis guns. A few tiles were missing from the roof, but the place was habitable. Some items of furniture – chairs, a bedstead, a wardrobe – had been requisitioned from the farmhouse, and a network of blankets and string provided a degree of privacy.

Mackenzie had made his quarters in an empty stall, a space piled high with boxes, maps and files, and lit by lanterns suspended from the wall. He had requisitioned an iron bedstead and a frayed-looking Persian rug for the floor. His batman brought them mugs of tea, which he fortified with shots of brandy from a hip flask. He did not care if the provost marshal disapproved.

'I haven't had a chance to thank you,' Mackenzie said, pulling up a dining chair with a ripped leather seat.

Westbrook sat down at the end of the bed. 'For what?'

'Saving two of my men. Another minute and they'd have suffocated.'

'I should have recognised that trap sooner. I've been away too long.'

'Too long?' Mackenzie laughed. 'That's a new one. Feeling nostalgic, were we?'

'I wouldn't say that.'

'But you're here.'

'So are you. I take it you volunteered?'

'Everyone out here is a volunteer.'

Mackenzie emptied his mug, all the while watching Westbrook over the rim. His report had been written in haste, in the immediate aftermath of the discovery. It had not been as orderly or thorough as his superiors would have come to expect. Perhaps they feared he was losing his mind, that the months of searching, exhumations and reburials had weakened his grasp on reality.

Westbrook drank the tea without comment. 'I'm sorry about the corporal,' he said.

'Hughes, yes. A good man. Never stopped complaining, but the best ones are like that often. He was in it for the extra pay, wanted to build up a nest egg before he went back to Leeds.' Mackenzie felt the wry smile freeze on his lips. 'Wife's got a little one on the way. I'll have to write to her tonight.'

He pushed his hands through his hair. In some ways it was harder commanding men in the field, now that they were expected to survive.

'You've had casualties before?' Westbrook asked.

'Fewer than most companies, and no fatalities until now. Our luck changed when we reached the Ancre. Since then hardly a day's gone by when someone hasn't come a cropper.'

Mackenzie reached for the brandy again, aware of Westbrook watching him.

Westbrook swilled the tea around the bottom of his cup. 'Just how long have you been out here?'

'Since the end of November.'

'That's a long time, for this kind of work.'

They *did* think he was mad. Or was it that they wanted him to be, so that they could dismiss his report as the product of a disturbed mind?

Mackenzie shrugged. 'I suppose I'm not ready for civilian life. Too much ...'

'Too much what?'

'Left unfinished, you might say. Someone has to take care of it.'

'And that has to be you? Why?'

Mackenzie considered telling Westbrook to mind his own business, but the man's scars rebuked him.

'We've all lost friends. We've all lost ...'

'Brothers?'

'Yes. Are we supposed to walk away, forget about them, because of an armistice? Are we supposed to pretend they never existed? That's not how a war should end.'

From outside came a bark of command. Mackenzie got to his feet and peered through one of the windows. At the end of what had once been a paddock lay a stack of old German munitions. Among them were several fat brown shells, each marked with three white stripes. The stripes indicated chemicals – phosgene or chlorine – that would vaporise upon detonation. Oblivious to the danger, some men were smoking a short distance away, incurring the wrath of a passing NCO.

'The French have given up in some places,' Mackenzie said. 'Did you know that?'

Westbrook watched the men in the paddock slouching away to safer ground. 'Given up?'

'Recovering the dead. Too dangerous. Fifteen million acres of Lorraine and Champagne are to be fenced off, for ever: *terrain interdit.*'

'A lot of land.'

'A lot of men. Half a million or more around Verdun, left to rot where they fell.'

The paddock outside was quiet now. A scrap of paper snagged on a coil of wire, twisting in the wind. The window overlooking it faced due east, towards the Serre Ridge.

'You're sure we shouldn't do the same? Even after—'

'Yes.' Mackenzie sat down again and reached for a cigarette. 'Though I expect we will in the end. We've five hundred and sixty thousand men still unaccounted for. At the current rate we should have them all decently buried in about a hundred and twenty years.'

Mackenzie offered Westbrook a cigarette. Westbrook refused it.

'Tell me about Two Storm Wood.'

Mackenzie lit up. 'You read the report.'

'It sounds like you had men trampling all over the scene. Why the hurry? You could have left things as they were.'

'We were brought in to deal with the dead, as quickly as possible. That's what we do, Major. We've thousands of Chinese up here, on salvage duty. If we hadn't acted, they'd have taken matters into their own hands.'

'It will be harder to establish the facts. I don't see how that helps anyone, except the men responsible.'

Mackenzie studied Westbrook through the veils of smoke. Of all the provost marshals in the British Army, why had he been chosen? What special qualifications did he have? Or was it just his bad luck?

'I don't think you understand: out here things can get out of hand in a minute. They damned nearly did.' Mackenzie shrugged. 'Military expediency, Major. It gets to be a habit.'

Westbrook pulled a notebook from his pocket. 'Besides the bodies, was anything else removed?'

Mackenzie shook his head. 'No one spent a minute more down there than they had to, you can be sure of that.'

'What were you worried about? The Chinese?'

'No, not them. It was ... what we found, for God's sake. My men have seen a lot – too much – but nothing like that. This was the work of a lunatic, or more than one. Perhaps my report didn't convey that clearly.'

'Barbarism isn't lunacy.' Westbrook wrote something in his notebook. 'Lunatics tend to be disorganised.'

'If you say so.' Mackenzie dropped the cigarette and crushed it beneath his boot, recalling the moment Sergeant Cotterell had left him alone, his faltering steps into the second room, the moment shadows became flesh. His feelings at that moment had not made it into his report, because he could not find the words for them. 'The last three, the way they were ... like some sick kind of offering. Madness was all I could think of – madness and depravity. If I'd found the men responsible, I think I'd have killed them on the spot.'

Westbrook stopped writing and regarded Mackenzie steadily. 'Let's stick to the facts, shall we? Tell me what you found.'

—— Sixteen ——

Amy knew where to begin. She left the Desmoulin farm at first light and took the dry-weather track to Colincamps, where the Labour Corps wagons were mustering, the horses blinkered, men hunched over in the back. She followed them east onto the old Serre road, hoping she would know the ruins of the village when she found them. According to the map, a German trench called Munich ran south from the church. At the end of the trench lay Two Storm Wood. Captain Mackenzie might have told her to stay away, but he had not told her why – or, at least, he had not told her the truth. Besides, Two Storm Wood was in the right place: two miles north of the River Ancre. Maybe Corporal Staveley was shell shocked or insane, but when it came to finding Edward, what he said made sense.

The site of Serre proved easy to spot. There was nothing left of the church, but Madame Desmoulin had described an old sugar refinery on the far side of the village. Amy found the remnants of its metal frame still standing, vats rusting among the mounds of rubble. There was nowhere any sign of reconstruction, no villagers returned to survey the task. But then what would they live on, Amy thought? Who would plough the land now? Were the old inhabitants even alive?

Two hours from her lodgings she was making her way south along a narrow communications trench towards the winding course of the Ancre. In places the walls had collapsed, nettles colonising the loose earth. Looping brambles now reached out from either side, catching on her coat as she worked her way past. She hummed to herself as she went – any tune she could think of, anything to stop her imagination getting to work.

A cluster of dead tree trunks marked the site of Two Storm Wood. Amy found it a short distance from the village, just where Captain Mackenzie had said it would be. The nettles all around were trodden down, the mud crowded with boot prints, but the trenches were deserted now. Nothing stirred but the clumps of wild grass on the slopes above. The wind made no sound in the limbless trees.

Amy followed the boot prints. Captain Mackenzie's men had already searched the area, he had told her. Most likely the prints had been left by his men, unless there had been others, since then. She thought of Staveley and his bands of deserters: men living in darkness, only coming up at night to scavenge, and kill. She had to remind herself that it was all a fantasy.

She came round a traverse and stopped. A wall of sandbags stood on one side of the trench, reaching all the way to the parapet. It was neat and intact, new. Slips of paper – scores of them – had been pushed in between the bags. Different colours and sizes, they flapped and fluttered in the wind.

On the lintel, two Chinese characters had been painted:

鍾馗

Amy pulled out one of the papers. It was covered in Chinese writing. It came to her that she was looking at a shrine, and what she held in her hand was a prayer.

She put the paper back carefully. Along the top of the sandbags lay a sheet of corrugated iron. She had seen one like it over the entrance to a dugout, the one where the rats had found them. There had to be a dugout here too. But the entrance had been blocked up.

There was a logical explanation – several explanations in fact. The dugout might be on the verge of collapse. There might be other dangers below ground: poisonous materials, perhaps even a risk of disease, of contagion. Had men died down there already? It would explain the prayers. What it would not explain was Mackenzie's silence.

She set to work. The sandbags were damp and heavy. The ones at the bottom were held firm by the weight of those above. The bags above the lintel were beyond her reach. She pulled with all her strength, but none of them would budge. Then she remembered the folding knife. She crouched down and stabbed into a bag two feet from the ground, kicking at the sand as it spilled onto the ground. Twenty minutes later she was crouching before a small rectangular hole, just big enough to crawl through.

Amy clipped the trench torch onto her belt and lit the storm lantern. She knew if she hesitated, if she let herself imagine, then she would turn and run. She sang to herself again – *It was a lover and his lass* – barely

124

remembering the words, then threw away the match and climbed down into the darkness.

The first thing she noticed was the damage: the supports were splintered and charred, though the exposed wood had not weathered much. She went slowly down a flight of steps, stooped over, holding the lantern in front of her. The air was cold. It smelled of mildew. From below came neither light nor sound.

That o'er the green cornfield did pass ...

At the bottom of the steps she found a brass switch screwed into an upright, the rim decorated with a delicate coiled-rope relief. The dugout had been equipped with electric light. She was tempted to try it, but checked herself. Edward had told her about the booby-traps the Germans often left behind when they abandoned a position. From behind the switch, wire ran up the wall for a few inches, then came to an end in a tuft of copper. The rest of the wiring had been stripped out.

She stepped down into a large room, her breath coming faster. The lantern played over concrete walls streaked with damp. On one side a doorway led into a second room. She fought the urge to go back – back to the air and the light – and forced herself to sing.

In springtime, the only pretty ring time ...

A kitchen table stood in front of her. There were chairs around it, two overturned. A faint, sickly smell reached her nostrils. She saw a gas mask, some six-inch nails and a fat coil of something that turned out to be a belt. Underneath, the wood was thick with clinging filth – an old German news-paper came up stiff with it. She held it up close to the lantern, but could not make out a date.

As she stepped away, her foot knocked against something heavy. The floor was strewn with bottles, cans, broken china. Then she saw the far wall. It was covered in dark stains: spatters, flecks, smears, in red-browns and greys. She crouched down, holding the lantern close. Some of the stains were thin, as if sprayed on, others were thick and granular. She dabbed at the nearest. A pale splinter came away on her fingertip. It wasn't dense enough to be concrete: it was bone.

She rose, stumbling against the table. The gas mask rolled onto the floor. The impact echoed like a shot. She swallowed, tried to calm her breathing.

There was movement in the other room.

'Who's there?'

She listened. Water was dripping from the roof, the impact humming around the concrete walls. That was what she had heard, she told herself: water.

The other room was the same size, but tidy and clean. The walls had been whitewashed. Even the ground beneath her feet felt smooth and hard, as if freshly mopped. It was as if she had walked into an operating theatre, or a morgue.

She walked round the walls. Inside some cupboards she found coffee cups, a stack of books in German. Between the leaves were some postcards: a naked woman sitting on a Persian rug, pinning up her hair; a group of young German officers smiling in front of a St Bernard dog.

On a wooden stool in the corner sat a wind-up gramophone. She lifted the lid. Inside there was a record on the turntable. The paper label was blue with silver lettering. She could not make out the words.

She cranked the handle. The gramophone record began to turn. She lowered the bulky metal arm. Through the undulating hiss an accordion struck up. A tenor began to sing: a sad French song that she knew she had heard before.

She looked at her fingers. Smudges of a dark residue coloured the tips. The name of the song came to her: '*Le Temps des Cerises*' – 'The Time of Cherries'. The needle began to jump, the tenor repeating the same two notes over and over. She brought the lantern closer: the disk and the arm, the whole interior of the gramophone, had been spattered with the same dark fluid.

The flame in the lantern began to flicker. She had been burning the oil too fast. It was running low. She checked her belt for the trench torch, then turned it on, to be sure it was working. Her hands were trembling. Her fingers slipped on the switch.

Shadows swept across the ceiling. Six inches above her head was a thick wooden beam, made from a single tree trunk. It ran down the middle of the room. Six-inch nails were embedded in it, one of them bent downwards.

Amy lifted the lantern and looked along the length of the beam. Near the middle she found a sharp prominence where a branch had been hacked off. Several strands of hair caught the light, stuck to the wood with dried blood. They were blond.

The needle on the gramophone jumped. The song went on, the singer's voice deepening as the mechanism wound down.

126

It was no good. She had to get out.

She ran back to the first room. The torchlight faltered and she was lost in darkness. She pounded the torch against her palm, the walls closing, the smell of death thickening in her nostrils.

The torch came back to life, its white glass eye pulsing. Her foot was on the first step when she heard the voices.

———

— Seventeen —

Mackenzie lit another cigarette. He did not want to talk about Two Storm Wood. It was as if the place had found its way inside him, its darkness spreading like a stain, infecting his thoughts and his dreams.

'Thirteen victims, all male.' He sucked up the hot smoke as the provost marshal listened in silence. 'Chinese clearly, which means the Labour Corps. The dugout was deep and pretty watertight, and the entrance was buried at some point, which explains why the rats didn't get in. There wasn't much evidence of maggots, either. The remains were partially mummified, which we don't see often. As to timing, they must have died last year, between March and August.'

Westbrook looked up from his notebook. 'That wasn't in your report.'

'Didn't need to be. It's obvious. The whole area was in British hands until the end of March. The Huns were twenty miles away, on the Hindenburg Line. They retook the Serre Ridge during the spring offensive last year and held it until August, when the Third Army pushed them out again. After that, it was always behind our lines.'

'What about 'sixteen, before the Germans withdrew? Maybe all this happened during the first Battle of the Somme.'

'Impossible. There were no Chinese here in 'sixteen. They didn't start recruiting until the year after that.' Mackenzie took another pull on his cigarette. 'Poor bastards didn't sign up for that, though, did they?'

Westbrook was still making notes, his writing laborious. The way he held the pencil, Mackenzie wondered if he had lost some feeling in his fingers.

'The report said you found no identification.'

'We didn't.'

'None at all? No tags, no pay books—'

'My men know what to look for.'

'Then how do you account for it?'

'I can't.' Mackenzie rubbed his eyes. 'Maybe the idea was to erase their identities – as individuals, as human beings. Taking away their tags would fit, wouldn't it? Soldiers have identities; meat doesn't.'

'Why would someone do that?'

'To make a point perhaps. The Huns took it badly – very badly – having non-whites pitted against them. It violated a sacred principle, as they saw it.'

'The imperial principle.'

Mackenzie nodded. 'It proved they were defending the supremacy of European civilisation, while we and the French were defiling it. They didn't give the African troops much quarter – and were paid back in kind, so I heard.'

'A matter of race before country.'

'Only a white man should be sent to kill a white man, in their book.'

'Interesting.' Westbrook stopped writing. 'But the Chinese weren't sent to kill anyone. They were recruited for labour.'

'Perhaps they put up a fight for once.'

'With picks and shovels?'

'It's been known. All their officers are British, after all. They must have done *something* to have ended up ... that way.' Mackenzie frowned. 'You don't look convinced, Major.'

'It's a strange way to assert the superiority of your civilisation,' Westbrook said, 'to mimic your inferiors. And the worst of them, at that.'

'What do you mean?'

'The phenomenon you observed has a name in China: *lingchi*. It's exclusively reserved for traitors – if it happened as you say. That makes the killers Chinese too.'

'The coolies? I find that hard to believe. They're a pretty decent bunch, from what I can see. Work hard and don't complain.'

Westbrook shrugged. 'China's infested with secret societies, gangs. They reach into all strata of society, even the lowest. Maybe that'll be at the root of it.'

Mackenzie shook his head. 'Somebody would have reported it, sooner or later. Nobody said anything, not in all the months since it happened. Things like this, people are bound to talk.'

'Maybe that was the point: to enforce silence.'

'Silence about what?'

Westbrook did not answer. The back of his hand brushed against his chin, as if he too had doubts. 'The victims were all Chinese – all thirteen?'

'I think so, yes.'

'You're not sure?'

'Sergeant Cotterell was in charge of removing them.'

'Then maybe it's Sergeant Cotterell I should talk to.'

'He's not here any more. I sent him back to his battalion.' Mackenzie dropped his cigarette end. 'He's in hospital now.'

'Injured?'

'A mental hospital.' Mackenzie watched the cigarette burn out. 'I thought he'd be more resilient. It helps out here, having no imagination. But then he started getting the terrors, wasn't sleeping a wink, chattering to himself. The next thing he disappeared. We searched the whole camp, eventually found him cowering under there.' He pointed under the bed where Westbrook was sitting. 'Blubbing his eyes out, he was. Some men snap without warning. You don't see it coming.'

'Who else cleared the dugout? Cotterell can't have worked alone.'

'He had another NCO with him. But you can't talk to him, either.'

'Why not?'

'We just buried him. Corporal Hughes.' One of the lanterns had begun to flicker. Mackenzie got up and adjusted the wick. 'A couple of their gangers helped out, but they can't tell you anything. You have to remember: it was dark, and we had to work quickly. By morning we'd have been mobbed.'

He cursed as the flame refused to rekindle.

'They told me you were thorough,' Westbrook said. 'Did you go back to the dugout later?'

'No. No one did. I had the entrance blocked up as a precaution.'

'Against what?'

'The Labour Corps didn't want it turning into a shrine.'

Westbrook's pencil tapped against the spine of his notebook. Mackenzie knew what he was thinking: that the whole operation had been slapdash, and that he, as the ranking officer on the scene, was responsible. From an office at the General Staff, or from Whitehall, it might have seemed that way. They had no idea that, in the absence of the enemy, the chain of command had become a thread.

'Labour Corps men work in sections, don't they?' Westbrook said.

'Same as regular infantry, yes. Why?'

'The Chinese too?'

'Yes.'

'So what you found, most likely, was a section plus one.'

'One of their gangers, I should think,' Mackenzie said. 'A corporal or a sergeant.'

'Or an officer.'

'An officer?'

'The idea hadn't occurred to you?'

Mackenzie shrugged. The idea *had* occurred to him, but it had only stuck when Amy Vanneck showed up, searching for her missing fiancé.

The flame in the lantern spluttered back to life. By the light of it, Westbrook's face was grey like wax, a sculpture, a work of art gone cruelly wrong.

'*Was* there an officer? Is that why you're here?'

'I know only what you've told me,' Westbrook said. 'What happened to the bodies?'

'They were buried at a concentration cemetery.'

'Where?'

'Mailly-Maillet, a mile south of here.'

Westbrook got to his feet.

'You're not going to dig them up?'

'The ground's wet. Every day could make a difference.' Westbrook began doing up his coat, his stiff fingers labouring over the buttons. 'If there's any chance of identification, we have to take it.'

'You're wasting your time.'

'I'll need a couple of men to assist me. One of them should be able to take dictation. And I may need to set up a temporary morgue somewhere.'

'You don't mean now?'

'Why not?'

'I don't have the men available. Besides, they may take some persuading.'

'Persuading?'

'They're volunteers, Major. And the whole business – Two Storm Wood – it's acquired a reputation. After what happened to Cotterell and now Hughes. Give me until tomorrow.'

Westbrook replaced his cap. 'What's the matter, Captain? Your men believe in ghosts?'

———

—— Eighteen ——

The voices were behind the walls. They were faint, as if carried over a great distance. Amy pressed an ear to the cold cement, heard short bursts of words – two voices, both male: talking, not shouting. What was the language? French? English? She strained to make it out, but the distance grew greater, the sounds fainter, until she could no longer be sure they were voices at all.

The eye of the torch pulsed in her hand. She had heard *something*. It wasn't in her head. Not an animal, either. It was as if the voices had been stored in the ground, echoes captured as on a phonograph, and her presence was the needle making it play.

A faint draught moved against her forehead. Were there tunnels down here, a way into them that she had missed? Maybe that was what Captain Mackenzie did not want her to find. She should call out, she thought, make her presence known. The men might come to her – men like Mackenzie's volunteers, tasked with clearing the battlefields, recovering the dead. They might know something, they might help her: ordinary men, not deserters, not ghosts.

She ran back to the steps, stumbling as she climbed towards the light. On the last turn the lantern fell from her hand and landed with a crash. When she looked up again, she saw a head silhouetted against the sky.

'Is that you, Miss?'

Amy recognised Corporal Reid, Mackenzie's company clerk. She did not try to answer him. Her heart was beating too fast.

Without further questions, Reid reached through the gap in the sand-bags and helped her out. It took her a moment to realise that they were not alone.

'And who's this?'

Before them stood an officer. He was tall, his eyes the same striking blue as Edward's, but the left side of his face was a misshapen mass of scar tissue. It was difficult not to look away.

133

'Miss Vanneck, sir,' Reid said. 'Her fiancé was missing in action. Came by a few days ago with a Miss ... ?' He turned to Amy.

'Page.'

'That's it. Still down there, is she?'

'No.' Amy put out the lantern. She hoped the fear did not show in her voice – fear that was only of the dark, and her own imaginings. 'She's gone back to Amiens.'

The officer was staring at her. The cover on his cap was red, the mark of the military police. Amy wondered if she had violated some provision of martial law and was about to be arrested.

He held out his hand. 'Major Westbrook. Provost marshal, Second Division.'

They shook. Amy had heard the name before, but she did not know where.

'May I ask what you were doing down there?' Westbrook said.

'This place, it used to be known as Two Storm Wood, didn't it?'

'Yes, it did. How did you know that?'

'I have a trench map. Vital military intelligence, I know, but I'm not giving it back, I'm afraid.'

'I can think of no reason why you should.'

Amy nodded. It seemed she was not about to detained, after all. 'Then I'll be on my way.'

'You haven't answered my question. What were you expecting to find, in the dugout?' Westbrook nodded towards the mass of ruptured sandbags. 'You went to the trouble of digging your way in.'

He did not sound angry or indignant, but curious. For the first time Amy had a sense that being there, on the battlefield, had earned her a sliver of respect.

'Someone told me I might find my fiancé. Under Two Storm Wood, he said.'

'Your fiancé?'

'He was missing in action. Captain Edward Haslam, of the Seventh Manchesters.'

Westbrook regarded her steadily. 'Fine battalion,' he said, 'so I've heard. Who told you to come here?'

Amy packed away the lantern and slung the haversack over her shoulder. She wanted to get away from these men, from their questions and their staring. 'A sergeant in the Seventh Manchesters – my fiancé's battalion. He said there were men still living underground, men who'd run away.' Reid kicked at the loose sand, as if the very idea was embarrassing. 'It's only a rumour, but I had to be sure.'

'Of course you did,' Westbrook said, as she nudged past him. 'Leads must be followed, even if they turn out to be false.'

'You don't think I'm insane, coming out here on my own?'

'Your friend's gone, you said. I don't suppose you had a choice.'

'You don't think I should go home and hope for the best?'

'Why should you?' Westbrook looked away. 'The exhumation companies do their best, but the task is ... well, immense. And they're short of volunteers. Soon the Chinese will be left to it, and most of them can't even read. What was your fiancé's name again?'

Amy put down the haversack. 'Haslam. Edward Haslam.'

Westbrook hesitated. 'And you think he might still be alive – is that why you've come?'

Reluctantly Amy shook her head.

'You've heard a rumour? An unconfirmed report?'

'I know what it means when someone is missing in action, Major.' Amy stared at the ground. 'I know I'm looking for a body.'

Westbrook walked over to the wall of sandbags. Amy had the impression he was not convinced. She watched as he pulled out one of the scraps of paper and examined it closely, his lips moving like a child with his first book.

Amy indicated the Chinese characters painted on the lintel. 'Do you know what that means?'

Westbrook did not look up. 'Zhong Kui. It's a name.'

'Zhong Kui?'

'A guardian spirit, a vanquisher of ghosts and evil spirits.' Westbrook replaced the paper and took out another. 'In life he was disfigured, and died by his own hand. In death he's said to command eighty thousand demons.'

'Why put his name there?'

'It's an evocation. Quite common.' Westbrook's fingertips absently traced the line of his jaw. 'Such spirits guard the passage from one place to another. Their presence keeps out evil, or keeps it in.'

'So, this place is a shrine?'

'Of sorts.'

'Why is it here? Is it because . . . ?' Westbrook looked up at her. 'I saw blood, down there on the walls.'

'Blood?'

'And bullet holes. I think that's what they were.'

Westbrook nodded. 'Thirteen men were killed, Chinese labourers. They were found a few weeks ago.'

Amy remembered the splinter of bone coming away on her finger, felt the same shudder of revulsion. 'Murdered?'

'It would seem so. Ten of them were shot, reportedly.'

'And the others?'

Westbrook did not answer. He was climbing through the gap Amy had made in the sandbags, moving stiffly and painfully. When he was on the other side he looked back at her. 'You came here on foot, Miss Vanneck?'

'I've lodgings in Bertrancourt.'

'Then we'll take you back in the wagon, when we're done.'

'There's no need,' Amy said. 'I know the road.'

'It's on my way.' Westbrook switched on a trench torch. 'I'm afraid I must insist.'

———

Westbrook spent twenty minutes underground. When he returned, it was almost as if the others were not there. He hardly spoke. His eyes were glazed, his skin shiny with sweat. They sat in the back of the wagon in silence for almost a mile.

'Forgive me, Miss . . .'

'Vanneck.'

'Impolite of me to . . .'

He frowned, as if the appropriate words, like conversation itself, were lost to him.

'May I ask how you know Mandarin, Major?'

Westbrook looked out towards the horizon. 'My childhood. A long time ago.'

'Is that why you were sent? Because you know the language?'

'They didn't explain. I received orders by post, from the War Office. I was two days out of the hospital. Another week, I'd have been demobbed.'

'They must need you very badly.'

Westbrook grunted. 'I was a detective before the war, at Scotland Yard.'

'Scotland Yard?'

'Does that surprise you? It surprises me, a little.' The wagon began to rattle violently as they went over a patch of stony ground. 'Why should Whitehall care about a few dead Chinamen? There must be more to it, but I can't imagine what it is.'

The mention of Scotland Yard had stirred a memory, but Amy could not grasp it. 'It was murder, you said.'

'I don't believe I used that word.'

'But if it was in cold blood?'

'Cold blood? Perhaps you're right. Perhaps that is it.' Westbrook touched at his shoulder. He seemed to be in pain. 'After all they've never set foot on a battlefield, have they, those gentlemen at the War Office? All they know of it is figures and maps. So I'm to hunt down whoever's responsible, though the task is hopeless.'

'Couldn't you have refused?'

'I wanted to. But I also want my old job back. And they were most insistent.'

Amy knew where she had heard his name before. '*Inspector* Westbrook, was that you?'

'You read the papers then.'

Amy had read the papers, in spite of her mother's best efforts. In particular she had followed the reports of the Tipton murder trial, alternately revolted and fascinated, as if discovering a sickly but forbidden fruit. The accused had been a solicitor from Portsmouth, the victims two adolescent boys found naked and garrotted in different locations in south London. Detective Inspector Westbrook's conduct of the case had been an object lesson in persistence. Lacking witnesses, he had canvassed every constabulary within a hundred miles of London, asking if the details of the case were familiar. An unsolved case on the south coast led back to Tipton, who had been questioned at the time. The same unusual knot found in London around the dead boys' necks was to be found in his conservatory, where the solicitor had used it to tie up his tomato plants.

'The men at Two Storm Wood, you said ten of them were shot,' Amy said. 'What happened to the others?'

The wagon lurched violently from side to side as they rode over a deep hole in the road. Amy held Westbrook's gaze.

'I'll know better tomorrow, when I examine them. They're buried not far from here, a mile or two from Bertrancourt.' If he was issuing an invitation, it was not one Amy was about to accept. 'It might be possible to find out if the wounds were inflicted before or after death. Or at least to discern the intention. It looks like a form of torture – the nails suggest as much.'

'Nails?'

'They were secured,' Westbrook said. 'The choice of victims may also reveal something, if we can establish who they were.'

He fell silent, as if aware of having said too much.

'I asked Captain Mackenzie about Two Storm Wood,' Amy said. 'He was very anxious I should stay away.'

'He was one of the first on the scene. His men dealt with the bodies.'

'He didn't say anything about that.'

Westbrook nodded, the hint of a smile on his lips. 'Captain Mackenzie thinks he may have made a mistake: he's afraid there might have been an officer among the dead, a white man. He's suspected it for some time. If your fiancé went missing last summer, on the Serre Ridge, there's a chance it could be him.'

Westbrook was watching her again, his eyes hidden beneath the peak of his cap. Then Amy understood: this was why she was being taken back to Bertrancourt. This was why they were talking about Two Storm Wood.

'You want me there when the bodies are exhumed,' she said. 'In case I can make an identification.'

Westbrook was testing her: testing her resolve, her purpose – as if he doubted both.

Corporal Reid looked back over his shoulder. He had been listening.

'It isn't something I'd normally ask of a woman,' Westbrook said.

———

138

Opium

—— Nineteen ——

England, July 1916

The sun was low, the shadows of the branches dancing over the bed, insects buzzing lazily among the apple trees, the air warm and heavy.

'Don't get dressed. Not yet.'

Amy sat up and drew the shirt off Edward's back. Before he could protest, her hands were on his shoulders, tracing the arcs of muscle beneath his skin. She pushed her fingers through the damp hair at the back of his neck, a gentle scent rising like freshly gathered grain.

'Amy?'

'Stay as you are. Don't hide behind all this ... *starch*.'

'You know we have to go. What's the matter?'

Recently she had begun to notice it: the way he became restless and awkward after they had slept together. Even on the warmest summer days, in his little rented cottage in Madingley, he would quickly pull on a shirt, or wrap a sheet around his middle. He would sling his legs over the side of the bed, look up at the narrow casement window and then start arranging things decently. He would even arrange the covers over her, as if too much exposure might be harmful to her skin. She did not know whether to feel protected or insulted, cherished or demeaned. But that afternoon, watching him fumble with a shirt button, she had felt a sudden distance between them that made her shudder.

'You know, you won't always be beautiful.' Her lips played over his neck. 'You'll have plenty of time to hide when you're old.'

'If I live to be old.'

The skin on his shoulders smelled of coal-tar soap and, beyond that, something musky and comforting. 'Why shouldn't you?'

'A lot of people won't. There's this war on, you see.'

'Really? I hadn't heard.'

141

He shrugged. 'Well, I expect it'll all be over by Christmas.'

They both laughed, even though they knew it was wrong to laugh, that the war was no laughing matter. It was something they had explicitly allowed themselves to do in private: a way to keep the terrible fact of the conflict at bay, to stop it infecting their brief hours together with mournfulness and guilt. The war was not their war. They had not made it, had not asked for it, did not approve of it. Why then should they treat it with reverence? How many lives would that save?

'It's almost six o'clock, Amy. You did say.'

They had to watch the time. A few weeks earlier, Kitty Page had run into Amy's mother and Aunt Clem on King's Parade. Kitty was supposed to have been out with Amy, a respectable chaperone. When questioned, she had been too flustered not to give the game away.

'I don't want to hear you lie, Amy,' her mother had said the next morning, 'so I'm not going to ask you where you were yesterday.'

Amy should have said it was none of her business, but she had only sat there, silent, transfixed.

'I will only say that if anything's going on between you and that ... musician' – she would not use his name, although Amy felt certain she knew it – 'you'd be well advised to call a halt, for your own sake.'

Amy's cheeks had burned. She had been seen with Edward somewhere, by someone. She had counted on the anonymity of a large town, but Cambridge, it seemed, was not large enough.

'You see, I know his kind very well.' Her mother had been going through her correspondence, slicing open envelopes with a letter-opener. 'I've seen them before: a nobody who wants to be a somebody. That's all it is, I'm afraid, even if you aren't old enough to see it yet.'

Still Amy had said nothing. She had been unable to defend him, to tell her mother that she was wrong.

'A young woman needs her family, Amy. The war has changed a lot of things, but not that.'

Amy had buckled. She had enjoyed leading a secret life as Edward's lover. At times, simply possessing that secret had made her feel powerful, privileged. Now she wished she could wipe the slate clean, go back to the way things were when she had nothing to hide. The day she went to Madingley and found

Edward in the graveyard she had been carrying a letter, since destroyed. The letter had said goodbye.

Edward turned towards her now and kissed her, one hand travelling to her shoulder, the other hovering beneath her breasts, as if unsure whether to caress them or not. She shivered, skin tightening, as finally she felt the gentle friction of his fingertips.

The church bells rang: six o'clock. Amy sat up. Aunt Clem was expecting her for dinner. If she was on time, she would not have to lie.

Edward sighed. 'So we're dressing after all.'

'I'd better.'

'It feels like you just arrived.'

'I'm sorry. It's—'

'For Aunt Clem's sake, I know.' He smiled. 'It doesn't matter.'

He picked up Amy's chemise and laid it on the bed beside her. Then he went downstairs, carrying his shoes.

Slowly, Amy began to dress. The clothes felt thick and clinging. Outside, the branches stirred so that she had the fleeting sensation of being watched.

When she got down to the kitchen Edward was dressed as smartly as if for church. The caps of his shoes were shiny, and he had brushed his hair. The pearl tiepin was in place. He stood by the window with his hands in his pockets.

'Is something wrong?' Amy said.

'No.' He turned to look at her. He was hiding something – some thought, some reflection. What was it? 'How about a drink?'

'You know I have to go.'

'Then I'll come with you.'

'There's no need, really.' She did not want him saying goodbye at Aunt Clem's front door. They might be seen. She put a hand on his shoulder and kissed him on the cheek. 'I'd best not be late.'

'I was thinking you could plead exceptional circumstances, just this once.'

She put her hat on. 'What exceptional circumstances?'

There was a hoarseness in his voice, an unfamiliar tension. 'You could tell your aunt and uncle that someone proposed to you.'

'I couldn't say that. They'd want to know who—'

In the middle of the kitchen table lay a small black box. Edward picked it up and opened it in front of her. Inside was a ring: a single sapphire set in a gold band.

'It was my grandmother's. I've not much in the way of family heirlooms, but ... well, I hope it fits.'

That was when it hit her: the proposal was his. She felt exhilaration – she would never forget it – a fleeting moment of pure joy.

'It's beautiful,' she said.

And then she realised what it would mean if she said yes, the price she would pay. Her mother would never accept an engagement. She would see it as an act of war. The doors of the Vanneck family would close, and Amy would be left firmly on the outside, with only Edward to depend on, a man she had known for just a few short months.

What she needed, she told herself, was time. With time, the family might come to see Edward as she did. Her Uncle Evelyn was going to be visiting them in Cambridge in a week's time. He had always been on her side. She could start with him. If he approved of Edward, anything was possible. Even her mother might relent at last.

Amy took the ring from the box. The stone was a fathomless blue, polished to a shine, as if newly made. She felt breathless, close to panic.

'Try it on,' Edward said.

She brought it to the tip of her finger. Her hands were shaking.

'I think it's ... too small.'

'Are you sure?'

She pushed the ring down, but only to the first knuckle. 'Besides, why the hurry? We're happy, aren't we? You don't have to make an honest woman of me, if that's what—'

'But I want to.'

'Make an honest woman of me?'

'I only meant ...' He held her hands together between his. 'I want us to be together all the time, Amy. And for ever. I don't want to hide any more – like we're hiding now.'

'I'm not hiding.' She could not look him in the eye. 'Haven't I always told you: I don't give a damn about the old conventions? When the war's over, we'll start again from scratch, just like you said.'

For a moment everything was still. Edward stepped back. 'So your answer is ...?'

She brought a hand to his face. This time it was he who could not look at her. 'Not yet. Soon. I love you, but we need time. Time to – to make it right.'

'Right?' He shook his head. 'Isn't it right already, what we have?'

'Yes, of course, but ...'

Edward sighed. 'They're never going to change their minds, you know, not about me. You can't win them round, Amy. In the end, you're going to have to ...'

She knew what he was going to say. She knew what she had promised, and yet it was as if she were standing on a precipice, unable to take a final step into the void.

Edward swallowed, nodded. 'But you're right. It's a big step. A lot to ask of you so ... soon.' He yanked open his collar. The tiepin made a high singing note as it fell onto the flagstones.

Amy had never seen him look so lost. For ever afterwards the memory of it pierced her heart. Without another word he walked over to the kitchen door and opened it.

Amy had snatched up the tiepin. 'Edward?'

He was already out on the doorstep. 'We should go now. You don't want to be late.'

They had cycled back into the town, Edward taking the lead. Amy had tried to catch up with him, but he was always too far ahead, pedalling hard. He had left her at the corner of her road, so that nobody would see him from the house. Amy had not needed to ask him. He already knew.

———

January 1917

... My family think my working at the telephone exchange is a great sacrifice on my part. They don't see that for most of the girls there, taking on 'men's work' means an escape from the drudgery of domestic service or a life spent confined to the home. The fact that my circumstances are different makes it hard for me to fit in, unfortunately. The girls are not mean, but they have always kept me at a distance. I am sure many of them think that is the only proper thing to do, that I have no interest in mixing with the likes of them.

Last Saturday I cycled out to Madingley, to look at the house again. I couldn't stop myself. I thought it would cheer me up to see it unchanged, even if you're not there any more. I thought it would be comforting to be reminded that it was all real, the time we spent there, those secret hours I long to have again, but which seem to grow more distant and fantastical every day, as if I only dreamed them.

It looks as if there are no new tenants. Nettles are growing in the little flower-bed outside the kitchen, and the bedroom window has no curtains. I tried the front door, knowing it would be locked, of course, and so it was. Still, I found myself fighting back tears. It was foolish of me, but I felt as if I was being shut out of more than just an empty cottage. The time I dream of is gone and will not come again, that was what the locked door seemed to say. If it hadn't been for some people passing, I would have battered it down.

I peered through the hedge into the orchard. It's the season, I suppose, but the trees look as if they are dying and will not fruit again. Perhaps it is not good for me, staying here now you are gone, but I can't think of being anywhere else. A trace, a memory, the knowledge that you once stood where I stand, walk where I walk, is better than nothing at all. I cling to those threads, breathing in this time but living in another, like some poor old widow who walks about in her wedding dress, carrying a bouquet of dead flowers. Only your letters, and my fear, bring me back to the present.

If you don't lead me out of this place, my love, I may never leave. Where else could I possibly go?

———

—— Twenty ——

France, March 1919

Amy was waiting outside the Desmoulin farm when Corporal Reid arrived with the wagon. She had been up since dawn, the dread building, solidifying inside her, until the weight of it seemed to press against her heart, making rest impossible. It was what she had come for: to find him. But the thought of the exhumation was too much, her imagination crowding with pictures she did not want to see. Even in her worst moments she had never dreamed that Edward would die in darkness, below ground, tortured, murdered. If she had stayed in England she might have lived forever in ignorance, imagining a swift death, free from pain. But it was too late for that now.

Corporal Reid regarded her warily as she hurried across the yard. She had seen that look before among Mackenzie's men, and others who worked on the battlefields. It was as if her grief and fear might infect them, breathing life into feelings they thought they had dispensed with.

'You ready then, Miss?'

'Yes.' Amy climbed onto the seat beside him. She knew she was not ready – not to look upon Edward's dead body, not to discover that he had been butchered under Two Storm Wood. She only knew she had no choice.

'Well then,' Reid said and cracked the reins.

———

South of Bertrancourt the road rose gently. It twisted around a large crater, then descended towards the Ancre, where solitary walls and lines of broken trees betrayed the site of streets, and where a church still stood intact, its stones pale grey like the sky. The mist was lifting.

Short of Mailly-Maillet they came to a crossroads. Opposite the shell of a farmhouse a signpost read BUCQUOY – SERRE. As they slowed down, Amy became aware of a new sound breaking over the rattling of the wagon: boots on mud – thousands of them, a tumbling, muted roar. She looked round: a column of men was trudging past the village with bags on their backs, a scruffy procession of solemn, dark-skinned Chinese dressed in wadded tunics or greatcoats. Some wore Shantung hats, ear-flaps wagging in time with their strides; others had caps or balaclavas. A few of them smoked as they walked.

'Where are they going?'

'Up to the Hindenburg Line.' Reid sniffed. 'The coolies do things different from the rest of us.'

'How so?'

'We make camp at the edge of a battlefield, somewhere already cleared, and work our way across. The coolies pitch up right in the middle and work their way out.' A gap opened up in the river of men. Reid cracked the reins. 'They don't care where they put their heads down. A graveyard's as good as any other place to them.'

Amy searched for an end to the column, but it snaked round a distant bend, unbroken. 'I thought they were superstitious.'

Reid shrugged. 'I got talking to one of them, a ganger. He said: Why would your ghosts bother us? It's not like we did them any harm.'

Amy looked into the faces of the men as they passed, searching for some sliver of insight, some sense of what they saw as they looked back at her. She was struck only by their difference: men from another world caught up in the ruins of hers, but cut off from its history and its suffering.

'Who are they?'

'Miss?'

'Why did they come? Do they have families? Some of them look so young.'

Reid blinked behind his milky lenses. 'I don't know. Never really thought about it.' An idea occurred to him. 'Work the docks back home, I heard. Shifting things. That's what coolies do, Miss: shift things and dig.'

'Dig?'

'Trenches and dugouts.'

'And that's all?'

'What else? Not their war, is it?'

The concentration cemetery lay south-west of the village. Over the previous month, Reid explained, the smaller cemeteries roundabout had been emptied and the dead reburied there. The new graves were marked with stakes, to which labels had been tied, bearing the names of the dead, their ranks and regiments. Others that Amy saw read only *East Kents*, *Private*, *Second Lieutenant*, *Canadian* and *Unknown*.

The thirteen men from Two Storm Wood had been buried at a distance from the others, one beside the other.

'We have to keep the coolies separate,' Reid said, pointing out the spot. 'No mixing with our boys. And their feet have to point east.'

'Their feet?'

'Always. A Chinaman isn't supposed to turn his back on his home, even when he's dead. That's one thing they *are* superstitious about.'

Major Westbrook was already there, walking from grave to grave, making notes in a book, while two other men from Mackenzie's company were unloading another wagon. Spades and shovels, stretchers, canvas, rope, rubber gloves and flasks of disinfectant were laid out in readiness.

The graves of the murdered men were in a line. The labels read *CLC Unknown*, and were numbered one to thirteen.

Westbrook watched Amy approach, the pencil motionless in his hand. 'You continue to defy expectations, Miss Vanneck,' he said, when she was in earshot. 'Corporal Reid and his comrades were sure you would change your mind.'

Westbrook had not shaved. Pale stubble dappled his jaw, broken up by patches of bald scar tissue. Like his injuries, it reinforced Amy's impression of him as someone who stood apart from the normalities of military life.

'Graves one to ten hold the men who were shot,' he said. 'Is that correct, Corporal Reid?'

'Yes, sir. Sergeant Cotterell must've got out the easy ones first.'

Westbrook stopped beside the eleventh grave. 'Then we'll start here.'

Privates Cavanagh and Fielding put on their rubber gloves and started digging. Progress was slow. The heavy clay clung to the shovels, and the men seemed to tire, the sweat running down their faces. As they dug deeper, water seeped into the grave, forming puddles under their feet.

After a few minutes a corner of pale fabric could be seen peeping through the ground. Westbrook threw off his coat and stepped into the hole. 'Take care. I don't want any damage, understood?'

He took Cavanagh's shovel and began scraping away at the soil. Little by little, a canvas bundle, secured with ropes, came into view. The material was soaked through. A large brown stain covered half of it. Amy did not notice the smell until she saw that Reid had a handkerchief over his mouth and nose.

'All right, lift him up.'

Cavanagh took one end, Fielding the other. They raised the bundle to shoulder height and rolled it onto a stretcher. In spite of the water, it did not seem heavy, but strangely shapeless – no visible breadth where the shoulders should have been, no tapering towards the feet. Edward had been tall, and broad. Amy told herself it could not be him.

Westbrook went to the next grave. 'This one and number thirteen. We'll leave the rest for tomorrow.'

Mackenzie's men seemed to think they'd got off lightly. They set to work quickly, keeping up an industrious rhythm. Westbrook paced up and down as they dug, now and again looking up at the church, which stood a hundred yards away. With its roof and spire intact, its walls and windows hardly damaged, it looked out of place among the earthworks and the ruins.

Cavanagh rested an arm on his shovel. 'Here it is, sir. This bugger's a big one.'

Amy stepped forward. The bundle at the bottom of the grave was longer and broader than the last, almost as big as Cavanagh himself. At one end she could make out a pair of feet pushing at the canvas. At the other end a bulge indicated the position of the head. As they slowly raised the body onto a stretcher, a trickle of dark fluid ran down the underside and dripped onto Fielding's boot. Amy felt hot, the skin tight across her forehead. Her vision clouded and for a moment she thought she would fall.

'You all right, Miss?'

Corporal Reid was standing close beside her. Amy straightened up. Cavanagh and Fielding were already starting on the last grave. They looked up at her between shovelfuls of earth, as if anxious not to miss the moment when she finally turned and ran.

Westbrook's attention was elsewhere. 'The church will be our morgue,' he said. 'I don't suppose anyone will object.'

———

They had to pull down a wall of sandbags to reach the doors of the church, which turned out to be unlocked. Inside it was cold and dark, the stained-glass windows glowing like jewels above them. The pews had been cleared away and stacked against the wall. The floor was strewn with rags and scraps of paper. Stained bandages balled up in one corner indicated the temporary presence of a dressing station. On the steps leading up to the altar a solitary boot lay on its side.

The altar table was the only piece of furniture big enough to lay a body on. They wiped it clean and moved it into the south transept, where the tall windows had been peppered with shrapnel, allowing in some extra daylight. Reid lit the storm lantern for good measure and hung it on a nearby nail. The stretchers were brought in and laid on the ground.

'We'll start with number eleven,' Westbrook said. 'Put him on the table.'

Still wearing their gloves, Fielding and Cavanagh picked up the first bundle. The canvas was pale and wet. As they carried it to the table it flexed and slackened like the skin of a maggot. It had been secured with three lengths of rope, the knots tight and hard – a kind that were never meant to be undone.

Westbrook took out a penknife and sawed through the ropes. 'Corporal Reid, I want you to write down everything I say.'

Reid fumbled in his satchel for a notebook and a pencil. Fielding lit a cigarette as he looked on, like a bystander at the scene of an accident.

'You men can go back to the wagon,' Westbrook said. 'I'll call you if you're needed.' The men left, as instructed. 'The same applies to you, Miss Vanneck, if you wish.'

Amy was staring at the bundles on the ground. Westbrook's voice came to her as if from far away.

'Miss Vanneck?'

Wing-beats clattered in the roof above them. A pair of pigeons swooped through the air and vanished into the shadows of the spire.

'No, I'll stay if …' Amy checked herself. This was no time for excuses, no time for conditions. 'I'll stay.'

'You're quite sure now?' Westbrook was watching her closely. Again she had the sensation of being tested. 'Nobody could blame you if—'

'No one else can identify him, can they? If it's Edward … in there.'

Westbrook looked at the bundle in front of them. 'Probably not.'

'Then I'll stay.'

It seemed to take a moment for her answer to sink in. He had been expecting her to back out, that was clear.

'Very well,' he said.

He pulled on a pair of gloves and unrolled the first two feet of the canvas. Reid let out a stifled grunt as the head came into view. It was twisted up and over to one side, as if trying to tear itself away from the rest of the body. Amy stepped back. The flesh was a pearly grey, the parted teeth standing out starkly between purple lips. The brown hands were crossed under the chin, palms outwards. Ragged holes were plainly visible in the wrists.

'Unknown number eleven. Flesh is partially mummified.' Westbrook crouched down to examine the back of the head. The short black hair was caked in dirt. 'No bullet wound.'

Reid began to write. The dead man appeared to be Asian, but such was the contortion of the features it was hard to be sure.

That can't be Edward. Amy clung to the thought. *That can't be him.*

Westbrook had begun to unroll the rest of the canvas when something caught his attention. 'Bring that light over here.'

Reid unhooked the lantern and handed it over. Beneath the yellow flame the body shimmered and twitched. The dead man's left forearm seemed to be covered in scales, like those on a lizard. They snaked around it from wrist to elbow, hooks and curls branching off left and right.

Westbrook bent closer until his face was inches away. 'Tattoo around right forearm. About fourteen inches long, in the form of a dragon and a tiger in combat. No tag.'

Reid kept writing, tilting the page towards the light. Westbrook pulled open the rest of the canvas. For a few moments the silence was broken only by the scratching of Reid's pencil.

'Body is naked,' Westbrook's voice was flat and steady, though his fitful breathing betrayed the illusion of calm. 'Wound to the wrist, consistent with the use of nails. The pectoral muscles have been removed with a blade – a sharp blade. The calf muscles of the right leg and the thigh muscles have been partially excised. The sartorius has been left intact. I suspect that was to keep the leg from separating under its own weight, at the hip. That would have brought matters to a close.'

Amy stared, a hand clamped over her mouth.

Westbrook took a pencil from his pocket and gently lifted a string of blackened flesh beside the thigh bone. 'Femoral artery is also intact. Extraordinary. Almost the entire *rectus femoris* has been excised, the *vastus lateralis* likewise, without severing the major blood vessels.'

Reid took a step closer, blinking as his bespectacled eyes sucked in the detail.

Westbrook moved further down the body. 'Lower leg, same … same approach. The gastrocnemius cut clean from knee to heel without any detectable damage to the arteries, tibial or peroneal. Most of the sural nerve is here as well.'

Reid had stopped writing. 'What's it all about, sir? Why the bother?'

Westbrook looked up. His eyes were bloodshot. 'To keep him conscious, of course. Maintain blood pressure. That way he could see his …' he caught Amy's eye, 'transformation.'

Amy turned and walked briskly to the door. She reached the corner of the building, just out of sight of Fielding who was tending to the horses, and vomited in three wrenching heaves. She steadied herself against the wall, her vision consumed by a swirling, granular fog, in the midst of which she saw Corporal Staveley, watching her from his hospital bed. Her insides heaved again, but there was nothing left in her stomach.

Slowly her vision cleared. She took some deep breaths and went back inside the church.

Westbrook was still standing beside the body, staring fixedly at the pared limbs and the exposed sections of ribcage. He looked up, blinking, as Amy approached, as if waking from a dream.

'Corporal, help me wrap him up,' he said.

Reid folded over the canvas and secured it with fresh rope. Then he and Westbrook placed the body back on the stretcher and carried it clear. The second bundle was heavier than the first, and longer, but Westbrook didn't summon help. He seemed to prefer working with Reid.

Westbrook cut open the second bundle. The body was lying on its front, naked, a tall man with broad shoulders, though the flesh was shrunken and cracked around the ribs and the hips. Amy knew she should move closer, but her legs would not carry her.

Reid took out his notebook again.

'CLC Unknown number twelve,' Westbrook said. 'Wound to the back of the skull.' He leaned forward, brought the lantern closer. 'Superficial. Lacerations, not a bullet wound.' He ran a gloved hand across an area of torn flesh and matted hair. 'Not a cause of death. Caused by something pointed but not sharp.'

His glove came away stained. The whole head was covered in dried blood, recently moistened by rain or the damp ground. The flesh was black.

'Puncture wounds through the wrists, same as number eleven. Get him on his back.'

Westbrook put the lantern down on the floor. As he did so, Amy saw something on the body glimmer. Westbrook saw it too. Still crouching, he examined the top of the dead man's skull.

'Give me a rag,' he said. 'A handkerchief – anything.'

Reid picked up one of the old bandages lying on the floor. Westbrook spat on it, then rubbed the moistened cloth over a small area of the scalp, cleaning off the dried blood.

He stood up again and threw the bandage away. 'Unknown number twelve has blond hair.'

Amy's fists clenched at her sides. The men were both looking at her now, expectantly. The vision came back to her of Edward sitting on the edge of his bed, a breeze blowing from the open window, the smooth warmth of his skin as she slid off his shirt. Then the shirt became the paper prayers lodged among the sandbags at Two Storm Wood, a wall of prayers to seal in the evil – a wall that had been breached.

'Miss Vanneck?'

The body had been rolled over. Westbrook was examining the head. Amy stepped forward. The brow of the dead man was familiar, the bumps and lines.

'This should make it easier,' Westbrook said. 'Here.'

He prized open the jaw with his fingers. Amy forced herself to look.

'The upper right canine: it's capped with gold. You see?'

Reid picked up the lantern and held it closer. Amy saw the bright metal glimmer in the black, shrivelled mouth.

She shook her head. 'I've never seen that before.'

'Are you sure? There are two gold fillings.'

'Quite sure.'

Westbrook stepped back. 'Then this can't be Captain Haslam.'

Amy could see now that the features were different: the jaw too prominent, the nose too broad. It was a European, but not Edward.

'No. It's not.'

The relief was like something bursting inside her. She stumbled. Westbrook moved to her side, but she held out a hand to keep him back.

'I'm all right. I'm all right.'

'You're very pale. You'd better—'

'Really. I'm all right, Major. Thank you.'

Reid was paying no attention. 'Something in here, sir.' He was bending close to the dead man, frowning behind his spectacles. 'In his throat.'

Westbrook went back to the table. At the back of the dead man's mouth lay something yellow or white, something that was not bone or flesh.

'A gag, do you think, sir?' Reid said.

'Perhaps.' Westbrook eased the jaw down and reached into the mouth with two fingers. Dark fluid welled over his fingertips. 'It isn't cloth, though.'

It was paper, balled up, slimy. His fingers could not get a grip on it, his efforts threatening to push it further down the dead man's throat.

Westbrook took out his pencil. 'I'll need yours too.'

Reid handed it over. With the two points Westbrook carefully pinched the obstruction and drew it out. Taking care not to tear it, he slowly flattened out the paper over a corner of the altar table. Amy saw handwriting in pencil, dense lines of it covering the page. It had to be a letter. After squinting for a while at the contents, Westbrook carefully folded it and placed it in the top pocket of his tunic.

'Is there a name?' Amy could not help thinking of a family somewhere – a mother, children, a lover – waiting for news that never came.

Westbrook covered up the corpse, starting with the head. 'Unfortunately not,' he said.

—— Twenty-one ——

Amy opened her eyes. She was lying in the back of a wagon, blinking into weak winter sunlight, hazy cloud twisting high above her, celestial, beautiful, like music. They were travelling quickly, Westbrook at the reins. There was no sign of Corporal Reid.

She lifted her head. Was she back on the road to Bertrancourt? She searched the horizon for a clue. All she could see was the same landscape of churned earth and yellowed grass – and for a moment she saw it covered in an endless field of wheat, as in her dreams.

Then it came back to her: the canvas bags and the mangled bodies. After the blond man, she must have passed out. Somewhere in a dream he had turned out to be alive. His head had rolled towards her, the mouth gaping in a voiceless scream – screaming for pity and for death. It was the horror that had woken her. She was still shaking.

She sat up further. Three bodies had been taken to the church, but she had only seen two. 'Major Westbrook?'

Westbrook pulled on the reins.

'What about the third body?'

He didn't seem to hear her. 'I'm taking you to a doctor in Acheux. We won't be long.'

'The last body, did you examine it? Number thirteen.'

Westbrook nodded. 'Another Chinaman. You're going to have to keep looking for Captain Haslam, I'm afraid.'

Corporal Staveley had given her the name of Two Storm Wood. He had been playing with her, giving her false hope – a madman's amusement. And yet, she was relieved.

The wagon had come to a halt. Westbrook was waiting. One of the horses shook its mane.

'I've taken you away from your duties,' Amy said. 'You must forgive me, Major. I don't need a doctor. I'm fine now.'

'I expect you could do with a drink, after what you've seen.' Westbrook took up the reins again. 'There's a hotel of sorts in Acheux. Billets for officers. It should still be possible to get a glass of brandy.' He turned a little so that she could see his face. 'I can take you back to Bertrancourt, if you'd prefer.'

She knew how it would look if she refused him: that he was too ugly to drink or be seen with, too disfigured for his company to afford any pleasure. Besides, she did not want to be alone, not yet.

She climbed onto the bench beside him. 'Acheux then.'

She thought she saw him smile as he urged the horses on.

They travelled for half a mile, passing through a small village called Forceville, where a burned-out field ambulance stood beside a crossroads, its wheels and engine gone. A small cemetery lay to the south.

'The dead men,' Amy said, 'did you learn anything, apart from how they died?'

'They were killed on the sixteenth of August or soon after that. We found the date on a letter. It should help with identification. Labour Corps officers didn't die in large numbers. There'll be a record that matches, somewhere.'

Edward had been reported missing on the seventeenth, the very next day. Twenty-five men from his unit had died in battle that day, according to the battalion diary. The obvious explanation was that the Chinese had been caught up in the same attack.

'What will happen when you have it?'

'The record?' Westbrook took a moment to consider the question. 'The men will get their headstones – the officer, at any rate.'

'And the men who killed them?'

'They're long gone. Or dead. Out of reach, either way.'

'How can you be sure?'

Westbrook rolled his right shoulder and grimaced. 'Captain Mackenzie was right about one thing: the Chinese didn't do this. To dismember the living is a trick of theirs, but it's reserved for traitors, their own kind. A British officer doesn't fit the bill. Besides, the use of firearms, the ostentation – leaving them up there to be found – that has to be the work of the Hun, unless we've missed something. There's no one else.'

Amy had heard of atrocities perpetrated by the German Army – civilians bayoneted, a sergeant crucified on a barn door. She had never known for sure if they had really happened. But there was no denying the evidence of her own eyes.

'You'll find the men responsible, won't you? You'll track them down?'

'What purpose would that serve?'

It was as if Westbrook was trying to provoke her. 'The purpose of … of justice. What we saw – what happened – it was … It can't just be forgotten.'

'Perhaps it would be better if it was.'

'Why would you say that?'

Westbrook stared at the road ahead. 'Civilians prefer to remain ignorant of what men do in war – most civilians anyway. They're eager enough to celebrate victory; they don't want too much knowledge about how it was won.'

Amy had no right to be indignant, but if Edward had been found at Two Storm Wood, she would have wanted to know who killed him. She would have wanted to look into the murderer's face. And then? Would she want revenge? If so, of what kind?

'Inspector Westbrook – the one I read about – would he have been satisfied with that? Wouldn't he say the dead deserve justice?'

Westbrook nodded slowly. 'Perhaps he would, at that. But then he was a civilian too.'

'So once the dead men are identified, you're finished here. Your work's done.'

He regarded Amy for a moment, as if trying to decide if she deserved the truth. He had once been handsome, imposing, she could see that. Now his self-respect was most likely hanging by a khaki thread. It would be harder to maintain in the civilian world, without the status of rank, and most likely he knew it.

'Not quite.'

'Then—'

'I would like an explanation. Such a … transgression: I would like to understand it. Sometimes there's more value in knowledge than judgement.' Westbrook smiled. 'Call it professional curiosity.'

'Why would someone stoop to such … ?' Amy could not find the words. 'I'll never understand it.'

Westbrook turned back to the road. 'It would be easier to perceive a motive if the chain of events was clearer. Unfortunately, the evidence is inconsistent.'

'The evidence?'

'Two Storm Wood was never far behind the German front line – that's what doesn't fit. Prisoners of war wouldn't have been held there for long. Normally they'd be escorted to the rear straight away. That means these victims were killed soon after capture: a spontaneous act. And yet the nature of the killings seems premeditated.'

Amy shuddered. 'Who could plan such a thing?'

'Without a witness, we'll never know. And we have no witness, at least not yet.'

'So what will you do?'

'I'll report to the War Office and await orders.'

'What if they send you home?'

'Then I'll go. Orders are orders.'

'Will you go back to Scotland Yard?'

Amy was curious to know what home meant to him: a place of warmth and shelter, or of dread, isolation, loneliness?

'That's up to the ministry.'

'What about your family?'

Westbrook cracked the reins. It was possible he had not heard her. He was prone to disappear into his own thoughts, Amy had noticed that. Or had she been indiscreet to enquire about his private life? His scars made him hard to read. All men had feelings and emotions, responses to those around them that would normally shape an encounter. But his were hidden, as if he were wearing a mask.

'I'm sorry,' Amy said. 'I've no right to pry.'

They went over a rise. Rooftops appeared in the distance, partly hidden behind a patch of woodland.

'This isn't England, Miss Vanneck,' Westbrook said. 'It's a battlefield. Etiquette is a little out of place.'

———

They reached Acheux as the sun was slipping beneath the clouds, the church tower and the rooftops standing stark against a mass of bruise-coloured clouds.

Amy had expected to find the town quiet, but the streets were crowded with soldiers and civilians. An event was in full swing. From nearby came the beat of drums and a frantic crashing of symbols. As they turned a corner they were met by the sight of six Chinese on stilts, firecrackers bursting around them. They were moving in a circle, pirouetting on one leg or pivoting off one another in a precarious mockery of combat.

Westbrook pulled the wagon up sharply. 'What are they doing here? Damned Chinamen are supposed to stay in camp.'

'Don't they have leave?' It was the first time Amy had seen the provost marshal look angry.

'No fraternising with the civilian population,' he said. 'Labour Corps general orders. It's asking for trouble.'

They left the wagon behind a hotel on the rue de Louvencourt and continued on foot. Outside the church the crowd was bigger and noisier. Many of the troops were holding pamphlets. Amy picked one off the ground and read a few lines of uneven type:

> *His return is upon us. Soon he will declare himself and*
> *all men loyal and true shall rally to his flag.*
> *SOLDIERS! BE READY!*
> *You ask: What was this war for?*
> *You ask: Why were you spared?*
> *It was for this!*
> *On the command, fall in!*

A procession of ceremonial dragons was edging its way along the street. The drums beat relentlessly. Dancers twisted and convulsed as if possessed. After the emptiness of the battlefields, Amy felt dazed.

Stalls had been set up on the streets, selling silk embroidery, imitation flowers and figures carved from bone. Amy saw horses, tigers and demons wielding swords. Soldiers were crowded round, anxious for souvenirs. They looked Amy up and down as she passed, as if trying to assess her value or her price.

'May I ask you something?' Westbrook said when they had turned a corner. 'What did Captain Haslam do before he joined up?'

Amy kept close by his side. 'Edward was a ...' What should she say? She could not call him a choirmaster. It felt naïve, ridiculous. 'He was teaching at a school when we met.'

'A reserved occupation. So he could have stayed out of it.'

'He was all against the war, as a matter of fact, on principle. He called it madness.'

'Did he? Madness?'

'Mass slaughter is no way to settle an argument, that's what he used to say. What's civilisation for, if it can't do better than that?'

'A pacifist.' Westbrook nodded thoughtfully. 'But then he met you.'

Amy stopped. 'I didn't talk him into it, if that's what you mean. I felt the same way about the war. I still do.'

'None of which explains the change of heart.'

Amy walked on. She did not have to suffer Westbrook's questions. She was not under the jurisdiction of military law.

'Perhaps he'd found something worth fighting for at last,' he said. 'Or perhaps he was afraid.'

'Afraid?'

'That you would think him a coward. You or your family.'

'What are you talking about? Why would you say that?'

'Forgive me, Miss Vanneck. It's simply ... I'm not clear in my mind about why you're here, why you didn't leave with your friend.' They stopped again by the side of the road as a horse and cart rolled by. 'I can believe you loved Captain Haslam, but I can't help feeling there's more to it than that. Guilt perhaps? Guilt demands suffering, self-punishment – like today, for instance. Why would you put yourself through it if not—'

'I'm not putting myself through anything, Major, not out of choice. I'm looking for my fiancé. There's all there is to it.'

They crossed the road, Westbrook offering no response. The gathering darkness obscured his limping gait and misshapen flesh. Amy found she could picture him the way he must have been before his injury: tall and strong, a young man in his prime.

'Of course he was here not so long ago, your husband-to-be.' He was gazing up at the rooftops. 'He would have walked these streets on his way to the line, or for some other reason. They were probably the last places he ever saw. For anyone who loved him, I suppose, that might make it hard to leave.'

It was Amy's turn to be silent. Until now, every man she had met had told her to go home, because she did not belong.

They reached a crossroads at the end of the street. A man in an officer's uniform was sauntering over, smoking a cigarette. Seeing the provost marshal, he quickly changed direction, but it was too late. Westbrook called him over.

'What's going on in this town? Your men should be in camp.'

The lieutenant took his hands out of his pockets and saluted. On his cap badge was a coiled silver dragon.

'A couple of the COs thought it would be an idea to put on a show, sir.'

'A show?'

'For the locals. Improve relations. Hearts and minds, and all that.'

A volley of firecrackers erupted behind them. Even amidst the smoke and the noise, Amy had a sense that the presence of a military policeman was an unwelcome intrusion.

'What's your name?' Westbrook demanded.

'Sloan, sir, Twenty-Fifth Company.'

Westbrook had to shout to make himself heard. 'Have you been here long, Lieutenant?'

'A few days, sir. I'm billeted at the hotel.'

'Can we get a drink there?'

'Dry as a bone, sir.' Lieutenant Sloan shot an uncertain glance at Amy, no doubt wondering what manner of consort she was. He pointed to a corner shop twenty yards away. Soldiers were slouching around outside, watching the parade with bottles of beer in their hands. 'There's an estaminet over the way. And another one further down.'

Westbrook shook his head. 'I meant a real drink. Is that whisky I can smell on you?'

'Just a little brandy, sir.'

'Even better. Well?'

Sloan frowned, as if the question were a complex one.

'Spit it out, man. We need more than a little plonk.'

Sloan swallowed. 'There's still a *maison tolérée* off the chemin de Varennes, sir. Run by a woman called Chastain. Officers only – used to be. Usually has a good bottle or two.' He looked at Amy again and seemed to lose his nerve. 'It's the only place I know, sir.'

Westbrook sighed. 'Then the estaminet will have to do.'

He turned to go, but Amy stood her ground. 'Why don't we follow the lieutenant's suggestion?'

'A *maison tolérée*? Do you even know what that is?'

Amy's hands were clasped in front of her. 'Yes, I do.'

The two officers exchanged glances.

'And you want me to take you there?'

'This isn't England, Major. Etiquette is a little out of place.'

Westbrook fell silent. He was trying to understand her, preferring, she sensed, to arrive at the truth unaided. 'You think your fiancé might have gone there. Is that it?'

'He would have walked down these streets on his way to the line, you said, or for some other reason. That was the other reason you meant, wasn't it?'

Westbrook nodded, both embarrassed and amused to have been caught out. After a moment he turned to Sloan. 'How do we find this place?'

———

Twenty-two

The officers' brothel lay at the far end of a cobbled yard, partly hidden behind a high brick wall. There was no light behind the shutters. They found the side door and knocked. Horses snorted and whinnied in the stables opposite, frightened by the fireworks erupting overhead.

A handsome, raven-haired woman opened the door.

'Madame Chastain?'

She glanced at Amy and frowned. '*Que voulez-vous?*'

'A drink,' Westbrook said. 'Some cognac.'

'*Ce n'est pas une taverne, Monsieur.*'

She tried to close the door. Westbrook jammed his boot against it. 'I know what it is.' He showed her a pair of banknotes. 'You can open my account with this. Lieutenant Sloan suggested we come here.'

At the mention of Sloan, the woman relented. She accepted the money and stood back from the door, her eyes still fixed on Amy. The hallway was dark and paved with stone. A sallow light was visible beneath a door at the far end. There was a smell of tobacco and stale lavender.

'*Montez au premier étage, s'il vous plaît.*'

Amy had always imagined that brothels were noisy. In the paintings she had seen, the people danced and played cards. But they were halfway up the stairs before she heard the sound of a gramophone above. For a moment the effort of climbing left her light-headed. It was days since she'd eaten a decent meal.

Madame Chastain was following them. '*A votre droite, si vous voulez.*' Her voice was brisk and businesslike. Did the red flashes on Westbrook's coat bother her? Or was it the unexplained presence of another woman?

A pair of doors opened onto a large salon. Thin curtains covered the windows. A fire was smoking in the grate.

A man in uniform lay asleep on a threadbare chaise longue, his tunic unbut-toned. Another had a girl on his lap: white chemise, black stockings, long black hair, already half-unpinned – a *fille soumise*, as they were known in France, a girl 'under the thumb' – the first Amy had ever seen: younger, plumper, altogether more ordinary than she had expected.

One of the soldier's hands was playing idly with the girl's jade earring, the other was on her thigh. Amy touched at her still-swollen lip, aware of how dirty and dishevelled she must look.

Westbrook threw down his kit bag and pulled off his coat.

'*J'ai seulement de l'eau de vie*,' Madame Chastain said.

'That'll do nicely. Miss Vanneck?'

Amy nodded. Outside, another rocket went up. She stepped towards the window and edged back the curtain. For a second or two the shadows that covered the yard vanished beneath a bright flickering light.

Standing just inside the gate was a soldier. He wore an overcoat and a cap pulled down low. She couldn't tell his rank. He was looking up at the house, at the windows, at *her*. A second later the rocket faded and he was lost in the gloom.

'Down there, did you—'

Westbrook was beside her. 'After a trick, no doubt.' He pulled the curtains shut. 'Expect I put him off. Or you did.'

'Me?'

'The ladies you see at these places – ones like you – they come armed with Bibles, preaching abstinence.'

Madame Chastain reappeared with the *eau de vie*. Amy perched on the edge of a settee. She tried to imagine Edward in a brothel like this one, but her memories of him would not be shoehorned into such a melancholy and soulless place.

Madame Chastain uncorked the bottle and poured out a single glass. '*Pour votre amie aussi?*' she asked Westbrook.

'*Oui, bien sûr*,' Amy said, speaking for herself.

The corner of Madame Chastain's mouth twitched, as if repressing a smile. She poured out a second glass.

'Better leave the bottle,' Westbrook said, but the bottle was empty.

'*J'en ai une autre.*'

Amy watched Madame Chastain disappear through a connecting door, wondering at what point in her life she had decided to take up her present line of business – whether she had been forced to do it for lack of an alternative, or if it had simply offered the best available return. Had she been a prostitute herself at any time? If so, she would have been an expensive one, a rich man's mistress perhaps.

Westbrook's glass was already empty. He was slouched back in an armchair, eyes closed. Amy took a mouthful of the *eau de vie*. It was strong and thick. Eagerly it burned its way to her stomach. In a minute a familiar unsteadiness began to cloud her senses.

'So, Miss Vanneck,' Westbrook said. 'Is it what you expected?'

'This place? No. It's more . . . unremarkable. I expected something exotic.'

Westbrook laughed. 'Most of the boys who came here, they didn't want anything exotic. They wanted to be comforted, mothered. The next best thing to going home.'

Amy looked around her at the worn furnishings, the landscape painting above the mantel, the faded rug with its floral pattern: the domestic ordinariness of it all made the battlefields seem far away.

'Of course they don't understand that in England,' Westbrook said. 'They think it's all cancan girls and debauchery.'

The mention of the cancan brought back a vision of Edward, half-dressed in his kitchen, knocking out the gallop from *Orpheus in the Underworld* on a row of bottles. In the legend, it was his beloved who died.

The girl in the corner was whispering, giggling. She had spotted the battered Englishwoman in the dirty dress. Perhaps Edward *had* come here – for comfort or for a girl, maybe this girl. For a moment the hand on the girl's thigh was Edward's hand, the amorous words his words. Amy shut her eyes. What did it matter? What did it matter if Edward hadn't 'played the game'? She felt sick. She took another mouthful of the *eau de vie* and turned away.

From behind the connecting door came voices, the clink of glass on glass. The soldier and the girl with the earrings crossed the room arm-in-arm, heading for a bedroom. Amy felt a draught. The connecting door swung half-open. On the other side Madame Chastain stood with her back to them. She was talking to someone. She had money in her hand, but she wasn't taking it – she was handing it over. The recipient was Chinese. He had a pale, angular face, more knowing and less tanned than most of the labourers Amy had seen.

He wore a civilian cap and the shapeless tunic of the corps. The money went into a hip pocket. Then he turned and left. The flames fluttered in the grate. The connecting door swung shut.

The room was growing dark when Madame Chastain returned with another bottle of liquor. She turned up one of the lamps, before refilling the glasses. Amy felt exhausted. She leaned back in the settee. She knew if she closed her eyes she would sleep.

'I'd like something else,' Westbrook was saying. '*Autre chose.*'

'*Autre chose?*'

'Whatever the Chinaman came to sell you.'

Westbrook had witnessed the transaction too.

'*Vous vous trompez, Monsieur.*'

There was a cough on the landing. Another girl drifted by, wearing nothing but a silk robe open to her knees. She looked like she was in a trance.

Westbrook put a hand on Madame Chastain's arm. She recoiled, but did not remove it. '*Regardez-moi, Madame. Regardez-moi.*'

Reluctantly she looked into his face. After a moment she nodded and turned away.

Across the town a volley of fireworks erupted like gunfire. Amy heard shouting, bestial bellows, screams of laughter, but they seemed far away. It was no good. She could not keep her eyes open. 'I have to ... I must go back to the—'

'You can sleep here,' Westbrook said. 'There are plenty of rooms.'

The last thing Amy remembered seeing was Madame Chastain setting a tray down on the table. There was a carafe of water, a glass, a small bowl of sugar and a flat brown bottle with the word *Papine* faintly visible on the label. To Amy it looked like medicine, except that they were not in a pharmacy.

'*Soyez prudent, Monsieur,*' Madame Chastain said. '*C'est fort.*'

———

Amy opened her eyes to silence. It was light outside. She was lying down, looking up at a stained plaster ceiling, breathless, heart pounding. The walls on either side of her were covered in floral wallpaper. She was no longer in the big salon. At some point she had moved – or been moved – to a bedroom. Her boots stood beside the bed.

She had been dreaming of Edward. She could not bring back a picture, a sense of the time or place; only his voice, calling to her – urgent, pleading, but muffled as if coming up through the ground. Then she remembered: she had been walking across the battlefield, except that a vast field of wheat covered everything, smothering the trenches and the wire so that she could neither search nor run. In the distance stood a man on horseback, watching her.

She sat up. Her mouth was so dry it felt as if her tongue would crack. She forced herself to her feet, head swimming gently, limbs weak and trembling as if she had shaken off a fever. The *eau de vie* had been stronger than anything she was used to. It had been a mistake to drink it on an empty stomach.

A clock on the mantel said seven o'clock. She had been unconscious for twelve hours.

There was a washstand and jug in the corner. She poured out some water and drank with her hands. After washing, she went out onto the landing.

Opposite, a door stood ajar. On the other side she found Westbrook asleep on the bed. It was not clear if he had spent the night alone or not. He was mumbling as he dozed, complaining, arguing. None of his words made any sense. The memory came back to her of a little brown bottle, the one Madame Chastain had brought in the night before. It had been opium in one form or another. What else could it have been? Amy would not have expected such a thing from a military policeman, but she felt no disgust, no disappointment. What had he been through to get his scars? What had he endured?

She had been anxious to be on her way, but she could let Westbrook sleep a little longer. She would wait in the salon.

As she turned, she noticed his tunic hanging on the back of a chair. Peeping out of the top pocket was a scrap of paper. She knew at once what it was: Westbrook had extracted it from the dead man's throat, the one they called *CLC Unknown number twelve*.

From outside she heard the sound of footsteps on the cobbles. An iron bolt rattled.

Amy thought of the dead man's name on an army ledger, listed as Missing in Action. She thought of a family somewhere, receiving the news, the slow death of hope in the long weeks that followed.

She plucked out the paper and held it to the light.

16th August 1918

Dear Ma,

This morning your package turned up with the socks and the shaving kit. Just the ticket, as I've been scrounging off Collie ever since I lost the last one. Sorry my letters have been short. The company has been moving forward, trying to keep the roads — and now a light railway — open over hellish territory. The Huns are a lot closer than usual. We often work at night to avoid the guns. Last week some shells came down on the camp at Beaumetz and caused quite a panic. The coolies scattered so far and wide the redcaps had to round them up.

There's been some bad business, and I'm not sure how it will play out. It's been on my mind a lot. I wish I had time to tell you. The Chinamen are good boys, by and large. There are a few bad apples. I heard deals were done with a prison in Shantung, felons and Boxers handed over for cash, but overall they are no more dishonest than the rest of the corps, and every bit as human. But these facts have not sunk in where they should. Some in the regular army seem to think of them as animals, which I won't stand for. Unfortunately Major Pickering has all the spine of a jellyfish when it comes to the rest of the army. If you ask me, they scare him worse than the Germans. That is why—

A cry went up outside. A man was yelling for help, his voice shrill. Westbrook sat up, blinking. He stared at Amy, then scrambled his way out of bed and hurried to the window.

Madame Chastain, dressed in a nightshirt and shawl, came running out into the yard. A groom, no more than seventeen, was outside the stables, pointing at something through the half-open door. One of the girls was outside too. She peered inside, screamed and kept on screaming. The groom dragged her away.

Westbrook ran downstairs, with Amy on his heels. Madame Chastain was frozen to the spot. She was muttering to herself: '*Pas encore, pas encore. Il est ici!*'

They moved past her towards the threshold of the stables. Westbrook eased back the door.

'*Il est revenu!*'

Blood on the walls. On the floor. Sprayed across an overhead beam. The cobbles were slick with it, the straw dark and glistening. As Westbrook stepped forward, Amy saw it well up around his feet.

A faecal stench mingled with the fatty butcher's smell. Amy clamped a hand across her nose and mouth. There were voices behind her, more people coming, calls for help, but she hardly heard them.

Westbrook shouted, 'No one comes in here!'

The dead man was tied to an upright beam opposite the stalls. He had a gag in his mouth, but Amy could still recognise the pale Chinese she had seen taking money from Madame Chastain. He was naked now, his limbs stripped of their flesh like three of the victims at Two Storm Wood.

Westbrook placed two fingers against the Chinese man's neck, then stood looking him up and down. 'Dead some hours,' he said.

All Amy could hear was the screaming in her head.

———

The army has starting enforcing the ban on forced-march tablets. Cocaine plays havoc with men's nerves, we are told, and corrodes the mind — quite unlike German heavy artillery, of course, which does neither of those things. Next they will take our rum, I suppose, so that we can all meet the enemy stone-cold sober and mindful of the high purpose that brought us here. And the Huns will be in Paris by Christmas.

You must not speak about this to anyone — not that you would. I don't want to give your family another reason to dislike me. More than that, I fear what Rhodes would think. An officer is supposed to be an example to his men. The commander can be strangely forgiving of weakness — I know this from experience — but this might count as betrayal. It is a fine thing to be trusted, to be favoured beyond your merits, but it is a burden too. Sometimes I think it will crush me.

Don't worry, Amy. I will give up all the poison when I am home. I'll have no more need of it then, because life will be easy. Meanwhile there will be other ways to get hold of what I need. The Chinese sell opium on the sly. I'm sure they will exploit this new opportunity. Then again, I've heard that some of them mix their opium with quinine and other poisons to make it go further. Men get sick or go blind. Can it be true? The Chinks would be lynched if that happened. They are not best loved as it is — because how can you love anyone when you don't know whose side they're really on?

———

— Twenty-three —

Westbrook spent a long time examining the floor. When he was done, he took a horse blanket from one of the stalls, threw it on the ground and reached into his pocket for a penknife. Madame Chastain had gone back into the house, but the others remained, watching.

'Help me get him down.'

Westbrook was half-dressed and unshaven, his eyes bloodshot, a sheen of sweat on his skin.

The groom stood on the threshold of the stables, staring at the body hanging from the upright beam. The dead man's head was twisted over to one side, his eyes shut. A bloody rag had been stuffed into the gaping mouth.

The groom shook his head. '*Je ne peux pas, Monsieur.*'

'I don't want him to fall. *Aidez-moi.*' The boy shook his head again and retreated towards the yard, where one of Madame Chastain's girls stood, frozen. Amy recognised the jade earrings, the round doll-like face. 'Damn it, someone has to help me.'

The girl ran away. Amy wanted to run too. Maybe if she shut her eyes, thought of other things, she could wipe away the memory of what she had seen.

Horses stamped and snorted in the stalls. They were expecting food.

Amy stepped forward. She was shaking. 'Tell me what to do.'

She forced herself to look again. The dead man's arms had been raised. His wrists were bound together and hooked over a four-inch nail at the back of the beam so that the elbows pointed forward. The way the ribcage jutted out, straining against the skin, reminded her of the tortured Christ – gruesome depictions in plaster and paint that had given her nightmares as a child.

Westbrook unfolded the blade of the knife and handed it over. 'I'll hold him. You cut him free. Can you do that?'

Amy moved slowly around the back of the body. With one hand she began sawing into the ropes, keeping what distance she could. But the ropes soon began moving beneath the blade. There was nothing for it but to hold them close with her free hand, her fingertips pressing into the flesh of the dead man's wrists. They felt cold.

Westbrook kicked the blanket into position. His breathing was unsteady. The groom was still staring from the yard. 'You, go and find Lieutenant Sloan. At the hotel. Tell him to come right away. And keep your mouth shut. *Ne dites rien à personne.* Understood?'

The groom nodded and hurried away, pulling up his collar. At last the ropes slackened and gave way. The Chinese man's arms slid lazily down and forward as if he were sleepwalking. Then he pitched forward into Westbrook's waiting arms.

———

Sloan arrived a few minutes later, pale and befuddled, still pulling on his tunic. He took one look at the body and retreated to a corner of the stables. After a couple of dry retches he managed to straighten up again and shuffle back.

'I'm sorry, sir. I wasn't—'

'Do you know this man? Is he one of yours?'

Covering his mouth with a handkerchief, Sloan looked into the dead man's face. 'Liu. Liu Dianzhen.'

'Who is he?'

'An interpreter. Keeps to himself, pretty much.' Sloan shrugged helplessly. 'Can't say I know much more. What in God's name happened?'

Westbrook squatted over the body. 'Death by a thousand cuts. Only in this instance no more than a dozen – hurried at that, judging from the loss of blood.'

Sloan looked down at his feet. A scrap of flesh, dark like liver, lay beneath the toe of his boot. He jumped. For a moment Amy thought he was going to be sick again.

'When? How long . . . ?'

'A few hours. He's cold. Some rigor mortis. The fireworks must have covered the noise.'

'The noise of . . . ? Oh God.'

Amy was sitting huddled in a corner. The house would have been warmer, but she sensed Westbrook wanted her with him.

'Is it what happened at Two Storm Wood?' she asked. 'Is it the same?'

'How could it be? We're not behind German lines here. There are no German lines.'

Amy was taken aback by the scorn in Westbrook's voice – as if there had never been any doubt about who was responsible.

'But you said—'

'A crude imitation. Two Storm Wood is public knowledge, for all Captain Mackenzie's efforts. Perhaps this is a message of some kind, a warning.' Westbrook covered the interpreter's face with a corner of the blanket. 'The killer worked alone, anyway. There's one clear set of footprints around the body, and only one.'

The rain was coming down outside, spattering on the cobbles. Thunder rumbled in the distance. Amy remembered standing at the window of Madame Chastain's salon, the moment when she realised she was being watched. 'I think . . . I think perhaps I saw him.'

Sloan looked up. 'Saw him? Who?'

'The man who did this. There was someone outside. He followed us here. Don't you remember, Major? Something about him—'

'Another Chinaman, was it?' Sloan said.

'No. I'm sure it was a white man.'

Westbrook folded his arms. 'She doesn't know what she saw. That could have been anyone.'

Sloan leaned closer to the body, one hand braced against his knee. His revulsion now contained, a certain fascination had begun to take hold. 'What was it caused those . . . ?' He grimaced. 'Those wounds? An axe or something?'

'A hatchet maybe. It would have to have been a sharp one. I'd say it was something more ceremonial.'

'Such as?'

'A sword.'

'A cavalry weapon?' Sloan frowned. 'There's no cavalry round here. Hasn't been for months.'

'Pass me your handkerchief,' Westbrook said.

Reluctantly Sloan withdrew it from his mouth and handed it over. Westbrook dabbed at the flesh of the dead man's right arm. The skin was covered in a dense, dark tattoo, worked into a pattern.

Sloan stepped closer. 'The tattoo? Seen a few of those, mostly on the older men. A dragon and a tiger in combat.'

Amy remembered Westbrook describing just such an image at Mailly-Maillet, on the body of the first man he had examined.

'Does it have some special meaning to your men, Lieutenant?' Westbrook said.

'I'm not sure. There's a story – can't say if it's true: convicts being brought in to make up the numbers, from Shantung Province. For the corps. Job lot, as it were. Commission paid.'

'And the convicts had tattoos like this?'

'Supposedly. They say the prison held a lot of men from the *Dádao Hui* – the Great Knives – one of those secret societies that kicked off the rebellion. Maybe it was their way of sticking together.'

Amy had been a young child at the time of the Boxer Rebellion, but she remembered the stories: Christian missionaries massacred in the countryside, merchants and diplomats besieged in Peking; then a war of reprisal by foreign powers that her Uncle Evelyn had described as 'atrocious'.

'You've had trouble from such men?' Westbrook said.

'Not in my company.'

'What about opium trafficking?'

'I wouldn't know about that, sir. Besides, to be frank ...'

'Not everyone sees opium as a problem?'

Sloan shrugged. 'Anything to give the men some relief, that's what they say.' He nodded towards the house. 'Like these places. They'd be shut down back home, quick as a flash. Out here, well, it's very different, isn't it?'

Amy could see the logic: addiction was the kind of problem people worried about in peacetime. It assumed a future that was measured in years, not weeks.

Westbrook pulled the blanket back over the body. 'Why would someone do this? Have you any idea?'

Sloan shook his head. He had gone pale. 'Work of a madman. What else could it be?'

———

Westbrook had the stables shut up, and posted the groom by the gates with instructions to keep everyone out. Sloan was sent to report the matter to his commanding officer. The *maison tolérée* was a civilian establishment, but nobody questioned the provost marshal's right to give orders. There was safety in obedience, protection in authority – at least, to Amy, it felt that way.

They went back to the house. Amy wanted to be gone from Acheux, but Westbrook seemed in no hurry to leave. As they crossed the hall, she wondered whether this new killing would complicate his investigation or simplify it.

Westbrook stopped and touched his nostrils. His fingertips came away red. 'Are you all right?'

He pulled a handkerchief from his pocket and pressed it to his nose. It took a minute to staunch the bleeding. Finally he sat down at the foot of the stairs. He was sweating, jumpy. The killing had unnerved him, unless some other sickness was at work. It was hard for him, conducting himself in a professional manner – Amy saw that clearly for the first time.

'There's something I want you to do,' he said. Her heart sank. Meeting Westbrook's requests always came at a price. 'I want you to talk to Madame Chastain. I need to know what she knows.'

'She bought something from the dead man. You saw it, didn't you?'

Westbrook nodded. 'It may go deeper than that.'

'Can't you talk to her yourself?'

'She's frightened of me. You've a better chance, woman-to-woman.'

'I'm afraid you're wrong there, Major,' Amy said. 'I'm the last person she'd talk to. She thinks I look down on her.'

'Do you?'

'I pity her girls. I'm not sure what I think about her.'

'Good enough.'

Amy shook her head. 'I'm sorry. This is not my affair. I don't want—'

'Something like this is everyone's affair. It's murder, isn't it? That's what your Inspector Westbrook would say.'

Amy could not answer. If the dead men at Two Storm Wood deserved justice, then so did the interpreter.

'I need to know what this man was doing,' Westbrook said. 'I need to understand why he died, and why now.'

Amy knew she had no choice. 'What do you want me to ask?'

———

Twenty-four

Amy found Madame Chastain in a bedroom at the top of the house. She had expected the decor to be luxurious, louche, befitting a purveyor of vice, but the room was cramped, the ceiling low. A vase of dead flowers stood on the windowsill opposite an iron bed. This must have been servants' quarters before the war.

Madame Chastain rose to meet her, a small firearm in her hand. 'What do you want?'

'I didn't mean to …' Amy felt as if something had been pulled tight inside her, so tight it might snap. 'I need to ask you some questions. It's important.'

The rain beat steadily on the roof.

'*Des questions sur quoi?*'

'About the man in the stables. Please put down the pistol, Madame.'

The older woman hesitated, then placed the weapon on a dressing table, the drawers of which were open. A suitcase lay on the bed.

'Are you going somewhere?'

'My sister in Abbeville, she is ill. *Vraiment*, Mademoiselle, I have nothing to tell you.' She went back to packing, throwing items onto the bed with little regard for order.

Amy noticed a clutter of framed photographs on the narrow mantelpiece. One was of a young girl, six or seven years old, with ribbons in her hair. The resemblance to Madame Chastain was unmistakable. The girl had her arms around a cat. The animal must have moved during the exposure, because its head was a blur. Where was the child now, Amy wondered? What did she make of her mother's line of business? Where was her father?

'The dead man, I saw him talking to you last night.'

Madame Chastain did not reply. She was struggling with one of the catches on the suitcase.

'He gave you something. Was it opium? Laudanum perhaps?'

179

Madame Chastain forced open the catch. '*Et alors?* It was what he wanted, your … *beau*.'

Her beau, her handsome one. Was the choice of words deliberately cruel?

'Major Westbrook is not my beau. My beau – my fiancé – he was missing in action, a few miles from here.'

Madame Chastain hesitated. 'He is dead then.'

'It seems so, yes.'

'Seems? You had hopes to find him alive?'

It took Amy a moment to answer, to find the words. 'Hope is hard to give up, Madame. Harder than anything.'

The older woman sniffed and went on packing her suitcase. 'It will die too, in the end, have no fear.'

'Perhaps it will.'

'And until then you must search, *non*?' Madame Chastain shook her head pitifully. 'But this is impossible. You will find nothing here, nothing for your comfort. Your dreams, they will grow darker, that is all. *Je suis désolée.*'

Voices echoed in the yard outside. Lieutenant Sloan and some of his men were carrying away the body of the interpreter. It was already wrapped in canvas, ready for burial.

'The dead man, did you know him?'

'Liu. Liu Dianzhen.'

'How long have you been buying opium from him?'

It was one of the questions Westbrook wanted Amy to ask.

'*C'est pour les clients*. The clients. Like your—'

'How long, Madame?'

'One month, two.'

'And before that? Who did you buy from then?'

'*Les chinois*, they are always near. Since two years. Someone always comes, though it is dearer now. *Très cher.*'

Madame Chastain's house had become known among the traffickers as a place where they could do business. Westbrook had suspected as much. 'Who killed him, Madame?'

'Liu Dianzhen? I do not know.'

'Then why are you leaving?'

'I told you, my—'

'Do you really have a sister in Abbeville?'

One of the girls was watching them from the corridor.

Amy closed the door. 'You're afraid you might be next, is that it?'

'You should think about yourself, Mademoiselle.' Madame Chastain opened another drawer, fretting as she searched through her garments. 'You know nothing of this place.'

'If you're afraid, then help us. If anyone can find this madman, it's Major Westbrook.'

'Find him?' Madame Chastain shook her head pitifully. 'To *find* him will not be enough, I think.'

'You're wrong. Major Westbrook knows his job. He was a detective before the war, at Scotland Yard. Murderers are his business.'

'Murderers?' Madame Chastain was still for a moment. 'Then he will be busy here, *n'est-ce pas?*'

'He can protect you.'

'He is sick. You cannot see it?'

'It doesn't matter. Who killed the interpreter?'

'I cannot help you.'

'You're hiding something.' Amy took Madame Chastain by the arm. 'Tell me what you know.'

'*Je ne sais rien.* Ask *les Chinois.*'

'The Chinese? What would they say?'

Madame Chastain regarded Amy steadily. Her eyes were pale, like stone. Out of nowhere, Amy felt an urge to hurt her.

'Maybe they will say Liu was killed by a demon. Because they are savage, *non? Primitifs.*' Madame Chastain shook herself free. 'How else to explain that he is not taken? How else to explain that the British Army cannot stop him?'

Hurried footsteps echoed on the cobbles outside. The rain was coming down in squalls, pushing against the thin glass of the casement window.

All at once Amy understood. 'There were others, weren't there? Other killings.' Madame Chastain said nothing. 'When? Before the Armistice?'

Reluctantly the older woman nodded.

'How many?'

'In Acheux? One I know of. Another ... *Il a disparu.* There were more, I think, in other places.'

'Who were they?'

'A man called Chen Te-shan. He came here one time, with another.'

'To sell opium?'

'Silk. Some of my girls bought . . . *les foulards*.'

'Scarves?'

'They found him in a wood – what remained. He had been . . . Like Liu. His friend they never find: his name was Zheng Tao.'

Amy's mind was racing. Westbrook did not understand why his superiors had sent him, but here was a reason: because they feared the killings would go on. If she was right, it meant they had information they had not been prepared to share, even with the provost marshal.

Amy felt sick. Westbrook's investigation was drawing her in, coiling itself around her, like the tattooed monsters she had seen on the dead men's arms.

'What makes you think Zheng Tao was killed too? Maybe he just ran away.'

Madame Chastain shook her head. 'Marie-France, one of my girls, she and Zheng were friends.'

'Friends?'

'They made plans to leave, for Boulogne, after his contract was finished. He save his money for her.'

The prostitute and the coolie, their bodies both put to the service of an insatiable war. In spite of their differences, Amy could see how the two might come together.

'When was this?'

'In the summer.'

'In August?'

'I think so.'

'Where is Marie-France now?'

'She was afraid. She left here. She thinks Zheng was dead because of her.'

'Because of her? Why? Why would she think that?'

Madame Chastain frowned, as if the question were too obvious to need an answer. 'Marie-France was of the white race, Mademoiselle,' she said.

———

—— Twenty-five ——

Coming down from the top of the house, Amy was struck by the silence. The last of the girls had left. The salon where she had spent the previous evening was empty, cold daylight spilling through the half-drawn curtains onto empty tables and vacant chairs. She went to the window and looked out at the gate. She had seen someone down there, but who? Why would he want to follow her, or Major Westbrook for that matter? She tried to recall some impression of the man's face, his posture, his build. Was there something familiar about them? All that came back to her was a sense of his presence, his intent – things that might all have been in her mind.

A draught was blowing through the ground floor. Someone had left the back door ajar. It bumped against the frame, rattling the latch.

'Major?'

There was a kitchen leading off the back of the hall. A pan of scorched milk lay on the stove. On the table sat a joint of meat, covered with a cloth, a carving knife beside it. Amy lifted the cloth. It was a ham, most of the meat already pared off, inches of yellow bone showing through the dark flesh.

She couldn't help herself. Her hunger was sudden and overwhelming. She picked up the knife and sawed at the meat, her only thought: to eat.

Amy stuffed the meat into her mouth. It was chewy and badly cured, with a texture like raw bacon – not of a quality to grace their tables at home. But it didn't matter. The meat would give her back her strength. It would keep her alive.

She was cutting another slice when she heard a footstep behind her – as if the stranger had walked right out of her thoughts. She spun round, raising the knife high, steeling herself to strike.

It was Westbrook. He was dressed now, though still unshaven. He did not flinch. Instead he made a tutting sound, as if disappointed. 'Use a knife like that and you'll only cut yourself.' He brought a hand up under hers. 'No cross-guard here, you see?' His fingertips teased at the edge of the blade. 'Without one, you'd lose your grip on the handle as soon as you hit cartilage or bone. Your fingers would slip down onto the blade, unless you let go.' He stepped back. 'It's useless for combat, unless you catch your man from behind.'

Amy pictured the knuckle-knife she had seen for sale in Amiens, the woman who had tried to sell it to her, as if it were the only natural choice.

She dropped the carving knife onto the table. 'You startled me. I thought—'

'I'm sorry. One is meant to cough, I suppose.' Westbrook regarded the flayed remains of the ham bone. 'Good to see you haven't lost your appetite.'

Amy turned away, wiping her mouth on her hands. She was ashamed: stealing food, devouring it like an animal, yards from where a man had been butchered. The meat had left behind a fatty carrion taste on her tongue. She hoped she was not going to be sick.

'Are you all right?'

She braced herself against the sink. What she needed was to cry, to give some voice to the shock and revulsion inside her. But no tears came.

'Do you get used to this?' she said at last. 'All this death – all this ... ? Does it become normal for you?'

'Normal?' Westbrook repeated the word as if it were unfamiliar to him. 'I suppose if it were normal, I wouldn't have been sent here.'

'You don't *know* why you were sent. Why should Whitehall care about a few dead Chinamen? Isn't that what you said?'

'They sent me to gather the facts. My feelings aren't important, if that's what you're getting at.'

Westbrook dragged a chair out from under the table. She heard him pick up the carving knife.

'Don't you understand?' Amy said. 'All this *tolerance*, this keeping up appearances. Like it's all a game. Where's the outrage? Can't you feel it any more?'

Westbrook sighed. 'In the face of extreme violence, men either become resolute or they submit. They master their dread – feed on it – or it breaks them. Moral outrage is quite useless, I'm afraid.'

He was digging at the meat, tracing the lines of sinew with the tip of the knife.

'And then there are some kinds of men for whom violence brings clarity. They embrace the elemental force of it. Rules and other abstractions . . . Well, I couldn't expect you to understand.'

'I don't. I don't *want* to understand.'

'Why should you?'

Amy turned away again. 'The things I've seen . . . they're unforgivable. Who could live with the guilt?'

'Not all men fear judgement, Miss Vanneck. Not yours or mine, and not God's, either.'

Amy nodded. 'That must be true. Their existence must be lonely then.'

Westbrook put down the carving knife and pushed the plate of meat away. 'Suppose you tell me about Madame Chastain.'

Amy knew she had no right to pick on the provost marshal. He was not to blame for the violence – he was a victim of it, all too clearly. And weren't his reasons for being there as good as her own: a desire to understand; distaste perhaps at the idea of simply walking away? In any case, how would it help her find Edward? Moral outrage *was* useless.

'I'm sorry,' she said. 'You must think me very naïve.'

'Frank, perhaps,' Westbrook said. 'Not a bad quality, in my book. Now tell me: what did the woman say?'

Sitting at the table, Amy shared what she had learned while Westbrook made notes. She had the impression he was satisfied, even pleased with her information. It was something, to know that she had been of some use.

'Do you think she told you everything?' he asked when she had finished.

'I think so. She's frightened, but I don't see why she'd lie. I found her packing. She said she was leaving for Abbeville.'

'She's just a customer. I doubt she has much to fear.'

'You think that poor man was killed because of opium?'

'Opium or money. That's all your Chinaman's here for – not King and Country anyway. I expect the interpreter trespassed on someone else's patch, or stole from the wrong people. Something like that.'

Westbrook's confidence struck Amy as brittle. It was as if he were trying to convince himself. 'You said the killing was a message. What if the message was meant for one of us?'

Westbrook looked up. 'What makes you say that?'

'It happened here, as we were sleeping,' Amy said. 'We were sure to find it. Maybe that was the idea.'

The notion had already hardened in her mind that Westbrook's mission, his digging and probing, had awoken a pitiless malevolence in the old battlefields, and now its focus was on him.

Westbrook closed the notebook. 'We must hope you're wrong.'

Flies had descended on the uncovered meat. Amy threw the cloth back over it. 'What will you do now?'

'Contact the Chinese base depot. As far as Two Storm Wood's concerned, they should be able to identify the dead, once I've given them a date. Their records may tell us how their men fell into enemy hands. There's no telling what information they might have.'

'So what happened here, it doesn't change anything?'

'I don't know. Should it?'

Amy frowned. 'The victims were Chinese in both cases.'

'All but one.'

'And the way they died ...'

'I told you: this was an imitation, designed to exploit a fear that already exists.'

'Are you sure?'

'No, I'm not.' Westbrook put down the carving knife and got up. 'But I didn't come here to police the Labour Corps. My orders were quite explicit on that point.'

Something felt wrong. Detective Inspector Westbrook, as portrayed in the newspapers, had been tenacious, meticulous, implacable – a man famous for leaving no stone unturned. And yet here was a stone he preferred to leave to others, on the hunch that it was of no value.

An idea came to her, a possibility that Westbrook had seemingly overlooked. 'Yesterday, at Two Storm Wood, you said the evidence contradicted itself. You couldn't see a logical chain of events, leading up to the massacre.'

'Not where the Huns are concerned, no. I can't make it fit, can you?'

———

—— Twenty-six ——

They found Captain Mackenzie with one of his squads on the far side of the Serre Ridge. He watched them as they climbed down from the wagon and picked their way across the stony ground. Nothing in his demeanour suggested that he was pleased to see them, or that Amy being in the provost marshal's company met with his approval.

At Mackenzie's feet stood a burial pit at least twenty yards long. His men were still toiling with spades and shovels, searching for the end of it. Along the bottom, a few feet down, lay a carpet of cloth and bones. Gaping jaws and half-submerged craniums betrayed their origins as human.

'There must be fifty men down there,' Westbrook said.

'More than that.' Mackenzie offered a perfunctory salute. 'Miss Vanneck.'

Unlike the last time, he made no attempt to hide the nature of his work, to cover the remains with tarpaulins or usher her from the graveside. By now he would have heard about Mailly-Maillet and her presence at the exhumations. In his eyes, she supposed, her innocence was lost.

'Are they German?' Westbrook asked.

'So far. A hasty burial, by the looks of it. We were after Kiwis. Found this lot instead.'

'How long have they been here?'

'Two years – three at most. Someone'll have to move them. They can't stay here.'

Amy felt cold. Westbrook had told her to keep quiet about the killing at Madame Chastain's, for the time being. He did not say why.

'So what can I do for you, Major?' Mackenzie said. 'I've already told you what I know.'

'I need to see the burial records for this area.'

'Burial records?'

'Miss Vanneck's idea. She thinks we may have missed something.'

Mackenzie regarded her coolly. 'Miss Vanneck is full of surprises. I'd never have guessed she'd show up at Two Storm Wood, for instance, not after our last conversation.'

Evidently it rankled that Amy had ignored his forceful recommendation to stay away.

'I explained my reasons, Captain Mackenzie,' she said.

'You thought you might find your fiancé underground, alive or dead.'

'I hoped so.'

'And did you?'

'Thankfully not,' Westbrook said. 'The white man you buried – yes, there was one – he doesn't match Captain Haslam's description. Too many gold teeth.'

Mackenzie coloured. 'Well, that's what comes of … You can't trust the ravings of a dying man.'

Amy looked up. 'Dying, did you say?'

'I'm afraid so. Corporal Staveley is dead. I took the liberty of making enquiries.'

'On my account?' Amy recalled the captain's vague offers of assistance. She had never expected him to honour them.

Mackenzie cleared his throat. 'Not exactly. I thought the man might have heard something about the incident, a rumour at least. I was too late. He died at the clearing station. They told me he'd been seriously injured in an accident.'

'A motorbike. He was badly burned.'

'So I understand.'

Sister Adams had been convinced that Staveley had been trying to kill himself. Amy shuddered. Had he made a second attempt? How long after her visit had it happened? A day? An hour?

'What exactly are you looking for, Major?' Mackenzie said.

Westbrook was staring into the pit. 'Anything relating to this sector in August last year. A matter of geography and chronology.'

'The files are still at Colincamps.'

'Perhaps one of your men could accompany us.'

'Corporal Reid's there now.'

'Then we needn't trouble you further.' Westbrook turned to go.

'Wait,' Mackenzie said. 'I'm coming with you. Sergeant Farrer?'

Farrer was standing a few yards away, holding a shovel, watching them.

'I'm escorting our guests back to Company HQ,' Mackenzie said. 'Do a head count here when the pit's fully uncovered, then carry on searching the grid.'

'Sir.'

'And look lively. I want those Kiwis found.'

By the time they reached Colincamps it was raining again. Water fell in threads from the stable roof, hitting the earthen floor and the mess tins that lay all around. Mackenzie's quarters were in one of the stalls. As she walked past, Amy caught a look of embarrassment on the captain's face, as if her presence where he slept was improper.

Corporal Reid was working at a large table planted across the central aisle. He stood up and saluted. Several trench maps lay open beside him, held down by stones. The flame of a lantern played over their surfaces.

'These are the latest we have,' Mackenzie said. 'Date from last June. I don't think they bothered after that.'

Westbrook put his cap on the table and stooped to examine the maps. The German positions had been drawn west of Serre, almost halfway to Colincamps, though the trenches were less elaborate than the old ones further east. Some were incomplete, coming to an end not at a strongpoint or a natural barrier, but in the middle of a field. Most of them had no names. The British lines were scarcely better ordered. Amy could detect the haste: battalions by night – labourers too – carving out what cover they could within range of enemy guns.

Mackenzie had an unlit cigarette in his hand. He waved it over the area of the battlefield. 'The Huns took all this in March, during their big offensive. The dugout at Two Storm Wood ended up two or three thousand yards behind them. It stayed that way until the East Lancashire Division started to push them back in July. They gave up the Serre Ridge a few weeks later.'

Westbrook ran his fingers over the tangle of blue and red lines. The long summer push had covered about three thousand yards. On the map, it was a little more than the span of his hand.

'When exactly was Serre taken?' he said.

Mackenzie looked at Corporal Reid. The company clerk pushed his spectacles up his nose. 'The Forty-second Division entered Serre-lès-Puisieux on the twentieth of August, sir. Unopposed. Huns had moved out the night before.'

'It's like I told you, Major, the enemy must have known they were going to yield. The whole business with the coolies was some gesture of defiance, which we were meant to find, Huns being Huns.' Mackenzie fished in his pocket for a box of matches. 'Or do you still think some Chinese gang was responsible?'

'I don't, as it happens.'

Mackenzie plucked the unlit cigarette from his lips. 'Because?'

'Call it a poor fit,' Westbrook said. 'Now, those burial records.'

Reid was dispatched to find them. He returned with a stack of brown folders. 'This is pretty much the lot, sir, for last summer.'

Stamps and labels read: *IV Corp, DGR&E* and *SECRET*.

'Thank you, Corporal.' Mackenzie struck a match. 'I can't think what these are supposed to tell us.'

Westbrook had already opened the first folder. Inside were the lists of field burials: names, units, dates, grid references or other indications of where the dead were interred. Amy noticed that very few were designated 'Unknown' or identified only by their regiment.

'One advantage of moving forward,' Westbrook said. 'You get to collect your dead there and then. Easier to identify that way. Am I correct, Captain Mackenzie?'

Mackenzie nodded. 'Very different in 'sixteen. After the big offensive, the bodies went unburied for six months. High Command only took action when it started to affect morale. There wasn't so much to identify by that time.'

Westbrook closed the first folder and opened another.

Mackenzie was growing impatient. 'Are you going to tell me what you are looking for?'

Westbrook placed a finger on the map. Amy watched him follow the grid references as they moved erratically forward, battle by battle, day by day, closer to the German strongpoint at Two Storm Wood.

His finger advanced to the site of the dugout, then passed over it, stopping on the other side. 'Walter Trench. Can you find that for me, Captain?'

'*Why?*'

Amy did not need to ask. She already knew.

'Do you know where it is?' Westbrook said.

Reid stepped forward. 'It's one of the old German lines, sir, outside Serre. A reserve trench. Here.'

His finger traced a dotted diagonal line around the west side of the village. At the southern end the word WALTER was obscured beneath a muddy smudge. It lay two hundred yards further up the ridge than the dugout at Two Storm Wood.

Westbrook took a final look at the graves registration report. Then he closed the folder. 'Which units were responsible for this part of the line?'

'We don't have that kind of information,' Mackenzie said. 'You'd have to talk to the Division HQ.'

'I was afraid of that.'

'The dead were all in the Labour Corps. How are the Forty-second going to help?'

'There may be witnesses.'

'Witnesses? How could they ... ?' Mackenzie opened the folder and hastily flicked through it until he found the page that Westbrook had been interested in. 'Fourteenth August. Burials: Corporal R. E. Callam, Private T. H. Nicholson, Forty-second Battalion, Machine-Gun Company. In Walter Trench, grid reference—'

'The men at Two Storm Wood died on the sixteenth,' Amy said. 'No earlier than that.'

'How do you know?'

'One of the dead men had a letter.'

Westbrook was already buttoning up his coat. 'It would be best if you kept this to yourself, Captain, until all the facts are in.'

'The sixteenth. So that's it.' Mackenzie shook his head. 'Those poor bastards were never POWs. The wood was in our hands when they died.'

'It seems Miss Vanneck's hunch was a good one.'

Westbrook was looking at her, but to Amy the acknowledgement felt insincere.

'Hunch? This was no hunch.' Mackenzie seemed to take the information as a personal affront. 'You've known about this all along.'

'Not so.'

'Someone *must* have known – someone in Whitehall. That's why they sent you, isn't it?'

'I'm not in a habit of questioning my superiors, Captain, war or no war.'

'If the Chinese weren't to blame, then that only leaves our boys. That's what this is all about. Nothing to do with the Huns.'

'So it would seem.'

'Couldn't just be about the Chinese, could it?' Mackenzie wasn't going to leave it at that. He wanted to make sense of it. He wanted to know. 'Are the killers still at large? Still a threat?' He must have seen something in Amy's face because he seemed to understand. 'Have they killed again?'

'I don't think so,' Westbrook said.

'What happened? Was it in England? Or over here?'

'Nothing's happened.'

'Are they here now?'

'There's no connection.'

'They must be among the volunteers? Who else is here? Do you—'

Westbrook slammed his fist against the table. 'I told you: *there's no connection!*'

Silence fell. Amy and Mackenzie exchanged glances. Westbrook's anger seemed to come from nowhere.

'A Chinese man was killed last night,' Amy said. 'In Acheux. Madame Chastain's. Perhaps you know the place.'

'The state of the body was superficially ... like the others, at Two Storm Wood,' Westbrook said.

'The three who were—'

'Yes. But the work of one man this time.'

'Are you sure?'

Westbrook nodded. 'The man dealt in opium. God knows what else. That'll be what did for him. He crossed someone, somehow.'

'How do you know?'

'I don't, not yet. I need to make enquiries with the CLC, get the names of the missing men. Should be easy enough, now we know the date.'

'I'll take care of that,' Mackenzie said. It was obvious he was not going to brook any argument. 'Identifications are my business.'

'Fine. You'll keep me informed?'

'Of course.'

Westbrook replaced his cap. 'There's one other thing, Captain: I need a revolver.'

'A revolver?' The request seemed to catch Mackenzie unawares. 'You don't have one?'

'I did.' Westbrook put his head to one side. 'It was damaged too.'

'Yes, of course.' Mackenzie was embarrassed. 'We've recovered a few. Reid?' The company clerk was already gathering up the files and stowing them away. 'Corporal, the major here needs a weapon. Perhaps you could show him what we have.'

Reid hurried away and returned with a Webley. It had been cleaned, but there were traces of rust around the thumb-catch and the sights.

'Does this work?' Westbrook asked.

'Tried it out myself, sir,' Reid said.

'You'll need ammunition.' Mackenzie found his own revolver and emptied out the cylinder. 'Take mine.'

Amy watched Westbrook load. In his hand each of the bullets made a rapid tapping sound as it entered the mouth of the chamber. One of them slipped out and fell to the ground.

———

Amy followed Westbrook outside. The rain had eased. Men in oilskins were leading a procession of wagons into the yard, they and their horses splattered with the same pale clay, as if made from it. The wagons were loaded with the familiar canvas bundles.

'They're for the Euston Road cemetery,' Mackenzie said. He had caught up with her. 'It's going to end up a big one.'

'I suppose you're going to tell me to leave. Am I right, Captain?'

'I've already offered you my advice. You're clearly determined to ignore it.'

'I'm sorry. I don't mean to get in your way.'

'What were you playing at the other day, leaving the road, running around over uncleared land? You could have been killed.'

His indignation was feigned, Amy could tell. Something troubled him, but it wasn't her disobedience.

'Our mule ran off. Something frightened it.'

'Something?'

'A stray dog probably. For a moment I thought ...'

Mackenzie looked at the ground. 'It's not unusual to hear things out here. Voices on the wind, that sort of thing. The imagination has too much to feed on.'

And when the dreams became too much, Amy thought, there was always opium. She was sure Edward had used it. Did Mackenzie use it too?

'Do you plan to remain here?' he asked.

'At Bertrancourt, yes.'

They had stopped by the wagon. Westbrook was waiting to give her a hand up.

'Then I suggest it might be more convenient if you were to billet here in Colincamps,' Mackenzie said. 'There's a farmhouse here that was just vacated. The roof's damaged, but otherwise it's perfectly habitable, at least by military standards.'

Amy looked at Westbrook. His hand remained outstretched.

'Miss Vanneck would be safer,' Mackenzie added. 'And she'd be on hand to make any identification.'

Colincamps was closer to the Serre Ridge, closer to where she needed to be. If Edward lay in an unmarked grave, that grave would be there.

'Thank you for all your help, Major,' Amy said.

It was her turn to offer a hand, but Westbrook was already climbing into the driver's seat. It came to her that he might see her decision as an expression of preferment – of Mackenzie over him, of a whole man over a disfigured one. She wished she could reassure him that nothing of the kind was on her mind, but words, she knew, would only make things worse. In any case it was unlikely he would have heard her over the squeak and rattle of the wheels.

—— Twenty-seven ——

The first thing Mackenzie pointed out was the heavy iron bolt inside the front door. The farmhouse was gloomy, daylight seeping in through shuttered windows and splintered glass. A scattering of furniture had been assembled in the kitchen, where a cooking pot hung above a soot-blackened hearth. A sour smell of wood smoke hung in the air, evidence of recent occupation.

'There's a pump outside in the yard. Still works, though I'd boil the water if I were you.'

A flight of stairs connected a narrow hallway to the first floor.

'Best not go up there. Roof tiles still loose. Could come down any time.'

Amy did her best to sound grateful, but the way Westbrook had left troubled her. The provost marshal made her uneasy: his work, his appearance – she could not deny it. But she felt safe with him at the same time, almost untouchable. By comparison, Mackenzie, for all his efforts, seemed out of his depth. Perhaps his work, day in, day out, had sucked the fight out of him.

'If anything turns up,' he was saying, 'any effects that might be Captain Haslam's, then at least we'll know where to find you. And the village is still patrolled, so you can be sure ...' His words petered out, as if he hadn't the confidence to complete them.

'Thank you.' Opposite the fireplace Amy saw a print of a young woman raising a glass. It was a calendar, four years out of date. 'I'm going to check the concentration cemeteries, see if I can find anything there.'

'I'll provide you with a list. They're not hard to find.'

'Thank you, Captain. I'll try not to get in your way.'

Mackenzie opened the front door. 'I'm sorry you had to get mixed up with Major Westbrook and his ... duties. He had no business dragging you into it all.'

Amy shook her head. 'I wasn't dragged. Major Westbrook ... he was trying to help, in his way.'

'I see.'

'He asked me if I had any reason to think Edward was alive. He seemed to think that was possible.'

Mackenzie frowned. 'But you don't have any reason, do you? With respect. I wonder that he asked such a thing.'

'I told him what Sergeant Staveley said, about Two Storm Wood. He took it seriously – seriously enough to want me there when he exhumed the bodies.'

Mackenzie dug his hands into his pockets. 'There's no mystery about it. Staveley must have heard the rumours. Imagination got to work. From what I gather, he wasn't right in the head.'

'Shell shock, the sister said.'

'I hope you understand why I didn't go into it all before. Some things it's better not to know.'

Amy did understand: she understood that, as far as officers were concerned, ladies should at all costs be shielded from the contemplation of unpleasant-ness, for fear of nervous collapse, even though it was women who brought them bloody and bawling into the world and nursed them when they left it.

'Of course,' she said.

Mackenzie nodded, satisfied, and turned for the door.

'There's something else I'd like to ask you,' Amy said. Mackenzie stopped. She had to steel herself. 'I want ... I need to know about trench raids.'

'Trench raids? Why?'

'I heard that Edward was good at them. I heard ...' Amy could not hold Mackenzie's stare. 'I heard he was good with a knuckle-knife.'

'I can't imagine who'd—'

'Please, tell me the truth.'

After a moment Mackenzie closed the door. 'All right. You've earned it, I suppose. What do you want to know?'

'Everything.'

Mackenzie nodded. 'Maybe we should get a fire going. Looks like we've got what we need here.' He crouched in front of the hearth and got busy lining the grate with kindling, binding the twigs and straw into tight bundles. 'Trench raids have two purposes: to demoralise the enemy and to gather intelligence, mainly about the state of the enemy defences. They're carried out at night – moonless nights are best – and they're dangerous. You have to get across no-man's-land without being detected, that's the first problem. Make a sound, trip on something, and up goes a flare. You're lit up in the open, nothing but a shell hole for cover, at best.'

Amy sat down. 'So you've led these raids?'

'No choice. Junior officers take turns. Some get more, by way of results. End up doing more than their share, I dare say.'

'What do you mean by "results"?'

Mackenzie struck a match and put it to the kindling. 'If you reach the enemy lines undetected, you don't have long. You make a mental note of everything you see: the condition of the wire, the parapet, the trench, craters, loop-holes – anything the enemy might use in defence. Then you push on until you find him.'

'What happens then?'

Mackenzie blew on the fire. A single tongue of flame danced in the grate. 'It depends on your luck, and your skill. You want to take one of them alive, if you can – an officer is the real prize. And documents, maps especially, if there are any about. But you have to be in among them before they know it, for any chance of that. Usually the best you can hope for is to bomb a dugout and run, before you're surrounded.'

'Aren't there always lookouts, men on guard?'

'Almost always. You have to spot them before they spot you. That's where the knuckle-knife comes in, or whatever else you've brought along. My sergeant major had a club – vicious, studded thing, hard as nails. Always aim for the mouth, he used to say. Hard to scream with a mouth full of broken teeth.' Mackenzie held out his hands to the flames. 'That fellow never had much finesse.'

Amy closed her eyes. She did not want to hear any more, but this was the truth of Edward's war, and she had to know it.

'And the knuckle-knife?' Amy said. 'How was that used?'

Mackenzie looked at her, as if unsure if he could have heard her right, then turned back to the fire. 'Never used one myself. In the right hands, a single thrust through the windpipe is preferred, so I'm told: sever the vocal cords, open the arteries. A silent kill. But you have to be focused, decisive, not a hint of hesitation or feeling – like a machine. Not many men can manage it, not close up, not even when their own lives are at stake. Goes against a deep-seated instinct, that's my belief: a taboo.' Mackenzie threw some more sticks on the fire, watched them start to smoke. 'So you go for the body instead, or use a bullet – which gives the game away, in either case. If a raid's really important, if there's something big brewing and you need information, you know who'll be sent: the men who are calm, the ones who won't hesitate to ...'

'Kill in cold blood.'

'Yes, just that. It's a fine line between a soldier and an assassin, but you'd be surprised how men cling to it – ordinary men, I mean.'

Amy remembered Edward walking from the churchyard where his mother was buried. *I know about death. I know what it does to the ones it leaves behind.* How far he had travelled, for her: how far into the darkness.

'Are you all right, Miss Vanneck?'

Amy's face was in her hands. She sat up. 'Yes. I'm sorry, go on.'

There was pity in Mackenzie's eyes. 'You must understand: these raids were vital. They helped us win the war. It wasn't only the intelligence, it was the effect on enemy morale. Mortar rounds and gas, fired from a safe distance, they're one thing; but an enemy who comes at you with a knife or a club, that's an enemy who'll never quit, who isn't afraid to die. They're the predators, you're the prey.'

Amy was silent. She found it hard to look at Mackenzie. In his frankness and decency she found something repulsive. She did not know why. 'The men on these raids, the ones with the knives and the clubs, the ones who break the taboo, do they feel guilty?'

'There and then? No. They tell themselves they're doing their duty, serving their country, avenging their dead comrades. They might even brag about their exploits, how may skulls they split, how many throats they cut. Because they want approval, absolution. Mainly they're simply glad to have got out alive.'

'And later? What happens later?'

Mackenzie took a while to answer. 'Maybe we're just beginning to find out.'

———

Unknown Number Twelve

—— Twenty-eight ——

France, June 1918

Haslam lay in darkness forty yards from the German line, his body pressed into the damp earth, making no sound. The rest of the platoon lay behind him, hidden in shell holes, waiting for the signal to move. His breathing was rapid but steady, almost normal. He could hear everything: the rattle of a tin cup, the clump of a sentry's boots as he came round a traverse, a muffled cough two trenches away. He felt a strange certainty that he was going to survive the raid: life had more in store for him yet.

Halfway over, a flare had gone up on their left. They had heard shouting in the enemy trenches. In the flickering light, rats could be seen dragging something through the wire, rattling a can that had been hung from a picket. They would have to sit tight until things calmed down. Haslam guessed half an hour would be enough. He hoped the cocaine would not wear off before then. Recently the effects had been more short-lived. Either he was growing more accustomed, or the batches were not as pure. He had injected a larger dose than usual that night, in the privacy of the officers' latrine.

The Huns were jumpy. Raids were more likely on a moonless night. Their sentries opened fire on ghosts or nothing at all. Rhodes wanted it that way: the enemy in a constant state of fear, never able to rest or sleep. The purpose of the raids was to gather intelligence, but their effect on morale was just as valuable. Mortar rounds and gas, fired from a distance, were one thing, but an appetite for hand-to-hand combat engendered a more insidious kind of dread. An enemy who chose the bayonet, the knife or the club was an enemy who had lost touch with self-interest, the calculating instinct for self-preservation – an enemy devoted to the collective cause, unafraid to die.

Haslam looked over his shoulder at the motionless forms of his men. They had been in the line for a month, the earth encrusting their tunics and their skin, thoughts of life beyond the war shrunken to nothing by the need to harass the enemy hour by hour, day by day. The battlefield had become their habitat. They used it as the serpent used the jungle, adapting in body and spirit to its requirements, its logic, with Rhodes as their mentor. In the officer manual it was written: *Make no-man's-land our land*. They had gone one better: they had made it *his* land.

The night before, a scout had discovered an enemy sap thirty yards forward of the German line. A narrow ditch snaked back under the wire. Such listening posts offered a way into the enemy trenches if they could be taken quietly. If not, Lewis guns would open up to cover their retreat, although in the dark at such a range it was anyone's guess who they would hit.

The wind was gusting, enough to mask the sound of their bodies as they crawled over the ground. Everything metal had been left behind or wrapped in cloth: belt buckles, water bottles, trigger guards. Privates Burgess and Salter had exchanged their rifles for clubs, long pieces of varnished ash studded with nails at the business end. Haslam had opted for a knife. The handle was made of brass with finger holes, like a knuckle-duster. Plain handles could slip when they hit bone or cartilage. He held it now reversed, the narrow eight-inch blade resting inside the sleeve of his coat.

Ten yards from the sap they heard movement: a boot scraping on the soil, the chink of metal on stone. They stopped. The Hun in the listening post was heading back to his lines. Staveley looked at Haslam urgently, wanting the nod to go after him before he could report. Haslam shook his head. Maybe they hadn't been spotted. So far, at least, there was no flare.

From the sap-head came a murmur. Two voices. They were changing over. Haslam waited again – ten minutes this time. Long enough for the new man to believe he was alone, with nothing to watch for but the slow arrival of dawn.

Haslam gave Staveley the nod. They crawled round opposite sides of the sap, while the men behind took up firing positions. Yellow light flickered across the southern horizon – artillery impacts ten miles away. For a moment Staveley's helmet was visible in silhouette.

A pebble rolled down the wall of the sap. Haslam didn't wait for a shot. He rose to a crouch. Two long strides and down, Staveley's dark form moving at the same instant.

He landed on both feet, stumbling over loose earth. He saw the rifle aimed at him before he saw the Hun. He seized the barrel and thrust it backwards so as to relieve any pressure on the trigger. Staveley came down behind the man, pulling his head back by the rim of his helmet. The German barely had time to gasp before Haslam went in with the knife: a single thrust through the voice box, lodging in the spinal column. He felt the warm spray on his fingers and his face. There came a violent, sucking sound. The rifle dropped to the ground. Haslam drew out the knife and let the body slump backwards into Staveley's arms, shoulders still convulsing. He had the impression the Hun was thin, light, probably no more than a boy. The enemy were running out of men of optimal fighting age.

Silently Staveley laid the body down. They listened. Thirty yards away in the German trench, somebody coughed.

The rest of the platoon did not need a signal. The silence told them enough. They edged towards the cover of the sap, Haslam leading the way on hands and knees. The rumble of distant guns rolled in. Light rain began to fall.

The ditch deepened, passing beneath the wire at an angle, then dog-legged towards a sandbag parapet. The last few yards were covered in corrugated iron. Ahead, Haslam could make out a ragged square of grey against the surrounding black. The grey flickered to yellow. He smelled smoke and something brewing that wasn't coffee. A grenade was the safest weapon, but it would cut down their time in the trench. And time was everything.

He eased closer. A few yards away two men stood by a brazier, rifles slung, bayonets fixed. They were heating a mess tin over the flames. The distance was too great for him to jump them both.

He reached behind him. Silently Staveley placed a grenade in the palm of his hand. One of the Germans sauntered away, holding a cup. The other sipped from the mess tin.

Haslam handed back the grenade. '*Hilf mir. Ich bin verletzt,*' he said wearily, swinging down from the trench. *Help me, I'm hurt*, a useful phrase.

The sentry looked round, the tin still raised to his lips. Haslam killed him the same way, grabbing him by the belt to break his fall, laying him on his back so that his feet kicked against nothing. He was bigger than the other man, and for a moment it looked as if he might manage a scream, but when Haslam went to smother his mouth, the bearded jaw went slack with nothing more than a gurgle.

The platoon split in two. Sergeant Farrer led a group to the left, Haslam's went the other way. The trenches were deep, but rough by German standards: the walls bulging and irregular, the wooden supports uneven and of different sizes. Where there should have been duckboards, their boots found mud and shallow puddles – more evidence the Huns were running short of supplies and skilled labour, just as they were running short of food.

Haslam hadn't gone a hundred yards when a muffled bang ruptured the silence, followed by a second. Farrer's men were bombing a dugout. The alarm went up at once. Voices echoed in the darkness. A white Very light soared upwards from the support line as Haslam hurried back the way he had come. The Huns knew they were being attacked, but they might not know exactly where. He swapped his knife for a revolver. Opposite the sap, his men took up firing positions on the back wall of the trench.

Haslam spotted the dugout. Two Germans, freshly bayoneted, lay sprawled at the entrance. As he approached, a third clambered out, retching and blinded, a pair of spectacles hanging off one ear. Burgess split his skull with the club; Farrer thrust a bayonet through the back of his ribs, the bones splitting with a muffled crack. Haslam switched on his trench torch and stepped over the body. Staveley followed him inside.

The air was full of dust. Scraps of shredded paper drifted past the beam of the torch. Men were coughing and moaning. The floor was covered in them: dead and wounded, blood pooling on the ground, a lower leg, minus the foot, lying beneath an upturned chair. Haslam looked around for maps, code books, any scrap of intelligence. He saw nothing. A shattered lantern hung from an overhead beam, the oil dripping slowly onto the ground.

He listened for rifle fire, heard none. There was still a little time before his platoon was trapped. He advanced further into the dugout, scanning the walls and the floor. At the far end a heavy kitchen table had been overturned, but the legs were turned away from the blast, as if to form a barricade. Haslam stepped closer, cocking the Webley.

'Hands up!'

A man was cowering behind the table. Haslam saw the insignia on his shoulders, realised he was looking at an officer. He kicked the man's foot. He sat up, open palms shaking. He had blood coming out of one ear. Otherwise he seemed unhurt.

'*Nicht schiessen.*' His teeth were chattering.

'Get up.'

The German stumbled to his feet. He was a staff captain, thin and tall – tall enough that he had to stoop under the roof beams. Haslam grabbed him by the collar and pressed the revolver into the nape of his neck. Staveley helped haul him up the steps of the dugout.

'Prisoner here!' he shouted. 'Keeping this one.'

The sky was bright with flares. Farrer's men ducked as a grenade exploded a few yards from the trench. Seconds later trench mortars answered from the British side, landing short of the support line. Haslam dragged his prisoner towards the sap, both of them stumbling over the bodies of the bayoneted men, their gaping wounds black in the stark magnesium glare.

The staff captain looked back. Haslam saw the stupefied terror in his face, knew there would be no resistance. The German officer would tell Rhodes everything he wanted to know.

Base Depot
Chinese Labour Corps
Noyelles-sur-Mer
23rd March 1919

Dear Captain Mackenzie,

With regard to your query about missing personnel in the Chinese Labour
Corps, I have ascertained that a Form B 104-83 was sent out on 16th September
1918 to the family of Lieutenant G. S. KELVIN of the 125th Company CLC,
previously of the Royal Garrison Artillery, advising that the same was posted
Missing in Action on 17th August. This is the only record I have been able to
identify which matches your criteria.

As for coloured labour, the CLC suffered a high number of losses during
last summer's advance, due to enemy action, disease and desertion. The 125th
Company lost thirty-seven men during the month of August, twelve of whom were
posted missing on the same day as Lt Kelvin. The company, presently on salvage
duties, is camped outside Bapaume, under the command of Major Pickering.

The names and numbers of the missing will be sent to the DGR&E as soon
as they can be determined. All recruits to the Chinese Labour Corps were finger-
printed by Scotland Yard detectives before embarkation from the port of Tsingtao.
This method of identification might be deployed as a last resort, if the condition
of the remains allows for it.

I have no information on the circumstances surrounding these reports. Should
this change, I will advise.

Sincerely,

Capt. J. Temple

Adjutant to the Commandant of Labour

—— Twenty-nine ——

France, March 1919

Many of the walls in the small town of Bapaume were still standing, though stripped to bare brick by explosives and shrapnel. A few patches of roof remained intact, but the windows and shutters had been blown out, and even the windowsills were gone. The town hall was the only structure the Germans had not left in ruins during their withdrawal to the Hindenburg Line. Instead they had buried a delayed-action mine in the cellar, which finally detonated nine days after the Allied troops arrived, killing thirty of them. Driving through the ruins, Mackenzie wondered how the town would ever be rebuilt: if it would not be simpler – easier – to start from scratch somewhere else, somewhere new and untainted by memories of war.

The Chinese camp was north of the town and easy to find, with the smoke from its fires rising high into the air. Hundreds of conical tents, canvas streaked and grimy, were crowded together on a slope above the Arras road. A sign by the roadside read:

SHANTUNG CAMP
125/150 CLC

Mackenzie had decided that he would be the one to deal with the Chinese Labour Corps. He wanted to discover for himself the names of the dead men and how they came to be lost, rather than rely on Major Westbrook's good offices. Why was he still in France, if not to identify the dead, to afford them dignity and recognition – not as an anonymous mass of men, but as individuals? Besides, he did not trust the provost marshal to share his information. Westbrook had never explained Whitehall's interest in Two Storm Wood. His investigation might be as much about hiding the truth as revealing it, though Mackenzie could only guess at the reasons of state involved.

And then there was Amy Vanneck. Had her arrival at Two Storm Wood been prompted by nothing but mischief or misunderstanding? Privately, Mackenzie was not yet convinced. She had been told of the place, she claimed, by a corporal in Haslam's battalion – a dying man, it had turned out. But the corporal's meaning was far from clear. Had he heard, from his hospital bed, about the discovery of the massacre? Or had his knowledge, in fact, pre-dated that discovery? In either case, his placing Haslam at the scene, however ambiguously, could not be dismissed out of hand. Westbrook must have thought the same. His interest in Miss Vanneck seemed to go beyond trying to identify a body. Did he sense, as Mackenzie did himself, that there was more to learn from her, that behind the dark eyes and the unflinching purpose lay secrets?

He drove the wagon off the road onto a track paved with railway sleepers. The horses pulled up, their hooves sliding on the slick wood. He had to coax them forward a few steps at a time. Thirty yards on stood a makeshift Chinese *paifang* – a traditional gateway – this one made from old telegraph poles and pieces of corrugated iron. The cross-beam was decorated with Chinese letters, formed with six-inch nails like the ones used at Two Storm Wood. No sentry challenged Mackenzie as he passed beneath it.

The smoke was thicker up here, tinged with the smell of boiled meat. A tall Chinese man came out of a tent, carrying a bayonet in one hand and a skinned carcass in the other – a rabbit perhaps, or something less palatable.

He found more Chinese men further on, of every size and build, all with the same dark, weather-beaten skin. Dressed in ragged tunics or long black overcoats, they squatted outside their tents, brewing tea over makeshift braziers. Some were reading newspapers, many smoked. They watched in silence as the wagon came to a halt and Mackenzie climbed down. Behind the silence, he sensed complicity. The men here *knew*. Perhaps the killer himself walked among them – was watching him even now. A trickle of sweat ran down the back of his neck. They might be interrogated, but among so many, where would the questions begin? Besides, would the Chinese talk? Would they side with white men against their own kind? Retribution would follow them home, far beyond the point where the British military could protect them – if it didn't come sooner.

Mackenzie felt for the revolver at his waist. He was surrounded on all sides, not an officer or an NCO in sight. This was the madman's turf, his domain. A single officer, lightly armed, could be easily disposed of. He would disappear, another nameless grave in a wilderness of nameless graves.

A track wound its way towards the crown of the slope, where a flagpole rose above the cones of canvas. A few yards further on, a Chinese man was playing a single-string violin, holding the small round bowl between his knees. To Mackenzie's ears the music was raw and ugly, but half a dozen coolies were listening. Chinese labour signed up for five years' service. Five years was a long time without the civilising influence of family. It was a year since he had seen his own, and that was too long.

A small parade ground was marked out with whitewashed stones. At the corner a sour-faced ganger with a cane in his hand was haranguing a section of men armed with shovels.

'I'm looking for your commanding officer,' Mackenzie said, as the men shuffled away. 'Major Pickering.'

The ganger did not salute. He studied Mackenzie's face, frowning openly, then raised his cane and pointed towards the far end of the parade ground.

The Company HQ was located in an Armstrong hut on the north side of the camp. Finding no guard, Mackenzie opened the door. He hadn't placed a foot inside when a dog bounded towards him, snarling. Mackenzie stumbled backwards. The dog, a bull mastiff, was pulled up short by a chain around its neck. The other end was secured to a bolt in the floor.

'Jasper! Down!'

An officer stood in the far corner, behind a desk. The dog whimpered, paced a circle in front of Mackenzie and slumped to the floor, its tail thumping against the boards.

'It's customary to knock,' the officer said. 'And generally advisable. Who are you?'

Mackenzie introduced himself. 'I'm looking for the company commander.'

The officer had a bookish, unsoldierly demeanour. He was middle-aged with thin hair, a grey moustache and spectacles in thick frames. 'Pickering's the name.' He gestured at an upright chair with a broken wicker back. 'Take a seat. Don't worry about Jasper. He only kills on command.'

Pickering's sense of humour, Mackenzie sensed, was a pre-emptive defence against those who would belittle him, a poor substitute for authority.

He sat down. 'I'm after information. The provost marshal's branch is investigating an incident, and I need help to identify—'

'What's happened?'

Mackenzie wasn't sure how much the other man knew. 'It concerns some members of your company.'

Pickering put an unlit pipe between his teeth. 'Who now? They haven't caught that fellow Chang Ju Chih, I suppose?'

'Who's that? A runaway?'

'A murderer. Killed a *fille de joie* in Amiens, and her three children. Last November, it was. Fine way to celebrate the Armistice.'

'I'm here about a Lieutenant Kelvin and twelve Chinese labourers.'

Pickering took a moment to respond. 'Lieutenant Kelvin is missing, presumed dead. Has been since the summer.'

'It's likely his body has been found.'

'Likely?'

'It hasn't been possible to make a positive identification. That's why I'm here. No tags were recovered.'

'Then how do you know you've got Lieutenant Kelvin, if you don't mind me asking?'

Mackenzie cleared his throat. 'According to the Commandant of Labour's office, the One Hundred and Twenty-fifth is the only company in the CLC to lose an entire section and an officer on the same day, at least in the area concerned.'

'The area being?'

Mackenzie showed Pickering the message from Captain Temple. 'West of Serre. An old German strongpoint known as—'

'Two Storm Wood. I thought so.'

'So you've been notified?'

'Not a word, officially. There've been rumours.' Pickering handed back the letter. 'Didn't know it was that number. Or that there was an officer – otherwise, of course, I'd have, you know ...'

Otherwise he would have made enquiries as to whether the dead were from his company. In the event, he had done nothing.

'Was it ... ?' Pickering stared into the bowl of his pipe. 'Was it as bad as they say? Were they ... ?'

'Most of the men were shot.' Pickering looked up hopefully. 'Kelvin wasn't one of them. He was singled out, along with two of the Chinese. We don't know why.'

'One hears these stories about China. Gangs, secret societies. They used to kill like that: slowly, like it was an art.' Pickering shook his head. 'Sickening. Are Kelvin's family going to be told? Perhaps it would be better—'

'That isn't my responsibility, Major. It's yours.'

Pickering's fingertips traced the furrows of his brow. 'He was a newspaper man, you know, before the war. In Shanghai. He wanted to join the infantry. Couldn't pass the physical. Only man in the company who could speak decent Mandarin. He was closer to the coolies than most officers, which was to his credit, it must be said.' He took off his spectacles and began polishing the lenses with a handkerchief.

'You have the names of the other missing men?'

'Of course.' Pickering sifted through a pile of papers for what Mackenzie assumed was the company war diary. After flicking through a few pages he turned it round so that Mackenzie could read for himself. 'There, the seventeenth of August.'

Mackenzie took out a notebook and pencil and copied down the list of thirteen names. Kelvin's was at the top, followed by an NCO called Niu Yun-huei. He would pass the information to Graves Registration, but that still left the problem of which men were which. As things stood, apart from Lieutenant Kelvin, their names would be recorded over a communal grave.

'It might still be possible to identify the dead individually,' Mackenzie said. 'At least some of them. I'd need volunteers from your company, men who knew them well – men with strong stomachs, needless to say.'

Pickering frowned. 'Not sure I like the sound of that. Given the state of things round here, it might be better to let sleeping dogs lie. We don't need a ruckus.'

The dead men had been stripped of their tags. A communal grave was what their executioners wanted for them – or no grave at all. Mackenzie was not going to let them have their way. 'The fallen deserve marked graves if there's any way we can provide them. That's always been the army's view. It's the reason I'm here.'

Pickering closed the diary and put it away. 'I doubt if the army was thinking of the coolies when it set you to work, Captain. They're only here for coin, after all. Isn't that so?'

'Perhaps. It's immaterial either way.'

'Immaterial, really?'

'If all Englishmen had been zealous to serve, there'd have been no need for conscription.'

Pickering sighed. 'Very well, I'll ask around. No doubt a few volunteers will step up. Some extra pay should do it.'

Mackenzie stared at the list of names. Pickering clearly had no idea that his men had been killed on the British side of the line. The possibility did not seem to have crossed his mind. Yet labourers rarely worked close enough to the enemy to risk capture.

'Where was your company operating the day Lieutenant Kelvin went missing?'

'As I recall, the whole company was busy building a light railway from Acheux, a priority assignment. The terrain to the east was utterly pulverised, nothing you could call a road for miles ahead, and the Third Army was pushing forward. Without the railway, most of the supplies would have had to go by mule.'

'But you must have been well behind the front line. Where exactly?'

Pickering replaced his spectacles, his small mouth twitching. 'Since the CLC came to France we've lost around two thousand men. If we'd always been *well behind the front line* we'd not have lost half that many.'

'Excuse the presumption, Major. So where were you?'

'North-east of Mailly-Maillet. We were close enough to the Huns that we lost men to shelling. Worked at night, when the lie of the land allowed.'

'Kelvin and the others were found more than two miles further east. Have you any idea what they were doing there? Did they get lost?'

Pickering's spectacles, though just polished, were evidently not polished enough. He took them off and began again. 'I only learned of this after the event, you understand. I wasn't on the scene that day. But a report came in that a huge stockpile of shells had been found, poison-gas shells. They were in some old German bunkers our boys had taken a day or so earlier. If the stockpile got a direct hit, it could have wiped out half a brigade. There was a concern the Huns might be targeting it with their big guns. Hence some urgency.'

'Gas shells aren't usually stored in forward positions.'

'Of course not. But Serre wasn't always a forward position. A year ago it was well behind the German lines, if only for a month or two.' Pickering put his spectacles back on again. His eyes, made large by the lenses, were red-rimmed. 'In any event, Lieutenant Kelvin went forward to assess the situation and see what could be done.'

'Taking twelve men with him.'

'Correct.'

'Why? If all he planned to do was take a look?'

'History does not relate. Perhaps he thought some temporary measures might be possible. Sandbags and so forth.'

Or perhaps the report did not ring true. It did not ring true to Mackenzie now. Had Kelvin been suspicious? Had he taken men with him for protection? If so, from whom? If he had been truly afraid, he could have stayed put. But then refusal to go forward, especially from a Labour Corps officer, would have been interpreted as cowardice.

'This report, where did it come from?'

'Someone turned up from the front lines, I believe, requesting assistance – an officer, in fact.'

Westbrook looked up. 'So this was not an order. Corps HQ knew nothing about it.'

'No, it was all very ad hoc. Events were moving fast at the time.'

'And the shells?'

'Shells?'

'The poison-gas shells. Were they removed?'

Pickering frowned. 'Not that I know of.' It was obvious the question had never occurred to him. 'Not by this company.'

'But they *were* found?'

'I couldn't say. As the front moved forward, I expect they ceased to be a threat. Serre was taken a few days later.' Pickering must have seen the impatience in the other man's face. 'Our objective was to complete the railway, Captain Mackenzie. Salvage was not our concern.'

A trickle of sweat ran down Mackenzie's temple. He was close to the truth, to understanding – ahead of Westbrook, ahead of Whitehall. A few steps more and it would be his. And he would see that it was shared, no matter how ugly.

'Major Pickering, do you know who brought Lieutenant Kelvin this report? Do you have a name?'

'No. What does it matter?'

'Please, Major. It may matter a great deal.'

Pickering shook his head. 'I told you, I wasn't there. Lieutenant Collins was in charge.' Pickering pulled out a pocket watch. 'He should still be at the dump, if you want to see him. He and Kelvin were friends. If anyone knows what happened, it'll be him.'

———

The salvage dump lay a few hundred yards from Shantung Camp, next to the light railway that the Chinese themselves had helped to build. Mackenzie would have preferred to go alone, but Pickering insisted they go together, bringing the mastiff with them. The site was surrounded by wire and guarded by sentries.

'A regrettable necessity,' Pickering explained. 'We've had a lot of thieving since civilians starting coming back. We suspect some of the coolies have been involved as well.'

Just inside the wire stood three piles of rifles, each higher than a man, the weapons numbering thousands. Demobbed infantry handed their weapons in at a depot. These were the rifles of the dead and wounded, recovered from the battlefields. Many would have been used to mark their graves.

'I thought the Chinese were supposed to stay away from the civilian population,' Mackenzie said. 'Isn't that army policy?'

Pickering scoffed. 'In theory. In practice, it's impossible to enforce a ban. In some places the locals are hostile – the Belgians especially – which makes things easier. In France the coolie has a better reputation. There's been fraternisation aplenty, a good few women involved and no small amount of commerce.'

'What do the Chinese have to sell, besides their labour?'

'You'd be surprised. They started out making baskets, used the reed matting they were given to sleep on. Then silk embroidery and imitation flowers, all manner of knick-knacks. But it makes them money.'

'What about opium?'

Pickering tugged on the chain, bringing the huge dog to heel. 'Opium?'

'Don't the Chinese know a lot about that?'

'Coolies are drawn from the lowest strata of Chinese society, Captain. Some latent criminality is to be expected. The important thing, as regards the war effort, is to limit the opportunity for the latent to become actual.'

They stopped in front of a rampart of shell casings. It was ten feet high and extended in an arc for a hundred yards, the brass sometimes yellow, sometimes rusted to a dark brown or caked in mud. Unlike the dead, this battlefield harvest would find its way back to England. It had a value that could be measured in cash.

'Lieutenant Kelvin was very protective of his men,' Pickering said, as they worked their way round, 'more than was useful. He was inclined to blame their failings on a few bad apples, and grant too much licence to the others. He refused to see your typical coolie for what he is: essentially bovine and amoral.'

'Did you have cause to reprimand him?'

'I might have said something once or twice.' Pickering tugged on the chain again. 'Come on, Jasper.'

'Were there arguments?'

'The CLC is a constituent part of the British Army, Captain. Junior officers do not generally argue with their superiors.'

'What was Kelvin concerned about? Anything in particular?'

Pickering bent down to pat the mastiff, which was alongside them, panting as it ambled past the mass of spent munitions. 'Kelvin became preoccupied with secondary matters. He tended to forget that the purpose of the CLC is to support the army and help it fight. It's not a branch of the Chinese Seamen's Welfare.'

'What secondary matters?'

'I still don't understand how this helps you.'

They rounded a corner. A platoon of Chinese labourers was trailing back from the railhead. A ganger tapped his cap with a cane. Pickering saluted, pulling the dog closer. By now the shell cases had given way to heaps of rusting iron: scraps of machinery, reels of wire, the scorched panels of a wrecked tank.

'Major Pickering? What secondary matters?'

Pickering sighed. 'Some coolies went missing. It was fairly obvious they'd done a bunk. They were seen in Acheux, consorting with the locals. The camp was nearby at that time, and the natives were . . . let's say, friendly.'

'You mean, women?'

Pickering grunted. 'And it wasn't as if we hadn't had runaways before. There are swarms of Chinks in France these days, so there are plenty of places to hide. Still, Kelvin insisted there'd been foul play.'

'On what evidence?'

'None at all, except his supposed knowledge of the men in question. They were not the types to run off, he said. He'd taken up various allegations of mistreatment before – rarely substantiated and often involving other labour companies.'

'Mistreatment by British troops?'

'I can't recall the details, but that was the gist of it. Then, quite some time later, a body was found, one of the missing coolies. That was when Kelvin went too far.'

'Too far?'

'He went over my head, if you must know. I learned – unofficially, mind you – that he even bypassed the Commandant of Labour. Took his wild allegations all the way to the adjutant general's office at Third Army – where doubtless they were given short shrift. Still, it would have done nothing for the reputation of the company.'

Or its commanding officer, Mackenzie thought. As if the lowly status of the Labour Corps wasn't bad enough.

'Did anything come of these allegations?'

Pickering shrugged. 'Can't say. I rather doubt it. The Third Army was heavily engaged at the time, making headway at last. Hardly the time for housekeeping.'

'And then Kelvin was murdered too.'

'Apparently. Still, I fail to see how any of this—'

'Who did Kelvin blame for the disappearances? Anyone in particular?'

Pickering shrugged. 'Part of the East Lancashire Division was in the area. So naturally he pointed the finger in their direction.'

A whistle went up from a locomotive waiting on the line. A dozen wagons stood empty behind it. Light rain had begun to fall, the drops turning to steam as they hit the engine.

'Here's your man. Lieutenant Collins!'

An officer in a trench coat stepped down from the driver's cab and saluted. He was short, with a sandy moustache and a florid complexion.

'Lieutenant Collins, this is Captain Mackenzie, attached to Graves Registration.' They shook hands. 'The captain has some questions regarding Lieutenant Kelvin.'

'George? Has he—'

'It seems his remains have been found.'

'Remains?' Collins blinked, then looked down at his boots. 'I see.'

'You were friends, I take it,' Mackenzie said.

'Yes, sir, he was a ...' Collins glanced at his commanding officer, 'a good man. I was holding out hope he'd been captured.'

'He *was* captured,' Pickering said. 'Unfortunately the Huns—'

Mackenzie interrupted. 'I've been told Lieutenant Kelvin took a section forward, the night he went missing. Can you confirm that?'

'Yes, sir. I saw them go. Our platoons were working side-by-side on the railway, laying down the ties. Then we got word of this problem on the Serre Ridge: a big store of Yperite shells just waiting to go up.'

Pickering's mastiff saw something behind them. It growled and began tugging on its chain.

'Who told you about these shells? Who asked for your help?'

'One of their chaps from the East Lancashire Division. They sent an officer, so we knew it was serious.'

'Who specifically?'

'Well, it was ... I'm not sure I—'

Pickering gave another tug on the chain. 'What difference does it make?'

'Think, please.'

'He was a captain in the Manchesters.' Collins pulled up his collar. The rain was coming down harder. 'Yes, that was it. I remember we'd seen him before.'

'What was his name?'

'Haldane or ...'

'Haldane?' Mackenzie reached for his notebook. 'Are you sure?'

Collins shook his head. 'No, I'm sorry, sir, that wasn't it. The captain's name was Haslam.'

———

Thirty

Mackenzie returned to Colincamps in the afternoon to find a letter from his sister. He set aside thoughts of Edward Haslam – thoughts that weighed on him heavily – and sat down to read.

For most of the war Hannah had written only now and again, but since the loss of her other brothers, her letters had become more frequent. It was not as if she had much to say. The flu epidemic was a mainstay: those in the district who had gone down with it and those who had died. Mostly she described her uneventful daily life, before moving on to news about their neighbours and friends. Perhaps, Mackenzie thought, dwelling on the day-to-day made it easier to keep her grief at bay. Or perhaps the very act of writing provided a respite from the suffocating gloom of a household in mourning.

At the end of her letter Hannah asked when he was coming home:

Will you be demobbed soon? It would make all the difference to have you here, safe and sound. I sometimes feel that life has stopped. No one thinks about the future any more. Making plans seems pointless. I dreamed the other night that I was going on an exciting journey. I turned up at the station with everything packed and ready, only to find that most of my companions were not coming. Then I found I didn't really want to go any more. That's how life feels now, for those of us who are left. There are too many empty rooms, empty chairs, empty places. How are we supposed to fill them?

Mackenzie sat down to write a reply. He tried to sound cheerful: he was in splendid health, getting plenty to eat, with a cosy billet and a good bunch of fellows under his command. As for coming home, he reassured her that it would not be long: a month or two at most.

He tore up that letter and started another. He needed more time, he wrote, to finish the job he had started. Men who had given everything – men like their brothers, Alan and Robert – deserved a marked grave if there was the slimmest chance of one. The thought of leaving them uncollected was unbearable to him.

He tore up that letter too. He couldn't expect his sister to understand. Was that even the truth?

He left the paper on the table and went outside. The sky was darkening, threads of rain suspended above the horizon. The squads would be making their way back to Colincamps by now, back to the vats of oily stew that waited for them. Company HQ would need to move forward in a day or so, as their allocated search areas moved further east. That would mean setting up camp on the battlefield itself, on ground that was dangerous and unsanitary. He wasn't sure how his men would take to that, or if they would take it at all.

He walked to the end of the yard and lit a cigarette, noticing as he threw the match away that there was smoke coming from the chimney of the farmhouse. Miss Vanneck left early most mornings, visiting the concentration cemeteries as they grew, grave by grave, row by row, ranging into territory worked by other units, as far as Gommecourt to the north and Achiet to the east. Nothing had turned up, of course, no remains bearing Haslam's rank and insignia, no grave with his name. Among the unidentified, only a dozen or so had been officers; and in each case it had been possible to establish at least their nationality, if not their regiment. In none of these cases was the information a fit with Haslam. And that was how things would stay. The area where Haslam had gone missing had already been cleared. But still his fiancée searched, heedless of what was reasonable. Mackenzie had found himself watching and waiting for the day when she would give up and go home, when Edward Haslam – his memory, his ghost – would finally release her.

Would that day be nearer, he asked himself, if she knew all that he knew about Edward Haslam's last day? Rumours might reach her anyway – no doubt darker and less ambiguous than the facts as they stood – but should he be the one to blacken her fiancé's name, to suggest, on the basis of evidence that was far from conclusive, that he was complicit in the atrocity at Two Storm Wood? She would hate him for it. He should expect no less. At the same time Mackenzie burned to know if it was true. What would remain of Miss Vanneck's love then? How much change could it stand?

The next step was obvious. Lieutenant Kelvin, the murdered CLC officer, had taken his complaints all the way to the adjutant general's office at the

Third Army: allegations of mistreatment and worse. There would be a record of them at headquarters in Péronne: names, dates, places – everything in writing, everything in the files. Did Haslam figure in those allegations? If so, how? Major Westbrook would find out. He would make the journey to Third Army and open those files. And then? Who would share in his discoveries? Who would be trusted with the truth? The public, the War Office, the Secretary of State? In spite of everything, Mackenzie had the feeling he would not be extended the same privilege, and neither would Amy Vanneck.

The smoke from her chimney told him she was back earlier than usual. He made his way over and knocked at the door.

'Hello? Anyone home?'

Nobody answered. He pushed at the door and found it unbolted. In the kitchen a travelling blanket had been laid across the flagstones in front of the fire. On top of it sat Amy's small valise and a canvas bag on its side, papers spilling out of it. They were letters, all of them written in the same hand. Some were still in their envelopes.

He squatted down, reached for the nearest one, curious to see who had written them. The letter was signed *Edward*. Edward Haslam, of course: the lover, the music teacher, the expert close-quarter killer. Mackenzie turned over the page. The letter had been written in a place called Madingley and was dated the summer of 1916. Back then, Haslam had still been a civilian.

You are in my thoughts all the time: the feel of your skin, the scent of your hair, your smile, the warmth of you as we lie together. A boat goes by on the river, oars slapping the water, and I'm bathing you, making suds on your shoulders and your belly. A woman passes me in the street, trussed up and straining beneath her laces and whalebone, and I'm picturing you, breasts pale and perfect, free to be touched, caressed, yielding to my touch. Just the memory of my desire for you ... I have to break into a run, there in the street, for fear I'll burst. Is this madness? I don't care. If it's madness, who would want to be sane?

In spite of everything, Mackenzie had never pictured Haslam other than as a soldier, one more young British officer among thousands. His words to Amy, though out of the past, brought him to life, if only for a moment. It was a life, it seemed to Mackenzie, more vivid and passionate than his own.

Rain was coming in through a hole in the roof, dripping onto the wooden floor. Hastily Mackenzie folded the letter away. He had no business prying into another man's love life.

He threw his cigarette end into the fireplace and stood up. As he turned to go, another letter caught his eye: it was dated from August the previous year, the month Haslam went missing, the month of the atrocity at Two Storm Wood. One sheet, the paper frayed, had been read more often than the others. He picked it up.

... I am sitting in the lee of a slope, invisible to the enemy. I have a good view to the west, over much of the land we have taken, towards a pile of rubble we still call La Signy Farm. In spite of the fighting there is a fine crop of wheat growing over it all. It will be ripe soon, but no one is going to harvest it. It will be rolled flat where it obscures the field of fire. The rest will be left to rot. The thought makes me absurdly sad. I shed real tears when I first saw it, sobbed like a child.

We're launching trench raids night and day. In two weeks our brigade has advanced the line a thousand yards. We're on the edge of the old Somme battle-fields now. Soon we'll be in the trenches we held two summers ago — I say 'we', but of course I was in England then. It's strange to reflect that the men who fought in those fields are there still, most of them, in the ground. It isn't clever of me, but I can't stop thinking about it. In my dreams I feel them reach for me with their skeleton arms, begging, pleading — I don't know for what: decent burial, perhaps. Did I tell you my old friend Bill Egerton is down here with the Medical Corps? I always could talk to him. Maybe he can find out what's wrong with me, help me sleep without these awful dreams.

Last night I dreamed I had seen the Devil in this place — just an ordinary soldier in khaki with mud on his boots and blood on his face. I looked into his eyes and saw the emptiness within. The memory makes me shudder. He was laughing at me, though he barely smiled; laughing in triumph. I know now why I was so against the war when I was back in England. I was afraid, of course, but not only of dying. I was afraid it might suit me too well. There must have been more anger in me than I knew.

Promise me, Amy, that whatever happens, you won't let them leave me here. This is the one thing I ask of you, my love, the very last thing — I know it's a lot. This land is his land, and if I leave my bones in it, it'll be as if I belong to him

for eternity. That's the nightmare I feel growing in my head, the one that suffo-
cates me in my sleep, as if I'm already there beneath this putrid soil.

Mackenzie felt a draught at his neck. He turned to see Amy Vanneck in the doorway. Her eyes were red, as if she had been crying.

He made no attempt to conceal what he had been doing. 'I wanted to understand,' he said.

'Understand what?' She crouched down and began gathering up her letters.

'Why you're here. Why you're doing this.'

'Didn't I explain?'

Mackenzie handed back the letter. 'Did you make him that promise – the promise to bring him home?'

Amy folded it away. 'This is the last letter I have. I never heard from him again. I don't think he received my reply.'

'I see,' Mackenzie said. 'I hope you'll forgive me the ... Out here, it's easy to forget ... hard to believe in anything good – that love exists, or endures.' He shook his head. What good did it do to talk like this? 'I should get back.'

He walked back to the door. He had been tempted to tell her about Haslam's dealings with the Chinese on the day of the massacre, but he was not tempted any more.

'There's something else, Captain.'

'Something else?'

'I heard from Kitty Page this morning.'

'I saw the letter come in. Is she well?'

Amy nodded. 'They found her brother's grave. She got word from the Directorate in Péronne. John's going be reburied in a military cemetery outside Rosières.'

'That's good news.'

'Which you had a hand in, it seems.'

Mackenzie shook his head. 'I merely passed on her enquiry and the known facts. They would have found him sooner or later, I'm sure.'

'Kitty asked me to thank you in any case. She plans to visit the cemetery, then she's going home.'

'I'm glad.' Mackenzie hesitated. Amy might be happy for her friend, but she was bound to feel even more isolated, even more alone, once Kitty Page had gone. 'I hope you feel able to do the same, Miss Vanneck, one way or another. Soon.'

He opened the door. The sun had dipped below the clouds. Soon it would be dark.

'What about you?' Amy said.

'Me?'

'Why haven't you gone home? You volunteered, didn't you?'

Mackenzie thought about his sister, pleading with him to return; how he had struggled to explain himself. 'I don't think I'll ever really leave this place if I leave it now. It's just a feeling, but it won't . . . I suppose the thought of what's waiting for me – I'm not ready to face it. I had two brothers, both younger. Both missing in action.'

'And you hope to find them?'

'Not much chance of that. They were lost miles from here, in any case.'

'Then . . . ?'

Mackenzie looked out into the yard. The rain was coming down harder. He saw Sergeant Farrer leading a team of mules under cover. 'It was always my job to look after them, when we were growing up. That's just how it was. When it mattered most, I failed them.'

'That can't have been your fault.'

'That's what I tell myself, but it doesn't seem to do any good.'

'You feel guilty all the same.'

Mackenzie nodded. 'Except when I'm out here, doing what I do. I feel guilty when I'm happy, when being alive feels good. It must be hard to understand.'

Amy shook her head. 'I understand very well.'

'How could you?'

She placed the last of the letters in her canvas bag and clipped it shut. 'I caused Edward's death. He'd never have come here if it wasn't for me.'

She stood up. They were standing very close in the darkening room. Mackenzie had only to raise an arm and he would be touching her, caressing the soft skin of her cheek. She was exhausted, the grief etched into her face, like a sickness.

He let the door swing shut. 'You're no more responsible for the war than I am. Less so.'

'But I could have kept Edward out of the war, if I'd been brave, if I'd married him when he asked me. But I was afraid of my family, afraid they'd shut me out.'

'They didn't approve of him?'

Amy shook her head. 'Worse than that. The Vannecks had been benefactors of the school where he worked. A few weeks after I put Edward off, my mother contacted the governors, brought pressure to bear.'

'He wasn't dismissed?'

Amy nodded. 'I didn't find out until last month, the day the major general's letter arrived. I heard my mother and father arguing. It was clear what she'd done.'

Mackenzie did not much like the sound of Lady Vanneck, but it was not his place to say so. 'That must have been hard for you, to hear that.'

'Edward had always been against the war. He swore he'd never take a life. He knew what a single death could do.'

Amy's hands were locked together, her eyes glazed. These were things she needed to say. Perhaps it did not matter much who heard them.

'People can change their minds,' Mackenzie said.

'That's what he said. He told me he had to do his bit, like the others. It didn't feel right, staying out of it, while others risked their lives. For a while I almost believed him.'

'It doesn't devalue his sacrifice,' Mackenzie said, 'the fact that he had no choice. If that were true, I wouldn't still be out here.'

'But he did have a choice: he could have refused to go, become a conscientious objector.'

'And gone to prison, most likely,' Mackenzie said.

Amy looked at him then. 'He'd have suffered that, but he couldn't do it, because of me.'

'Because you'd have shared the stigma, the disgrace?'

'It would have forced me to choose between him and my family: him and the world I knew, the world I'd always said I wanted to change.' Amy hung her head. 'He didn't think I loved him enough for that. He was afraid of the choice I'd make.'

———

—— Thirty-one ——

The ganger sat on a stool in the middle of the stables, a few feet from where his comrade had been killed, though the bloody straw had been burned and the cement floor scrubbed clean. Sergeant Shen Xinfeng was a riveter, and reputed to be the oldest man in the company – his papers said thirty-seven, but no one believed that. By the light of the lantern he looked at least fifty, the lines on his face dark and deep, like wounds. From what Lieutenant Sloan could gather, he enjoyed the status of a father figure among the rank-and-file. He helped them with letters home, the ones who could not write. And he knew Liu Dianzhen. It was from Liu that Shen had learned his rudimentary English. That did not make the two men confidantes or friends, but it was the best Sloan could do; the interpreter had been a solitary man, by coolie standards. The commanding officer had reacted to his death by ordering a curfew and searching the camp for illicit weapons: nothing had been found but everyday tools and pocket knives.

Sloan stood waiting for the business to begin. The last place he wanted to be was back at Madame Chastain's, but Major Westbrook had insisted. The ganger had to be questioned somewhere private, he said, and that ruled out the camp. The provost marshal was not an easy man to refuse. Sloan would have done as instructed, even if he had not been taken aside and told in strict confidence about Westbrook's mission: that it had been ordered from high up in London and had to be kept secret.

Westbrook was pacing up and down in the shadows, now and again touching at his shoulder. Sergeant Shen watched him warily as he rolled himself a cigarette. He knew where he was and what had happened there. It was enough to make anyone nervous.

'Just tell the major what you know,' Sloan said, 'and there won't be any trouble.'

Shen licked his cigarette paper, eyes still fixed on the more senior officer. Sloan felt himself grow warm. He did not want to look bad in front of the major, although he could not help noticing that the man seemed on edge.

There was grime on his collar, and since their last meeting he had acquired a Webley, which he kept not holstered, but in the pocket of his greatcoat where he could reach it quicker.

Westbrook stopped pacing and walked into the light. 'You and Liu Dianzhen, how did you meet?'

Shen's tongue resumed its progress along the edge of the cigarette paper. 'The Empress.'

'Empress? What are you—'

'*The Empress of Asia*,' Sloan said. 'It's a liner. Works the Pacific to Vancouver. Our whole company were aboard. Ten weeks at sea.'

'So you never met Liu before, in China?'

Shen waved the suggestion away. 'Liu from Weifang.'

'That's two hundred miles south of Tianjin,' Sloan said. 'Shen's from Tianjin, isn't that right?'

Shen put the cigarette in his mouth and began patting his pockets. Reluctantly Sloan supplied a light.

'Tianjin,' Shen said finally. 'Liu from Weifang.'

'Do you know who killed him?'

Shen rolled his shoulders as if the question were a burden, the latest of many and heavier than most.

'He was killed right here, in these stables.' Westbrook looked back at where the interpreter had been found. The only trace of the killing was a dark patch on the upright beam. 'Not a quick death, not at all.' Shen's gaze was on the floor. 'Who would want to do that? You must have thought about it. You must have an idea.'

Shen pulled on his cigarette – a little unsteadily, Sloan noted. 'No.'

'Did he have enemies?' Sloan said. 'He must have crossed someone, somehow.'

Shen squinted through the smoke, as if surprised to see that Sloan was still there. 'In this land ... many men are killed by strangers.'

'That's different,' Sloan said. 'That's war, and the war's over. This was murder.'

Westbrook showed no interest in joining the argument. 'Did Liu say anything? Was he scared? You'd be wise to tell us.'

'You could be next,' Sloan said. 'Any one of your kind.'

Shen shook his head again. 'Liu not scared. Liu was sad. He have a wife in Weifang, young wife. And a daughter, four years. Liu have news last month: his daughter die of fever.' Shen took another puff of his cigarette. 'Only time I see him cry.'

Sloan looked at his feet. He had not been told about Liu's daughter, but then it wasn't his custom to worry about the coolies' private lives. It was enough trouble keeping them adequately fed and free from disease, so that they could work.

'You know Liu sold opium, of course,' Westbrook said.

'When he can. Business not good, he says.'

'Trouble with the competition, I expect.'

Shen frowned. 'Trouble?'

'From others in the same line. The army's going home. It must be getting hard to find buyers. Customers like Madame Chastain must be worth fighting for.'

It was an explanation that made a kind of sense, but Lieutenant Sloan was not convinced. The violence seemed out of all proportion to the gain. Liu had been little more than a peddler. His patch, if he had one, could not have been worth much.

Shen smoked silently for a few moments, as if trying to decide if the provost marshal was worth enlightening. 'Liu does not fight. For opium? No. Few buy now, little money. Nothing to fight about. Liu say he give up soon.'

'Did he steal?' Sloan said. 'Maybe the goods he sold were stolen.'

'No.' Shen spat out a loose strand of tobacco. 'Think what you want: Chinese kill Liu Dianzhen. White man not guilty.'

'That's enough of that,' Sloan said. He was at a loss. They were getting nowhere. The way he saw it, the killing could only be the random act of a madman, prompted perhaps by some deep-seated hatred of the Chinese race, but quite beyond Shen or anyone else to explain.

Westbrook walked over to the door and looked up at the house. It was getting dark, but there were no lights behind the shutters. 'Shen belonged to a secret society, didn't he, in China? That's why he had that tattoo on his arm.'

Shen sighed. 'That very old. Long time ago. Liu a young man then, a boy.'

'But a boy who took part in the rebellion.'

Shen shook his head. 'He never talk of that. All that past. No Boxers now, no gangs.'

'Once a Boxer, always a Boxer. Their victims are still dead, aren't they?'

'The rebellion was getting on for twenty years ago, Major,' Sloan said. 'Small beer compared to the last show, in any case.'

The provost marshal still had his back to them. Sloan saw that his hand was in his pocket now, on the handle of the Webley. His other hand was braced against the wall.

'The other men in your company, what do they say?' Westbrook said. 'Who do they blame?'

'You want names, for court martial. They have no names.'

'That's not what I asked, damn it.'

After a moment Shen carefully placed his cigarette end on the floor and ground it out with his foot. 'They say there is evil here. In the ground. Dead men with no grave, spirits have no rest. Too many.' He gently thumped a fist against his chest. 'Go into men's hearts, take their souls.'

'Demons and devils,' Sloan said. 'The coolies' explanation for all ills, I'm afraid, Major. Deductive reasoning's not a strong point.'

Westbrook did not seem to hear him. 'And then? Then this? This ... butchery?'

Shen did not answer, but merely frowned, as if the question betrayed a faintly pitiful lack of understanding.

'The major wants to know why Liu was killed in such a ... particular way,' Sloan said, going along with Westbrook's line, for the sake of appearances. 'Why would our killer do that?'

'To show what he *can* do.' Shen put his head on one side. 'To show what he has become.'

'Show who, for God's sake?' Sloan said.

———

— Thirty-two —

Amy lay on the kitchen floor, her head propped up on her bag of letters, waiting for the night to end.

She had found an iron bed in the next room, but it was better keeping close to the fire. The warmth made her drowsy, and yet she had hardly slept. She tried to think of Edward, the young man she had met in a college chapel, the lover of music and ideas; she tried to think of him in bed, their secret love-making in a quiet little cottage that overlooked an orchard, but her memories were pierced by the picture of a knuckle-knife. She was back in the kitchen at Madame Chastain's, listening to Major Westbrook explain the shortcomings of the carving knife: *No cross-guard here, you see?* You'd lose your grip as soon as you hit bone. She had no doubt he was speaking from experience. She thought of the butchered interpreter and a shudder of revulsion went through her. The few days she had spent in Major Westbrook's company had left her feeling soiled. Violence was at the heart of it – violence witnessed and violence done. But what about Edward? How would she have felt if she had seen him in action, on one of those trench raids Mackenzie had described? Would her feelings – her love – really have gone on, undimmed?

Pale-blue light was reaching beneath the kitchen door when at last Amy fell asleep. It was white when she awoke again. A piece of paper lay on the threshold. Her first thought was that it must be a note from Captain Mackenzie, but then she saw the ungainly, schoolroom hand, like a child's, and knew she was mistaken.

Miss,

They say you have come here for your sweetheart, to find his carcass and give it a decent burial. It took some guts to come. This is why you have been spared. But this is not a place for the likes of you. It is a place for Jezebels and whores. I would not want you to be used like one of them.

229

Did Captain H send you to cover his tracks? Is that your plan? To put a cross with his name on it above a body that fits? So that those he wronged will not think to look for him?

If not, then you have been duped. You will not find your sweetheart here. The serpent is safe in Whitehall or some bordel *in gay Paris, where he sat out the worst of the fight while his comrades were cut down. It was his ten pieces of silver, the price of his damned soul. We were warned that there would come a Judas among us, and so it proved.*

Go home then, Miss. Leave the dog to us. We will find him. Then you will have something to bury, when we have done with it.

In truth,

A comrade-in-arms

After half an hour's break the prisoners of war were ordered to fall in, before being led out of Colincamps along the rue du Bois. Mackenzie watched them shuffle past, a hollow-eyed ragtag company of three hundred men, halfway between soldiers and tramps. They had been shipped in to rebury the German dead. Fresh appeals for volunteers had not produced much in the way of numbers, even when sweetened with the promise of early repatriation. So the prisoners had been put on cemetery duty without their consent. The Irish troops escorting them had their bayonets fixed.

Mackenzie turned away. A breakfast of fried eggs was cooking up in the stables, the welcoming smell drifting out across the yard. He planned to invite Miss Vanneck to share it with him. He was halfway to the farmhouse, his cap in his hand, when she came out through the door. She hurried towards him, breathless, face flushed. For an exhilarating moment Mackenzie thought he himself might be the cause of her excitement. But then he saw the piece of paper in her hand. She had been reading something, though it wasn't possible she had received another letter. The military post had not arrived, and the nearest civilian post office was in Doullens, several miles to the west.

'Captain Mackenzie?'

'Good morning, Miss Vanneck.'

'I found this. It was under my door this morning. Someone left it there.' Her hand was on his forearm. 'It says Edward's still alive.'

'Alive?'

'Here.'

He took the note. The paper was coarse and cheap, little thicker than newspaper. The writing was large and heavy, each letter separate, like a schoolboy's. He read in silence, then handed the note back. 'Burn it. It's all lies.'

'How do you know? How can you—'

'Someone doesn't want you here. A woman's place, and all that. It's vile and I'm sorry about it, but you shouldn't take any notice. As I understand it, Captain Haslam was an outstanding officer. He would never have abandoned his men.'

Amy snatched the note back. Her hand was trembling.

'Why would . . . ?' She frowned at him, as if bewildered at his willingness to hurt her. 'Why would anyone write these things if they weren't true?'

'I have some breakfast waiting. Join me, please. You must be hungry.'

'I'm not hungry.' Her eyes narrowed as she looked into his. 'Captain? What aren't you telling me?'

'I don't know what you mean.'

'Have you heard these things before?'

'Certainly not. I told you, I made enquiries at your fiancé's battalion. His brother officers were very clear that he had served with honour and distinction.'

'His brother officers are all dead.'

Mackenzie shook his head. To Miss Vanneck, the accusations in the note meant little. If anything, they spelled hope. Her fiancé's honour was of small account. Still, Mackenzie felt bound to defend it. 'The army doesn't take desertion lightly. There would have been a hue and cry within hours.' Amy watched him, stony-faced. 'There's something you should understand: Captain Haslam's commanding officer enjoyed a remarkable reputation among his men. They seem to have regarded him as invincible, a man of destiny. When he became a casualty, I expect they preferred to believe he'd been the victim of a plot rather than something more rational. That's all there is to it.'

'Are you talking about Colonel Rhodes?'

'You'd be doing Captain Haslam no service giving credence to these lies. What greater insult to his memory could there be than to think of him as a coward?'

Amy's red and coarsened fingers tightened around the note, and for a moment Mackenzie thought she was going to screw it up. Instead she tucked it away inside her blouse.

'I know Edward was not a coward.' Her voice was quiet and steady. 'If he abandoned his battalion, it would have been for a reason – a good reason. Perhaps Colonel Rhodes can tell me what it was.'

Mackenzie shook his head. 'There are always a hundred reasons to run away. An officer stays because it's his duty, and because his men are counting on him.'

The wind tugged at Amy's unkempt hair. She turned away.

'Miss Vanneck, wait.'

Her arms were folded against her chest. He could see her – cold, huddled – buckling under the weight of dashed hopes.

After a few paces she stopped, as if the very act of walking was too much for her. 'You read Edward's last letter, the one where he dreamed about the Devil. Do you think he was starting to lose his mind?'

'There's no suggestion Captain Haslam was anything but a dedicated and effective officer right up to the end,' Mackenzie said.

'Corporal Staveley said Edward was living underground, in no-man's-land, in the old tunnels and dugouts.'

'I told you before: no such thing ever happened. Even if it did, why would anyone stay down there now?'

Amy looked out across the land, its ragged furrows dappled by the shadows of clouds. 'Couldn't he be in hiding? The provost marshals would be looking for him, wouldn't they, if he'd run away? Maybe there *are* places out there, underground – places a man could exist.'

Mackenzie hung his head. When would she give up hope? Was the faint possibility of finding Haslam alive going to keep her here for ever? If she found his body and gave it a decent burial, then she might be free, but there was very little chance of that now.

'If Captain Haslam was a fugitive, we would know,' he said. 'He's listed as missing, presumed dead. That's the end of it. No one's looking for him now. Only you.'

He reached for Amy's hand. It lay cold and motionless in his own.

'I have to write a letter,' she said, pulling away. 'I mustn't waste time.'

'A letter?'

'To Amiens. Will you send it for me?'

'Of course, but can't you see, this can only—'

She did not want to hear it. 'Maybe Edward did run away,' she said. 'The note could be true. Maybe he had no choice. My uncle used to say there are so many secrets in Whitehall, it's enough to drive a man mad. Maybe this is one of those secrets.'

Amy hurried back to the farmhouse. Mackenzie watched her go. His breakfast was waiting, but he found he no longer had any appetite.

———

—— Thirty-three ——

He had to knock loudly four or five times before Madame Chastain came to the door. It was starting to get dark.

'*Qu'est-ce que vous voulez?*'

'It's me.'

'Monsieur Westbrook?' The chain on the door remained in place.

'I saw a light.' His breath made clouds in the damp air. 'I thought you said you were leaving.'

'Soon. They say we are safe, now all *les Chinois* stay in their camp.'

'Who said that?'

'Is it true?'

'I don't know. I need to come in.'

He was shivering. His skin felt hot and tight, maybe the beginnings of a fever.

'There is nothing here, Monsieur. The girls, they are gone.'

He pulled his lapels close around his neck. 'I didn't come for a girl.'

—————

She lit a fire in the upstairs sitting room, kneeling before the hearth while he sat hunched on the sofa, still in his coat, holding a glass with both hands. The last of the *eau de vie* was gone. All that was left now was some red wine that was too young and thin to be warming. The shutters stayed closed.

'Liu Dianzhen, have you learned who killed him?'

'Not yet. The man had no enemies, they say.'

'Then why did he die?'

He stared into his glass. 'Because of a tattoo, or because of his race. Mostly because he was unlucky.'

'So you know. You know who is guilty.'

'No, I don't. But I think ... I'm rather afraid ...'

'*Oui?*'

A few pale flames were rising in the grate. They cast fleeting shadows across the walls. 'I know his kind. He's a prisoner here. Because of what happened. He can't get away or he would have done. He can't go back.'

'*Alors, il est fou.*'

'No, not insane, Madame. Liu's killer believes he is damned, that he was led into damnation, by design.'

Madame Chastain threw a bunch of kindling onto the fire. 'You will find him? You will stop him?'

'Or he'll find me. Either way, it won't be long.'

He gulped down some wine and glanced at the window. Had he heard movement outside or was it just the rain? If he looked across the yard, would he see a figure standing there, as he had that first night?

In the fireplace the flames were sickly and shrinking. Madame Chastain kindled them with a pair of bellows, pausing to dab her forehead with the back of her hand. She had strong shoulders and graceful hands, the nails pale against tanned skin. On her wedding finger there was no ring.

'You never married, Madame?'

She hesitated. 'Many years ago.'

'You don't wear a ring.'

She glanced at her left hand, as if to be sure. '*Non*. My husband, he left us.'

'Us?'

She hesitated. These were things she did not usually talk about, he sensed, especially not with clients. 'We had a child, a daughter: Louise.'

'Where is she now?'

'She is dead, Monsieur. *La scarlatine*. She was three years old.'

'I'm sorry.'

She nodded. The wound had not healed, he could see that. Perhaps it never would. Perhaps the best that could be hoped for was to grow accustomed to the pain. She picked up the bellows again.

'The Chinaman, the interpreter, he lost a daughter too. She was about the same age, his friend told me. That was a fever too.'

'*La scarlatine* takes many children, Monsieur. It is a curse.'

The wood was damp. It began to hiss and pop.

'Will you tell me about it? I'd like to know.'

'About the sickness?'

'About losing a child.' Madame Chastain did not reply. 'I expect it's wrong of me to ask.'

She shook her head. 'No. It is not *usual*, but it is not wrong.'

'You must forgive me, Madame.'

'Please, my name is Suzanne.'

'S-Suzanne.' He stumbled over the word, as if it were difficult or unfamiliar, though it was just a woman's name. 'Can you tell me?'

She put down the bellows. 'Before Louise, I lived, but I did not know what it was for, my life. I dreamed of being happy, but I did not know how that would be, how to find it. You understand me?'

'I think so.'

'After Louise, I did not have these questions. My life was her life. It was for her.'

'And then? When she was gone?'

'I had not the questions any more, or the answers. I had nothing, only living – the burden of it. I think it is the same for many people, to lose what you love most.'

He was silent for a moment. 'And so you're here.'

'Yes, I am here.' She wiped her hands on her apron. 'Are you married, Monsieur?'

'No.'

'There is somebody waiting, in England?'

'Not any more. There was a girl. She broke off our engagement.' He gestured towards his face. 'Understandable, given my injuries. She had enough patriotism to wait until the war was over.'

'I am sorry, Monsieur. You loved her?'

'Of course I . . .' He fell silent again. 'I don't remember. I remember wanting her – from the moment I laid eyes on her: thin summer dress, twirling a parasol on her shoulder, spoiled, bored.'

'In England?'

'No. We were on a boat from Cairo: her lot in first class, of course, me sweating it out in second. We met in secret – had to, what with me having no title. It was two years later she agreed to marry me. I suppose by then I'd earned it.' He remembered her final letter: she feared he'd been to brothels in

France, brothels like this one, and couldn't stomach the thought of it – as if that was the real reason she was abandoning him. 'Damn it, what is this filth?'

He threw his glass into the fire. It shattered and hissed. He covered his face with his hands.

Madame Chastain got up. '*J'apporte la teinture, tout de suite.*'

She hurried out of the room and returned with a tray, set out as before, except that the bottle was bigger. He watched her as she poured out the water and mixed in the sugar, before adding drop after drop of the dark-orange liquid. It was a stronger dose than last time. She understood his requirements without having to be asked.

'I'm sorry,' he said. 'I didn't mean to frighten you.'

'*Ce n'est rien, Monsieur.*'

'John, please.'

She nodded.

'Who'll supply you,' he said, 'now that the Chinese have gone?'

'No one. I am finished here.'

'Where will you go? To Abbeville?'

'No. Far away. I do not know the place. But I will go.'

Madame Chastain handed him the glass. '*Santé.*'

She watched him drink. When the glass was empty she reached up and touched his face. For a moment they neither moved nor spoke.

'Rest now, *mon ami*,' she said. 'Forget.'

———

—— Thirty-four ——

London, March 1919

For a moment Sir Evelyn Vanneck thought his taxi had arrived outside the wrong house. Standing silhouetted in the window of the library – a room he rarely entered these days – was a young woman. He had not been expecting any visitors, and certainly not at this hour. By the time he had paid the driver and climbed out into the foggy street, the curtains had been drawn and the stranger could no longer be seen.

His housekeeper opened the door. 'A young lady, sir. She insisted on waiting.'

'What's her name?'

'Page, sir. A friend of your niece, she said.'

Sir Evelyn took off his coat and instinctively touched his tie, only then recalling his recent exchange of letters with Amy's mother. He had just returned from Italy and had written to enquire if his representations to the colonel of the Manchesters had borne fruit – if Amy had received any more information about her fiancé's loss. Connie Vanneck had written back that Amy was not at home: she had gone on holiday to Paris with a friend. No explanation or comment was offered, which could only mean that Connie did not approve. The news had taken him aback. It did not seem entirely appropriate – or in character, for that matter – for Amy to be sightseeing and drinking in cafés while Edward Haslam remained unaccounted for. On the other hand, if it helped her get over her loss, Sir Evelyn had told himself, perhaps it was not such a bad thing. Either way, who had the right to judge?

He cleared his throat and went into the library.

'Miss Page?'

The girl was younger than he had expected – not much more than a child. Her limbs were long and willowy, her untidy reddish hair tied up in a single plait. Her cheeks were freckled. She stood by the unlit fireplace, her hands clasped in front of her.

'Thank you for seeing me, Sir Evelyn. I'm sorry to arrive unannounced.'

Her clothes were visibly unkempt, as if she had been wearing them too long.

'Have you news of my niece? Is she still in Paris?'

'Paris?'

'I understood from her family that she decided on a change of scene. Sightseeing, the Louvre – take her mind off things?'

'We were neither of us in Paris, Sir Evelyn.' Miss Page's gaze dipped towards the Persian rug. 'We weren't in France for pleasure.'

'Visiting friends then?'

The girl spoke softly. 'I went to find my brother's grave, near Amiens. The location was lost, by the army. I was fortunate, though: they found it in the end, identified his remains. I saw them reinterred. I'm afraid Amy hasn't been so lucky.'

Sir Evelyn felt himself grow pale. '*That* was where she went? To Amiens?'

'And to the battlefields, where Edward went missing.'

'The battlefields? Good God, where is she now?'

'Still there. A little place called Colincamps, near the River Ancre, just behind the old front lines.'

'She's not alone?'

'There are volunteers, a labour company – for the time being anyway.'

Sir Evelyn shook his head. Amy's mother could not have been more wrong. He had been picturing the City of Lights, days of gaiety and culture; not the ravaged wastelands of Picardy. How could Connie have been so badly mistaken?

'Please sit down, Miss Page,' he said. 'Let me offer you some refreshment.'

'Thank you, no. I mustn't be long.'

Sir Evelyn slumped into an armchair. 'I had no idea Amy was in France for *that* reason. Stupid of me – I should have guessed.'

Kitty sat down on the edge of the sofa. 'She wanted to see you before she left, but you weren't in London.'

'No, I wasn't.'

'She couldn't wait, I'm afraid. She was worried her parents might try to stop her.'

Sir Evelyn shook his head. 'I'll have to inform them, all the same. It wouldn't be right to keep them in the dark.'

There was a faint blush on Kitty's cheeks. 'I'm sure they've already guessed, Sir Evelyn. You see, Amy received a letter from the colonel of Edward's regiment.'

'Major General Barnard?'

Kitty nodded. 'It told her where Edward's battalion had been posted when Edward went missing. Amy said she was going to go there. You see, she'd promised to find him, no matter what.'

'His remains, you mean?'

Kitty nodded. 'Lady Constance was all against it, I'm afraid. She never cared for Edward. I expect you knew that.'

Sir Evelyn nodded. Connie's attitude had been sadly predictable: she had convinced herself that Haslam's sole interest in Amy was as a means of advancement, that her daughter was being duped. There was a whiff of scandal about the affair, a suggestion of impropriety, but the young man had never stood a chance, either way. Sir Evelyn had thought about speaking up for him – at their one meeting he had seemed decent, if a little awkward – but had decided it would do no good. The fact was he had never been on the best of terms with his sister-in-law. Connie was beautiful and elegant. He had met crowned heads of Europe who were less regal. Everyone had thought his brother Charles, an awkward suitor at the best of times, a very lucky man when he had finally won Connie's hand, but what had struck Sir Evelyn from the beginning was a lack of warmth. Time had not changed his perception. The new Lady Vanneck could be gracious, but at some time during her young life all emotion and spontaneity had been drained out of her, to be replaced by a preoccupation with status and appearances. Amy had no hope of living up to her, in that regard. Looking back, it was this that Sir Evelyn had found interesting: not simply that his niece was intelligent, but that she was so completely overshadowed, like some rare plant that struggles to survive in the dark.

All the same, it was surprising, even distasteful, to discover that Connie had lied to him. Evidently Amy was not in Paris. It was not a great lie, as lies went, but it had kept him out of the picture when he might have been of some use. He found himself unable to stifle a feeling of admiration for Amy. She was doing the right thing by the man she loved. And this time he would help her, in whatever way he could.

'Is this why you came here, Miss Page, to tell me Amy's whereabouts?'

'No, Sir Evelyn. I came because Amy needs a favour. She said you may be the one person in England who can help her.'

———

—— Thirty-five ——

France, March 1919

He knew the names of the dead men now, but it did not help. Mackenzie had done the paperwork, sent the information to Graves Registration and to Major Westbrook in Acheux, even copied down the appropriate Mandarin for the head-stone inscriptions. None of it helped him put Two Storm Wood behind him. He had carried out his duty, which was to identify the victims and see to their burial, but that was no longer enough. The crime, the madness and depravity of it, seemed to cling to him like a stain. If there were justice – the facts uncovered, the guilty punished – then he might be free of it. But what chance did he have of bringing that about? Still the dead, or his conscience, refused to let him rest. As for Miss Vanneck: her presence, her hopes, made it even harder to walk away.

Mackenzie was alone, watching the farmhouse from the shelter of the stables, when a message arrived from the Directorate in Péronne. It asked for a report on progress. His company was to complete its searches along the Ancre as quickly as possible and proceed to a section of the Hindenburg Line eighteen miles further east. Mackenzie immediately sensed official impatience in the language, a dissatisfaction perhaps with the pace of his work. His impression was confirmed when the dispatch concluded with a summons to headquarters for 'additional briefing'.

He did not like the idea of leaving, not when there was still work to be done – more graves to find, boggy terrain that needed a second search – but he knew his men would not complain. Further east the land would be alive again, or at least recognisable. There would be trees in bud, spring crops growing, villages damaged perhaps, but habitable. The battlefields – the Somme and the Ancre – would be behind them at last, and so would their ghosts. But what of Amy Vanneck? He would tell her again to leave, for her own safety. He would give her whatever assurances she wanted with regards to information. But he knew it would not change anything.

That same morning a letter arrived from Lieutenant Aldridge. It was the first time Mackenzie had heard from him since the incident at Miraumont, and the booby-trap that had killed Corporal Hughes. He had expected to hear that Aldridge was in England by this time, but he wrote from the Château de Naours, a French military hospital north of Amiens:

I was lucky to be sent here. Their surgeons are some of the best, when it comes to facial wounds. The French have developed some wonderful new techniques, and they are getting more skilled every day. Anywhere else I would have lost my right eye, but they operated for two hours to save it, and now my sight is almost back to normal. There are some pretty bad injuries here, things no surgeon could completely put right – gueules cassées, the French call them: broken faces. They say some of them will get tin masks to hide the wounds, painted to look like real flesh. The others will go to live in special places where they don't have to worry about people staring.

Most of the staff here are nuns. It's a bit hermitic – terribly quiet. Nobody comes here, except medical people. Fortunately there's a smattering of English personnel too, including a very personable MO by the name of Bill Egerton. He served with the East Lancashire Division and was wounded himself last year. He came back to study the new surgical techniques.

My ribs are pretty much healed, so they are sending me home at last. I'd planned on stopping by to say farewell to the company and to you. I was damned sorry to hear about Hughes. But the doctors have forbidden it. They say I must go straight back to England, on account of my nerves. I have nightmares, you see, and times when I'm not quite myself. All that.

I expect you will carry on with the clearance work for a while yet. There are a couple of large Allied cemeteries outside Amiens. I passed them on my way here. Very orderly and well kept, gardeners at work on the grass and the flowers. They say the wooden crosses will be replaced with white stone, all lined up in tidy ranks. It will look peaceful and elegant. Does it matter that the fighting itself was so very different? The reality has to be hidden, I suppose, like the broken faces beneath the masks, or it becomes too much to bear.

As Mackenzie was reading, a raindrop landed on the paper. Away to the south-west thunder rumbled. He thought of Amy: he had seen her a few hours earlier, setting off in the direction of Bucquoy. The ground was more dangerous when it softened. Shells and mortar rounds shifted, becoming more susceptible to pressure. He hoped she would stick to the road.

Bill Egerton: it was then he remembered where he had seen the name before. He had glimpsed it in one of Captain Haslam's letters – the ones he had been caught reading without permission: *Bill Egerton is down here with the Medical Corps. I always could talk to him.* It had to be the same man.

Mackenzie folded the letter away. Did they talk: Captain Haslam and the surgeon? If so, what had they talked about? What confidences had they shared? It was a stroke of luck, the first to come Amy Vanneck's way. If nothing else, there might be some comfort to be had from meeting someone else who felt her fiancé's loss.

Mackenzie watched one of his squads returning to camp, where steam and a smell of boiled potatoes rose from the cookhouse, and began to have doubts. False hope was a drug, like opium: it staved off pain for a while, only to double it when the effect wore off. Amy Vanneck was already addicted. Should he feed her habit? Or would it be kinder to say nothing about Egerton at all?

———

The Surgeon

—— Thirty-six ——

France, June 1918

They got back from the raid with four men wounded. Private Mottram was stretchered to the dressing station with grenade fragments in his shoulders and arms. The others walked. No one was left behind, living or dead.

Haslam sat down to write the report. Every detail of the raid had to be recorded: the condition and layout of the enemy defences, the state of the wire, the number and disposition of enemy troops, the actions of Haslam's men. Rhodes often cross-examined his officers on their version of events. Anomalies and omissions displeased him. Sometimes he would simply sit and listen, motionless, eyes unfocused, as if his mind were elsewhere. It took a while for Haslam to understand that he was in the fight, at the point of contact with the enemy, at the collision of flesh and steel. Besides that, Haslam found it helped him to omit nothing, to tally every act of violence, ascribing it a military context and a military rationale. The temptation to dwell on it was easier to ignore then. He could even sleep without opium – which was just as well, because Rhodes did not tolerate its use on the front lines. Even the men regarded it with disdain: the expensive vice of the rich, decadent and weak.

It was almost dawn when Haslam finally left the dugout and made his way to Battalion HQ, passing a wiring party as it scurried back to safety among the earthworks. The enemy had put up a barrage after the raid, hoping to forestall a larger attack. The guns were silent now, but dust still drifted over the line, spun into eddies by the wind. Haslam wanted to hand over his report and be done with it.

He reached the bunker as the regimental sergeant major was coming out. The German prisoner was behind him, followed by Private Ingham and Corporal Staveley. Even in the darkness, Haslam could see that the German's face was swollen and he was bleeding from the mouth. He was younger than

Haslam remembered – probably his own age, his uniform ill-fitting and dirty. He wheezed as he breathed, as if in pain.

'Why's he still here?' Haslam said. 'He should be in the rear by now.'

'Some nuts is hard to crack, sir,' the regimental said. 'You can't always tell. Gave it up in the end, though.'

Corporal Staveley nudged the German in the back. 'Let's be having you.'

The German saw Haslam and stumbled over. 'My name is Haffner. Captain Georg Haffner.'

His voice was shaky. As he spoke, blood spattered across his chin.

'Haffner?'

Private Ingham grabbed him by the shoulder. 'The captain doesn't care what your fuckin' name is.'

The prisoner must have seen a flicker of recognition in Haslam's face.

'Haffner, Haffner. Like the symphony, *ja*?'

'All right.'

'Mozart, *ja*? Wolfgang Amadeus—'

'All right. I know.'

Then the prisoner was showing Haslam a photograph, thrusting it in his face: a little girl of four or five, sitting on her mother's knee.

'*Bitte, bitte.*'

Haslam pushed it away. 'Pull yourself together. These men will escort you to the rear. Nothing's going to happen to you.'

'Move it!' Corporal Staveley levelled his rifle.

The German raised his hands and stumbled on. At the corner of the comms trench, he looked back. Haslam turned away, muttering under his breath. What did Mozart have to do with it? What did Mozart have to do with anything?

He lit a cigarette and stood there, smoking. Like the cocaine, the tension of the raid was only now bleeding out of him. In its place came visions he did not want to see, sounds he did not want to hear. He should go back to his dugout and rest. Inspections would begin in less than an hour, the ceaseless work of improving their defences. The cigarette was half-finished when he saw that the German officer's photograph was lying on the ground. The fool must have dropped it.

He picked it up and looked at it. He saw a trace of resemblance in the young girl's face. It was there in the eyes and the breadth of the brow. She would be missing her father, waiting for him, eyes tight shut in prayer every night.

Haslam threw the cigarette away. Maybe it wasn't too much trouble to give the picture back.

At the far end of the comms trench he passed Corporal Staveley coming the other way.

'Where's the prisoner?'

'Left him with Ingham, sir,' Staveley said, a hint of impatience in his voice, as if the question were uncalled for.

'Alone?'

'I thought he could handle it, sir.'

Haslam walked on, his pace quickening. By the time he reached the end of the trench he was running.

A track lay in front of him, curving through the ruins of a farm. A barn there had served as a first-aid post until a shell collapsed the roof. A pair of service wagons rattled past at speed, coming from the direction of Divisional HQ, but there was no sign of Ingham or the prisoner. The handover point would be half a mile away at least. Ingham was a regular on raiding parties. More than once he had volunteered. When it came to clearing dugouts, no one was more fearless. It was said he notched kills on the handle of his club.

Haslam picked his way among the bombed-out buildings. Untidy rows of graves lay on the far side, where men who had died of their wounds were buried. Beyond that was an older cemetery, damaged by shelling. In the lee of what had once been the farmhouse he found Captain Haffner lying. His face and half his body were hidden beneath his trench coat. It was just as Haslam had feared: the prisoner's throat had been cut.

———

'What makes you so sure it was Private Ingham? Have you talked to him?'

Major Blomfield sat squarely behind a table at Battalion HQ, marking grid references on a map. The unsteady glow of a kerosene lamp threw shadows over the rough chalky walls.

'I don't want to talk to him, sir. I want him charged.'

Blomfield did not look up. 'Did you witness the killing?'

'I didn't have to. Ingham had sole charge of the prisoner. Who else could have done it?'

Blomfield was a good second-in-command: energetic and unthinkingly loyal. It was no great handicap that he was stupid. Rhodes had enough brains for both of them.

'I expect something went wrong,' Blomfield said. 'Hun pulled a weapon. Get our chap's side of the story. Only fair, after all.'

Haslam felt feverish, bile rising in his throat. Ingham would lie — there had been a struggle, or the prisoner had run away — lies that Blomfield would be happy to believe. He had not reported the matter for fear of retribution, Ingham would say: field punishment or the loss of leave. And then it would all be forgotten. One less Hun to worry about.

Out of nowhere, Haslam had a vision of Amy, her hands caressing his bare shoulders: *Stay as you are.*

'Ingham's a damned useful fellow,' Blomfield added. 'Wouldn't want to lose him on a hunch.'

'It's not a hunch, sir. A flagrant breach of . . .' Haslam found it hard to keep his voice steady, 'of the laws and usages of war. I'm going to take this up with the CO.'

Blomfield tossed his pencil onto the table. 'Not looking like that, I hope.'

Haslam looked down. The front of his uniform was black and shiny from collar to belt. A raw, fatty smell hit his nostrils — a smell of blood. There was more blood under his fingernails and on the cuffs of his shirt. It was etched into the lines of his hand.

Blomfield's tone softened. 'Get cleaned up, get some rest. Leave Ingham to me. I'll look into it, all right?'

'No, sir. This won't wait. The prisoner was tortured and unlawfully killed. The CO must be told right away.'

Blomfield's stare grew cold. 'I'll let him know then. You can go now.'

Haslam turned to find Rhodes standing at the foot of the steps. Haslam had not heard him arrive. His boots were shiny and his uniform as spotless as the lieutenant's was filthy. From the look of it, he had just shaved. Was it possible he had slept through the raid, the interrogation, everything?

Haslam saluted.

'Take charge of the inspections, would you, Major?' Rhodes said. 'I want to hear what Lieutenant Haslam has to say.'

Blomfield looked surprised and not a little affronted.

'Very good, sir.'

He got up and left. Rhodes took his place behind the table. Briefly he rubbed his eyes. They were bloodshot. 'Well, let's have it.'

'We took a prisoner, sir. A Captain Haffner. He—'

'Your report, Lieutenant. I meant your report. On the raid.'

Haslam realised he was still clutching it in his hand. He placed it on the table. Rhodes read it carefully, his gaze shifting to the trench map and a set of aerial photographs beside it.

'Congratulations,' he said finally. 'Your prisoner gave us the position of every machine-gun nest between here and Grévillers, and we've an excellent idea of their forward strength. A good night's work, and no losses. I'll admit I was concerned for a while.'

'Concerned, sir?'

'You were gone a long time. I was starting to think the Huns had set an ambush.'

Rhodes had been watching and waiting all through the night. Haslam should have known. Still, there was something almost touching about Rhodes's concern.

'We just had to bide our time, sir.'

'Of course. Timing's everything.' Rhodes undid his Sam Browne and slung it on the table. The leather holder held a German pistol, a long-barrelled Mauser that had been recovered on a raid. The men said it had a longer range than its British counterparts, though Rhodes had to buy the ammunition for himself. 'You heard about Captain Holt, I suppose?'

'No, sir.'

'His fever's much worse. It's the field hospital for him – a month, I'd say, at least. You'll have to take over C Company.'

Haslam was unprepared. Officer or not, he had never thought of himself as suited to command. Hierarchies, he had come to see, were distasteful to him, the inherent notion that one man was better than another. He had assumed Rhodes knew this. He seemed to know everything else.

'Yes, sir. Thank you, sir.'

Rhodes's stare came to rest on Haslam's soiled jacket. 'Better take that off, though. Can't have the new man smelling like a butcher's boy. Give it to Burgess.'

Rhodes's batman was sent for. He took the tunic away. Rhodes gestured towards a supply crate that served as a chair. 'Now, you were saying?'

Haslam sat down. He couldn't help thinking about the men he had killed on the raid, the sound of his knife as it pierced their flesh. 'The prisoner was killed. I found his body. He'd been roughed up, too, tortured.' He forced himself to sit up straight. 'King's Regulations demand the humane treatment of prisoners. Private Ingham, for one—'

'Private Ingham was at Nieuport, during the Battle of the Dunes, with the Northamptons. Did you know that?'

Haslam shook his head.

'The Huns cleared the forward trenches with flame-throwers, liquid fire. Ingham's pals tried to surrender but they were killed anyway, burned alive with their hands up. You can't blame him if he tends to be unforgiving.'

'Unforgiving? Captain Haffner was a prisoner of war.'

'So he was. Our prisoners of war are starved and beaten, and used as slave labour at the front. Officers generally fare a little better, but what use is that, to the likes of Private Ingham? What's he supposed to make of our officers sticking up for theirs?'

Haslam's head was spinning. Outside, above ground, the sun would be coming up, but down here, underground, it was always night. 'There are rules, sir. Decency. Isn't that what we're fighting for?'

Rhodes reached into his top pocket and took out a booklet bound in yellow canvas. Haslam recognised the 42nd Division officer manual. It was new. Copies had been issued a few weeks earlier. His own was in his dugout.

'Fifty pages from our divisional commander on an officer's duties,' Rhodes said. 'Not one word about prisoners. What we do have is item seven in *Maxims for the Leader*.' Rhodes pushed the booklet across the table. 'Why don't you read it out?'

'I know what it says, sir.'

'Read it. Page eight.'

Haslam picked up the booklet and found the page. He read aloud: '*Be blood-thirsty, and never cease to think how you can best kill the enemy or help your men to do so.*'

'Edward?' Haslam looked up. It was the first time Rhodes had used his first name. 'Look around you. This is not a gentleman's war. The gentlemen are all in the rear.'

Haslam shook his head. 'We're not savages.'

Rhodes laughed. 'Savages? That's a word the powerful use about the weak. It justifies enslaving them, or worse. It means very little here. You know this. You've worked it out for yourself.'

Haslam put the manual back on the table. He had not noticed before, but the blood on his tunic had penetrated all the way to his undershirt. A thin red stain discoloured the fabric above his sternum, like the wrapping on a joint of meat. 'This war will end one day,' he said. 'We'll take this back with us, to England, to the people we . . . It'll stay with us for ever.'

Rhodes sighed – not a sigh of impatience, but of recognition and regret. 'If we're to be judged, who'll judge us? Who would have the right? The Vannecks of this world? It seems to me they've judged you already, Edward. And that judgement brought you here. Or am I mistaken?'

Edward shook his head. He did not have the strength to resent Rhodes's intrusion into his private world.

Rhodes pulled a hip flask from his pocket and unscrewed the cap. 'Do you still care what they think?'

'No, I don't.'

'Then at least the war's done something for you. Here.' Rhodes offered the flask. 'It's early, but you've earned it.'

Haslam took the flask, held it to his lips, but he could not bring himself to drink. A drink would seal the bargain, cut the last ties to the old world, the old life.

There was a knock. Burgess returned, carrying an officer's jacket. It was clean.

'Should be a decent fit, sir,' he said, holding it up at the shoulders.

Haslam looked at the stripes on the sleeve. 'This isn't for me. It's for a captain.'

Burgess looked at Rhodes. 'No mistake, I don't believe, sir.'

'I expect the paperwork will come through in a week or so,' Rhodes said. 'No point in waiting.'

'Congratulations, sir,' Burgess said.

Haslam put the jacket on. It felt new. But if that was the case, then who had paid for it? It could only have been Rhodes. It was not the act of a commanding officer; it was the act of a friend.

'What do you think, Burgess? Does Captain Haslam look the part of a company commander?' Rhodes said.

'I'd say so, sir. Most definitely.'

Somewhere above ground a shell went over, followed by a second. Distant shouts of command funnelled down into the dugout. Burgess was dismissed.

'C Company is yours now,' Rhodes said. 'Two hundred and forty men. Can they count on you?'

'Yes, sir.'

Rhodes got to his feet. 'I'm sorry about the Hun, truly. But what he gave up will save your men's lives when the time comes to attack, which I've no doubt it will. Would you be prepared to forgo that advantage for the sake of a Whitehall rule book? More to the point, would you want your men to know it?'

'No, sir.'

'They need to know there's no sacrifice you won't make to keep them alive. And if they do, they'll return the favour, believe me – not just now, but for ever.' Rhodes put his cap on. 'These are bonds of blood, Edward. They're even stronger than the bonds of family.' He put an arm on the younger man's shoulder. 'I'm telling you this because I know you've never really had one – a family, I mean – until now.' He smiled. 'Now, let's get to work, shall we?'

The hip flask was on the table. Haslam handed it over.

'Finish it,' Rhodes said.

———

A minute later Haslam stepped out into the daylight. Up and down the line inspections were under way, work parties being organised, rations distributed. His company awaited him in the second line: veterans and new recruits, husbands, brothers, sons. With Captain Holt evacuated, they would be wondering where he was.

As he set off, his hand brushed against something in his trouser pocket. It was the photograph of the German officer's wife and child. He tore it up and let it fall to the ground.

July 1918

... Every time a letter arrives from you, the sight of it — the envelope, your hand-writing, knowing it's from you — the elation is hard to describe. In an instant the dread lifts, and it's as if I can breathe again. Because I know that you are alive and unharmed, and for the rest of the day I am cheerful and busy, and hopeful that the end of this dark time is in sight.

But your last letter worries me. I can only guess what prompted it, the strain you are under. Those dreams: the Devil and the dead. What can they mean but that you are in desperate need of rest? I don't doubt you have driven yourself to extremes in the service of your men. You were never one to give yourself half-heartedly — which I always loved about you until this moment, when it makes me afraid.

As to what you asked of me, though I dread to think of it, still I give it with all my heart. If the worst happens, the battlefield will not be your resting place, not while I have breath to prevent it. It is promised and decided, and we need never speak of it again. From what I hear — it cannot all be lies, can it? — the German Army is crumbling. If so, our luck needs to hold only a little longer and this torment will be over.

When the war is done we will take the time we spent apart, and everything that took place in it, and lock it away, bury it like a tomb in the desert, where no one will ever find it. We will live as if the war had never happened, and there will be no one to stop us. The battlefield will not follow us. It will stay in France. One morning we will wake up in each other's arms and hear the sounds of a sweet English summer — the wind on the wheat fields and the chirping of the birds — and it will be as if the time we spent away was just a dream.

—— Thirty-seven ——

France, March 1919

'You go over one at a time.' The redcap planted a hand on the canvas roof. He was speaking to each driver in turn. 'Dead slow, got it?'

Three hours out of Amiens the supply column had ground to a halt. Along the skyline, through clouds of exhaust, Mackenzie glimpsed the ruins of grand buildings. To left and right an expanse of muddy water divided the formless masses of rubble.

'What's the hold-up?'

'The bridge.' A crooked smile formed on the driver's lips. 'Hope you can swim, sir.'

Across a narrow neck of the Somme the sappers had made a crossing out of railway sleepers, and a narrow wooden viaduct for troops on foot. Beside the viaduct a sign read BREAK STEP. On the far side, where a great mill had once stood, there was now a triangular segment of wall, three storeys high, its blown windows offering views of the sky. Mackenzie had first been through Péronne two years earlier. The mill had been standing in those days, roofless and burned out, but with the external walls intact. An Indian cavalry post office had stood opposite. But the place had changed hands twice since then, in both cases after bitter fighting.

The bridge dipped and swayed as the truck crawled over. They made a turning and headed down a long avenue lined with piles of debris, past the shattered remains of provincial grandeur. On the upper floors of turreted houses, Mackenzie glimpsed striped wallpaper, iron bedsteads, wardrobes, a porcelain washbasin in mid-air, supported only by its pipes – all open to view. Where walls remained, teams of civilians were at work shoring them up or picking through the debris. Their ancient wagons, stopped at odd angles, looked out of place beside the lines of staff cars and motorcycles, like newly arrived foreigners, ignorant of local custom. Old men stopped and stared as the column rolled by. The air had a charred, sickly smell.

In the main square, opposite a statue upon which several British battalions had carved the date of their arrival, stood an Armstrong hut with the words TOWN MAJOR painted on the door. Mackenzie got down from the truck and made his way over. Inside, two junior officers were playing backgammon in a fog of tobacco. Another lay under a blanket, coughing. Nobody looked up.

'Where do I find the deputy adjutant general?'

Mackenzie was due at the Directorate, but the 'additional briefing' could wait.

A young lieutenant got to his feet. 'Do you mean Major General Crompton, sir? He's not with us any more.'

'Demobbed?'

'Dead, sir. Went down with the flu last week. They took him back to Étaples, but he only lasted a couple of days. Are you looking for a billet?'

'Not now. Who's his replacement?'

'Colonel Ormsby. He's set up opposite the citadel.' The lieutenant pointed towards the door. 'Up Piccadilly, turn right onto Park Lane, about a hundred yards down.'

Mackenzie went back outside. Blue smoke from the trucks was still spiralling through the square. He remembered a narrow lane that had been renamed Oxford Street. A short way down there had once stood a red-brick mansion with a courtyard in front. It had hardly been damaged and was serving as an officers' club. He searched for it now. He wanted a drink to steady his nerves. The club had boasted a decent cellar and more: an Australian captain called Perry had offered him cocaine and Indian hemp.

Mackenzie went up and down the street, but the mansion had vanished. The artillery – there was no way of knowing whose – had done for it, once and for all. He could not even identify the place where it used to stand.

The adjutant's office was housed in an old tannery, which had been made habitable with the aid of a corrugated-iron roof. Colonel Ormsby sat writing behind a trestle table, wearing a pair of spectacles, while a pair of junior GSOs hovered at his shoulder. An ornate china coffee cup, doubtless recovered from the rubble, served as an ashtray. Motorcycle riders came and went, holding envelopes or bearing satchels.

Mackenzie introduced himself. The colonel did not look up. 'What can I do for you? I'm a little pressed, as you can see.'

257

Ormsby was old, even for a man of his rank: at least sixty, haggard and narrow-chested – a veteran, Mackenzie suspected, of distant colonial wars, conflicts that had once gripped the popular imagination, but which now seemed like mere skirmishes, punitive expeditions against spear-waving primitives without a howitzer or a machine-gun between them.

'I'm looking for information regarding some allegations of misconduct,' Mackenzie said.

'Your men playing up, are they, Captain?'

'No, sir. The allegations would have concerned men of the Forty-second Division.'

The colonel shot him a sceptical glance. 'I think you'll find the Forty-second is in Belgium – what's left of it.'

'This would have been last summer, sir.'

'Last summer?' Ormsby stopped what he was doing. 'What's this all about?'

Mackenzie had hoped his request would go through on the nod, that he would be shown to the relevant files without having to explain himself. He saw now that Ormsby was not the type to let that happen.

'I'm hoping to shed light on some unlawful killings, sir. You might recall the incident. I sent in a report to your office.'

'This office? I'm afraid I don't recall—'

'The dead were discovered in the Fourth Corps sector, west of the Serre Ridge. A place called Two Storm Wood.'

Ormsby had stopped writing. One of the other staff officers looked at Mackenzie and then looked away again.

'And what's your interest, Captain?'

'I've volunteered to assist in the investigation,' Mackenzie said. The lie had been rehearsed. It would not help him to be candid, to admit he wanted the truth about Edward Haslam and Lieutenant Colonel Rhodes before it could be buried, for Amy's sake and for his own – because he felt sure it *would* be buried as soon as it saw the light of day, if only to protect the reputation of the army.

'What investigation?'

'The War Office has sent over a provost marshal: Major Westbrook.'

'First I've heard of it. We should have been informed, but then . . .' Ormsby's gaze came to rest on the piles of documents and letters on the table. 'It's entirely possible my predecessor omitted to inform me.'

'You've just taken over, sir?'

'Correct. Rearguard action, really. A few months from now, the Third Army will have ceased to exist. And then what'll become of us?' Ormsby tapped his papers on the table and handed them to one of his staff. 'That'll do for now, gentlemen. We'll resume later.'

The GSOs left the room.

'So, what have you learned? I'm interested.'

'We've succeeded in identifying the dead. It may be possible to discover who killed them.'

'I see. And what do you want from me exactly?'

'I'm interested in reports of violence against Chinese labourers – incidents that came to light last year.'

Ormsby picked up a bulging file and carried it to a stack of wooden cabinets. For the next few moments the business of filing seemed to absorb him completely. 'Go on,' he said finally.

'Do you recall a Lieutenant Kelvin, of the One Hundred and Twenty-fifth Chinese Labour Corps?'

At the mention of the Chinese, Ormsby appeared faintly amused. 'Should I?'

'He reported the loss of two men to the adjutant general's office. I'd like to see those reports.'

'The files will be halfway to London by now. You'll have to talk to the War Office.'

'I'm afraid there isn't time, sir.'

'Time? You're in a hurry, are you, Captain?'

'Yes, sir. I am.'

Ormsby shrugged. 'Then why don't you talk to Kelvin?'

'He's dead. His body was found at Two Storm Wood.'

Ormsby was still for a moment. Then he closed the drawer and locked it with a key. 'You look like you could do with a drink, Captain. There's one place that hasn't shut up shop. We might be in luck.'

He didn't wait for Mackenzie's assent. A moment later they had left the building and set off up a narrow side street opposite the old fortress. Fifty yards on, they passed through a gate into a well-swept courtyard. The buildings around were badly damaged, but the main house still had most of its roof. An NCO met them at the door.

'One for the road, Sergeant, if that can be arranged,' Ormsby said, handing over his coat and umbrella.

'Of course, sir.'

'The usual for me. Brandy for the captain. We'll be in here.'

Ormsby led the way into what had once been a dining room. The dining table was still there, although a wall of books six inches high lay across the middle, suggesting it had been retained by British officers only for ping-pong. A fire burned low in the grate.

'I won't be sorry to see the back of this place. I don't think anyone will.' Ormsby sat down and gestured for Mackenzie to do the same. The armchairs had their insides spilling out of them, as if sliced open by shrapnel. 'Still, the prospect of life among civilians is almost as daunting. Once war has opened a man's eyes, he can never close them again, no matter how hard he tries.'

Reluctantly Mackenzie sat down. 'Lieutenant Kelvin: do you remember the details of his report?'

'More or less. A couple of coolies disappeared. One of them turned up dead, name of Chen, as I recall.'

'Chen?'

Ormsby shrugged. 'There was a woman involved. All second-hand reports, largely circumstantial. I'm not sure I see the relevance.'

'Kelvin thought the men had been murdered by British troops.'

'Hearsay.'

'Did he give you any names?'

'Of course not. He held the Seventh Manchesters responsible – specifically their commanding officer, Lieutenant Colonel Rhodes.'

Mackenzie knew the name, remembered a man on a horse, sabre held aloft: a touched-up photograph in a newspaper, a caption that read *The Hero of Bazentin Ridge*. He had been Edward Haslam's battalion commander, a brave man, a man to be feared – the best kind in war.

'But he offered no credible witnesses,' Ormsby said. 'No more than his own suspicions in fact. It was notable that we heard nothing from his commanding officer by way of support. Quite the opposite.'

Mackenzie saw Major Pickering tugging at the lead of his oversized dog. *He refused to see your typical coolie for what he is.*

'Did your office take steps to investigate?'

'Captain Mackenzie, the Third Army never consisted of fewer than eighty-five thousand men – the equivalent of a large town. In any case, an investigation would properly have been a divisional matter, especially when prompted by a less-than-reliable source.'

There was a knock at the door. The mess sergeant entered with their drinks on a tray. Mackenzie was tempted to drain his glass in one. As he brought it to his lips, it struck him that Ormsby had not, in fact, answered his question.

The colonel was watching him. 'I have the feeling you're chasing shadows, Captain. Where's all this getting you?'

'Two Storm Wood was in British hands at the time of the killings. Did you know that?'

'No, I didn't. I guessed as much from the import of your questions.'

'Are you surprised?'

Ormsby took a sip of whisky. 'Disappointed. All in all, I've lost the capacity for surprise, when it comes to war.'

'What were Kelvin's grounds for accusing Colonel Rhodes?'

Ormsby lit a cigarette. Mackenzie recognised the crisp, nervous gestures: the hasty inhalation, the way the case snapped shut. A man kicking against his own insignificance. 'It went like this: some Frenchwoman – a prostitute, I expect – was assaulted by a Chinaman. I don't recall if she was violated or not. Frankly, if a whore . . .'

His voice trailed away for a moment, as if having second thoughts.

'Go on.'

'Well, by way of retribution, some of Rhodes's men abducted a bunch of coolies off the street – although one of them escaped. That's how Lieutenant Kelvin was able to identify the offenders as belonging to Rhodes's unit. He confronted Rhodes about it and came away less than satisfied. Apparently Rhodes was firmly of the view that the Chinese Labour Corps was full of criminals, and that only firm measures would keep them in check.'

'So Kelvin thought Rhodes was complicit?'

Ormsby twitched, spilling whisky onto his hand. 'Kelvin had this idea that the Chinks had been taken to please Rhodes. Like some sort of sacrificial offering. Ludicrous!'

261

Mackenzie watched the whisky run down Ormsby's knuckles. He didn't seem to notice it.

'What happened to the other man?'

'No one could say. Certainly Kelvin couldn't.'

'He suspected the man had been killed. Then Chen's body turned up, and he knew.'

'*Thought* he knew, Captain. Pure conjecture.'

'One death, one suspicious disappearance. It should have been enough for an investigation.'

'Not in the prevailing circumstances. That was Major General Crompton's view.'

'So you did nothing. The provost marshals' branch did nothing.'

'Consider it, Captain: no hard evidence, only the testimony of a coolie, doubtless cooked up as an excuse for being absent without leave. No realistic prospect of a successful court martial. Every prospect of disrupting a highly effective battalion in the midst of offensive operations – not to mention causing a panic that might undermine the effectiveness of the Chinese Labour Corps, and potentially force its withdrawal altogether.'

'Why wasn't Rhodes simply summoned to explain himself, if only to refute the allegations? If only to clear his name? Isn't that normal procedure?'

Ormsby shook his head. 'Too great a risk to morale. He was sure to take it badly. His *amour propre* was highly developed – that much we did know. He probably wasn't the sort of chap one wanted in one's club, to be candid, but his military record was exemplary. So was his battalion's. At a less critical time, things might have been different. But the priorities then ...'

Mackenzie looked into his empty glass. 'Another Chinese man was killed in Acheux a few days ago. Butchered, much like the others. However this began, it isn't over.'

Ormsby's breath came and went, marked by a thin, barely audible wheezing. 'Well, that's ... It only goes to show ...'

'Show what, sir?'

'Rhodes was injured months ago, badly. Evacuated to England. Thought unlikely to live.'

'Perhaps he recovered.'

'You can't seriously believe he's mixed up in all this.'

'Can't I?'

'Just because Lieutenant Kelvin is dead, just because he ... *suffered*, doesn't make his suspicions valid. Kelvin was a journalist by trade. He wrote stories for a living. As I understand it, he was turned down for a commission in the infantry, and no doubt resented it bitterly. Add to that a somewhat romanticised view of the Chinese under his command and you have a recipe for ...'

'For what, sir?'

'Fantasy. Dangerous fantasy. To go behind his commanding officer's back was outrageous. He was lucky not to be charged.'

Mackenzie looked up. An ugly thought had occurred to him: if Rhodes had exacted revenge on Lieutenant Kelvin, he must have learned about the allegations. Someone, most likely at Third Army HQ, had sent word. If so, that breech of military protocol had translated into a death sentence for thirteen men.

'You admired Rhodes, didn't you, sir?'

'I never met the fellow. I admired his record. Physically brave, tactically astute, exemplary in his gathering and use of intelligence. The sort you want on your side when you're out there on the front line. He had his critics, naturally. Strong leaders always do. But his men were devoted to him – and devotion, let me tell you, is not easily won. When his luck ran out, theirs did too.'

'Did you tell him about Kelvin, sir? Was it you who tipped him off?'

'That would have been quite improper, Captain. I did no such thing.'

Mackenzie was unconvinced. But then again, Ormsby's predecessor might have been the one responsible, or any number of headquarters staff – perhaps even Kelvin's CO, miffed at being circumvented by a junior officer.

'You said Rhodes had critics. Who were they?'

Ormsby pushed back in his chair. His gaze drifted towards the windows. Rain was beating against the glass. 'Do you know, Captain, I was nineteen years old when I saw my first battle? Well, it was more a skirmish, you'd say. That was more than forty years ago. But it left me in no doubt about the squalid nature of war, and since then I've never seen any reason to revise my opinion. Soldiering is admired because it's hazardous. But imagine if it wasn't. How would we soldiers be thought of then? As necessary, perhaps – the way butchers are. But I doubt if they'd pin medals on us.' He looked at Mackenzie. 'War is a contest of violence, not virtue. Like a force of Nature, it makes its own laws. Not everyone on the staff understands that. They define an ideal officer as one who follows King's Regulations at all times.'

'And Rhodes didn't?'

Ormsby smiled. 'Ill-considered orders had a habit of not arriving, so it was said. There were more troubling stories as well, I'll admit.'

'What kind of stories?'

'Regarding the treatment of prisoners. And then there was the suggestion that Rhodes was cultivating a following, replacing loyalty to King and Country with loyalty to himself.'

'Which would be treasonous, if it were true.'

'Perhaps so.'

'How did you learn about it?'

'Rumours, and letters home, of course. One of his company commanders had developed an opium habit, by the sound of it. He was less than discreet about Rhodes's style of leadership.'

Mackenzie frowned. 'Which company commander? You don't mean Captain Haslam?'

'Yes, Haslam. That *was* his name.'

Mackenzie got to his feet. He felt light-headed. For a moment he thought he was going to fall.

'Are you all right, Captain? You don't look entirely well.'

Ormsby's voice sounded far away, hectoring, clucking. Mackenzie wished he could shut him up, once and for all. So many honest men dead, and yet the old liar lived. Of course, if Rhodes had known about Kelvin, it was more than likely he knew about Haslam and his opium habit. Why wouldn't the sympathetic Colonel Ormsby have passed on that information too?

—— Thirty-eight ——

A day later Mackenzie was standing at the corner of the rue d'Albert, going through the burial lists with Lieutenant Harding. Harding's squad was trailing by on the road, making its way back to camp from Serre Road Cemetery No. 2. At the end of the war the plot had held four hundred and seventy-five graves; since then the number had swollen to seven thousand. Of these, nearly five thousand had no name. It was going to make a strange kind of graveyard, Mackenzie thought, so impressive and yet so incomplete.

One of the wagons was carrying a passenger.

'Major Westbrook?'

The provost marshal climbed down. Mackenzie was immediately struck by his ragged appearance: it looked like he hadn't shaved properly since their last meeting. Against the grey shadow, the scar tissue stood out all the more starkly. His eyes were bloodshot and puffy, as if he hadn't slept.

'I need to speak to Miss Vanneck.'

'She isn't here.' Mackenzie handed the lists to Lieutenant Harding. 'Give these to Corporal Reid, would you?'

Harding saluted and left. The last of the squad shambled past in silence.

'So where is she?'

'I couldn't say.'

Amy Vanneck was at that moment on her way to the Château de Naours, where her fiancé's friend Bill Egerton worked as a surgeon, but the provost marshal's brisk tone made Mackenzie wary. As he saw it, he had offered Amy his protection in so many words, and he was not about to renege on the commitment while his company remained in place.

'Is she coming back?'

'I'm not sure. We've had orders to move east. There's not much more we can do for her.'

'You haven't found her fiancé, I take it?'

'I'd have let you know if we had. You got my note?'

265

After his interview with Major Pickering, Mackenzie had felt obliged to share what he had learned with the provost marshal. Already he wondered if he hadn't been too hasty.

'That's why I'm here. Your information changes everything. You've done well.'

Mackenzie was not reassured. That Edward Haslam had played some role in the massacre had brought Amy Vanneck under the provost marshal's scrutiny again. Was that somewhere she wanted to be?

Westbrook looked back up the way he had come. The sun was a red smear on the horizon. He was shivering. It crossed Mackenzie's mind that he might be coming down with Spanish flu, except that flu victims turned blue within hours of the first symptoms, and Westbrook was deathly pale.

'Have you something to eat?' Westbrook said.

'Of course. Follow me.'

They made their way back into the village. The narrow road was rutted and deep in mud. Any more rain and it would flood completely.

Westbrook turned up his collar. 'Have you talked to her?'

'Miss Vanneck? We've had a few words.'

'What did she have to say?'

Mackenzie wanted to tell Westbrook to mind his own business – except that it was his business now. 'She had questions about the war, about what went on. She talked about her fiancé. She was clearly devoted to him.'

'Was?'

'What do you mean?'

'Are you sure that's all that brought her here? Devotion?'

It was love and it was guilt, a mix more potent than either by itself. But Westbrook did not need to know that. 'What else?'

'Perhaps she has special reasons for thinking he's alive.'

'Are you serious?'

Westbrook rubbed the back of his hand across his chin. Mackenzie did not like the menace in his voice. 'If she thought there was a chance he'd deserted – that he was hiding out here somewhere – then she might come, hoping he'd sniff her out.'

'That's preposterous. You think she's played us for fools?' Mackenzie shook his head. 'From what I hear, Haslam was a decent officer. Certainly not the type to run. It's a malicious rumour, nothing more – one Miss Vanneck's heard, unfortunately, but only a short while ago.'

'How did she hear it?'

'Some spiteful note turned up, unsigned. It gave her hope for a while, but there's nothing to it.'

'Did it say he was alive?'

'Something about a bordello in Paris, or Whitehall. Pure fantasy.'

'I'd like to see it.'

'The note? I told her to destroy it. I expect she has.'

The faintest of smiles formed on Westbrook's lips. 'You must care for her a good deal.'

'I certainly don't—'

'It doesn't matter. What matters is finding him.'

'Not likely, I'm afraid. His brigade was under attack when he went missing. The records are clear. Shelling on both sides. I expect he was blown to pieces.'

'Perhaps, perhaps not.'

'I don't think you understand.' It was maddening: Westbrook's reluctance to accept the only rational view. 'The idea that there's nothing left of a man – nothing to find, nothing to bury – it's very hard for a civilian to accept. It doesn't mean she *knows* something. It doesn't mean Haslam's alive. In any case, if he were alive, why would he stay around here where he might be recognised? He'd have to be insane to . . .'

Westbrook had fallen behind. He was looking back up the road again. On either side stood the blank brickwork of barns and stables. Mackenzie had been talking to himself.

'Is something wrong, Major?'

'Did you hear that?'

'Hear what?'

'A horseman. Out there.'

Mackenzie looked towards the edge of the village. He couldn't see anything. 'We should get a move on.'

'I saw him, on the road. Couldn't see his face, though. Keeps his distance, for now.'

Mackenzie offered no comment. He was not sure what to believe any more. Too long on the old battlefields and it became increasingly difficult to distinguish imaginings from reality. Hadn't he warned Miss Vanneck and her friend about that very thing? And then there was paranoia. It often went hand-in-hand with shell shock. Some men showed the first signs of it weeks or months after coming out of the line: a harbinger of complete mental collapse. Perhaps Two Storm Wood had reopened some old wounds, as it had with Sergeant Cotterell – Cotterell who had ended up cowering in corners, pleading with shadows.

'Do you really think Haslam's your man?' Mackenzie said. 'He's the butcher you're after?'

Westbrook touched at his shoulder. 'Your information ties him to the victims on the day they died. He's the reason they went forward to Two Storm Wood. Wasn't that your conclusion?'

'Yes, Haslam was the messenger, but—'

'His is the only name we have.'

'No, there's another. What about his commanding officer: Lieutenant Colonel Rhodes?'

Westbrook stopped. 'Rhodes?'

'I went to Third Army, checked up on Lieutenant Kelvin's allegations. I told you, he was exercised about the treatment of his men, even suspected murder.'

'You went to Péronne? Who did you talk to?'

'The deputy adjutant general, Colonel Ormsby. Apparently Kelvin singled out the Seventh Manchesters, and Colonel Rhodes in particular. He thought the killings were a kind of tribute – that Rhodes had inspired them in some way. It's clear he wasn't a conventional commanding officer.'

'Which you think counts against him?'

'I didn't say that. But Rhodes had a reputation for ruthlessness, and for requiring personal loyalty from his men.'

'Perhaps he gave loyalty in return. Perhaps that's why his men loved him. What exactly did Kelvin witness?'

'In person? By all accounts, nothing.'

'Then it's all speculation.'

'It gives Rhodes a motive for Two Storm Wood. What motive did Haslam have?'

Grimacing, Westbrook rolled his shoulder. Mackenzie heard something click.

'Who can say? A need to protect the honour of his battalion? Maybe he held a personal grudge. Kelvin was a combative sort, by the sound of it. Either way, we know Haslam was on the scene. We should put his name about now. Maybe somewhere there's a witness to what he did.'

It was getting dark. The end of the lane was lost in a blue haze. For an instant Mackenzie thought he heard the distant sound of hoof-beats.

'Rhodes should be questioned. He has to be.'

Westbrook shook his head. 'Colonel Rhodes is dead. Died of his wounds in England a few weeks ago. Haslam's all we have. Without him, we'll never know the truth.'

They were outside Mackenzie's billet. A handful of NCOs were brewing tea over a brazier, smoke billowing across the yard. Mackenzie sensed expectation in their murmurs, in the clink of the tin cups and the hiss of the coals. How many of them shared Westbrook's conviction? How many believed in Haslam, the sadist, the madman, the phantom?

'Haslam is dead,' Mackenzie said. 'I'd put money on it. How could you find him anyway? Too much time's gone by.'

Westbrook looked around the yard. 'There are still thousands of men working out here, Captain, men from every regiment, every brigade. Let them know who we're looking for, and why. That might smoke him out. Perhaps he won't like the idea of being blamed for Two Storm Wood.'

It would make a fine parting gift to Amy Vanneck, Mackenzie thought, blackening her fiancé's name with what remained of the British Army – when it was only a matter of days since he had insisted the man had nothing to be ashamed of.

'That's something you'll have to do for yourself. We've orders to pull out. Now, if you'll excuse me. You can get something to eat in the cookhouse.'

Westbrook grabbed Mackenzie by the arm, fixed him with his maimed stare. 'I still want to speak to Miss Vanneck. I think you know where I can find her.'

'I've already told you, I don't.'

Westbrook loosened his grip. 'There's no point trying to protect her, you know. You'd only be wasting your time. Captain Haslam is either a renegade or a dead man. Either way, I don't see a happy ending there, do you?'

Thirty-nine

The Château de Naours was hard to find. A long, low building two storeys high, it lay to the west of the village, surrounded by woods. From the lane, all Amy could see was a line of plane trees, at the end of which stood a pair of iron gates set in an ancient brick wall.

The gate was not locked. In a stable yard a French military ambulance stood waiting. Amy was halfway to the main house when a man with cropped white hair came hurrying round a corner, pulling on his jacket.

'*Attendez, attendez. Que voulez-vous, Madame?*'

He had to be the gatekeeper. Amy was conscious of her appearance: the tangled hair, the muddy dress, the broken nails and swollen hands. She explained that she had come to see Captain Egerton.

The gatekeeper was unimpressed. '*Vous avez le mauvais endroit, Madame.*' The way he said *Madame* was heavy with irony. He took her by the arm and forcefully led her back towards the gate.

'Please. He was a friend of my fiancé. He's a doctor here.'

Captain Mackenzie had given her the details. She and Egerton might share some reminiscences, he had suggested. That was the most she could expect.

'*Vous voulez un médecin? Allez à Amiens.*'

Amy pulled her arm free. 'I need to see Captain Egerton. I've come from England. My name is Vanneck.'

The gatekeeper frowned. Then the frown was gone. '*Ah, Monsieur Bill. Le médecin anglais.*' He turned, content now for her to follow. '*Je vais vous le chercher.*'

Steps led to the doors of the château. They were met by an old woman wearing the habit of a nun. One of her eyes was purplish-white, like the inside of an oyster shell, and had no pupil. She and the gatekeeper held a brief conversation over the threshold. After a few moments she closed the door.

'*Vous devez attendre ici,*' the gatekeeper said.

Amy waited at the bottom of the steps. Rows of tall sash windows looked down at her, shutters open but curtains half-drawn. Captain Mackenzie had explained that the hospital catered for men with facial injuries, men who often preferred not to be seen. She wondered how many they were, and if any of them were watching her at that moment.

The wind stirred in the trees. The château, like the village, had not been touched by the war, except that the grounds were untidy: the lawn overgrown, grass growing in patches on the paths, tall weeds obscuring the rose bushes. After a few minutes a man stepped outside wearing a white coat unbuttoned over a khaki uniform. He was tall, with deep-set, darkly shadowed eyes. The old nun watched from the doorway.

'Good morning.' He looked puzzled. 'I'm Captain Egerton. I'm sorry, I wasn't told your name.'

Amy hurried up the steps. 'Amy Vanneck. I'm Edward Haslam's . . .' She checked herself. 'I don't know if he ever—'

'Miss Vanneck. Yes, of course.' The stranger was staring, no doubt taken aback by her appearance. 'I'm sorry, I never expected . . .'

'Please call me Amy.' They shook hands. The gatekeeper grunted and headed back to the stable yard. 'I'm so sorry for turning up like this. I should have written. But I just learned you were here. I can come back, if you're busy.'

'There's no need.' Egerton said. 'What can I . . . ?'

She tried to explain calmly why she had come: in the hope that he could tell her about Edward's last few days and weeks, if he could shed any light on his disappearance. 'You're the only officer I've found who even remembers him. His battalion, most of them—'

'Yes, I know. The Seventh fared badly on the Hindenburg Line.' Egerton looked over his shoulder. 'Sister, would you tell Doctor Fabian that I'll have to consult him later? Explain that I have a visitor from England.' The old woman left. 'Would it be all right if we were to walk in the grounds, Miss Vanneck? The sisters aren't very keen on visitors, I'm afraid.'

They set off along a gravel path that skirted the building. Egerton's demeanour struck Amy as awkward, as if he wasn't sure what to make of her, or if he should be talking to her at all.

'Please forgive the way I look,' Amy said. 'I've spent quite a long time on the battlefield, close to where Edward went missing.' Egerton glanced at her, disbelieving. 'It's too far to go back to the town every day.'

'You weren't alone?'

'I had a friend with me, but she ... she had other obligations in England.'

All Egerton managed to say was 'I see.'

'From Edward's letters, I had the impression you saw quite a lot of him. Last summer, before ...'

'I wouldn't say a lot. We were in the same division, but different brigades. We only met up now and then, usually when we were in reserve, for a drink and so forth.'

'Weren't you one of his oldest friends?'

'I suppose I was. We lost touch after school, but it was good to meet up again, in spite of the circumstances.'

'Edward once said that whatever was on his mind, he could always count on you to understand.'

'That was kind of him.'

'I'm not sure,' Amy said, 'if he always thought the same of me.'

Egerton's face wore a pained expression. Perhaps, like so many men of his class, he was uncomfortable with any display of emotion and dreaded even the suggestion of it.

'Edward seemed different towards the end, you see. He wrote things in his letters – strange things.' Amy reached into her bag and took out Edward's last. 'Here, see for yourself.'

Egerton held up a hand. 'No, really, it wouldn't be right.'

'Please. Perhaps you can help me to understand.'

He took Edward's last letter and read it, frowning. They were standing at the far corner of the building, where the branches of a tall cedar brushed against the walls. Above them, on the top floor, one of the casement windows nudged open. Pigeons clattered up into the sky.

'Did he ever talk to you about this?' Amy asked. 'About these terrible dreams? I can't help thinking that he'd given up hope, that in some way he was trying to say goodbye.'

'Really, you mustn't ...' Briskly Egerton folded up the letter. 'You mustn't take this kind of thing at face value. Edward was just out of the fighting when he wrote this. I expect he was in a pretty black mood. We all had them. It's only unusual to see it written down.'

'He was all right then, when you saw him? His letters became ... I could sense that the war was overwhelming him, that he couldn't cope.'

'He showed some signs of strain – which was to be expected. Men find ways to deal with it. He had his.'

'In his last letter he said he thought you could help him sleep. What did he mean?'

Egerton hesitated. 'If I remember rightly, he was after sedatives: calm-the-nerves sort of thing. Quite common.' He handed the letter back, the action brisk, like a full stop. 'The fact is, for the thinking men – men like Edward – it was hardest: the realities of combat. If you can understand that.'

Amy carefully replaced the letter in its envelope. She felt the tears pricking her eyes. They would not help her. Egerton was uneasy enough, as it was. 'When I read that letter, I can see he's ashamed. In his dream the Devil's laughing at him. He's laughing because he's won.'

Egerton's hands were dug into his pockets. It was as if he wanted to comfort her, but couldn't. 'Whatever he was going through, you should not be in any doubt that Edward ... that he loved you. That I remember clearly. You were always in his thoughts. I think ... I think he measured himself against you, in everything. And that never changed.'

'This is the last letter I received. Whatever he was going through, he didn't feel able to share it, not with me.'

Amy kept her eyes on the ground. If she looked Egerton in the face, the tears would return. She busied herself putting the letter away in her bag. When she glanced up again she found Egerton's attention focused on the roof of the château. He seemed dismayed, disappointed. It could only be her questions, the pain she hadn't managed to hide.

'It was a very volatile time,' he said. 'The whole front was moving. And the division had been in the line a long time. The strain was ... I expect his letters went astray. Or maybe ...'

They were walking back towards the doors. The conversation would soon be over.

'Maybe what?'

'Sometimes thinking back to one's home, to one's loved ones, bringing it all back, it's too much. Too difficult. Like trying to live in two worlds at once. It can make it harder for a soldier to do what he has to.'

Amy stopped. 'Captain Egerton, did Edward ever talk to you about deserting? I've heard some rumours.'

Egerton turned. 'What rumours?'

'It doesn't really matter, I—'

'Who did you talk to?'

'Nobody. I received a note. Here.'

Another scrap of paper came out of the bag. This time Egerton read it without protest.

'Outrageous! You should destroy this at once.'

'That's what Captain Mackenzie said.'

'Captain Mackenzie?'

'He commands a labour company, clearing the battlefields. He says this is a slander, designed to drive me away.'

'I expect he's right. Please allow me . . .'

Before Amy could protest, Egerton had torn up the note and thrust the pieces into his pocket. Then he continued towards the door of the château and the safety of his patients.

Amy followed. 'But there has to be a chance—'

'There isn't, I'm sorry.' Egerton took a deep breath. This was hard for him. 'I was nearby when it happened, when Edward became a casualty. A surprise German attack at night, west of Serre. Our battalions were both in the reserve positions, next to each other. We sent companies forward to retake the trenches in front. I heard a report that Edward had been hit – quite reliable, I'm afraid. A mortar round. Someone else had to take over his company.'

'But . . .' Amy's head was swimming. The strength had gone from her legs. 'They said he was *missing*.'

'If he wasn't found later in the day, he would have been listed as missing. Or if his identity was lost for any reason. Or if he was misidentified. It was a frantic time: everything on the move – even the clearing stations and the hospitals. Record-keeping wasn't a priority, I'm afraid, and where there were records, they could easily go astray.'

'So you don't know where he is. You don't know where he died.'

'No one does. And the likelihood is no one ever will.' Egerton cleared his throat. 'So there's really nothing to be gained – and nothing to be learned – by your staying out here, in France. I wish there was something else I could tell you.'

They had reached the foot of the steps. Amy told herself to breathe, to stay calm. They had been telling her to give up, from the beginning. They had been telling her it was hopeless. What was one more voice, among so many?

'Thank you for seeing me,' she managed to say. 'I mustn't keep you from your work.'

She offered her hand. Egerton shook it.

'Goodbye, Miss Vanneck. I hope ...' He frowned. 'I hope the future is brighter for you.'

Amy walked away towards the gates, but she had only gone a few paces when she heard Egerton calling after her.

'Perhaps you could tell me where to reach you, in case I hear something more specific. In case ... in case something surfaces.'

Amy gave him the poste restante at Amiens and her aunt's address in Cambridge, feeling, as he hastily wrote them down, that his request was unexpected, and wondering what new information could possibly surface after what he had already told her.

———

Forty

Madame Chastain opened the door and stood back to let him in. He looked into her face for some sign that she was unhappy to see him again – frightened perhaps – but saw no emotion at all. 'Are you in pain?' she said, as he stepped into the hallway.

He nodded, although the pain that day was bearable. He had come because he could think of nowhere else to go. The hotel was cold and cheerless, and the strangers who passed him on the stairs or in the corridors were always careful not to meet his eye. Even without the *filles de joie*, the house off the chemin de Varennes felt further from the desolation of the battlefield – more like a home, even if it was not his own.

But things were not the same. Along one side of the hallway were items from the house, stacked up and ready to move: chairs, rolled-up rugs, piles of linen and books tied up with string. He had never noticed the books before.

'What is all this? You're leaving?'

Madame Chastain nodded. 'It is time.'

He thought better of arguing with her. Even if she managed to find more girls, without the presence of the army it would be hard to make a living. And that was if the civilian authorities did not shut her down. 'Where are you going?'

'To Normandy. It is not so far. But it is far enough.'

They climbed the stairs. On the landing above stood a washstand and jug and a stack of pictures propped up against the wall. His footsteps boomed on the bare boards. He had stood in many ruined houses, shell-blasted and bullet-ridden, and experienced nothing like the same sense of loss.

'How are you going to move all this?'

Madame Chastain sighed. '*Je ne sais pas.* I must find a wagon, and a horse.'

'Are you going alone?'

She opened the door of the salon and gestured for him to enter. Her gentle formality seemed to him like an echo from a past time. 'I have no choice.'

The furniture in the salon was where it had been, as if trying to make him welcome. Only the curtains were missing. He went to the window: a patch of pale sunlight drifted across the yard, but there was no horseman, no sign that anyone had followed him.

A gust of wind whistled over the crumbling walls.

Perhaps there had never been a horseman, except in his head. Sleeping, waking – it was getting harder to tell them apart. At times reality was unfocused, a film stretched over shifting depths, but then the present would snap back into place, raw and unforgiving. At the hospital the doctors had described the side-effects of opiates. He might hallucinate, they said. He might experience extremes of mood – panic, euphoria, dread. All things considered, it was to be expected that he should suffer a degree of disorientation and memory loss. It did not mean he was losing his mind.

But he felt afraid now: afraid of the horseman, of his own failing strength, of what awaited him at the end of his mission. Fear was a stone in his gut, growing colder, heavier. At night he had visions of sinking into the earth, with its undiscovered bodies and unmarked graves. He heard the screams of ghosts. Why now, when the Huns were long gone, when he had one enemy instead of thousands? In the war, within range of German guns, he had never experienced dreams like these. By day, the old battlefield worked on him differently, with its emptiness, its pitiless silence. It was the silence of abandonment, of men left behind – the dead and the broken.

Madame Chastain brought in the tincture, the sugar and the water. This time there was a dusty green bottle on the tray beside it.

'Cognac? I thought you'd run out.'

'This bottle I have many years,' she said. 'I forget it is there.' She poured out two glasses. 'But the Papine, this is the last. If you need more—'

'I don't *need* it.' He folded his arms. Without the fire, the room was cold. 'It helps, that's all.'

Madame Chastain expressed no scepticism. He liked that about her. Human fears, needs, desires – they were simply facts of life, like the landscape or the weather. Shame had no place with her, no traction.

She handed him a glass. The brandy was rich and strong, an old vintage. He had come to such pleasures late in life.

'When will you be done here?' Madame Chastain said. 'When will they let you go?'

'They?'

'The army.'

He smiled fleetingly. 'When I'm done here.'

'When the guilty ones are punished?'

'When the facts are known. It won't be long now. I see more clearly than I did when I was strong. I see the loathing.' He shook his head. 'I don't deal in judgement.'

Her dark eyes were downcast. Where had she come from, he wondered? Was Chastain even her real name? He watched her pour out a glass of water and open the tincture of opium, adding the drops one at a time. Soon the water had turned a golden brown. He finished the cognac.

'This place in Normandy, you have family there?'

'I went there one time, as a child. A holiday. I was happy.'

'So you don't know anyone?'

'It is what I want.' She tipped sugar into the glass and stirred it with a long silver spoon. 'They cannot hate me for what they do not know.'

'I suppose not. Then how will you live?'

'I will buy some animals. I will raise them. I will have the soil and the sky. I will make a new start. How do you say it: a clean stone?'

'A clean slate. You think that'll be easy?'

'No. It will be hard. But I am not afraid of work, are you?'

'No, I'm not afraid of work, honest work. There's nothing I'd like better in the world.'

'Then do it.' Madame Chastain picked up the glass. The tincture gave off a faint tarry smell. 'What keeps you here?'

———

He must have slept for a while. Through half-closed eyes he saw a room full of people: men in khaki and young women drifting in and out of his vision. He heard snatches of conversation, bright laughter, a moan. In a dream he saw

278

Eleanor on a couch, straddling a Chinese man, her dress and petticoats pulled up around her waist. This was the real reason she had left him, of course. He had been too naïve to see it at the time. The Orientals had wiles when it came to seducing women, so he had heard: tricks and seductions. It was the key to their fecundity. And weren't white women always preferred? What had Eleanor said about playing the game? He recognised the music on the gramophone: it was '*Le Temps des Cerises*'. The Chinese man looked at him and laughed, and then Eleanor laughed too. The whole room was laughing. He held a revolver in his hand, but it was heavy and he could not summon the strength to pull the trigger.

He opened his eyes and the brothel had become a ship, tilting slowly from side to side. He went to the window. The town had vanished. In its place there was only mud and wire as far the eye could see. Even the duckboards were gone.

He managed to sit up. His eyes would not focus and he had a bitter taste in his mouth. He needed something to take it away. He called to Madame Chastain, but she did not answer. He heard her voice downstairs: no girls, no alcohol, she was saying. Her *maison tolérée* wasn't open for business. But someone wasn't taking no for an answer. The door slammed. Something heavy – a kit bag or a suitcase – hit the paved floor.

He saw the sugar. It had been spilled across the tray. He dropped to his knees and lapped it up like a dog. Thirsty, he gulped down water from the carafe.

Footsteps on the stairs: another customer, or another dream. He hoped it wasn't a doctor. He had seen too many doctors. One of them had told him not to 'trust his feelings' for a while. It only occurred to him later, when he looked in the mirror, that the doctor was worried about suicide. What was his name? Price, was it?

He eased himself back on to the couch, only to find he was no longer alone. A man was standing beside him with his back to the light. It came to him that he should hide the bottle of tincture. He reached out for the bottle, but it wasn't there any more.

The man was turning it over in his hand. 'You have to be careful with the likes of this, sir.' The voice was a northerner's. His face was a blur of shadow. 'It'll scramble your brains.'

279

A joke, was it? A piece of shrapnel could scramble your brains too. The proof was right in front of him.

'Let not your heart turn to her ways,' the man said. 'Her slain are a mighty throng.'

'Proverbs, Chapter ... Chapter—'

'Seven.'

The northerner stepped closer. His clothes gave off a greasy, ferrous smell. It mingled with a fug of leather and wet straw. There was a tag on the shoulder of his tunic, white letters on red. It took an effort to focus. The letters spelled: MANCHESTER.

He rolled over onto his side, away from this man and his damned scripture. He was in no mood to be companionable.

'You came here to find someone. Isn't that right, sir?'

No need to reply. This was another dream. The northerner, like the horseman, did not exist. No need to worry about causing offence.

'You won't find him here, I don't think, sir.'

'Find who?' He did not want the man's opinion. What would it take to shut him up? A bullet perhaps? Could a bullet kill an imaginary man? 'What are you talking about?'

'We've been waiting for you. It's time.'

He glanced round, hoping to find that the northerner had disappeared, like Eleanor and her Chinese lover and all the people he had seen. But the shadowy bulk was still there, more solid than anything else in the room.

'What do you want?'

'We want to begin, sir. There's work to do, promises to keep. No more of this.'

The bottle was still in the man's hand. It had no business being there. He was not the one who had paid for it.

'Damn it, hand that ... I order you to ...'

He reached for the bottle. His arm felt heavy. The whole room was swaying. His fingertips brushed feebly against the glass.

'You remember me, don't you, sir?' the man said, but his voice was already far away.

———

When he opened his eyes again, he was alone. He looked at his watch, but the hands were too slender to read. The clock on the mantel was large and steady. It tick-tocked insistently in his head, loud enough that he wished it would stop. Four o'clock.

The bottle of tincture sat on the tray where Madame Chastain had left it. All around, the cushions and the throws were undisturbed. When he awoke he'd had the sensation of emerging from a crowd. In fact he had been alone all afternoon in an empty room – Madame Chastain's last customer.

What had become of her? He hoped she had gone out to buy food. Hunger was gnawing at his insides. Some more cognac would be welcome too.

He gulped down the last of the water. A thought, a memory, was pushing its way into his addled consciousness, like a voice shouting through a wall. Was it something he was supposed to remember? He closed his eyes and it was before him: the tunic, the shoulder tag, the word MANCHESTER.

He picked up the tincture bottle. It was *not* how Madame Chastain had left it. He pulled out the cork and turned it upside down. Not a drop was left.

He got up, steadying himself against the arm of a chair. His limbs were heavy. He went over to the window. Flecks of rain were falling against the sooty glass.

The soldier was standing at the far end of the yard with his back to the house. A few nights before – the night the interpreter had been killed – someone had been standing in the exact same spot: the same man, or another? He seemed to sense that he was being watched. He turned up his collar and walked out through the gates.

'You! You there!'

The window would not open.

Head swimming, he grabbed his coat and hurried onto the landing. He had to keep both hands on the rail to keep from falling down the stairs. He was almost at the bottom when he felt the stickiness on his palms. They were smudged with blood. His own blood? He looked for signs of a wound, but it was too dark to see. He felt no pain.

He pulled open the front door, saw a spray of blood across the inside wall.

'Suzanne?'

There was more blood on the skirting board and the wallpaper above. Still wet to the touch.

Three doors gave off the hall, all closed. The last had a smear of blood twelve inches above the handle. It was the door into the kitchen. He pulled it open.

She lay on her side, eyes open. A wide apron of blood was spread out across the flagstones. It had travelled the length and breadth of the room along the gaps in between them.

He knelt down. Her throat had been cut, the incision – a single stab – just wide and deep enough to sever the artery. A perfect trench-raid kill, harder to execute than the standard thrust beneath the ribcage, but quicker and quieter.

Let not your heart turn to her ways.

It was her blood he had smelled on the northerner, Madame Chastain's blood. He reached down and closed her eyes.

The drug weighed on him, fighting to keep him from the here and now. He urged himself across the yard and back onto the chemin de Varennes. On either side the houses swelled and twisted, as if being stretched on a frame. Acheux was a small town. The killer couldn't be far away.

The Webley was heavy in his pocket. The iron weight of it helped clear his mind. A shot to the head – simple, clean, final. The revolver was a weak compromise of a weapon, but he had always been blessed with an exceptional aim.

Madame Chastain had been his friend. She had cared for him, against all the odds. He saw now that it had been a kind of miracle – unexpected, undeserved. Now she was dead because of him: because he could not be allowed to leave, to take what she had offered him. The picture of her lifeless eyes filled him with rage, and the rage gave him strength. For the first time in days, he felt no pain.

The street was empty. His grip tightened on the Webley, his thumbs playing over the hammer. He longed to shoot, to experience the shock of energy, the power over life. He had missed that power. The soldier's lot was to be stronger than other men, and more circumspect. He took the gun out, let it rest against his side. In the ideal soldier, the impulse to kill was stronger than the impulse to live.

He looked over his shoulder. His heart jumped. He saw a flash of khaki. It was two hundred yards away, heading out of town, following the lane as it bent slightly to the east. After a few paces, it was gone.

He broke into a run. The rain masked his footfalls as he rounded the corner. Trees and bushes obscured his view. The choked ditches ran high with water.

The road turned south again, straightening out into empty fields, scarred with earthworks and traces of wire. No sign of anyone. He came to a stop, breathing hard. The rain ran into his eyes. He wiped them on his sleeve.

Up ahead he caught sight of a gap in the hedge. A narrow track ran over the ditch. He raised the revolver two-handed and advanced. The track was overgrown. Long stalks of grass crowded in from the sides and sprouted from the middle. As he drew closer he could make out hoof-prints in the mud.

At the end of the track, forty yards from the road, stood the ruins of a farmhouse. Trees nestled against the walls. The branch of an ash poked through the space where once there had been a window. No one had lived in the place for years.

He moved down the track, his footfalls cushioned by the grass. He was greeted by a stale smell of wood smoke, but it wasn't coming from the house.

The stables stood to one side. They looked habitable. A flight of wooden steps led up to a door on the first floor: a groom's quarters, in its day. A narrow window, still glazed, was set to one side. The door rocked noiselessly on its hinges.

We've been waiting for you. It's time.

He cocked the revolver and moved up the steps. They were loose and rotten, but quiet underfoot. Before the last one he stopped, trying to slow his breathing. *Open the door, take aim, fire.* Once it started, there would be no time to think. Like landing in a Hun trench, no room for thought or feeling. Action, only action.

He sensed movement, a subtle shift of weight somewhere on the other side of the clapboard wall. It would be dark in there, dugout-dark – best cleared with Mills bombs. But he only had the Webley.

One deep breath. He yanked open the door, stepped inside.

Take aim, fire.

Table. Upright chairs. A stove. On one of the tables a strange metal contraption like a giant sewing machine. He lowered the revolver. Nobody there.

He took a couple of paces. The machine had a large iron wheel at the side. It was not until he saw the pots of ink and the stacks of paper that he understood what it was. Some of the papers had already been printed. Crumpled copies lay scattered across the floor. In the dim light he read: *all men loyal and true shall rally to his flag. SOLDIERS! BE READY!*

His eye was drawn to something hanging on the wall: a cavalry sword, sheathed in a plain metal scabbard. He put down the revolver and drew out the blade. It was straight and true, polished to a shine: a weapon designed not for the cut, but for the thrust. He tested the end. A bead of blood welled up on the tip of his finger.

He extended his arm. The weapon was perfectly balanced, an extension of the body as natural as a limb. Light danced over the rippling steel. Holding it, he felt restored.

Newspaper cuttings plastered the wall: photographs, trophies. Faded headlines shouted at him from the shadows: VALIANT CAVALRY TURNS THE TIDE.

He stepped closer. Groups of officers and NCOs posed like schoolboys in orderly rows. THE HEROES OF BAZANTIN RIDGE. Mounted men in turbans, lances slung across their saddles, grinned at the camera. A German officer's cap hung from a nail, a bloody tear in the crown. HAND-TO-HAND IN BUCQUOY, LANCASHIRE MEN BREAK THE HUN. In every story he read the name of Rhodes: Captain Rhodes of the Deccan Horse, Major Rhodes of the Manchester Regiment, Lieutenant Colonel Rhodes, battalion commander of the valiant Seventh.

Something stirred beneath his feet. A gentle thud.

One photograph was bigger than the others. It had been cut from the *Pictorial Review.* An officer sat astride a black horse with a white star on its forehead. He was looking down at the camera, sword in hand: a handsome, clean-shaven man, eyes deep-set, the beginnings of a smile on his lips. No hint of a pose, no pretence. A picture of complete belonging. The photographer, the photograph, the readers of the *Pictorial Review*: they were all his. This was his war, his stage, made for him.

From beneath his feet came another thud – louder, angrier. He ran back down the stairs, still holding the sword. The stable door was shut. The noise on the other side grew more insistent: someone trying to break out, or break in.

He pulled back the door. A horse was tethered in the furthest stall. It jostled against its confinement, hindquarters knocking against the walls. A saddle lay waiting on a rack, polished, spotless.

The horse was powerful and tall: seventeen hands. Even in the stormy gloom, the white star on its forehead was bright.

———

Forty-one

At Sailly-au-Bois one of the horses pulled up lame and the carter would not risk the other any further. Amy walked the last two miles to Colincamps, her shawl pulled over her head, her clothes wet and heavy. No one passed her on the way.

She had thought to spend another night in Naours, where a small, half-timbered inn had reopened to civilian guests, but after the encounter with Bill Egerton, she had felt a need to go back.

Egerton's story should not have surprised her: Edward had fallen on the Serre Ridge, killed by a mortar round. It was a story that conformed with what she had been told before, except there was a difference: Egerton had spoken to witnesses, to Edward's comrades. Their reports could not be doubted, even if they were no longer alive to confirm them. The unyielding certainty of that fact drove Amy back towards the battlefields, as if Edward were still there, waiting for her. She felt the need to reassure him that she would not abandon him, even now.

Colincamps was deserted. Where the camp had stood there were now only wheel tracks, cigarette ends and scraps of rubbish. Captain Mackenzie's billet and the Company HQ stood empty. The only sign of life was a pair of civilians trying to repair a roof on the other side of the road.

Amy nodded to herself. She had been hoping for some company, for a chance to share what she had learned, for a little hot food – though she knew she had no right to them. But she was alone now. This was how it would be from now on. She was beyond the point where anyone could be expected to help her. The essential facts were known. To go on with the search, from cemetery to cemetery, from grave to grave, meant crossing a line from devotion to madness – and the mad were shunned, as if their affliction were catching, or their inner ruin too troubling to witness.

The rain ran down her face, carrying dirt and grit into her mouth. Standing outside Captain Mackenzie's old billet, her wet skirt flapping against her shins, she asked herself how long she would be able to endure, and how the end would come. Would she simply run out of money? Would her family take her away and lock her up? Or would she one day cease to care, to feel anything when she thought of Edward, his smile, his touch, his love? In which case, what feelings would she have left?

At the door of the farmhouse something caught her eye. A white envelope was pinned to the door, just above the latch. On the front she read the words: *Miss Amy Vanneck.* Across the bottom was written: *If uncollected, please deliver to POSTE RESTANTE, AMIENS.*

She pulled off her gloves and opened the envelope.

Dear Miss Vanneck,

As you know, my company has been designated a new sector on the Hindenburg Line. I have received orders to decamp with immediate effect. Our work on the Ancre is incomplete, but the passage of time and the shortage of manpower make it essential that other battlefields are subject to a preliminary search without further delay. I am confident further searches of the Serre Ridge will take place at a later date, and I will make it my business to inform you if anything of significance is found. In the meantime I must once again urge you to leave the old battlefields and find lodgings in Amiens or another town where you will be safe. I am truly sorry that our acquaintance must be cut short, and that our sudden departure makes it impossible to say goodbye in person.

There is something else you should know. In your absence, Major Westbrook came here asking for you. He has certain new information regarding Captain Haslam, which he wishes to discuss. I did not tell him your whereabouts, and he will be none the wiser, should you decide against seeing him. For what it is worth, I can see no value in raking over rumours and conjectures that your fiancé is not here to confirm or deny. But that must be a decision for you. Major Westbrook is still billeted at the Hôtel du Grand Cerf in Acheux.

I have taken the liberty of leaving certain excess supplies in my vacant quarters, in the hope that these may be of use. It is my hope that you will feel able to return to England soon, and that awaiting you is some part of the tranquillity you once knew. I also hope that we may meet again in happier circumstances.

Yours most sincerely,

Capt. James Mackenzie

Amy let herself into the stables. She found a neat pile of blankets on a table, under which lay several tins of bully beef, another of jam, a loaf of bread and a bottle of red wine. Her body ached for rest, but the thought that there was more to learn – that Major Westbrook had information he wanted to share – was like a spark in the darkness, a small, cold flame of hope. She could not ignore it.

All the same, that Westbrook had come looking for her made Amy uneasy. In the beginning she had thought it was only his appearance that made him frightening, her aversion being unworthy and unkind. But there was more to it than that. His forensic demeanour, so practical and direct, masked a soul in turmoil – a conflict she could perceive, but not understand. At moments she had wondered if he were truly in his right mind. And the way he had driven away that day, without a word, had done for any notion that they were friends. She wondered how he had come by his injuries, in what brutal fight. She wondered how he had taken to the business of war, and an instinct inside her said: *Stay away.*

She stood for a moment, staring out across the empty yard towards the farmhouse, abandoned, lifeless. Then she put the bread and the wine into her bag and walked out of the village on the road to Acheux.

———

—— Forty-two ——

Kent, England, March 1919

The telephone operator could not get through. Rather than wait for an exchange of letters, Sir Evelyn travelled down to Farningham by car, trusting to luck that he would be received. It wasn't that he was anxious to see Lieutenant Colonel Rhodes. The very thought of the man, his legendary bravery and ruthlessness, was unnerving. He was a man born to command, and yet so utterly different from those who *did* command, like Sir Evelyn himself – a fact that would be all too obvious to both of them. But a promise had been made, and Sir Evelyn had no intention of going back on it.

According to her friend, Amy had heard – she did not say from whom – that Edward Haslam was still alive and in hiding. There was even a suggestion that he had been taking secret orders from Whitehall before he disappeared. Amy wanted Sir Evelyn to find out if there was any truth to these rumours, any shred of hope. She was clutching at straws, almost certainly, but his own views on the matter were neither here nor there. Besides, Haslam's commanding officer had been highly unconventional, by all accounts: arrogant, brilliant, delusional, or some combination of the three. Was it possible the two men had come into conflict – a conflict so severe that Haslam *had* considered desertion? Could things have gone that far? But then, if Edward Haslam really was alive, what kind of existence would he be leading? What possible future could he offer Amy?

Sir Evelyn had written to the War Office, asking for help: had there been, he asked, any kind of trouble in the 7th Manchesters the previous summer, any hint of desertion or mutiny – anything out of the ordinary? He had been surprised when a note came back by return. It stated that the relevant files were 'confidential at present', and that it would not therefore be possible to answer his query. Sir Evelyn wrote again, this time to a personal contact in the financial secretariat. This yielded a solitary nugget of information: Haslam's commanding officer, Lieutenant Colonel Rhodes, was still alive and undergoing medical treatment at a military hospital in Kent. It was the only line of enquiry left.

The hospital was a large red-brick mansion hidden away behind tall, ivy-covered walls. A lake stretched away to the south. Sir Evelyn spotted a procession of men in wheelchairs being pushed around the grounds, taking advantage of a break in the weather. They wore their uniforms, with the occasional civilian addition of a scarf or a pair of mittens. Some distance away, rooks were nesting, their harsh calls echoing across the valley. In spite of its size, the place felt lonely.

Major Richardson, the hospital director, was a bald, bespectacled man close to sixty. He came hurrying down the stairs, struggling to do up the top button of his tunic.

'Sir Evelyn?' He held out his hand. 'The War Office said you might be coming, but they didn't say when.'

'I'm sorry. I tried to telephone.'

'Ah, a problem with the local exchange, I'm afraid. How can I help?'

'The War Office didn't explain?'

'They only said you were interested in one of our patients.'

'I am: Lieutenant Colonel John Rhodes.'

Richardson hesitated. 'Rhodes.' The name seemed to trouble him. 'Yes, I see. Perhaps you'd better ... Are you family, by any chance?'

'No. My concern is a matter of military record.'

'I see. My office is this way.'

In silence the director led Sir Evelyn through a series of narrow corridors to where an NCO sat typing at a desk. The building had an unappetising smell of boiled vegetables and bleach, but at least the patients were hidden away. He had no desire to meet their pitiful stares.

Major Richardson's office was a panelled room overlooking a walled garden. Tidy rows of vegetables were growing where once there would have been roses and lavender.

'I expect you'll want to see the colonel's file?' Richardson said.

Sir Evelyn was surprised. He had assumed that medical records were confidential, as in civilian life. But then this hospital was a military establishment, and no soldier was allowed to have secrets from the War Office. 'I'm sure that won't be necessary. I'd simply like to speak with him, with your permission.'

A look of confusion crossed Richardson's face. 'I'm sorry, but I'm afraid that's impossible.'

'Is he ... ? Has he succumbed to his wounds?'

'Not as far as I know.'

'Then ... ?'

'He isn't here, Sir Evelyn. You weren't told? We informed the War Office some time ago.'

'Then where is he?'

'I couldn't say. Please do have a seat. Let me take your coat.'

A pair of leather-bound armchairs stood opposite the window. Sir Evelyn sat down. The portrait of a grand lady in a green ballgown stared down at him from above the fireplace.

'He left some weeks ago,' Richardson said, 'of his own accord. Simply vanished. We've had no word of him since.'

'I thought he was badly injured. Near death.'

'He was. He was hit by a grenade at close quarters. But that was last autumn. He underwent a series of operations, all quite successful. I attended some myself, as a matter of fact.'

Sir Evelyn nodded on cue. 'I hear you're doing some remarkable work here,' he said, although he had not, in fact, heard anything.

Richardson had been hovering around his desk, as if unsure whether to sit down or not. The compliment seemed to make up his mind. 'Physically, his convalescence was excellent.'

'Physically?'

Richardson pulled up a chair. 'His mental state was harder to read.'

'Did he suffer brain damage?'

'We were trying to establish that, when he disappeared. His essential brain function seemed unimpaired. There was certainly some memory loss – entirely to be expected with head injuries – but beyond that ... Let's just say, there was cause for concern. In any event, we'd not planned to discharge him for a good while. It seems he took matters into his own hands.'

Sir Evelyn suppressed a shudder. Colonel Rhodes convalescing in a hospital was one thing; Colonel Rhodes at large, whereabouts and intentions unknown, was another.

'If I could find him, would he talk to me?'

'I see no reason ...' Richardson's expression darkened. 'He could be unco-operative. He also exhibited a degree of suspicion towards the War Office and authority in general. So ... I couldn't promise.'

'You said something about memory loss. When it comes to the war, are his recollections clear?'

'For the most part. He struggled to remember names, as I recall.' Richardson frowned. 'I think it would be best if you talked to Captain Price. Psychiatric matters are an interest of his. I'm a surgeon, as you know – cranial work. Price is your man.'

Before Sir Evelyn could stop him, Richardson had sent the NCO to find his colleague. When he returned to the office, he had a slender green folder under his arm. Sir Evelyn was on the verge of excusing himself. If Rhodes's where-abouts were unknown, there was nothing to be gained from investigating his mental state.

'Yes, paranoia,' Richardson said, looking over the contents of the file. 'That was the first red flag. Rhodes told the nurses that his injuries had been inflicted by a traitor.'

'A traitor? Why would he think that?'

Richardson frowned. 'I don't think he had a reason.'

'Didn't anyone ask?'

'We humoured him, of course: asked why anyone would want to kill him – besides the Germans, of course.'

'And?'

'He said he planned to find out. We left it at that.'

Sir Evelyn remembered what Amy had heard in France: rumours that Edward Haslam had been taking secret orders from London. If the rumours were true, what exactly would those orders have involved? Haslam had pros-pered under Rhodes's command. He had risen rapidly to command a company of his own, advancement that would surely have been earned. There could have been no greater mark of trust.

Richardson sat back in his chair. 'An irrational sense of persecution, it's not unheard of in cases like these, especially if combined with shell shock. In the end we decided to move him onto a busier ward, give him some companions to talk to – Captain Price's idea, and it seemed to work, after a fashion. He struck up a friend-ship with another patient, though it was more a case of listening than talking.'

Sir Evelyn's gaze drifted towards the window. The more he heard about Rhodes, the more difficult it became to picture him, to pin him down. Nothing about the man was ordinary. If the same singularity had extended to his subordinates – to Edward Haslam – then anything was possible.

'Things started going downhill again after his last operation,' Richardson went on. 'The shock of his altered appearance, I think, was profound. Sadly, it seems his fiancée had much the same reaction.'

'Rhodes was engaged? I'd no idea.'

'They seem to have kept a low profile. Some issues of station, I believe, not to mention ...'

'Heritage?'

Richardson nodded gratefully. 'A touch of the tar brush' was the expression Sir Evelyn had heard bandied about the ministry, although, as far as he could tell, there was no evidence that Rhodes was of mixed race.

'In any case, the young lady broke it off.' Richardson wrinkled his nose and sniffed. 'Of course, one mustn't judge.'

'Unfortunate. Was Colonel Rhodes very ... ?'

'Hard to tell. He never talked about the girl, never talked about England, either – or India for that matter. All he talked about, if he talked at all, was the battlefield, the front. In his mind, that's where he was. Understandable, I suppose, after so long.'

'I expect he was concerned for his men.'

'Yes,' Richardson said, but with an unmistakable lack of conviction.

'Why did he leave? Have you any idea where he went?'

'I'm afraid not. Some inner crisis brought it on, no doubt. As I say, there was the contretemps with his fiancée. And then his companion on the ward, the one I mentioned, he died quite suddenly. That might have been the trigger.'

'Is it possible he returned to France?'

Richardson took off his spectacles. The idea was apparently new to him. 'Well, it couldn't be ruled out. Rhodes has very little by way of family in England. He started out in the Indian Army. Fancied himself in the Guards, I gather, but couldn't land a commission.' There came a knock at the door. 'Ah, that'll be Captain Price.'

Richardson's colleague was ten years his junior, a small, cave-chested man whose uniform hung off him like an older brother's hand-me-downs. He smiled as he shook Sir Evelyn's hand, brushing at the hem of his tunic as if trying to iron out the creases.

'Sir Evelyn has come about Colonel Rhodes,' Richardson said.

'Have you found him?' Price asked, seating himself in the other armchair.

'I wasn't aware that he was missing until now.'

'We've notified the War Office,' Price said, 'and his regiment, and the police, just in case.'

'In case what? Why the concern?'

Richardson folded his arms. 'Captain Price thinks Colonel Rhodes has some long-standing neuroses. The normal restraints, compunctions, they couldn't be counted on. Is that fair, Arthur?'

Price nodded. 'This is a man inured to violence, and in his present state of mind – the paranoia, the talk of betrayal – I believe he's quite capable of it.'

Sir Evelyn frowned. 'A soldier, capable of violence? What use would he be, if he wasn't?'

'This is different. He may seek out violence because he needs it.'

'Needs it?'

'As a form of affirmation. Violence, in some cases, becomes bound up with self-esteem – an expression of power, if you like. And, due to his injuries, it's likely Colonel Rhodes's self-esteem is at a very low ebb.'

Sir Evelyn was unfamiliar with Price's language, but the dubious message was clear: the hero of Bazentin Ridge was mentally unbalanced – and dangerous.

'If you were so sure of this, why didn't you place him under guard? Why was he allowed to simply—'

'He showed no sign of wanting to leave,' Richardson said. 'Besides, Captain Price's ideas were entirely conjectural at that stage.'

'And now?'

The two doctors looked at each other. In the end it was Richardson who spoke. 'We were recently forwarded some correspondence from Rhodes's old tutor, a Dr Blake. It seems he wrote to the War Office several years ago.'

'To no effect,' Price added.

'Rhodes was educated at home for most of his upbringing, outside Calcutta. We knew something of his history, of course, but there was a lot we didn't know. It's not what you'd call a happy story.'

'Go on.'

294

It was starting to get dark. Richardson turned on a reading lamp. The desk was bathed in yellow light. 'John Rhodes's parents were missionaries. You knew that?'

'They were both killed, so I heard, when they were out in India.'

Richardson shook his head. 'Not in India, Sir Evelyn. They died in China. It was a couple of years before the Boxer Rebellion proper – one of the first attacks on Christians.'

'They were hacked to pieces,' Price said, 'literally. People avoided talking about it afterwards, but Rhodes's uncle apparently said it was a very gruesome business.'

'The kind of thing the Chinese do well,' Richardson said. 'Bloody savages.'

'And that wasn't even the worst of it.'

'How could anything be worse than that?' Sir Evelyn said.

Price braced himself against his knees, as if the painful memories were his own. 'From Rhodes's point of view, only this: he may have been the one who actually killed his father. Reportedly, when the Chinese broke into the compound, Rhodes's father told him to run and fetch his revolver. In his panic, Rhodes opened fire on the rebels. Eleven years old. Terrified out of his wits. Certainly not a steady hand.'

Sir Evelyn closed his eyes. 'He shot his father.'

'Yes, and nobody else. The way his tutor heard it, the rebels thought it was the funniest thing they'd ever seen. They fell about laughing.'

Sir Evelyn cleared his throat. He wished he was back in London, in the safety of his house or his club, far away from this clinging darkness. He wished his niece was there too. 'At least they didn't kill him,' he said.

Price shook his head. 'No, they let him wake up to what they'd done, to their handiwork. I'm not sure that wasn't worse. Dr Blake didn't go into details, but he did refer to certain barbarous practices in China, tortures reserved for traitors and the like: flaying alive, partial dismemberment. Rhodes may have seen the results, if not the execution. After that, he was removed to the care of his uncle in Delhi, along with his infant brother.'

Sir Evelyn swallowed. 'It's an awful story. I assume there's more.'

Price nodded. 'At his uncle's, the older boy's behaviour took a troubling turn: torture of animals, a decidedly unhealthy fascination with vivisection. Boarding school was out of the question. In any case, after all that had happened, John's uncle was determined to keep him close. So the tutor was sent for, all the way from Oxford. For the rest of his formative years it seems Rhodes was in good hands. Unfortunately the damage had already been done.'

Richardson took some papers from the file and handed them to Sir Evelyn. 'Dr Blake – he was back in England by this time – wrote to the War Office to warn them that John was mentally unstable and should, on all accounts, be kept out of the army.' There were three letters, more than a dozen sheets of pale-blue paper, covered on all sides with meticulously tidy handwriting. 'Obviously, claims like that have to be backed up. So Dr Blake went into considerable detail.'

'Not that it did any good,' Price said.

'Rhodes proved an outstanding officer,' Sir Evelyn said. 'He ended up commanding a battalion and was probably destined for the General Staff. This Dr Blake was clearly worried about nothing.'

Richardson held up his hands. 'Captain Price was speaking from a medical standpoint, Sir Evelyn – from the standpoint of the patient, not the war.'

This time Price did not endorse the director's words. 'Rhodes was still a child, in India, when he began to display what we would call psychotic behaviour. A young servant almost lost an eye. It's all in the letters. If he hadn't been out in India, it's more than likely he would have fallen foul of the law. The way I see it, there was a struggle going on inside him between the child raised by God-fearing Christians and the child traumatised by exposure to extremes of violence.'

'Dr Blake was clearly a very decent sort,' Richardson said. 'Fond of his old pupil. I think he was trying to keep him from harm when he wrote those letters. He believed Rhodes was moral at heart. But the events in China had unleashed forces within him that no amount of distance and tranquillity could banish.'

Sir Evelyn found he resented the easy way these men of medicine pronounced on the inner workings of their subject. 'I'm not surprised the War Office took all this speculation with a pinch of salt,' he said, 'if you'll forgive me.'

'I think there was more to it than speculation, Sir Evelyn, regrettably.' Price sighed. 'When he was fourteen years old, John Rhodes started receiving letters from one of the British territories in China. His servants found them hidden under his mattress. They were in English but unsigned. They taunted the boy for cowardice, for not avenging his parents' death – described their fate in the most lurid terms and then spelled out the appropriate retribution.'

'Retribution?'

'Torture, mutilation. The stuff of nightmares. Rhodes's tutor questioned him about the letters, about who could have sent them. He was shocked that the boy could have been exposed to anything so hateful. But Rhodes appeared to know nothing about them.'

'He didn't know who'd sent them?'

'No, he claimed not to have *seen* them before. He was oblivious to their very existence. And he was telling the truth, as he saw it. His tutor was quite sure about that. Why would he lie when he wasn't at fault?'

'Troubling certainly,' Sir Evelyn said. 'I don't see what it proves.'

'It proves nothing. But that wasn't the end of the matter. Some time later, the envelopes were examined more closely. The postmarks, it turned out, weren't from China at all. They were from the local post office in Calcutta.'

'I don't understand.'

'Rhodes wrote the letters,' Price said. 'He wrote the letters and posted them to himself. Such a fragmentation of consciousness is an indication of deep disturbance, not the kind that simply goes away.'

'But in the war Rhodes served with distinction, and bravery.'

'The war might have suited him, Sir Evelyn,' Price said. 'In war, violence and retribution are rewarded, provided they're directed at the enemy. Peace, on the other hand, offers him very little, especially now: disfigured and doubtless in pain.'

Sir Evelyn got to his feet. 'He should be found, then. He must have had some notion of where he was going. Unless he's wandering the countryside.'

'We did search the vicinity,' Richardson said, 'with the help of the local constabulary.'

'You mentioned a brother. Have you—'

'We don't even know his name. Certainly the War Office has no information. But we think Rhodes had a plan of sorts.'

'People talk over their plans. What about this friend he had on the ward? You said they talked for hours.'

'Indeed. It's quite possible he shared his thoughts with Major Westbrook, who could have been very useful to us. He was a Scotland Yard detective before he joined up, regaled us all with some fine case-histories. Unfortunately, as I said, Major Westbrook is no longer with us. He died of a stroke.'

'Rhodes vanished soon afterwards,' Price said. 'It's possible he stole Westbrook's uniform, and his effects, because we never found them.'

———

Vortex

—— Forty-three ——

France, August 1918

Edward Haslam felt something on the back of his hand: a solitary ant was crawling over his knuckles. He looked down: more ants, fat and black, were climbing up the side of the shaving bowl. A handful were already drowning in the soapy water. He caught movement in his peripheral vision, turned: beside him the wall of the trench was coming alive. Thousands of the insects were pouring out of it. They teemed around his feet, glistening like oil. He shuddered. He had seen such things in his dreams: the battlefields infested, heaving, sated on flesh. But he was awake now. He dropped the razor. The creatures were teeming over his skin, under his uniform, on his legs, his arms, his neck, their pincers hungrily probing, stabbing. They were in his ears and his nose. He clawed at his face, tore off his jacket, tried to brush his skin clean – seeing, understanding in the same moment that the insects were not there. A handful were floating dead in the shaving bowl, that was all. And yet when he closed his eyes he could feel them still, a voracious insect army, intent on stripping the flesh from his bones. He stood staring at his naked arms, trying to force the illusion from his mind.

He might have been steadier if it hadn't been for the lack of sleep. But they had been in the line for ten weeks – far longer than usual – and his supply of laudanum was completely exhausted. As for the forced-march pills that he always took before raids and patrols, he was down to his last handful. Cocaine for action, and opium for calm: he had learned to balance the two, spacing out the highs and lows, establishing a rhythm that his body and mind had come to rely on, a narcotic shield that made it possible to function. With the right help, he could appear in control, normal – as much as could be expected from an officer with his reputation, an officer with an unusual appetite for the kill.

But now he was out, and until they were relieved – until the whole brigade moved to the rear where the sellers operated, in the brothels and the estaminets and the officers' clubs – there was little hope of resupply. He thought he could hide the craving, but he was not prepared for what followed: smarting eyes, stomach cramps, bouts of nausea, pain in his joints so bad that at times he found it hard to get up. Parkes, his batman, had asked if he was ill. Haslam had said it was a touch of summer flu, that he was over the worst. Even if Parkes believed him, it was only a matter of time before the secret was out. And then what? Rhodes would take a dim view of an officer resorting to such props. He would see it the same way the men did: as a sign of weakness, a betrayal. Haslam had written to Bill Egerton, dropped him a hint a mile wide, but like the Chinese who worked the small towns to the west, he and his supplies of morphine were out of reach until the order came to withdraw.

Haslam splashed his face and neck with water, trying to clear his head. The afternoon was humid, tall clouds gathering on the horizon, the atmosphere charged and heavy. In two days it would be their turn to man the front lines again and continue the push – another chance to fulfil the divisional motto and *Go One Better*, another chance to add to his tally of kills. He let the water run down his face as the thought sank in: he would not survive another attack in his current condition – not unless he hung back, kept himself safe, let his men do the dying instead. He thought of Amy receiving the news, and a pang of guilt went through him, one sharper than the prospect of death.

Inside the dugout his batman was ready with his revolver and his Sam Browne. 'Anti-gas drill in ten minutes, sir.'

Haslam took a deep breath. 'Thank you, Parkes.'

'Will that be all, sir?'

'Yes, thank you.'

'Promised one of the lads some help with a letter, you see, sir.'

Haslam frowned. Parkes had no need to explain himself. 'Fine. Dismissed.'

Parkes saluted and left. Haslam buttoned up his tunic and went to collect his helmet. Tucked behind the inside band he found a slip of paper covered with writing. He carried it over to the lantern. The hand was tidy but over-sized, like a child's. Haslam recognised the words. They were from the Epistle of St Peter:

Be sober, be vigilant; because your adversary the DEVIL, as a roaring lion, walketh about, seeking whom he may DEVOUR.

He left the dugout, still holding the paper. The distant thump of guns studded the air. His stomach squirmed. His secret was out. It had to be that.

'Parkes!'

Perhaps his batman could tell him who had left the message. But Parkes did not answer.

'Damn it, where are you?'

If he let the matter go – a blatant challenge to his authority – he was finished. Everyone would know the story was true: Captain Haslam was a useless addict.

He marched off towards Battalion HQ, ignoring the men assembling for drill behind Mark Copse. He arrived as Rhodes was returning at the head of a scouting party. He made a point of exploring the surrounding country in person, even when in reserve, as if it were his personal estate. It was a hallmark of his command, a facet of his genius – or so Haslam had always believed. In his current state, with his current needs, he found it hard maintaining faith in anything.

'Captain Haslam, just the man.' Rhodes was red-eyed and out of breath, though it detracted nothing from the air of purpose that made instant followers of ordinary men. Haslam was relieved to observe no obvious disdain. 'Huns left us a present in an old support line.' Rhodes pulled a trench map from his coat pocket. A black square had been drawn on one of the dotted red lines that indicated redundant earthworks. 'This is the place. A dugout at Two Storm Wood.'

'Booby-trapped, sir?'

'Big stockpile of Yperite. One direct hit and we could have a gas cloud the size of Paris.'

The way Rhodes spoke, there was something stagey about it, as if he were acting the part of a British commanding officer. Still, it wasn't like him to exaggerate. The Epistle of St Peter would have to wait.

'I'll organise a working party, sir.'

'No. Those shells could be leaking or unstable. I want the Labour Corps to handle it.' Fighting men were always worth more than any other kind. Rhodes would risk them in battle, but nowhere else. 'There's a Chinese company restoring a railway line from Acheux, the One Hundred and Twenty-fifth. We haven't time to go through the Commandant of Labour. We need those shells cleared tonight, before we move up to the line.'

'Did you say the One Hundred and Twenty-fifth, sir?'

'Yes. Their CO's a Major Pickering. Labour Corp bureaucrat, best ignored. There's another man we should talk to, an Australian. He'll help us, I'm sure.'

Haslam was not listening. In the 125th was a Chinese cook called Chang. Haslam had bought tincture of opium from him in Contay on his way up to the line. Chang Ju Chih. He made a mental note of all such transactions: the name, the time, the place. It was not strictly rational, but he felt more secure, having the list of sources in his head.

'His name's Kelvin – Lieutenant Kelvin.'

'Kelvin, sir?'

'You know the man?'

'No, sir.'

'He's their best, I've heard. Should be in the infantry.' Rhodes seemed to know a lot about the One Hundred and Twenty-fifth, but then his hunger for local knowledge had never been confined to the terrain. 'Our kind of officer. Send your best man to talk to him, bring him back for a dekko, see what he thinks. Lieutenant Hadfield might be the man for the job.'

Haslam saw his chance. 'Perhaps I should take care of this myself, sir.'

'You?'

'The company can manage without me for an hour or so. The extra rank might carry a little more weight, sir.'

Rhodes studied Haslam for a moment. 'Yes, I suppose it might at that.' He handed Haslam the trench map. 'Remember: get Kelvin. Don't take no for an answer. We need this done.'

Haslam found the Chinese to the south of Colincamps. The clank of their iron tools could be heard from half a mile away. Six hundred men toiled in teams, levelling the ground, unloading sleepers and rails, levering and hammering them into place. A small locomotive stood at the end of the finished track, its funnel smoking, its wagons fully loaded.

He walked along the track, hoping for some sight of Chang, but his memory was hazy, and it was far from certain he would recognise the man, even if he found him. Haslam went slowly, studying each face in turn, hoping that he might himself be recognised, that Chang might spot him and understand what he had come for. The craving gnawed at him with every step.

Two hundred yards on, a small crowd had gathered. Haslam did not see the officer until he was almost beside him. He was organising the evacuation of two men on stretchers. There had been an accident: broken bones, crushed limbs. One of the Chinese sobbed like a child as he was loaded onto the back of a cart. The officer gave orders in Mandarin and the cart rolled away. Haslam wanted to keep hunting for Chang, but it was too late.

'Can I help you, sir?'

Reluctantly Haslam returned the officer's salute. 'I'm looking for Lieutenant Kelvin.'

'That's me.'

Haslam had expected an imposing figure, but Kelvin's build was slight. He had sunken cheeks and wore spectacles.

'Captain Haslam, Seventh Manchesters. We're in reserve below the Serre Ridge.'

'Yes, I know, sir.'

The Australian's tone was wary, almost hostile. It did not bode well.

'We've found a big store of gas shells in an old German dugout. We need it cleared.'

Kelvin volunteered nothing.

'So can you help us?'

'We're at full stretch on the railway. Our orders are to finish it quick as possible, sir. You'd have to talk to Major Pickering. He's back at camp.'

Haslam remembered Rhodes's orders: *Don't take no for an answer.*

'Look, the Huns could target this dump at any time.' He pulled out the trench map. 'There'll soon be thousands of men moving through this area, day and night. If—'

'If the shells are deep in a dugout, sir, that'd be the safest place for them.'

'That depends on the state of the dugout. This one's old. Can you come and take a look at least? Work out what we'd need? Then we can clear it with your CO.'

Less than a mile away a British field battery opened up. All down the line, the Chinese looked up from their work.

'I appreciate it's a little dangerous.'

'That's not the point,' Kelvin said. Haslam had struck a nerve, as intended. 'We have our orders: the railway's the top priority.'

The Australian wasn't inflexible, he was scared. How could Rhodes have got it so wrong? Haslam looked back up the line: in the distance, partly hidden on low ground, he could make out the conical tents of the Chinese camp. Wisps of white smoke were rising from a fire.

'Your men don't work in the dark, do they, Lieutenant?'

'No, sir. Of course not.'

'Then you could come with me when they're done for the day.' He handed Kelvin the trench map, as if to seal the arrangement. 'Major Pickering couldn't object to that, could he?'

———

It was evening when Haslam returned to the railhead. In his pocket were two bottles of Papine. At least, that was what the labels said. Both the paper seals had been broken, and it was all too possible that Chang had diluted the contents – with what, Haslam did not want to think. The cook was a sly, hard-faced man, the kind you did not want to cross. He claimed the bottles were his last, and charged a hundred francs for each – three times the old price. Haslam had paid up without complaint. Now the flat bottles were in his trench-coat pocket with his fingers wrapped around them.

Kelvin was waiting for him with twelve Chinese labourers. Swarthy, strongly built men, they carried tools and wore their coats slung over their shoulders. Several sported tattoos on their sinewy forearms.

'A lot of men for a dekko, Lieutenant.'

The Australian shrugged. 'We might manage some temporary measures, sir, if they're needed.'

'Good thinking.' Haslam was relieved that the Australian was not going to need more persuading. The sooner the job was done, the sooner he could give his body what it needed.

On the horizon, muzzle-flashes dimly flickered in the haze. Sporadic shelling was going both ways, deterring supply and reinforcement, the intensity building. Rhodes had said the Huns weren't up to a major counter-attack, and he was never wrong about such things.

'Let's get moving then.'

They travelled for a mile along the old road, then turned north towards La Signy Farm, where an incline would hide them from any spotters on the Serre Ridge. Haslam watched the Chinese for signs of fear or protest, but saw none. They shuffled along in silence, heads bowed, seemingly preoccupied with where to put their feet. In his pocket the bottles were solid and heavy, impatient for use. He found himself trying to calculate how long it would be before he could dose himself; how long it would take to reach Two Storm Wood on foot, assess the situation and get back to his battalion. If the removal operation started that night, it might be hours before he could get away. And each hour would feel like a week.

His limbs began to shake, then cramp. The sweat was pouring off him, running into his eyes, down his cheeks. He could not stop thinking about the laudanum. A few drops in a cup of water and all the pain would be gone. The craving churned inside him. It circled his chest and squeezed so that it was hard to draw breath. The bottles clinked together as he stumbled on, promising to set him free.

At the end of Southern Avenue, a few yards from the reserve line, it came to Haslam that he could not hold out any longer.

He turned to Kelvin. He was glad of the twilight. 'I have to check in with my company. Wait here. I won't be long.'

Before the Australian could protest, Haslam had gone around a traverse and was running towards his dugout. In the distance he could hear the roll being called. It meant the dugout would be empty – not even Parkes to worry about.

Below ground a handful of lanterns, turned down low, glowed in the musty darkness. He found a china cup and tried to fill it from his canteen, but the canteen was empty. He threw it aside, found a mess tin with a finger's worth of tea at the bottom. It would have to do.

His bed was a stack of pallets along the far wall. He sat down, unscrewed a bottle of Papine and poured out a large dose. The bitterness almost made him retch, but he kept drinking, dousing the craving, emptying the mess tin in five long gulps.

He closed his eyes and waited for the calm to reach him. In a few moments his insides began to relax. A flood of warmth spread outwards from the pit of his stomach. He was no longer shivering. When he breathed, he felt the cool air flow deep into his lungs. He took off his helmet and lay back, stretching out his legs. His muscles relaxed. He was stronger, lighter – almost at ease. He thought of Amy. He could picture her face more clearly this time: her smile, her voice. He could hear her sweet laughter. What was it that had made her laugh? Was it something he said? He allowed himself to daydream, to taste for a moment what had once been his.

He closed his eyes.

———

In a dream, he heard Amy scream. She was kneeling on the ground, tearing at the earth with her bare hands. He woke up suddenly and squinted at his watch. An hour had gone by since he had left Lieutenant Kelvin and the others at the end of Southern Avenue.

He grabbed his helmet and ran out of the dugout, ignoring Parkes and a pair of NCOs playing cards at the table. He found Southern Avenue deserted. Kelvin and his men had left.

A sentry was watching from the fire step opposite. A full moon hung low in the eastern sky.

'Twelve coolies and an officer. I left them here. Have you seen them?'

'Damned nearly shot 'em, sir.' The sentry said. 'Didn't know the password.'

'And? Where are they now?'

The sentry jabbed a thumb towards the front lines. 'Gone forward, sir. More than half an hour ago. Somethin' about gas shells, the officer said. A likely story, I thought, but then he said it were your idea, sir.'

Haslam turned again towards Serre. Flag Avenue ran north-east across the old battlefield. It was six foot deep, but only wide enough for one man to pass. His head felt clearer than it had for days. The laudanum had bought him time. Completing his mission would buy him more – but now, out of nowhere, he had doubts. *A likely story, I thought*, the sentry had said, and with reason. Why would the Huns keep gas shells so near their front line? The artillery that fired them would have been at least seven thousand yards to the rear. Come to that, why did it have to be Lieutenant Kelvin who dealt with them? Nothing about the Australian seemed exceptional. How did Rhodes even know his name? Maybe it was the laudanum, or the note in his helmet, but the whole business felt odd. Rhodes, Haslam felt sure now, could have told him more than he had.

The comms trench petered out in the belly of a wide crater. Rusty bullet casings lay all around, marking a spot where a machine-gun had once been deployed. Haslam climbed up the far side and moved swiftly across the open terrain. The chalky soil was pale in the moonlight, the remains of old wire black like shadows. He kept his torch off, relying on the light from the sky. Up ahead, a line of shell-blasted trees was black against the night sky.

He reached the old German fire trench and hurried up the far side, following a path of beaten-down grass and barley stalks. The support line was barely twenty-five yards further on, deeper but equally neglected. He climbed down and stopped to listen, expecting to hear the scrape of a spade or a word of command. He heard nothing. Where were Kelvin and his men? Could he have missed them? Had they already returned by a different route?

He switched on his torch and picked his way north along the trench. Debris lay all around: shattered duckboards, a tangle of telephone cable, twisted sheets of corrugated iron. Coming round a traverse, he almost tripped over an ammunition box lying on its side, a single German stick-grenade half-sunk into the soft earth. Opposite, a handful of shovels were stacked against the forward wall. Into the handles were burned the letters CLC.

'Kelvin? Lieutenant Kelvin!'

It went against Haslam's instincts to shout, to give away his position without knowing who might hear him. His gaze came to rest on the wooden frame of a dugout, a gas curtain, brown and filthy, hanging from the lintel. This had to be the place. Slowly he eased the curtain back. On the other side lay darkness and silence.

Rhodes had warned him: the shells could be leaking. Normally it took detonation to turn liquid Yperite into a cloud of toxic vapour. But in a confined space, without ventilation, escaped chemicals might slowly evaporate, their concentration building over time. Maybe Kelvin and his men had not understood the danger until it was too late.

Haslam put on his gas mask and headed down the steps. Even through the filter he could smell gunpowder – and something beyond it: a raw, faecal stench. The beam of his torch swung through the darkness; the inside of the dugout was blurred through the dusty eyepieces of the mask. It was hot. The sweat ran down his forehead and into his eyes. Where were the shells? He saw no sign of them.

He reached the bottom step. 'Lieutenant Kel—'

Blood. It was on the opposite wall, red, glistening – fresh blood. Haslam stepped closer. The torch beam travelled unsteadily across the concrete surface. Blood was all over it: sprays of blood, smears, smudges – blood and paler fragments of flesh and bone, like coffee grains. His breath roared in his ears. He lowered the torch, knowing what he was going to find, but afraid to see it, afraid to understand.

They lay crumpled against the foot of the wall, hunched over. He saw a pair of hands, dusty, tanned, bound together at the wrist, as motionless as if made of clay. He forced himself to count the bodies, to search for signs of life. There were none. The exit wounds had knocked out teeth, cheekbones, eyes. Ten men, all Chinese, shot at extreme close range. Where were the others? Where was Kelvin?

He couldn't breathe. The mask was stifling him. He yanked it off, took a couple of deep breaths.

Haslam felt the vibration in the soles of his feet. A thread of dirt fell onto a kitchen table. Somewhere on the surface a shell had detonated. Then he heard something else, behind him. He spun around, fumbling for his revolver.

To his right was the entrance to another room. Faint light and shadows played over the floor. He heard the splash of water, a harsh abrasive sound – excited, erratic, like an animal burrowing into the ground.

He turned off the torch and stood in the darkness, listening. There came the snatch of a tune, someone humming. *A hymn*. He took out the revolver and stepped slowly towards the sound.

Two lanterns on the floor. A bucket. Two men on their hands and knees. They were scrubbing the cement floor with brushes, working their way to the far end of the room. Scummy red water ran along a shallow drain. Above them, hidden in shadow, hung the carcasses of freshly butchered animals.

Then Haslam saw the faces, saw Kelvin. They weren't animals.

Private Ingham heard footsteps and looked round. 'Who the fuck was that?'

Sergeant Farrer put down his brush and stared into the lightless space where Haslam had been standing. He reached into his belt and drew out the knuckle-knife.

310

Haslam scrambled out of the dugout. He did not know where he was going. He only knew he had to get out, get away. Because it was his fault. Because he should have seen what was coming. The opium had dulled his brain – not just today, but for months. He had not seen what he was falling in with, what it meant to be a member of Rhodes's 'family'. But he should have seen it. Now it was too late – too late to make amends, too late to unsee what he had seen.

Rhodes was standing a few yards away. He was staring up at the moon and the stars, his cap in his hand, breathing hard.

Haslam heard a voice in his head: *Shoot him.* He raised the Webley.

Rhodes turned. In the moonlight his flesh looked dead, like marble, his eyes lost in darkness. 'Edward?'

'What have you done?'

'Done?' Rhodes sighed. 'What I swore to do, years ago. A debt of honour. I'll explain it to you when the time is right.'

'Explain? Thirteen men, damn you ... And those three ...'

'I did it for us, Edward.'

Haslam shook his head. What did Rhodes mean by *us*? The regiment? The army? The white race? He did not want to hear the answer.

'Don't pity them, for God's sake,' Rhodes said. 'A pack of gangsters, dealing stolen morphine and opium – the same opium that's eating you alive.'

So he knew. When had he found out? How long had he known?

'If I take opium, it's so I can look at myself in the mirror. It's so I can live with what I've done, thanks to you.'

Rhodes replaced his cap. 'Don't be weak, Edward. You had it in you all along, just as I knew you did. And thank God for it. Now, put the revolver down before somebody sees you.'

The handle of the Webley felt greasy. Haslam tightened his grip. 'What about Kelvin?'

'Kelvin? He was one of them, or as good as. He tried to get me court-martialled. Doing the Huns' work for them, you could say, which made him a traitor.' Rhodes's voice became softer. 'He could have ruined everything: everything we've worked for, died for. His kind will always stand in our way, if we let them.'

Shoot him.

'Lieutenant Colonel Rhodes, I'm placing you under arrest. You're hereby relieved of your command, effective immediately.'

Rhodes took a step closer. 'What are you playing at, Edward? Is it the opium talking, or the cocaine?' Slowly his head tilted to one side, as if unsure what he was looking at. 'Do you see things that aren't there sometimes? Tell me. Do you hear ghosts in the darkness? Do they speak to you, tell you what to do?'

'You're insane.'

'Things like that happen out here, Edward. It's nothing to be ashamed of. It signifies a kind of receptiveness, an ability to sense the currents beneath us, the truths we can't yet see.'

Haslam cocked the trigger. 'Get moving. Now!'

'Haven't we always understood each other? Didn't you sense it: the way we see the world the same way? That was no accident. That was Fate. You can't turn on me now.'

Haslam had stopped listening. Rhodes could not see it, did not understand. Why did the dead men matter? They had no value, unless it was value to him. He was at one with the battlefield, where scruples and sentiment had no place – only purpose and victory. He mistook his narrowness of vision for clarity.

He raised the revolver. He did not care that his hand was shaking. 'Your last chance.'

Rhodes became very still, like some mythical creature turning to stone. It crossed Haslam's mind that a bullet might not stop him.

'Where are we going, Captain?' Rhodes said. 'You won't get far with that thing in my back. Do you think the men will let you walk by?' He shook his head. 'No. Your only chance'd be to run, to slip away and disappear. And hope none of them find you.'

Haslam's mind was racing. If they found him, he would end up like Kelvin: that was the message. 'Start walking.'

Rhodes shrugged. 'I suppose it's what Lady Vanneck always wanted: for you to vanish. So someone will be happy. And I expect her daughter will be happy too – when she finds out what you've become.'

'A murderer, you mean?'

'No, a traitor.'

Rhodes gave a nod, just small enough that Haslam knew it was meant for someone else. He hurled himself against the wall of the trench as Sergeant Farrer lunged at him from behind. The blade of the knuckle-knife pierced Haslam's trench coat a few inches above the pocket, slicing into the soft flesh of his flank, snagging on the bunched fibres. Haslam swung back with his elbow, striking Farrer hard in the throat.

Farrer staggered forward, letting go of the knife. As he went by, Haslam brought down the butt of the Webley on the back of his head. Farrer fell, moaning, but the force of the blow knocked the revolver from Haslam's hand.

Before he could reach for it, Rhodes's boot came down on top, pressing it deep into the soil. Rhodes shook his head. 'You've lost your touch, Captain. A damned shame.' He reached across his body for the Mauser, unclipping the holder that hung from his belt.

Haslam stumbled backwards. On his left the entrance to the dugout gaped like a black mouth. *Not down there.* He turned to run. His foot hit something hard. He staggered, looked down, saw the ammunition box lying on its side. The stick-grenade was still beside it, barely visible in the gloom.

Every possible course of action played out in his mind in the time it took to blink, resolving into one: he seized the grenade by the handle and flipped off the cap at its base. With his other hand he pulled the fuse cord.

Rhodes cocked the Mauser. 'Edward? Don't make me shoot you in the back. We can still put this right, you know.'

He's lying. Haslam felt the faintest vibration in his hand. The grenade was live, not a dud, as he'd feared. In the core a fuse was burning, rising towards the charge, a journey of four and a half seconds.

He counted to three, then turned. '*Hilf mir. Ich bin verletzt.*'

'What did you say?'

The stick-grenade was already on its way, describing a half-circle as it covered the short distance to Rhodes's chest. Haslam just had time to bring his head down before the blast hit him.

A fragment slammed into his helmet, metal against metal. He fell to his knees and over, ears roaring, a pain above his left knee welling up until he was screaming.

The trench was full of dust. Where Rhodes had stood there was nothing but a pale cloud. Haslam forced himself to sit up. There was blood on his trousers and his boots. It was running down his face.

'Colonel?'

His voice sounded distant, as if sealed behind glass. Then he saw Rhodes: he was lying on his back, motionless.

The voice in Haslam's head said: *Finish him.*

He took a few deep breaths and dragged himself over. The Mauser lay on the ground a few feet away. He reached for it, only then seeing what the grenade had done to Rhodes's face. He wasn't going to last the night, if he wasn't dead already. Haslam dropped the Mauser and began to crawl away.

He had not gone more than twenty yards along the trench when he heard the distant thud of artillery.

'Two tens,' he said under his breath – a reflex, Rhodes's example. *Know the sound of enemy weaponry. It can be useful.* A feeling of nausea broke over Haslam.

A piercing note, like a tiny bell. Then the ground beyond the parapet erupted into smoke and flame. The impact tore Haslam's breath from him. All along the skyline, shells gouged out the earth.

He crawled back the way he had come, wanting only to escape. He got as far as Flag Avenue before his vision failed and the darkness closed over him.

———

—— Forty-four ——

France, March 1919

The light was fading. The country all around was flat and empty: no woods or hills to mark her progress, no way of telling how far Amy had to go. Behind her the village of Bertrancourt had long since disappeared behind a curtain of rain.

Her limbs were numb with fatigue. Her boots were letting in water, but she kept moving, intent on reaching the provost marshal and learning what he knew. The way was muddy and cratered. In the twilight it would be easy to get lost. She wished Kitty were still with her. On the open road she felt vulnerable, like the soldiers who once crept along it on their journeys to the line. But the soldiers were long gone.

The rain caught up with her. She pulled her shawl over her head and hurried on, anxious for some glimpse of Acheux. Thunder rumbled in the distance, so softly she couldn't be sure she had really heard it. Crossing and recrossing the old battlefields, she had seen and heard many things — possible and impossible — as if the emptiness drew out her imaginings and made them real.

A horse whinnied. She stopped, squinting through the rain. It had to have been a big animal, by the sound of it, like the Cleveland bay her father used to ride, with its seventeen hands. Hooves pounded the earth, the gait changing from trot to canter — except now the sound was behind her. Did the horse have a rider? Was it running wild? She couldn't see. She was about to call out, when a memory came back to her: Kitty in the hamlet of Beaussart, shouting at a man who didn't answer, a man holding the reins of a horse. She had the same sensation — the clear sensation of being in danger.

Silence fell. She heard only the rain and her own unsteady breathing.

The road began to climb. Poplars crowned the top of a slope. Beneath them stood an army service wagon. It was pitched over at an angle, one of its rear wheels suspended three feet off the ground. It had run into a shell crater. The

315

horses were facing her way, struggling against their harnesses and the twisted tongue of the wagon.

The driver was pulling things off the back, grunting with the effort, making clouds with his breath. He was trying to lighten the wagon's load so that the horses could drag it out. He didn't notice Amy approaching. She was a few feet away when she realised that she knew him.

'Sergeant Farrer?' He looked up, startled. 'You remember me, don't you?'

The soldier stared at her with his big, joyless eyes as if she were a stranger, or a vision. Was he frightened? Perhaps, like Bill Egerton, he was shocked at her dishevelled state.

'Thought you'd gone home, Miss, like your friend. Shouldn't be out here on your own.'

Amy wondered why the sergeant had not moved on to the Hindenburg Line with the rest of Captain Mackenzie's volunteers. She glanced into the back of the wagon: instead of the long canvas bundles she had seen so often, there were stacks of grey wooden boxes. 'I'm going to Acheux. Can I help? It looks like you're stuck.' She didn't want to go on alone if she could help it.

Farrer wiped his nose and mouth on the sleeve of his coat, then nodded towards the horses. 'You lead 'em on. I'll give it a push.'

Amy took the reins and coaxed the horses forward while Farrer, standing knee-deep in water, put his shoulder behind one of the wheels and heaved. He was strong. On the third attempt the wagon rolled forward, righting itself as it cleared the rim of the crater.

He inspected the horses, gently running his hands over their legs and fetlocks. When he was sure they weren't hurt, he got busy loading up the wagon again.

'You jump up, Miss. I can take you to Acheux.'

'Is it much further?'

'A mile or so.'

She climbed aboard, accepting his offered hand, though the cut-off mittens were caked in filth and sticky to the touch. He turned the wagon round.

They sat for a minute in silence. Then Farrer said, 'Heard any word of your young man, have you, Miss?'

'I heard he died here.'

Farrer looked at her. He was thinking, she supposed, that this had been obvious all along, and wondering how she could ever have imagined otherwise.

She felt the need to explain. 'It's possible to have hope, without knowing you do. You can hope against your will. That word *missing*, it leaves open too many possibilities.'

The road was running downhill again. Trenches had been dug on either side, the bulging parapets and parados like the swellings around a lesion.

'How d'you find out?'

Amy explained about Bill Egerton, Edward's friend in the East Lancashires. She told Farrer about her visit to the hospital outside Naours. It eased the pain a little, putting it all into words.

'Captain Egerton treated some of our lads,' Farrer said. 'He were one of the good ones. What did he tell you?'

'He was very close at the time, when the Germans attacked, the night of the sixteenth. He heard reports from Edward's company. They said he'd been killed by a mortar round.'

'Egerton was wounded.'

'That's right. It must have been soon afterwards, I suppose.'

Farrer shook his head. 'No, he were pipped at La Signy Farm, when we took it back. Dressing station got strafed.' There was a strange insistence in his voice. 'Fancy him saying that. Why'd he lie?'

'Lie?'

'He and Haslam were old friends. It all tallies, when you think about it.'

'Tallies? What does?'

'Where did you say he is? Naours?'

'At a French military hospital.'

Farrer nodded. The news of Captain Egerton had cheered him up somehow. 'That tallies, an' all. I can't wait to tell the colonel.'

Amy did not understand. Nothing Farrer said made any sense.

'The colonel?'

'Rhodes. The CO. Saved my life. Would have saved more, if they'd let him. Like on the Hindenburg Line. Missed him then.'

'They told me Colonel Rhodes was badly wounded. Isn't he in England?'

Farrer shook his head. 'He came back to us, like he promised. To lead us out of here, and on.'

Amy felt uneasy. 'What did you mean about Captain Egerton? Why shouldn't I believe him? Why would he lie?'

Farrer hunched his shoulders, writhing in his bulky coat like a schoolboy with a secret. 'That's a question, in't it? That's a question.'

'To stop me searching, is that it? To save my feelings?'

'Oh no, Miss, not that. He lied to save his old pal's skin.'

'His old . . . ? You can't mean Edward?'

Farrer cracked the reins. The horses surged forward. Ahead the road ran dead straight. 'You're not the first to be taken in, Miss.' He was shouting over the noise of the wheels. Amy saw him reach inside his coat. 'The colonel trusted him. The serpent is beautiful and comes in many guises.'

The serpent is safe in Whitehall or some bordel.

A tremor went through her, a shock of understanding: it was Farrer who had written the letter, the one Bill Egerton had torn up in front of her.

She looked at her hands. The sergeant's mittens had left dark-red smudges on her palms.

'Let me down. Let me down, please. I can walk from here.'

'We're nearly there, Miss.'

'Let me down!'

The road was a blur beneath her, the horse's hooves smacking down on mud and grit.

'What's your business in Acheux?' Farrer said. 'That place is all Chinamen and whores.'

'I'm going to meet a provost marshal, Major Westbrook. He's expecting me.'

For a moment Farrer looked impressed. Then he laughed and shook his head. 'Do you know what Major Westbrook is, Miss? Have you no idea?'

'What are you talking about?'

Amy edged towards the far end of the bench. The fall wouldn't kill her, if she could avoid the wheels. But her skirts were wet and heavy. And if she broke an ankle, what then?

'The provost marshal's no more than a ghost. *Was* a ghost. Burned off like the mist. You're going to see the colonel now.'

Amy didn't try to understand. She rose. Her bag fell from her lap and burst open on the road, the wine bottle inside it shattering. She planted both hands on the edge of the bench, steeling herself to vault clear.

Farrer grabbed her by the hair. 'Where d'you think you're going?'

He forced her down again, and closer. His grip was like iron. Amy twisted round. Her fists and nails wouldn't be enough.

She swung at him with her elbow, making contact with his chin. Farrer's head snapped back with a choking sound. She reached inside his coat, found a knuckle-knife: brass loops for the fingers, a narrow, tapering blade six inches long. But Farrer's grip was round her arm. He forced it back. In a moment the blade was pointing backwards over her shoulder. She looked into his face, saw no strain, no fear, no hatred. He was all calm and purpose, a man about his work. She could not fight him. She could not win.

A thought, a chance. She let her body go slack. The knuckle-knife fell from her hand. 'Have you forgotten?' she said. 'The colonel is expecting me.'

Farrer blinked. His grip weakened. It was enough. She sank a heel into his shin and hurled herself off the wagon.

Her body slammed against hard ground. Grit and blood were in her mouth. Wrenching pain encircled her ribs.

She forced herself to her knees. The world was turning. She couldn't see Farrer. The wagon was rolling on ahead of her, slowing down, the reins slack. She scrabbled for a stone, hurled it at the horses. It travelled through the air in a slow arc, sideways. One of the animals skewed leftwards, then both of them galloped on.

Amy picked herself up. *Get off the road.* She clambered over the shallow embankment. She needed cover: a shell hole, a trench, a sliver of dead ground. It would be dark soon. In the dark he wouldn't be able to find her.

A tangle of collapsed wire and rusty pickets loomed up on her left. Wire meant defensive positions, earthworks. She ran for a gap, stooping low, hems catching, tearing. She risked a look back: the wagon had come to a stop. There was still no sign of Farrer.

She slid down onto a fire step, clinging to tufts of grass. At the bottom of the trench the water was six inches deep. He'd hear her running through it.

She edged along the forward wall, stepping where the water was shallowest, stopped at the corner, listened: nothing.

She went round a traverse, then another. A communications trench opened up on her left, heading in the direction of Acheux. She ran down it, stopped again. It was bound to get shallower as it went, and without the traverses to hide her she could be spotted from fifty yards away. She turned back, kept going along the firing line, deaf to everything but her own breathing and the hammering of her heart.

She rounded another traverse. The water was only puddle-deep. The floor of the trench was rising. A few yards ahead it ended in a heap of ruptured sandbags and coils of wire. Turn round or go up again and make a run for it? Maybe Farrer was too far away now to see her. Maybe he wasn't looking for her anyway.

She didn't want to go back.

She took a deep breath and dragged herself up the back wall of the trench. There were buildings up ahead, the edge of the village. Just a few hundred yards.

A muffled thump stopped her in her tracks. A flare sliced through the air. It hung above her, greenish and blinding, a coil of smoke twisting underneath. The trail pointed to a spot outside Acheux, directly in her path.

She ducked down into the trench, running back towards the road, not caring about the noise any more. A narrow gap opened up on the forward wall: what soldiers called a sap. She had missed it before. It would lead to a listening post between the two front lines. She could hide there. Those places were made for hiding.

Movement behind her: a splash, boots on mud. No time to think.

She threw herself into the sap. It was narrow, shallow, sheets of corrugated iron for a roof. She was on her knees, crawling forward: ten yards, twenty. The sap opened into a pit five feet deep, nettles crowding the sides. She stopped, listened: nothing but the steady beat of the rain. Farrer had lost her, gone back along the firing line. She let herself breathe.

Then she heard it: a scratch on the wet earth, a faint grunt of effort, then another. She peered back along the sap. Ten yards away light fell from a gap between two sheets of iron. Another grunt. Farrer's pale face loomed out of the darkness, the big, boyish eyes fixed on her, expressing nothing. Another day's work. The knuckle-knife was between his teeth.

She scrambled up out of the listening post, grabbing at nettles, kicking into the stony ground for a foothold. She needed a weapon: a rock, a piece of wood. Smash his skull before he could climb out after her – if she could bring herself to do it.

An iron picket was sticking out of the ground. It came loose with a tug, but the wire was still attached. She pulled at it, trying to work it free. The wire was stiff and rusty. It cut into her fingers. *Hurry!*

An animal snort brought her head up. Riding over the broken ground towards her was a man on horseback.

Amy couldn't move, couldn't think of any possible escape. The horse was bigger than she had imagined it, massive and black, with a star on its forehead. Its motion was fluid and sure. It came on like a boat on the water. The rider wore the uniform of a British officer, a sword at his side. Then she saw the sunken cheek and the scar-ravaged temples. It was Major Westbrook – except that he was different now: upright, strong, as if remade.

He drew closer, then stopped on the far side of the wire, barring her way. The last time she had seen him, at Colincamps, he had ridden away without a word – ridden away from an ungrateful woman who had rejected him.

She let go of the picket and turned to run. Farrer was there, climbing out of the listening post. She was trapped: no way past them, no way through the wire.

'Colonel Rhodes, sir,' Farrer said.

The towering horse expelled a breath. The rider did not speak.

Amy did not understand. 'Major Westbrook?'

Farrer took Amy by the hair. 'Haslam's woman, sir. She's found him for us. Hiding out at Naours in a French Army hospital.' The horse took a step closer. 'She'll clean up nice enough.'

The acolyte, eager to please.

'Farrer.'

'Sir.'

'Sergeant Farrer.'

'Colour sergeant, sir. I took care of the horse. Knew you'd be wanting 'im.'

'Good of you.' The rider unsheathed his sword. It was narrow and grey. 'Now let go of her.'

'Sir?'

'Miss Vanneck. Let her go.'

Farrer released his grip. 'We can't let her walk away. She'll warn him.'

'I know. Step back.'

Farrer did as he was asked, making room, excited now at the prospect of what came next.

321

'Your fiancé tried to kill me.' Was Westbrook talking to Amy or to himself? 'I never understood why. We were cut from the same cloth. I thought he would go with me, to the end.'

Amy backed away. 'Please.'

A shadow fell over the rider's face, as if he had just remembered something painful beyond bearing. 'I see now what I failed to see. You helped me to see it, Miss Vanneck, for which I thank you.' He looked up at Sergeant Farrer. 'That was a good woman in Acheux.'

'Sir?'

'You cut her throat.'

'The whore-keeper?' For the first time Farrer sounded nervous. 'She peddled her girls to the Chinks – white girls. Sold her poison to you.'

'You shouldn't have killed her.'

Farrer stared. 'I brought you to yourself, sir. I set you free.' He opened his arms wide. 'And now for the new beginning: the one you promised us.'

Rhodes shook his head. 'Look at this place. Nothing good can spring from poisoned ground – no new world. You must make your own way home.'

Amy tried to run. In a moment Farrer had her round the neck, his knife hard against her windpipe.

'Let her go.'

'We can't be doing that, sir. She'll give us away. We need more time. To gather our strength.'

'All that's done with.'

'No, sir. You can't leave us here. We gave up everything.'

'Yes, you did. So did I.'

'We've unfinished business: the cause. You came back.'

'For Captain Haslam, not for you.'

'It was a promise. *You promised.*'

The rider drew closer. His horse pawed the ground. Farrer was trembling. Amy could feel it in the point of the blade. Her skin punctured.

'Have you forgotten what they are? The likes of her? Them's that made the war and watched us fight it?' The sergeant was screaming. 'Have you forgotten what they owe us?' Farrer twisted Amy's arm behind her back, brought the knife up below her chin. 'Do I have to slice her too? Is that goin' to bring you to your senses?'

Amy tried to twist herself free. Farrer pulled her head back, baring her throat for the knife. At that same moment she saw the great horse rising, clearing in one bound the belt of wire. The earth beneath her trembled as the massive hooves came down. Rhodes was leaning out of his saddle, his sword pointing forward like a lance, pointing at *her*. She closed her eyes.

A spray of hot blood hit her cheek. Farrer shrieked, then fell. Amy was free.

She ran. When she looked back, Farrer was on the ground, arms flailing, struggling towards the cover of the sap, half his face bright with blood. The horse was turning, making ready for another charge. Farrer pulled something from his belt and took aim.

Amy stumbled. A shell hole opened at her feet. She lost her footing, fell. Behind her: a hollow, metallic thud. The bright light of a flare swept the air. A single, guttural grunt. The horse was whinnying, in terror or pain. She cowered by the lip of the crater, her face in the dirt.

Then stillness, rain, the flickering light of a flare still burning on the ground. Hoof-beats, steady now, coming closer. Sergeant Farrer had to be dead. Now Rhodes was looking for her. Should she let him find her? Could she trust him?

The horse went by her, then stopped. The saddle was empty.

Amy crawled to the edge of the shell hole. Rhodes was lying on his back a few yards away, his head twisted hard to one side, his mouth open. She placed a trembling hand against his throat. There was no pulse.

The horse sniffed the ground and began to graze on a clump of grass, as if nothing very much had happened. Amy got to her feet. Her whole body was shaking.

'Easy now,' she whispered, edging step by step towards the beast.

———

Forty-five

A ragged moon lit the twelve miles to Naours, flooded wheel-ruts stretching like silver ribbons over the land. Amy's stiff, bloodied hands shook as they held the reins, but now it was as much from the cold as from the shock. Hope drove her on, hope given to her by a murderer, grounded on the discovery of a lie – if that's what it was. There was nothing else to hold onto, nothing else that mattered. The struggle with Farrer, the appearance of Colonel Rhodes, they were already fading like a bad dream. If there was anyone behind her, she did not see them.

Exhaustion weighed on her, but her mind would not let go: Bill Egerton had lied to her. The surgeon was hiding something: was it Edward himself? It seemed impossible that she could have been close to him and not felt it. She had walked by so many nameless graves. Had she walked past his? Or had he been there, at the Château de Naours, watching her from an upstairs window? Was he one of those men so badly disfigured they were afraid to be seen?

Her thoughts spun in circles: Egerton had been shot during the battle for La Signy Farm, Farrer had been sure about that. Amy knew the place from Mackenzie's trench maps: a site between Bertrancourt and Serre. Edward had mentioned it in his last letter, in July – a pile of rubble, he had called it. She had read that letter a thousand times, but when it came to La Signy Farm, she could not be sure of the exact words. Had it already been taken? Wasn't that what he had written? She wished she could check. But the letters were lost now. They lay where they fell on the road to Acheux. She did not dare go back for them.

If Egerton had been wounded in July, how could he have been at the front in August? According to Captain Mackenzie, they had sent him back to England for treatment. Had La Signy Farm changed hands again, later? Had there been another battle for that same pile of rubble? How could Farrer have been sure of anything? How could she?

The streets of Naours were empty. Bands of clouds slid past the moon, gathering, thickening. By the time the church was behind her, she could hardly see the road.

A yellow light flickered beyond the hedgerows. It had to be the château. The rain was in her face when at last Amy recognised the avenue of plane trees, standing tall in the darkness. She climbed off the horse and led it towards the gates.

The horse snorted and tugged at its reins. Amy peered into the yard. The light was hidden now. The military ambulance she had seen before had gone. She tried the gates: they were locked and chained. There was no way in. She searched for a bell to pull, but found nothing. She called out into the gloom. No one answered.

The wind gusted in her face. The horse lurched backwards as if afraid, almost dragging her to her knees. She let go of the reins, took hold of the iron bars, rattled the gates with her last ounce of strength. She called Edward's name, called for Egerton, screamed for someone to let her in. Rainwater, spilling from the stable roofs, splattered into the yard.

She screamed until all that was left was a sob. 'Why don't you answer? Why don't you answer me?'

Her legs gave way beneath her. Her strength was gone, like a bowstring gone slack. She looked down, saw only water, circling and black, loops of wire, the white flesh of drowned men. She hung on the bars, clinging to consciousness, then fell.

Out of the swirling darkness: voices, hushed, urgent. A man, a woman. She was back in the dugout at Two Storm Wood, listening to the dead come alive. She had to get out or become one of them.

She shuddered, tried to force herself awake. A pupil-less white eye was staring back at her. She was hallucinating. Or she had lost her mind.

'*Dépêche-toi! La fille ne doit pas être vue ici.*'

The eye belonged to an old woman. Amy had seen her before, at the door of the military hospital: one of the sisters, blind in one eye. What did she want? What was she plotting?

A pair of strong arms pulled Amy to her feet. It was the gatekeeper, but he seemed real. She could smell his pipe tobacco, the dusty staleness of his clothes.

'What are you doing? Let go of me!'

'*Venez, vite!*'

The gatekeeper was dragging her. She was awake now, but her limbs were too weak to resist.

'*Et le cheval aussi,*' the nun said.

They wanted the horse too, the girl and the horse: loot from the battlefield – their property, their due. Scavengers. No interest in friend or foe, right or wrong. They took whatever came within reach – seized it and fed, like hungry dogs.

Amy tried to scream, but the gatekeeper's hand was over her mouth at once.

The nun brought a finger to her lips. '*Taisez-vous! Nous savons pourquoi vous êtes ici, Mademoiselle. Nous savons!*'

They knew why she was here. The gatekeeper released her. Then the old nun was beckoning for Amy to follow – not towards the hospital, but away from it. It was not a dream or a hallucination. It was real.

'Captain Egerton, I want to see Captain Egerton,' Amy said.

The nun shook her head and beckoned again. The gatekeeper gave Amy an impatient nudge in the small of her back, then took up the reins of the horse. The animal snorted, but allowed itself to be led away down the avenue.

A hamlet of low farm buildings stood on the opposite side of the road. Amy could follow the others or she could leave. It was as if they had read her mind and knew what she would choose.

The gatekeeper tied up the horse at the far end of a small courtyard. The nun stood in a doorway cut into the side of an ancient, half-timbered stable block. Dim yellow light spilled out onto the cobblestones. A window above was shuttered. Just as at Bertrancourt, people lived in these stables – servants, grooms – at least in peacetime, though these stables looked older and sturdier.

'Where are you taking me?'

They led her up a flight of wooden steps. At the end of a short passage was another wormy-looking door, ajar. Candlelight flickered across a cracked plaster ceiling. Amy crossed the threshold. There was a single bed, a wash-stand, a small iron stove. A single candle burned in a saucer. Above it, a garland of dead flowers was nailed to a roughly hewn beam.

'*Attendez.*'

The door closed. She was alone. Amy sat down on the bed.

It was still raining outside. A faint blue light bled through the shutters. Beyond it she could make out the tiled roof of a barn. Whose billet was this? Whose bed? Her gaze came to rest on a small stack of books. On a shelf above it sat a shaving brush, a comb, a small square mirror with its corner chipped off, a cut-throat razor.

Something moved on the other side of the door. She got up again. Her head was clearer now. Footsteps on bare boards. A familiar rasping sound: metal being sharpened on a stone. Scavengers. Why had she trusted them?

She seized the razor. The footsteps were closer now, slow, deliberate.

She tried to open the razor, but her fingers were covered in cuts from the wire. She couldn't close them round the edge of the blade.

More footsteps. Beneath the door a shadow fell. She put the razor to her mouth, took the blade between her teeth and drew it back.

The latch slid up. The razor would be useless at a distance – useless against a trench knife or a bayonet. She had to strike from close up, before her enemy knew where she was. She had to cut his throat.

She slipped behind the door just as it opened. A man shuffled into the room: no khaki, no uniform. He wore a crumpled waistcoat over a white shirt. She caught sight of a beard flecked with grey. He was holding something in front of him. *It must be now.*

She stepped forward, the razor poised. One swift cut before he could stick her. He wore no collar. It gave her a bigger target.

The man turned. In his hand he held a tin mug. He had his back to the light, but even so, she knew him, knew those eyes, that brow, that mouth.

The razor fell to the floor.

'Hello, Amy.'

For a moment her lips wouldn't form the word.

'*Edward?*'

He nodded, as if making a reluctant confession. 'They told me you fainted. I've some tea for you. You should sit down.'

She heard nothing, sensible only to the fact of him standing before her, changed but alive. His presence pressed in on her, stifling, electrifying, so that she could hardly draw breath.

'Come on now.' His voice, breathy and low, the faintest tremor in it.

Without meeting her eye, he put down the cup and moved to her side. She felt his hand on her arm. At once the pressure inside her was lifted. Breath flooded into her. She threw her arms around him, held him close, just wanting to know that he was really there – not another empty dream.

'Amy?'

She pushed away from him. She could not help herself: her right hand connected with his face, the slap so hard he almost lost his balance. He stared at her, stunned, a trace of blood on his lips. Then his arms were at his sides, his chin down, as if waiting for another blow. She launched herself at him, fists clenched, but the anger had already broken over her.

She clung to him again, unable to speak.

'I'm sorry,' he whispered, and held her close. She heard him sigh, his whole body quake, felt his tears on her cheek and her neck. Then he was sobbing, fighting it and cursing himself, but unable to stop until she had held his face in her hands, held him steady and kissed him.

They stood together for a long time, until the dawn had coloured the room and the steady hiss of rain had given way to the slow tapping of water as it dripped from the roofs. Somewhere a way off, a wagon moved on the road.

'I dreamed you might come,' Edward said finally. 'I never thought you would.'

'I promised. Did you think I'd forget?'

'It was wrong to ask you, very wrong. I wasn't ... in my right mind.' He looked at her. There were lines around his eyes, and shadows. He seemed twice the age of the man she used to know. 'It was the hardest thing, seeing you down there with Bill.'

'Outside the hospital? When I was here before?'

He nodded. 'I was watching, from the attic.' He wiped his nose on his sleeve. 'I wanted to scream your name.'

'Why didn't you?'

He slowly shook his head. He seemed to have no answer, or the time was not right to share it.

He saw the wounds on her hands. 'What's this, Amy? What happened?'

'I'm all right. They're scratches. They'll heal.'

'And you're so thin.'

'So are you.'

'It's cold in here. You're shaking. Lie down. I'll get these cuts cleaned up. Then I'm going to get you a doctor.'

She sat down on the bed. Edward put a blanket over her shoulders. She felt strangely weightless, her body hollowed out and fragile, as if coming out of a fever.

'Can you hold this?'

He brought her the tea, though it was barely warm, and placed it carefully into her hands – glad, she sensed, that there was something to occupy them besides all the questions.

She watched in silence as he busied himself fetching water and soap and a cloth. Her story could wait. What were her moments of fear and danger next to his, anyway? If she had faced a small part of what he had faced for nearly two years, then it was one less difference, one less barrier between them.

She blinked. The doubt lingered in her mind that none of this was real, that any moment she would wake up at Madame Chastain's and find him gone.

'You're coming with me now, aren't you?' she said. 'You're coming home?'

He set down a basin of water at her feet. 'You're not drinking.'

She took a mouthful of tea. The cup rattled against her teeth. Both were real enough. 'You're in hiding here. Is that it?'

Edward nodded. 'That was how it started. Bill did the paperwork. At the hospital I'm Eduard Lébèque, medical orderly. It's kept me safe. Nobody comes here, except medical men.'

His voice was different from the way it used to be: deeper, hoarser. Everything about him seemed older. Even his skin was thinly stretched over the bones of his skull. The softness had all gone. Amy caught a glimpse of herself in the little mirror. She must have looked older too.

'Egerton's been a good friend to you – better than he made out.'

Edward shook his head. 'You don't know the half of it. I was in a bad way when he found me. My wounds were superficial, but it was more than that.'

'You mean opium?'

He nodded. 'How did you know?'

'You told me, in so many words. You wrote about needing the Chinese, about them supplying things you couldn't do without.'

'Did I say that?' He shook his head. 'Careless.'

'It was in one of the last letters I received. I didn't fully understand it at the time, but it became clearer out here. A lot of things have.'

Edward crouched down in front of her, soaked a strip of cloth in the water and began to clean her wounds. 'It started with forced-march pills – cocaine. I found I couldn't face battle without them, especially not ...'

'The raids?'

He looked up at her. 'That's right. The raids. But then I couldn't rest, couldn't sleep. I started taking laudanum when we were in reserve. It felt like an escape, to begin with. It went on from there.'

'Did Bill Egerton supply you as well?'

'Bill? No. He's the one who weaned me off. Small shots of morphine – they keep plenty here for the patients. A little less each time. It hasn't been easy. I've had lapses, but I'm off it now. It's helped that I daren't draw attention to myself, for his sake as well as mine.'

'No one's after you, Edward. They all think you're dead.'

'Of course. Officers don't abandon their men. But I had no choice.'

'I don't care if you did. Did you think I would care, Edward?'

He did not seem to be listening. Amy had the sense that he was talking as much to himself as to her.

'They'd have killed me, torn me to pieces. I took away the thing that bonded them and gave them hope. I was lucky to be wounded; lucky to be picked up by a stretcher party before anyone knew what had happened. I woke up in a dressing station. I realised no one had taken my name. If I could get away, I'd be listed as missing. So I took off the same night. Later on, Bill helped me get in here. It felt like Providence, more than luck. As if I was meant to do what I did, and meant to end up here – to make amends perhaps.'

Amy brought a hand to his cheek. 'It doesn't matter now. You're alive. That's what matters.'

He dried Amy's hand with gentle dabs of a towel. 'We should get some disinfectant on these. I've got bandages.'

He took the basin away. Why didn't Edward tell her how he had missed her? Why didn't he tell her what it meant to see her again? Was it for the same reason she didn't: because there was too much to say, too much to tell?

He emptied the basin and returned with a first-aid kit in a canvas satchel.

'Why didn't you write to me?' she said. 'Did you think I wouldn't keep your secret?'

'Hold out your hand.' He placed a pad of gauze on her palm, then wrapped the bandage around it, cutting and pinning with practised speed and precision.

'Did you think I'd be ashamed of you?'

'For running away? No.'

'Then why ... ?'

'Because ...' He looked up at her, then went back to work. 'Because I knew you'd wait for me. I was afraid you'd wait for ever. And ... I couldn't take that from you as well.'

'There are worse things than waiting. I'd have known you were alive.'

Edward reached for another bandage, took hold of her other hand. The cuts weren't so bad. He ran his finger over them, as if to test their depth. She shuddered at his touch, just as she had the first time they met. The shock of finding him still coursed through her.

'And you'd have stuck with me,' he said. 'A criminal and an addict. You'd have followed me to the bottom: whatever the disgrace, whatever the hardship.' His head sank into her lap. 'I'm not worth that, Amy. I never was.'

'It was the war, Edward. Edward? Whatever happened, you aren't to blame – or we both are. You came here because of me, I know that. It's my fault.'

He did not seem to hear her. 'I used to think about our time together. I thought if I could hang on to those memories, I could hang on to the way I was. But by the end they didn't feel like they were mine any more. When I wrote to you ... about the fields and the wheat, that's what it was. I knew it was all lost – lost to me, nothing left to go back for.'

For a moment Amy thought he would break down and cry, but before she could reach for him again he was on his feet. This moment had already happened in his mind, she felt sure. And he knew that tears would not help. They would only make it harder to set her free.

'Come home with me,' she said. 'Come home. I won't let you down again. I've made my choice.'

'But you don't know me, Amy. Until I came here, I didn't know myself. One thing you can say for the battlefield: you find out what you're made of. You find out what's underneath.'

The tears pricked in her eyes. 'But I've been here too, and I know, I understand – enough, at least. Enough to know it wasn't your fault.' She saw his eyes close. 'Now let's leave this place and never come back.'

Edward did not reply. His back was to her as he packed away the first-aid bag. 'You didn't explain how you found me.'

Amy felt dizzy and short of breath, too weak to try and make him listen. 'Bill Egerton. He said he was in the line when you were killed. I found out that couldn't be true.'

Edward shook his head. 'He should've known better than to try and fool you. I told him you were sharp.'

She hung her head. 'I *was* fooled. It was Sergeant Farrer who wasn't. Edward, please—'

He turned. 'Farrer? You've seen him? Does he know who you are?'

The fear in his voice sent a jolt through Amy's heart. She nodded. 'He's the reason I came back here.'

Edward dropped the bag and went straight to a trunk lying in the corner. He threw open the lid and pulled out a revolver. He flipped open the cylinder: it was fully loaded.

'If Farrer knows—'

Movement. The creak of a board. They both heard it: footsteps easing up the bare wooden stairs.

The door onto the landing was ajar. Edward snapped the cylinder shut and took aim. The footsteps stopped. A faint metallic *snap*. Something hard and heavy rolled along the wooden floor.

'Amy, get—'

The Mills bomb clanked against the back of the stove and detonated.

Amy felt the blast go past her, a fury of fire and iron. The flue above the stove came down, smoke and soot billowing. Edward was on the floor, clutching his leg. He was shouting at her, but she couldn't hear him. The whole room had come adrift: it stretched and rolled as if riding on an ocean. She dropped to her knees.

Farrer stood in the doorway. The right side of his face was caked in blood, his ear sliced in two from front to back. Rhodes's blade had missed him by an inch. He pulled the knuckle-knife from his belt.

Amy's knee brushed against something hard. She looked down, saw the revolver. Edward was still shouting at her, beckoning with an outstretched arm, racked with pain. Farrer stepped into the room.

Sound rushed back like a breaking wave.

'Throw it to me. Throw me the gun!'

Amy grabbed at it. Her bandaged fingers wouldn't reach around the trigger. She juggled it into her left hand, pulled back the hammer with a heavy *click*.

The sound caught Farrer's attention. He looked at her with the same expressionless eyes, as if she were a window someone had forgotten to close.

The revolver danced in her hands. Her whole body shook. She tried to take aim.

'Amy, throw me the gun, for God's sake!'

Her finger locked around the trigger.

Farrer shook his head. 'You won't shoot me, Miss. A bit o' mud don't make you a soldier.'

'Amy!'

She pulled the trigger. The gun leapt in her hand. Farrer rocked backwards. His knife fell to the floor. She had hit him, but she couldn't see where. Farrer clawed at his throat.

He came to rest against the jamb. He looked lost, breathless, his head hanging forward. Absently his right hand reached into the pocket of his greatcoat. He pulled out another grenade and put the pin between his teeth.

Amy's second bullet hit him in the chest. His body lurched and twisted away. His hand was down by his waist again, with the grenade still in it. He frowned at it drunkenly, as if surprised to see it there. Then, with his other hand, he reached for the pin.

Amy's third shot opened a hole beneath his eye.

———

Dear Amy,

I asked after you at Heveningham and received the news this morning that you
had gone back to your aunt and uncle in Cambridge. I was happy to hear you are
recovered from the fever and, I trust, from the trials of last month. I think your
idea of undertaking a course of medical study is a good one. An agile mind needs
occupation, especially in the aftermath of tragic events. Setting aside the past will
never be easy, when so many holes have been torn in the fabric of the future.

From your mother's communication, I see that you have followed my suggestion
and refrained from sharing with her or your father the full extent of your discoveries in France. I think, in the circumstances, this is wise. It has certainly made
things easier with respect to the War Office and prevented events from running
ahead of us. I am now able to report on the fruits of my labours on Edward's
behalf.

The deaths of Sgt Farrer and Lt Col Rhodes have been under investigation by
the provost marshals' branch – the French authorities having satisfied themselves
that it is not a matter for them. I understand that some important information has
come to light, much of it supplied by Captain Mackenzie of the 21st Middlesex,
whose acquaintance I believe you made in France. This information implicates
men of Rhodes's battalion – and, by extension, Rhodes himself – in the unlawful
killing of an officer and a dozen other ranks serving in the Chinese Labour Corps
last summer. This information, together with Rhodes's war record and the testimony of doctors who later treated him during his convalescence in England,
make it entirely plausible that Edward's life was in imminent danger when he was
reported missing from his unit.

I am happy to tell you that I yesterday received informal assurances from the
War Office that no action will be taken against Captain Haslam, should it come
to light – formally, I mean – that he is alive. The one condition attaching to this
assurance is that Lt Col Rhodes's misconduct should not be made public. The man,
after all, is not alive to defend himself, and was recently buried with full honours
at Bertrancourt Military Cemetery. The matter, I may add, might cause some

334

embarrassment, involving as it does foreign nationals, especially if it were to be misrepresented in the press.

I will of course inform Edward of the War Office's position without delay. I had hoped that you and he would at last be able to continue your lives together where you left off two and a half years ago. Nothing would have been more welcome to me. Sadly, it seems that Edward is not yet ready to resume his former life in England, assuming such a thing would ever be possible. I do not know if he has communicated this to you himself, but my understanding is that he will be staying at the military hospital where you found him, at least for the time being. The work being done there is valuable, the patients being severely wounded veterans, and he feels a need to help them as best he can. This was, of course, before news of the War Office's decision came through. Wherever and whenever Edward finally settles, I hope that you can accept his choice with equanimity, knowing that your actions have given him back both his freedom and his honour, and that nothing more could have been asked of you, or of anyone.

I will let you know at once if anything further transpires. In the meantime, I pray you may find something of the peace and happiness to which your steadfast devotion entitles you.

Affectionately,
Evelyn

—— Forty-six ——

England, May 1919

'He's certainly been lucky with the weather,' Aunt Clem said. 'How like your uncle to have the heavens on his side.'

Amy sat by the window in the upstairs drawing room, gazing across the road towards Vicar's Brook. She sat there often these days, utterly still, lost in thought. Aunt Clem and her husband never knew whether it was best to leave her in peace or break the silence with conversation. It was a silence that Amy had brought with her from France.

'Yes, it's very like him,' she said.

The tall trees crowding the banks were in leaf, the new growth vivid against a blue sky. It was the first warm day of the year.

Until now the weather had given Amy an excuse to stay indoors, to pass up the long constitutionals that her aunt and uncle swore by. Such observances felt unnatural now, as if she were playing a part, living out a life that belonged to someone else. Too much had happened simply to carry on as before. The battlefields of the Ancre still held her prisoner. She had no idea when they would let her go.

But she would have to step out now, if only for fear of seeming ungrateful. She would walk past the places she had once shared with Edward, and be reminded of how he was. Would those places lose their power one day? If so, when would that be? She looked down at her hands. The scars on her finger and palm were now ragged white lines, with here and there a hint of purple. They were the only visible reminders of her time on the battlefields, but they would be there for the rest of her life. Next to them, Edward's pearl tiepin was pristine, as if freshly made.

Aunt Clem was anxious that Amy should rebuild her social life as quickly as possible. She brought Amy along to functions at the university. There had been a soirée at her house, replete with 'new people'. A young lieutenant in the Berkshires, recently demobbed, was among the guests at a dinner party.

Amy did her best to behave as expected, if only for her aunt's sake, but the sense of detachment would not leave her. At times, polite conversation was such an effort, it left her feeling faint. It did not help that the other guests studiously avoided any reference to her recent past. How much they already knew about it, what rumours they had heard, Amy did not know (that she had killed a man, she thought, was not yet generally known), but it was enough to make them wary. Her experiences, she supposed, were ones a young woman was not supposed to have. For all Aunt Clem's efforts, it was clear they did not know what to make of the Vanneck girl, or what to say to her.

As for Lady Constance, she had welcomed her daughter back to England with a show of warmth and a busyness that was surprising. It became clear that she had decided, in the light of recent events, to pretend that nothing very much had happened and simply carry on as if that were the case. It was the safest, the least embarrassing approach. Even the news of Edward's survival was treated as an occasion for joy and congratulation. Amy was content to go along with the pretence. She had seen little of her mother in any case, just enough to satisfy appearances.

Aunt Clem was fluffing up cushions now and reassembling the scattered newspapers. The front page of *The Times* carried a report on the release from prison of several conscientious objectors. The government had agreed to free them all by the end of the year.

'Do you think he's taking the train back to London tonight?' she said. 'Perhaps he might be persuaded to stay over.'

'I shouldn't think so. He's always so busy.'

The letter had arrived yesterday: Sir Evelyn had business at Trinity and would be pleased to call on them, if convenient. The arrangement seemed uncharacteristically last-minute. Amy wondered if it could really be just a social call.

Her last days in France were still a chaos of sharp, fragmented memories. Between bouts of fever there were endless questions: from the French *Gendarmerie*, from two different military policemen, from someone representing the Commandant of Labour and from Uncle Evelyn himself, who wanted a full account of her encounter with the late Colonel Rhodes. By that time Amy had been removed to a civilian hospital in Amiens.

Some memories never left her: Farrer, the smell of him, the wide, empty gaze; the feel of the revolver in her hand, the cold weight, the balance and precision of the mechanism. She remembered using it, wanting Farrer's death, the hatred that flared inside her. Those recollections came unbidden: when she stood before the mirror, preparing to wash; when she lay down at night to sleep, and in her dreams.

And she remembered Rhodes, restored briefly to himself, gliding to the kill on his beautiful horse, death in his eyes. In those moments she felt closest to Edward, as two people who had taken the same dark road and found themselves alone together.

One of her visitors in Amiens was Captain Mackenzie. His interrogation was the fullest of all, if only because she found him the easiest to talk to. He was apologetic about his failure, as he put it, to see Major Westbrook for what he was – a failure that had put Amy in grave danger. He had been blinded by the man's bravery and decisiveness, soldierly qualities that he had witnessed for himself. Had it been otherwise, he might have asked himself if Two Storm Wood had anything to do with Whitehall, with uncovering the facts. He might have come to see that the object had only ever been Edward Haslam – his exposure or his punishment – and that Amy had been unwittingly recruited to the same end. Captain Mackenzie, it turned out, had been thinking a great deal about Colonel Rhodes.

'Is it true he saved your life?' he had asked.

'Yes, but I can't forgive him, not for the massacre, or the rest.'

Mackenzie had nodded. 'Of course not. Do you think it was forgiveness he was after?'

'Perhaps not. Perhaps he knew it was too late for that.'

'And Sergeant Farrer? I understood he worshipped Colonel Rhodes. What happened? Why did he turn on him like that?'

Amy's memories of those final moments were incomplete. 'It was about a promise,' she said. 'A broken promise. That's all I know.'

Sitting alone by the window now, Amy found herself hoping she would meet Captain Mackenzie again, if only to see if he had managed to put the past behind him, or if the ghosts of the battlefields still haunted him. Of course he assumed that she and Edward would now be reunited, married, carrying on where they had left off two years earlier. Amy did not share with him her doubts – doubts that her uncle's last letter had done nothing to lessen.

Her thoughts were interrupted by the sight of a taxi pulling up outside the house. The railings and the trees obscured her view, but it could only be Uncle Evelyn. A glance at the clock revealed that he was almost an hour early. She watched him climb out, wearing an unfamiliar felt hat and carrying a cane.

Aunt Clem must have seen him too. She was hurrying down the stairs, shouting at her husband to prepare himself and giving orders to the maid.

'Amy!' Now she was calling to her niece. 'Amy, it's him. Sir Evelyn's brought ... Amy, come quickly!'

She got to her feet. The man with the cane looked up at the house. It was not her uncle, it was Edward. Sir Evelyn followed him out of the taxi and paused to pay the driver. Aunt Clem threw open the door. There were greetings and apologies, Sir Evelyn saying something about an earlier train, Aunt Clem assuring him that he had not arrived a moment too soon.

Edward stood at a distance, looking up at the window. Without the beard, he looked younger again, although not as young as the choirmaster Amy had once known.

'Don't just stand there, come in.' Aunt Clem's voice was hushed, as if sharing a secret. 'Amy's going to be so happy to see you. *So* happy.'

Edward hesitated, leaning heavily on his stick, as if unsure if that could really be true.

Amy got to her feet, her hands pressed against the glass. She was afraid the light would change and she would see that she had been mistaken, that it was not Edward after all. But the light did not change. The face looking up at her remained his.

She turned from the window and hurried downstairs. On her way out of the sitting room she cast a final glance at the tiepin in her hand and put it down on the mantelpiece.

———

Calcutta
21st November 1897

Dear Ralph,

Your letter arrived this afternoon. I have for a long time put off answering the important question that it poses, because in truth, dear friend, I did not know what I should say. I also believed, as I do now, that these decisions should ultimately rest with Emily and yourself. Whatever my feelings on the matter, it would not be right for me to set conditions, when it is you who have made a home for the child, and I who have relinquished him.

That said, I have recently become convinced that, all things considered, it would be best to make a clean break of the kind you suggest. Though family ties should never be severed lightly, such is the burden of the past in this case – such is its power to infect the mind and the character – that the price must be paid. John, who witnessed those terrible events in China, has already begun to show troubling signs of a disturbance that no amount of care seems able to remedy. Should he not improve or, heaven forbid, grow worse, I cannot say that to maintain a connection would not prove more of a burden than a blessing. John cannot unsee what he has seen. He cannot banish the sights and sounds that were seared into his mind that day. It may be too late for him, but it is not too late for his infant brother, he whom Providence or the Good Lord kept from all harm. He has been given a chance to live untroubled by the crime that took his parents and the nightmares it must surely engender, and we should not take that chance from him.

If it is still your wish then, let him be raised as your own son entirely, as Edward Haslam, and know that you have my blessing and my eternal thanks.

Your old friend and comrade,

William Rhodes

———

Acknowledgements

A number of people gave their time to read and comment on this book at various stages, and I could not have managed without their generosity, insight and candour. In rough chronological order these are: analytical psychologist Christopher Zach, who read the first and several subsequent drafts, making invaluable suggestions each time; crime writer David Young, author of the award-winning *Stasi Child* series; actor and audio entrepreneur Martin Simms; supportive readers Claudia Geithner, Jonathan Scherer and Deborah Carey; my agent Nicola Barr, who herded the various sacred cows in the manuscript with an irresistible combination of clarity and charm; and finally the editorial team at Harvill Secker, including publishing director Liz Foley, who was the first publisher to lay eyes on the manuscript, and editorial director Jade Chandler, who took on the book and honed the final drafts with brilliance and sensitivity. I would also like to mention Starling Lawrence at W.W. Norton & Company for championing *Two Storm Wood* in America, and Camille Grace for correcting my French. My sincere thanks to them all.